LEE BROOK

A Harvest of Sorrow

MIDDLETON
PARK PRESS

First published by Middleton Park Press 2024

Copyright © 2024 by Lee Brook

All rights reserved. No part of this publication may be reproduced, stored or transmitted in any form or by any means, electronic, mechanical, photocopying, recording, scanning, or otherwise without written permission from the publisher. It is illegal to copy this book, post it to a website, or distribute it by any other means without permission.

This novel is entirely a work of fiction. The names, characters and incidents portrayed in it are the work of the author's imagination. Any resemblance to actual persons, living or dead, events or localities is entirely coincidental.

Lee Brook asserts the moral right to be identified as the author of this work.

Lee Brook has no responsibility for the persistence or accuracy of URLs for external or third-party Internet Websites referred to in this publication and does not guarantee that any content on such Websites is, or will remain, accurate or appropriate.

Designations used by companies to distinguish their products are often claimed as trademarks. All brand names and product names used in this book and on its cover are trade names, service marks, trademarks and registered trademarks of their respective owners. The publishers and the book are not associated with any product or vendor mentioned in this book. None of the companies referenced within the book have endorsed the book.

First edition

ISBN: 978-1-917228-17-6

This book was professionally typeset on Reedsy.
Find out more at reedsy.com

Whilst Middleton Academy Primary School doesn't exist,
Middleton St Mary's Primary School does.

I dedicate this novel to the staff.

Contents

Prologue

The old farmhouse loomed against the darkening sky, its decrepit form a jagged silhouette in the twilight. Alanna shivered, pulling her jacket tighter around her shoulders. The place reeked of decay and forgotten memories.

"Come on," Ronan urged, his hand warm against the small of her back. "It'll be an adventure."

Alanna hesitated, eyeing the sagging porch with trepidation. "I don't know, babe. This place gives me the creeps."

Ronan flashed that cocky grin of his, the one which usually made her heart flutter. Now, it only intensified her unease. "Don't be such a pussy. I've got a surprise for you."

A chill ran down Alanna's spine, having nothing to do with the autumn air. She'd heard rumours about couples using abandoned buildings for... well, she wasn't ready for that. Not here. Not like this.

"Maybe we should leave, babe," she suggested, taking a step back.

Ronan's grip on her arm tightened, not painfully but with an insistence that brooked no argument: "We've come this far. Don't chicken out now."

Reluctantly, Alanna allowed herself to be led up the creaking steps. Each board protested under their weight, the splintered wood threatening to give way. The front door hung askew on rusted hinges, scraping against the warped frame as Ronan pushed it open. A gust of stale air rushed out, carrying the musty stench of decay and abandonment.

Alanna hesitated at the threshold, her eyes struggling to adjust to the gloom within. The interior sprawled before her, a labyrinth of shadows and neglect. Tattered cobwebs adorned every corner, gossamer strands glinting faintly in what little light filtered through grimy windows.

As they ventured inside, the floorboards groaned beneath their feet, an eerie chorus of creaks and pops that seemed to echo through the empty rooms. Dust motes swirled in the beams of moonlight coming in from above, dancing in the stagnant air. The acrid taste of mould coated Alanna's tongue, making her gag slightly.

"This is mental," Alanna whispered, her voice sounding unnaturally loud in the oppressive silence. "What if someone catches us?"

Ronan snorted. "Who? This place has been empty for years. Nobody cares about Lower Thorpe Farm now."

They picked their way through what must have once been a living room. Her fingers trailed along a wall, encountering the tacky remnants of peeling wallpaper. Fragments crumbled at her touch, falling to the floor with soft whispers. In the silence, even their breathing seemed thunderous, ragged with apprehension.

Alanna's skin crawled, imagining spiders and who-knew-what-else lurking in the darkness.

A skittering sound from a darkened corner made Alanna flinch. Rats, or worse, she imagined. The oppressive atmosphere pressed down on her, a physical weight that made every step an effort. She wiped her clammy palms on her jeans, fighting the urge to flee back into the open air.

"There," Ronan said, pointing to a door set into the far wall. "That's where we're headed."

Alanna's stomach dropped. "The cellar? No way, babe. I'm not going down there."

"Don't be such a baby," Ronan scoffed. "It's perfectly safe. I checked it out last week."

"You what?" Alanna stared at him incredulously. "You've been here before? Why didn't you tell me?"

Ronan shrugged, avoiding her gaze. "Wanted it to be a surprise, didn't I? Come on, it'll be fine."

Before Alanna could protest further, Ronan yanked open the cellar door. A gust of dank, musty air hit them, carrying with it the unmistakable scent of rot. Alanna gagged, covering her nose and mouth with her sleeve.

"Jesus, babe, it stinks down there!"

"It's an old cellar, what do you expect?" Ronan replied, already descending the stairs. "Stop being so dramatic and follow me."

Alanna stood frozen at the top of the stairs, every instinct screaming at her to run. But Ronan was already swallowed by the darkness below, his footsteps echoing hollowly.

"Babe?" she called, her voice trembling. "I really don't like this."

"For fuck's sake, Alanna!" Ronan's exasperated voice drifted up. "Get down here!"

Taking a deep breath, Alanna steeled herself and began the descent. The stairs creaked ominously under her weight, and she clung to the damp wall for support. The darkness pressed in around her, suffocating.

At the bottom, she fumbled for her phone, switching on the torch function. The beam of light cut through the gloom, revealing a space cluttered with broken furniture and discarded junk.

"Babe?" she called again, her voice small and scared. "Where are you?"

"Over here," came his reply from somewhere to her left. "I found something. Come check it out."

Alanna swept her light in that direction, catching a glimpse of Ronan's excited face before he disappeared behind a stack of rotting crates.

"Wait there," he instructed. "I want to make sure it's safe first."

Alanna stood rooted to the spot, her heart pounding. The silence was oppressive, broken only by the scurrying of unseen vermin. She played her light around the cellar, trying to quell her rising panic.

The beam fell on something which made her breath catch in her throat. A table, draped with a sheet stained a sickening crimson. And underneath... a small mass.

"Babe," she whispered, her voice barely audible. "Babe, we need to go. Now."

"Hold on," came his distracted reply. "I've almost got it."

"No, babe, you don't understand," Alanna insisted, her voice rising in pitch. "There's something... wrong here. We need to call the police."

"What are you on about?" Ronan emerged from behind the crates, frowning. His eyes followed her trembling finger to the sheet-covered table. "Oh. Oh, shit."

He approached slowly, his earlier bravado evaporating. Alanna wanted to scream at him to stop, to grab him and run, but fear had paralysed her vocal cords.

Ronan reached out, his hand hovering over the edge of the

sheet. Alanna shook her head frantically, willing him to stop. But with a sharp intake of breath, he yanked the fabric away.

The scream that tore from Ronan's throat would haunt Alanna's nightmares for years to come. He stumbled backwards, crashing into a pile of rusted tools.

"We're leaving," he gasped, grabbing Alanna's arm and yanking her towards the stairs. "Now, Alanna!

"Oh god."

"We need to call the police."

They scrambled up the steps, tripping and stumbling in their haste to escape. Alanna's mind reeled, unable to process what she'd glimpsed in that fleeting moment.

They burst out of the farmhouse, gulping in great gasps of fresh air. Alanna's legs gave out, and she collapsed onto the wet grass, retching. Ronan paced frantically, phone pressed to his ear.

"Police," he barked into the device. "I need the police. There's... oh God, there's a body. A child. At Lower Thorpe Farm in Thorpe near Middleton, just off the A654. Please, you need to come now!"

Alanna curled into herself, sobs wracking her body. Ronan knelt beside her, wrapping an arm around her shoulders. His voice cracked as he continued to plead with the emergency operator.

"Please hurry," he begged. "Oh Christ, please hurry."

As the wail of distant sirens pierced the night, Alanna clung to Ronan, both of them trembling. The old farmhouse loomed behind them, its secrets no longer hidden in the darkness.

Chapter One

The morning sun beat down relentlessly on Elland Road Police Station, turning the building into an oven. Inside his office, Detective Chief Inspector George Beaumont leaned back in his chair, tugging at his sweat-soaked shirt. The fabric clung to his skin, a constant reminder of the oppressive heat wave gripping Leeds.

June and July had been a nightmare for weather. If it wasn't raining, the sun was blistering. Isabella had been tempted to put the heating on, but George had laughed at the situation.

He squinted at the computer screen, the glare making his eyes water. Summer cases. Petty thefts, drunken brawls, domestics gone wrong. Nothing earthshaking, but the paperwork still needed doing.

At least nobody had died, he thought.

A sharp rap on the door broke his concentration. Newly promoted Detective Sergeant Tashan Blackburn stood in the doorway, his usually composed face tight with tension.

"Sir," Tashan said, his voice clipped. "We've got a situation."

George's pen clattered to the desk. "What kind of situation?"

Tashan stepped inside, closing the door behind him. "Body

found in a derelict farmhouse. Near Middleton."

George's stomach clenched. "Adult?"

Tashan shook his head, his eyes dark. "Child, sir. Young."

The word hung in the air, heavy as lead. George pushed back from his desk, chair legs scraping against the floor.

"Christ," he muttered. "Details?"

"Couple of teenagers found it last night. In the cellar." Tashan's jaw clenched. "Uniforms secured the scene. Dr Yardley's on her way."

George nodded, grabbing his jacket. "Let's go."

They strode through the bustling station, a bubble of grim purpose amid the everyday chaos. Outside, the heat hit like a physical blow.

"I'll drive," Tashan offered, fishing keys from his pocket.

The car's air conditioning sputtered weakly as they pulled into traffic. George stared out the window, watching Leeds blur past. His thoughts spiralled, professional instincts warring with a father's dread.

"How young?" he asked quietly.

Tashan's knuckles whitened on the steering wheel. "Initial report says... toddler, maybe."

George's eyes closed, and an unbidden image of Olivia flashed before him. He pushed it away, focusing on the road ahead.

The drive to Thorpe seemed interminable. When they finally pulled up to the cordoned-off farmhouse, a crowd of onlookers had already gathered, most of them the press. Uniforms kept them at bay, their faces a mix of morbid curiosity and genuine concern.

"Vultures," Tashan muttered as they ducked under the police tape.

"Indeed."

The farmhouse loomed, a decrepit sentinel guarding its grim secret. Paint peeled from weathered boards, and windows stared blankly like sightless eyes.

Inside, the air hung thick with dust and decay. Their footsteps echoed hollowly as they made their way to the cellar entrance. A young constable stood guard, his face pale.

After being handed forensic gear and being signed in, George took a moment to breathe. Child murders were the worst.

"Down there, sir," the young constable eventually said, jerking his head towards the stairs. "Dr Yardley's already started her examination."

George nodded, steeling himself. "Right. Let's see what we've got."

The cellar air hit like a slap, cool and dank. Portable lights cast harsh shadows, creating a nightmarish scene. And there, at the centre of it all...

George's breath caught. The body was so small, so fragile. A little girl, no more than three or four. She lay on a metal table, limbs akimbo like a broken doll.

Dr Lindsey Yardley straightened, snapping off a pair of latex gloves. Her face was a mask of professional detachment, but her eyes betrayed a flicker of something darker.

"Gentlemen," she greeted them. "I wish we were meeting under better circumstances."

George forced his gaze away from the child. "What can you tell us, Lindsey?"

Lindsey sighed, running a hand through her short blonde hair. "Female, approximately four years old. Severe malnutrition and dehydration. Multiple contusions and abrasions in various stages of healing."

She paused, her voice hardening. "There's evidence of sexual abuse."

George's fists clenched at his sides. Tashan muttered a curse under his breath.

"Cause of death?" George managed.

"Preliminary findings suggest blunt force trauma to the head," Lindsey replied. "But I'll know more after the post-mortem."

George nodded, his throat tight. "Time of death?"

"Based on liver temperature and the state of rigour, I'd estimate between 48 and 72 hours ago." Lindsey's eyes narrowed. "But she'd been dead well before those kids found her."

George forced himself to approach the table, to really look at the victim. Her skin was waxy and mottled with bruises. Dark circles ringed sunken eyes. And her hair... lank, matted strands of what might once have been tawny.

Like Olivia's.

The thought sucker-punched him, leaving him breathless. He gripped the edge of the table, knuckles white.

"You alright, sir?" Tashan's voice seemed to come from far away.

George straightened, shoving the personal horror deep down. "Fine," he said curtly. "Dr Yardley, anything else stand out?"

Lindsey frowned, gesturing to the child's arms. "These marks here. They're not consistent with the other injuries. Almost looks like..."

"Restraints," Tashan finished grimly.

George's jaw clenched. "She was held captive."

"For a significant period, I'd wager," Lindsey agreed. "The malnutrition alone suggests weeks, if not months."

The implications hung heavy in the air. A child tortured and abused for God knew how long before being discarded like trash in this godforsaken cellar.

"We need to ID her," George said, his voice hard. "Missing persons, dental records, DNA, whatever it takes."

Tashan nodded, already pulling out his phone to relay the orders.

George turned to CSI manager Stuart Kent, who stood quietly observing the scene. Kent's salt-and-pepper hair could just be seen beneath his hood. Despite the grim surroundings, his piercing brown eyes remained sharp, missing nothing.

"Stuart," George addressed him, "I want every inch of this place gone over with a fine-tooth comb. If the bastard who did this left so much as an eyelash behind, I want to know about it."

Kent nodded, his expression grim. He shifted his weight, favouring his left leg—a reminder of an injury sustained during the Bone Saw Ripper case two years prior. "Already on it, George. My team's setting up outside. We'll process the scene inch by inch, floor to ceiling."

He paused, gesturing to the damp walls with a gloved hand. "This environment's not ideal for preserving evidence, but we'll do our best. I've got specialists coming in to check for trace DNA, fibres, the works. If there's anything to find, we'll find it."

George nodded, grateful for Kent's thoroughness. The man's methodical approach had cracked more than one seemingly impossible case. If anyone could wring evidence from this godforsaken place, it was Stuart Kent and his team.

George turned back to Lindsey. "How soon can you get me a full report?"

"I'll start the post-mortem as soon as we get her back to the lab," she replied. "You'll have preliminary findings by end of day, full report within 48 hours."

"Can't you do it any earlier," George said.

Lindsey's eyebrows rose, but she nodded. "I'll do my best."

As the pathologist began preparing the body for transport, George climbed the cellar stairs, desperate for fresh air. Outside, he leaned against the farmhouse wall, gulping in deep breaths.

Tashan appeared a moment later, his face grim. "SOCOs are on their way. I've got uniforms canvassing the area; see if anyone saw or heard anything suspicious."

George nodded, grateful for his partner's efficiency. "Good. We need to notify the press, too. Someone out there knows something about this girl."

"You want to do the statement?" Tashan asked.

George hesitated. Usually, he'd jump at the chance to appeal directly to the public. But this case... it hit too close to home.

"No," he decided. "You handle it. Just... keep it factual. We don't need a media circus."

Tashan's eyes narrowed, studying his boss. "You sure you're alright with this one, sir?"

George straightened, squaring his shoulders. "I have to be, don't I? That little girl deserves justice, and we're going to get it for her."

As they walked back to the car, the sun still blazed overhead, but George felt cold to his core.

"Whoever did this," he said quietly, "whatever sick bastard could hurt a child like that... we're going to find them, Tashan.

And when we do, they'll wish to hell they'd never been born."

Tashan nodded, his face set in grim determination. "Yes, sir. We'll get them."

They climbed into the car, the air conditioning a welcome respite from the heat. As Tashan started the engine, George's phone buzzed. A text from Isabella.

"Everything OK? I tried calling your office, but they said you were out."

George stared at the screen, his throat tight. How could he explain? How could he put into words the horror he'd just witnessed, the evil they were up against?

He typed out a quick reply. "Got a bad case. Might be late. Kiss Olivia for me."

As they pulled away from the farmhouse, George's thoughts churned. Somewhere out there, a monster walked free. A creature capable of inflicting unimaginable suffering on an innocent child.

He'd seen a lot in his years on the force. Murderers, rapists, the worst humanity had to offer. But this... this was different. This was a level of depravity that chilled him to his very soul.

The image of the little girl's broken body flashed before his eyes. So small, so vulnerable. Like Olivia. Like Jack. Like every child who deserved to be protected, to be loved.

George's jaw clenched, a muscle ticking in his cheek. He'd find the bastard responsible. He'd bring them to justice, no matter what it took.

For that little girl in the cellar. For every child who'd ever suffered at the hands of evil. For the sake of his own sanity.

He had to.

Chapter Two

The air conditioning hit him like a wall as George Beaumont strode into Elland Road Police Station, a stark contrast to the oppressive heat outside. He made a beeline for the Missing Persons Department on the first floor, his mind racing with the image of the small, broken body in the farmhouse cellar.

Kalani Akana looked up as George entered, her dark eyes widening at his expression. "DCI Beaumont," she greeted him, her lilting Hawaiian accent a jarring note in the sombre atmosphere. "What can I do for you?"

George didn't waste time on pleasantries. "I need you to run a search, Kalani. Female child, approximately three years old, reported missing within the last month."

Kalani's fingers flew over her keyboard, her brow furrowed in concentration. "Any other parameters?"

"South Asian descent," George added, remembering Dr Yardley's preliminary assessment.

The computer hummed, seconds ticking by like hours. Finally, Kalani's sharp intake of breath broke the silence. "I've got a match. Dania Bhati, reported missing three weeks ago."

George leaned over her shoulder, scanning the report. His stomach clenched as Dania's photo smiled up at him, all chubby cheeks and bright eyes. "Christ," he muttered. "Why didn't this get more attention?"

Kalani shook her head, her expression troubled. "It did get some coverage, but... well, you know how it is. Pakistani kid from a working-class area? It didn't stay in the headlines long."

The bitter truth of her words tasted like ash in George's mouth. He straightened, committing the details to memory. "I need everything we've got on this. The family, the circumstances of her disappearance, everything."

As Kalani compiled the information, George's phone buzzed. Tashan's text was brief: "Car's ready when you are, sir."

Ten minutes later, they were on the road, the Bhati's address punched into the GPS. George stared out the window, his mind churning. How do you tell parents their child is dead? How do you describe the horror they'd found in that cellar?

The Bhati's home was a modest terraced house in Beeston on Marsden Mount. As they pulled up, George saw a curtain twitch. News travelled fast in neighbourhoods like this.

Hassan Bhati opened the door before they could knock, his face a mask of dread. "You've found her," he said, his voice barely above a whisper.

George nodded, his throat tight. "Mr Bhati, I'm DCI George Beaumont. This is DS Tashan Blackburn." They both showed their warrant cards. "May we come in?"

Hassan stepped back, allowing them entry. The house smelled of spices and cleaning products, a jarring combination. In the living room, a woman—Alize Bhati, George assumed— sat rigid on the sofa, her eyes fixed on them.

"Please," George began, but Alize cut him off.

"She's dead, isn't she?" The words came out flat, emotionless. "Our Dania. She's gone."

George met her gaze, unflinching. "I'm so sorry, Mrs Bhati. We found Dania's body this morning."

The wail that tore from Alize's throat was primal, a sound of pure anguish. Hassan rushed to her side, enveloping her in his arms as she broke down.

George and Tashan stood awkwardly, giving the couple a moment to grieve. Finally, Hassan looked up, his eyes red-rimmed but focused. "How?" he asked. "How did she...?"

George hesitated, weighing his words carefully. "We're still investigating the exact circumstances."

Hassan nodded, his jaw clenching. "What do you need from us?"

"Information," George replied. "Anything you can tell us about the day Dania disappeared, anyone who might have had contact with her."

Alize stood abruptly, mumbling something about tea before fleeing to the kitchen. Hassan watched her go, his expression pained. "It was supposed to be a normal day," he began. "Dania was at nursery, at Middleton Academy Primary School. Alize was meant to pick her up, but—"

"There was an accident," Alize interjected.

Tashan looked up at the grieving mother, his notebook at the ready. "An accident?"

"Two cars had smashed on Dewsbury Road," she explained.

An RTC? Can you give us the exact date, time, and location?"

Alize nodded towards her husband and then went back into the kitchen. Hassan recited the details whilst Tashan jotted them down, his pen scratching against the paper. "I'll verify this information, boss," he murmured to George.

George turned back to Hassan. "So Alize was delayed. What happened next?"

Hassan's fists clenched in his lap. "The school... they made a mistake. They let someone else take Dania. Some stupid teaching assistant. By the time Alize arrived, my little girl was gone."

George leaned forward, his voice gentle but insistent. "Mr Bhati, I need you to think carefully. Is there anyone—family, friends, anyone—who might have had reason to hurt Dania?"

Hassan's head snapped up, his eyes flashing with anger. "No! Never! Our family loved Dania. No one would ever..."

"I understand," George cut in, holding up a placating hand. "But we have to consider every possibility. Can you give us the names and addresses of family members and close friends?"

For a moment, Hassan's face contorted, rage flashing in his eyes. He leapt to his feet, fists clenched at his sides. "How dare you!" he shouted, his voice echoing through the small room. "These are our family, our friends! They loved Dania! They would never—"

George remained seated, his expression impassive. He'd seen this reaction before, the anger masking pain and help-lessness. He met Hassan's furious gaze without flinching.

"Mr Bhati," Tashan interjected, rising slowly with his palms out in a placating gesture. "We understand your anger. We do. But we have to explore every avenue to find who hurt Dania. Wouldn't you want us to be thorough?"

Hassan's chest heaved as he glared at Tashan, then back at George. The detective's calm demeanour seemed to infuriate him further. "You people," he spat. "You always suspect the family first, don't you? Because we're—"

"Because statistically, it's often someone close to the vic-tim," George cut in, his voice level. "Not because of your ethnicity, Mr Bhati. We'd be asking these same questions of any family in this situation."

Tashan took a step closer to Hassan, his voice gentle but firm. "Sir, please. Sit down. Take a breath. We're on your side here. We want justice for Dania as much as you do."

For a tense moment, it seemed Hassan might lash out physically. But then, as quickly as it had come, the fight drained out of him. He sank back onto the sofa, burying his face in his hands.

"I'm sorry," he mumbled. "I'm sorry, it's just... our little girl..."

Tashan sat beside him, placing a comforting hand on his shoulder. "It's OK, Mr Bhati. We can't imagine what you're going through. But we need your help to catch whoever did this."

Hassan nodded, wiping his eyes. He looked up at George, who still hadn't moved. "Fine," he said quietly. "I'll give you the names. But I'm telling you, none of them could have done this. None of them."

As Hassan began listing names and addresses, George noted them down, his mind already mapping out the investigation. "And your immediate family," he pressed. "Parents, siblings?"

Hassan's expression darkened. "My father is in poor health. He can barely leave the house, let alone..." He trailed off, shaking his head. "And my brother, Bilal, he travels for work. He was in Dubai when Dania... when it happened."

George nodded, making note of the alibis. "What about Mrs—"

"They're all dead," Hassan interrupted, his eyes darkening further. "She has no family."

George narrowed his eyes and made a mental note. "And

your work, Mr Bhati? Mrs Bhati's?"

"I work nights," Hassan replied. "At a curry house in Bradford." He provided the name and address of one George had been to before. Great food, incredible atmosphere. "Alize works part-time at a shop on Dewsbury Road near the doctor's surgery. We... we arranged our schedules around the children's school hours."

The pain in his voice was palpable. George fought to keep his own emotions in check. "Mr Bhati," he said, leaning forward. "I want you to know we're doing everything in our power to find who did this. If you think of anything, anything at all, no matter how small or insignificant it might seem, please call me."

He handed Hassan his card, watching as the man's fingers closed around it like a lifeline. As they stood to leave, Alize reappeared, her eyes red and swollen. She said nothing, but her gaze bored into George, a silent plea for justice.

Outside, the heat hit them hard. It was like a punch to the gut. George paused on the doorstep, Alize's muffled sobs echoing behind him. He turned to Tashan, his expression hard.

"We find this sick bastard," he said. "And we find him soon. Yeah?"

Tashan nodded, his own face set with determination. "Yes, sir. Where do we start?"

George's thoughts spiralled, piecing together the puzzle. "The school," he decided. "We need to know who picked up Dania that day. And I want background checks on everyone on that list Hassan gave us. Family, friends, co-workers—no stone left unturned."

"Shall I get Yolanda on CCTV."

George nodded.

As they climbed into the car, George cast one last glance at the Bhati's house. The curtain twitched again, a fleeting glimpse of a grief-stricken face. He swallowed hard, pushing down the wave of emotion threatening to overwhelm him.

"Let's go," he said to Tashan. "We've got work to do."

Chapter Three

George and Tashan pulled up to Middleton Academy Primary School. As they got out of the car, the change in temperature from the air-con inside and the fierce heat outside took George's breath away.

Children's laughter echoed across the playground, a cacophony of joy that felt jarringly out of place given their grim purpose.

George headed towards the gate and was hit by a wave of nostalgia. This had been his school decades ago. The building stood unchanged, its windows reflecting the summer sun, but instead of being white, the facade was now blue. The scent of cut grass mingled with the unmistakable aroma of school dinners wafting from the hall.

"Brings back memories, eh?" Tashan remarked, noticing George's expression.

George nodded, his eyes scanning the familiar landscape. "Some good, some not so much."

They walked towards the main entrance. George noticed they'd changed the way you got in. He preferred this way. Before, you had to go all the way around.

"How's Olivia doing?" Tashan asked as they navigated the corridors. "Starting school soon, isn't she?"

George's face softened momentarily. "Next year. She's excited and keeps asking for a 'big girl backpack' like her brother's."

Tashan chuckled. "And Jack? He settling in OK?"

"Most days," George replied. "Though he's not keen on maths. Takes after his old man there."

Their banter ceased as they pressed the button of what appeared to be a doorbell camera and waited to be allowed entrance.

"Hello?" a voice asked.

"Detective Beaumont and Detective Blackburn here to see Mrs Gledhill. My colleague, DC Patel, called ahead."

"Come in."

After signing in and collecting their badges, a stern-faced woman in her fifties greeted them with a grim nod. "Detectives," she said, ushering them inside her office. "I can't tell you how devastated we are about Dania. Such a bright little girl."

Mrs Gledhill exuded an air of stern authority; her salt-and-pepper hair pulled back into a tight bun that accentuated the sharp angles of her face. Her steel-grey eyes, magnified slightly by wire-rimmed spectacles, seemed to miss nothing as they swept across the two men. She wore a crisp navy blazer over a white blouse, her outfit as meticulously ordered as the papers on her desk. A thin gold chain around her neck and a simple wedding band were her only concessions to adornment.

George sat, his face impassive. "We need to understand exactly what happened the day she was taken, Mrs Gledhill."

The headmistress sighed, clasping her hands on the desk. "It was a terrible mistake. A young Asian woman came to collect Dania, claiming to be her aunt from Pakistan. She said

Dania's mother was in hospital and her father was with her."

"And you let her take the child?" Tashan's voice held a hint of incredulity.

Mrs Gledhill flinched. "Not me personally. It was our new teaching assistant, Chelsie. She... she didn't follow proper protocol."

George leaned forward. "We'll need to speak with Chelsie. And Dania's teacher."

"Of course," Mrs Gledhill nodded. "I'll have them sent in."

Chelsie arrived first, a young woman barely out of her teens. Her eyes were red-rimmed, hands twisting nervously in her lap. She was full of nervous energy. Her mousy brown hair, hastily tied back in a messy ponytail, framed a round face dotted with freckles. Wide, hazel eyes darted about the room, never settling in one place for long. She wore a brightly coloured cardigan over a floral dress, an outfit clearly chosen to appeal to young children but now rumpled from a long day of chasing after her charges. Her fingers constantly fidgeted with a silver charm bracelet on her wrist.

"I'm so sorry," she blurted before George could speak. "I never meant... I should have checked. Oh God, poor Dania."

George's voice remained neutral. "Walk us through what happened, Chelsie."

The girl took a shaky breath. "This woman came to the door. She was Asian, young, maybe mid-twenties? She said she was Dania's aunt and that her mum was in the hospital. I... I should have called to verify, but she seemed so worried, and I had parents mingling wanting to talk to me. I... I let Dania go with her."

"Did you see what kind of vehicle they left in?" Tashan asked.

Chelsie shook her head. "No, but we do have CCTV." She narrowed her eyes. "We did tell the other detective it was a white van. We didn't see the registration, though, because it was dirty. I'm sorry, I should have paid more attention."

George leaned forward, his elbows on his knees. "Chelsie, I need you to think carefully. Can you tell us more about the woman who picked up Dania? Any details you remember could be crucial."

Chelsie nodded, her brow furrowed in concentration. "She was... pretty, I guess. Dark hair, tied back. She had an accent, but it wasn't strong. More like she'd lived here a while, you know?"

So not recently from Pakistan? George thought.

"What about her clothes?" Tashan prompted.

"Uh, jeans, I think. And a blue top. Oh, and a headscarf. Not a full hijab, just... covering part of her hair."

George nodded encouragingly. "Any distinguishing features? Scars, tattoos, jewellery?"

Chelsie shook her head. "I don't... wait. She had a small mole, just above her lip on the right side."

"Good," George said. Now, did she seem familiar with the school? Did she know where to go and what to do?"

"Yeah, actually," Chelsie replied, surprise colouring her voice. "She came straight to our door when people picking up children normally get confused about which one to come to. I didn't think anything of it at the time..."

Tashan made a note. "And Dania? How did she react to this woman?"

Chelsie paused, her face clouding. "She... she seemed OK at first. But thinking about it now, she was quieter than usual. Dania's normally such a chatterbox."

"Did anyone else see this woman?" George asked. "Other staff, students, or parents?"

"Mr Farooq, the caretaker, was sweeping up sand," Chelsie said. "And there were a couple of Year 6 girls hanging around. I can't remember their names, but they're always coming to check on the rabbits and chickens."

"One last thing," Tashan interjected. "In the days before this happened, did you notice anything different about Dania? Her behaviour, her appearance?"

Chelsie thought momentarily. "She'd been quieter lately. And... now that I think about it, she had a bruise on her arm a few days before. She said she fell in the playground, but..."

George and Tashan exchanged a glance. "Thank you, Chelsie," George said. He made a note. "We'll need you to work with a sketch artist, Chelsie. Can you do that?"

"Yes, of course. Anything to help."

As Chelsie left, her shoulders slumped with guilt, George exchanged a glance with Tashan. The fear in her eyes was palpable—fear for her job, fear of the consequences of her actions.

Their next interviewee presented a stark contrast.

Abbie Illingworth's presence brought a sudden warmth to the room, catching George slightly off guard. Her chestnut hair fell in loose waves around her shoulders, framing a face that could have graced magazine covers. Striking blue eyes, rimmed with long lashes, met George's gaze directly, their depths clouded with concern for her missing student. She wore a simple yet elegant emerald-green blouse tucked into black trousers, the colour complementing her fair complexion. A delicate silver necklace drew attention to the graceful curve of her neck. George found himself having to consciously refocus on the task at hand.

"I wasn't on door duty that day," she explained, her voice tight with emotion. "I had my PPA time. If I'd been there..."

George cut her off gently. "This isn't your fault, Miss Illingworth. You couldn't have known."

Abbie nodded, but the guilt in her eyes remained. "Dania was such a sweet girl. But... there were issues at home. We were keeping an eye on her."

George's interest piqued. "What kind of issues?"

"Nothing concrete," Abbie said, her blue eyes still shimmering with unshed tears. "Just... little things. She'd come in tired sometimes or a bit unkempt. We were monitoring the situation."

George made a mental note. Neither Chelsie nor Mrs Gledhill had mentioned this. "Can you be more specific?"

Abbie took a deep breath. "It was little things at first. Dania would come in without a smile on her face, or wearing the same clothes as the day before. Then there were days she'd be really quiet, almost withdrawn."

"Any signs of physical abuse?" Tashan asked gently.

Abbie shook her head. "Nothing obvious. But about a month ago, she had a bruise on her arm. Said she fell, but... it didn't look like that kind of bruise." She paused. "I did report it."

George nodded, making notes. "How did Dania get along with the other children? And the staff?"

"Oh, she was a lovely girl," Abbie said, a fond smile briefly crossing her face. "Always kind to the other children, eager to help. The staff all adored her. Except..."

"Except?" George prompted.

Abbie hesitated. "There was an incident with Mr Farooq, the caretaker. Dania seemed scared of him for a while. We thought it was just because he'd told her off for running in the corridors, but now I wonder…"

Tashan leaned forward. "Did you notice any changes in Dania's behaviour or academic performance over time?"

Abbie nodded. "Her reading was improving rapidly, but then it just… stopped. And her artwork changed. It used to be all bright colours, but in the last few weeks, she has been using a lot of dark colours. Blacks and greys."

"What about her attendance?" George asked.

"It was good overall," Abbie replied. "But there were a few unexplained absences in the month before she… before she disappeared. Her mum said she was ill, but Dania always seemed fine when she came back."

George made a note to check the exact dates of these absences. "Did you have many interactions with Dania's parents? Or any other family members?"

Abbie shook her head. "Mostly her mum at pick-up time. Her dad came to one parents' evening. Oh, and there was an uncle who picked her up once or twice. Dania didn't seem to like him much."

George and Tashan exchanged a glance. "This uncle," George said carefully. "Can you describe him?"

"Tall, well-dressed. He had a beard. Dania called him Uncle Bilal, I think."

"How long had this change in Dania been going on would you say?"

Abbie bit her lip. "A few months, maybe? I've been having trouble sleeping, worrying about her. And now…" Her voice cracked.

George softened his tone. "You did everything you could, Miss Illingworth. This isn't on you."

As Abbie left to compose herself, George mulled over the discrepancies in their accounts. The genuine distress in Abbie's eyes contrasted sharply with Chelsie's fear and Mrs Gledhill's concern for the school's reputation.

"We need to look into this Uncle Bilal. And I want to know more about that caretaker."

Tashan nodded grimly. "This case just got a whole lot more complicated, didn't it?"

"Yeah," George agreed.

Their final interview was with Mrs Mellor, Abbie's nursery partner. Mrs Gledhill had told them earlier that the nursery children were allowed to wander between classes, so it made sense to interview her.

Mrs Mellor carried herself with the weary dignity of a long-serving educator. Her grey hair was cut in a practical bob, and laugh lines around her brown eyes hinted at a warmth that her current serious expression couldn't entirely mask. She wore a comfortable beige cardigan over a floral print dress, clothes chosen for practicality rather than style. Reading glasses hung from a chain around her neck, and a chunky wooden bangle adorned one wrist, bearing the marks of years of wear.

"There's something you should know," she said immediately, which shocked George. The older woman's face was etched with lines of worry and something else—reluctance? "Dania... she told me something. About her uncle."

George leaned forward, his heart rate quickening. "What did she say, Mrs Mellor?"

The teacher squirmed in her seat. "She said he... touched her. Inappropriately. But she was so young; children that age often misunderstand—"

"And you didn't report this?" Tashan's voice was sharp.

Mrs Mellor flushed. "I... no. I was afraid of causing trouble. You know how it is with the Asian community—"

George held up a hand, cutting her off. He didn't want racial prejudice clouding the investigation, but this was a lead they couldn't ignore. "We'll look into it, Mrs Mellor. Thank you for coming forward now." He narrowed his eyes and stared at Mrs Melllor for a long moment before saying, "I need you to tell me exactly what Dania said about her uncle. Every detail you can remember."

Mrs Mellor shifted uncomfortably. "It was during free play. Dania was with the dolls, and she... she said her uncle played a 'special game' with her. When I asked what kind of game it was, she said it was a secret, but it made her tummy feel funny."

Tashan leaned forward. "Did she say anything else about this 'game'?"

"She mentioned he'd touch her 'special places'," Mrs Mellor said, her voice barely above a whisper. "I... I should have reported it. I know that now."

George nodded, his jaw tight. "Did you ask her to point out where these special places were?"

Mrs Mellor shook her head.

"Not even on the dolls?"

"No."

"Were there any other behaviours or comments that concerned you?" George asked, grinding his teeth.

Mrs Mellor thought momentarily. "She started having accidents again, even though she'd been fully toilet trained. And she'd get very clingy at drop-off times, especially if her uncle was there."

"Tell us about her interactions with her parents," George

prompted. "What did you observe during drop-offs and pick-ups?"

"Her mum seemed... distracted, most of the time. Always in a rush. Her dad was gentler with her, but he didn't come often. The uncle, though..." Mrs Mellor trailed off.

"The uncle?" Tashan pressed.

"He'd come maybe once a week. Dania would go very quiet when she saw him. Not scared, exactly, but... subdued."

George made a note. "Did you ever address these concerns with anyone? Other staff members or Dania's parents?"

Mrs Mellor's face flushed. "I mentioned the toilet accidents to her mum. She just said Dania was going through a phase. I talked to Abbie about the clinginess, but..." She shook her head. "I should have done more."

"One last question," George said. "In your professional opinion, how was Dania's overall well-being and development?"

Mrs Mellor sighed. "She was a bright child. Ahead in her language development, good social skills. But in the last few months, she seemed to regress. More tantrums, trouble concentrating. I thought it was just a phase, but now..."

As they stood to leave, Mrs Mellor's face hardened. "Whoever did this... they're monsters. And that girl, Chelsie—we should never have hired her."

George and Tashan settled into the chairs opposite Mrs Gledhill once more, her desk a barricade between them. George leaned forward, his voice level. "Talk us through your child safeguarding policies. How are they implemented on a day-to-day basis?"

The headmistress straightened, her tone clipped and professional. "We have comprehensive safeguarding measures in place. All staff undergo mandatory training annually. We have strict sign-in and sign-out procedures for visitors and a clear chain of reporting for any concerns."

"And yet," Tashan interjected, "a child was abducted from your care. How did that happen, given these 'comprehensive measures'?"

Mrs Gledhill flinched. "It was... an unfortunate lapse. As I said, our new teaching assistant—"

"We'll get to her in a moment," George said. "Have there been any other safety incidents or concerns at the school?"

A pause. Mrs Gledhill's fingers drummed nervously on her desk. "Nothing of this magnitude. We had an incident last year where a non-custodial parent attempted to collect a child, but it was quickly resolved."

George's eyebrows rose. "And how was it resolved?"

"The staff member on duty followed protocol, refused to release the child, and contacted the custodial parent immediately."

"Unlike in Dania's case," Tashan noted dryly.

Mrs Gledhill's lips thinned. "As I said, it was a lapse. One we deeply regret."

George leaned back, studying her. "Tell us about your hiring and training process. For new staff like Chelsie, specifically."

"We conduct thorough background checks, of course. References, DBS checks, the works. New staff undergo training, including safeguarding procedures, before they start."

"And Chelsie went through all this?" Tashan asked.

Mrs Gledhill nodded. "Yes. She passed all checks with flying colours."

George made a note. "What about your communication protocols with parents in emergency situations?"

"We have an emergency contact list for each child," Mrs Gledhill explained. "In situations like illnesses or injuries, we always call the primary contact first, then work our way down the list if necessary."

"But in Dania's case," George pressed, "no one called to verify the story about her mother being in hospital?"

Mrs Gledhill's face tightened. "As I said, it was a lapse in judgment. One we're addressing."

"How?" Tashan asked. "What changes have you implemented since Dania's abduction?"

"We've retrained all staff on safeguarding procedures," Mrs Gledhill said. "We've implemented a new sign-out system requiring photo ID for anyone collecting a child who isn't a known parent or guardian. And we're installing additional security cameras."

George nodded, standing. "We'll need copies of all your safeguarding policies and procedures, as well as staff training records."

Mrs Gledhill's eyes widened. "Is that really necessary? We're cooperating fully—"

"It's necessary," George cut her off. "We'll also need access to *all* your security footage from the day Dania was taken."

"I also need to discuss with you the very interesting conversation we've just had with Mrs Mellor. I'd like to know why we weren't informed immediately about Dania's disclosure regarding her uncle."

The headmistress's face paled. "Disclosure? I... I don't understand. What disclosure?"

"According to Mrs Mellor," Tashan interjected, his voice cold, "Dania told her that her uncle played 'special games' with her. Games that made her 'tummy feel funny'. Games

26

that involved touching her 'special places'."

Mrs Gledhill's hand flew to her mouth, her eyes widening in shock. "Oh my God," she whispered. "I had no idea. Mrs Mellor never..."

"Never reported it?" George finished for her, his tone sharp. "Never followed proper safeguarding procedures? Never thought to mention it to you when a child in the school's care went missing?"

The headmistress seemed to shrink in her chair. "I... I don't know what to say. This is... it's unforgivable."

George straightened, crossing his arms. "You're damn right it's unforgivable. A child made a clear disclosure of sexual abuse, and it was ignored. And now that child is dead."

Mrs Gledhill flinched at his words. "I assure you, Detective, if I had known..."

"But you didn't know," Tashan cut in. "Because your staff failed to follow protocol. The very protocols you assured us were so comprehensive."

George watched as the reality of the situation sank in. Mrs Gledhill's professional demeanour crumbled, replaced by genuine horror and distress.

"What... what happens now?" she asked, her voice barely above a whisper.

"Now," George said, his voice hard, "you give us every piece of information you have on Dania Bhati. Every note, every observation, every scrap of paper with her name on it. And then you pray that there's nothing else your staff has failed to report."

* * *

Twenty minutes later, and after receiving all the information they needed for now, George got up to leave but paused at the door, his hand on the handle. He turned back to Mrs Gledhill, his eyes narrowing slightly. "One more thing. We need to speak with Mr Farooq. Is he around?"

Mrs Gledhill shook her head. "Not at the moment. He'll be at home until two-ish, I expect. Just around the corner near the chippy."

Tashan made a note of the address while George pressed on. "Tell me about Mr Farooq. What's his reputation here at the school?"

Mrs Gledhill's brow furrowed. "Mr Farooq? He's been with us for years. Reliable, hard-working. Why do you ask?"

George kept his expression neutral. "Just covering all bases. There haven't been any issues with him? Complaints from staff or students?"

"None whatsoever," Mrs Gledhill said firmly. As with all our staff, Mr Farooq underwent rigorous checks before being hired—references, DBS checks, the works. He's always been above board."

George nodded slowly, exchanging a glance with Tashan. "I see. And in all his time here, nothing's ever raised a red flag?"

Mrs Gledhill's posture stiffened. "Detective, if you're implying something about Mr Farooq, I can assure you—"

"I'm not implying anything," George cut in smoothly. "As I said, we're just being thorough. Thank you for your time, Mrs Gledhill. We'll be in touch if we need anything else."

As they left the office, Tashan leaned in close. "She seemed pretty quick to defend him, didn't she?"

George nodded. "Yeah. A bit too quick, if you ask me. Let's pay Mr Farooq a visit, shall we? I've got a feeling he might have more to tell us than Mrs Gledhill lets on."

"She also seemed more worried about covering the school's arse than about Dania."

George nodded grimly. "Noticed that too. Let's get those records. I want to know exactly what kind of training Chelsie had, and why it failed so spectacularly."

Outside, the playground had emptied, and the children were back in their classrooms. George and Tashan walked to their car in silence, both processing the information they'd gathered.

"We also need to talk to Dania's father again," George said as they climbed in. "About his brother. Something's not adding up here."

Tashan nodded, his expression grim. "You think the uncle could be involved?"

George sighed. "He's certainly looking good for it," George replied. "But let's not jump to conclusions."

As they pulled away from the school, George's mind raced. The image of Dania's small, broken body flashed before his eyes, driving home the urgency of their mission. They had to find her killer, and quickly!

Chapter Four

George and Tashan stood on the doorstep of Mr Farooq's modest terraced house. The paint peeled from the door frame, and a faint smell of curry wafted from inside. It made George's stomach rumble.

George rapped his knuckles against the wood, three sharp knocks.

Footsteps shuffled behind the door. It creaked open, revealing a man in his fifties, his salt-and-pepper beard neatly trimmed, his dark eyes wary.

"Mr Farooq?" George asked, flashing his warrant card. "DCI Beaumont. This is DS Blackburn. We'd like to ask you a few questions about Dania Bhati."

Farooq's eyes widened slightly. He nodded, stepping back to let them in.

The living room was small but tidy. Family photos lined the mantelpiece, a life's story told in frozen moments. George and Tashan settled onto a worn sofa while Farooq perched on an armchair, his posture stiff.

"Mr Farooq," George began, his voice level. "We're investigating the disappearance and death of Dania Bhati. As the school caretaker, we believe you might have information that could help us. Before we begin, I want to make sure you understand your rights. You're not under arrest, and you're free to stop this interview at any time, but any information you can give us would be extremely helpful. Do you understand?"

Farooq nodded, his hands clasped tightly in his lap. "Yes, I understand. I want to help. Poor little Dania..."

George leaned forward slightly. "Let's start with some background information. Can you confirm your full name, date of birth, and address for the record?"

"Amir Farooq," the man replied. "Born 15th of May, 1968. This is my current address."

Tashan jotted down the details in his notebook as George continued. "How long have you been employed at Middleton Academy Primary School?"

"Fifteen years now," Farooq said.

"And your job responsibilities?"

Farooq shrugged. "I'm the caretaker. I maintain the building, fix things, and keep the grounds tidy. I'm there before the children arrive and after they leave." He paused. "I sometimes help out during the day if an emergency fix is needed."

George nodded. "Any previous employment we should know about?"

"I worked in a factory before this. Nothing exciting."

"Now, Mr Farooq," George said, his tone sharpening slightly. "I need you to walk me through the day Dania disappeared. Every detail you can remember."

Farooq's brow furrowed. "It was a Tuesday. I remember because I always clean the gutters on Tuesdays. I arrived at 6 am, did my usual morning rounds. Around 3.15, I was in the nursery playground, fixing the waterfall."

"And did you see Dania?" Tashan asked.

Farooq nodded slowly. "Yes... yes, I did. She was with a woman. I assumed it was her mother or an aunt."

George leaned forward. "Can you describe this woman?"

"Young, maybe late twenties. Dark hair, wearing a head-scarf. She seemed... familiar with the school. Walked like she knew where she was going, which is unusual for nursery."

"Did you hear any of their conversation?" George pressed.

Farooq shook his head. "No, they were too far away. But Dania seemed... quiet. Not her usual chatty self."

George exchanged a glance with Tashan. "Mr Farooq, how well did you know Dania?"

"Not well," Farooq replied. "I didn't interact much with the children. But Dania was... noticeable. Always smiling, always talking." He closed his eyes. "A cute kid."

"Were there any incidents between you and Dania?" George asked, his voice carefully neutral. "Anything that might have scared her?"

Farooq's eyes widened. "Scared her? No, never! I... I did tell her off once for running in the corridors. But I wasn't harsh, I swear."

George nodded, making a mental note. "Let's talk about the school's safeguarding procedures. What can you tell me about them?"

"We have strict rules," Farooq said. "No adult is allowed in the building without signing in. Children can only leave with approved adults. We have regular training sessions."

"And your role in implementing these procedures?"

"I make sure all doors are locked during school hours. I report any suspicious activity to Mrs Gledhill. But mainly, I watch. I'm always around, you see. I notice things."

George leaned back slightly. "Have you ever had any

concerns about safety at the school?"

Farooq hesitated. "Not... not really. Though lately, there have been some odd characters hanging around outside. Nothing I could put my finger on, but..."

"Can you elaborate?" Tashan asked.

"Just... men and women I didn't recognise. They were watching the school. I reported it to Mrs Gledhill, but she said not to worry."

George's eyes narrowed. "When was this?"

"A few weeks before Dania disappeared. It stopped after she went missing."

The detectives exchanged another glance. George pressed on. "Did you know any of Dania's family members? Her uncle, perhaps?"

Farooq shook his head. "I saw her parents at pick-up sometimes. Never met an uncle."

"One last thing, Mr Farooq," George said. "We need to account for your movements in the days before and after Dania's disappearance. Can you walk us through that?"

For the next ten minutes, Farooq detailed his routine. Work, home, mosque on Fridays. Nothing out of the ordinary.

"Is there anyone who can corroborate this?" Tashan asked.

"My wife, my colleagues at the school. The imam at the mosque."

George stood, signalling the end of the interview. "Thank you for your time, Mr Farooq. Is there anything else you think might be relevant? Anything at all?"

Farooq hesitated and shook his head. "No, I don't think so. I wish I could be more helpful."

"You've been very helpful," George assured him, handing over his business card. "We may need to speak with you again.

If you remember anything, no matter how small, please call me."

As they left the house, Tashan turned to George. "What do you think?"

George's jaw tightened. "I think we need to find out more about these men and women watching the school. And I want to know why Mrs Gledhill didn't mention it."

* * *

The afternoon sun cast long shadows across the playground as George and Tashan returned to Middleton Academy Primary School. The children's laughter and shouts had faded, replaced by an eerie quiet that seemed to echo the gravity of their task.

Mrs Gledhill met them at the entrance, her face a mask of professional concern. "Detectives, thank you for coming back. The girls are waiting in my office."

George nodded curtly. "And their parents?"

"We've asked permission to interview the children alone," Mrs Gledhill admitted. "I thought it pertinent."

Tashan's eyebrows shot up. "That's not standard procedure, Mrs Gledhill."

"I understand," she replied, her voice tight. "But these girls are our best witnesses. I didn't want their recollections tainted by parental influence."

George exchanged a glance with Tashan. It wasn't ideal, but time was of the essence. "Fine. But you'll be present as an appropriate adult, and we'll record it."

They entered the office to find two girls perched on chairs, eyes wide with a mix of curiosity and apprehension. George softened his expression, crouching down to their eye level.

"Hello, girls. I'm George, and this is my friend Tashan. We're police detectives, and we need your help. Is that OK?"

The girls nodded, exchanging nervous glances.

"You're not in any trouble," Tashan added, his voice gentle. "We just want to ask you about something you might have seen."

George pulled up a chair, keeping his body language open and non-threatening. "Can you tell me your names and how old you are?"

The first girl, a freckle-faced redhead, spoke up. "I'm Poppy. I'm eleven."

Her friend, darker-skinned with braided hair, followed. "Destiny. Also eleven."

"Nice to meet you both," George said, offering a reassuring smile. "Now, can you tell me what you usually do after school?"

Poppy shrugged. "We hang out in the nursery playground sometimes. Wait for our mums."

"And is that what you were doing on the day Dania disappeared?" Tashan asked.

The girls nodded in unison.

George leaned forward slightly. "Can you tell me exactly what you remember about that day?"

Destiny bit her lip. "We were by the waterfall. Poppy forgot her jumper, so we went back for it."

"And did you see Dania?" George prompted.

Poppy nodded vigorously. "Yeah, she was with a lady. Not her mum, though."

George's pulse quickened. "Can you describe this lady for me?"

The girls exchanged glances again. Destiny spoke first. "She was pretty. She had dark hair, kind of curly. She had a scarf on her head, but it didn't cover her face."

"What did her face look like?"

Destiny shrugged. "Pretty. Like magazine-pretty."

"Beautiful," Poppy added.

"Anything else?" Tashan pressed gently. "What was she wearing?"

Poppy scrunched up her face in concentration. "Blue top, I think. And jeans. Oh, and she had a mole! Right here." She pointed to a spot above her lip.

George nodded encouragingly. "That's excellent, Poppy. Did you hear the lady speak? What did her voice sound like?"

"She sounded nice," Destiny offered. "Like... posh, sort of. But not too posh."

"And Dania?" George asked. "How did she seem when she was with this lady?"

The girls' expressions clouded. "Quiet," Poppy said. "Dania's usually really chatty, but she wasn't saying much."

"Did she look scared?" Tashan asked.

Destiny shook her head. "Not scared. Just... different. Like when you're at someone else's house, and you don't know how to act."

George made a mental note of the astute observation. "Have you ever seen this lady before? Or since?"

Both girls shook their heads.

"What about anyone else unusual hanging around the school?" George pressed. "In the days before or after?"

Poppy's eyes widened. "There was a man! In a white van. He was parked outside for ages one day."

Destiny nodded in agreement. "Yeah, I remember him. He

gave me the creeps."

George and Tashan exchanged significant looks. "How come you remember him?"

"Because he was parked on the lines where you're not supposed to park," Destiny said.

Tashan asked, "Can you describe this man?"

The girls provided a vague description—old but not really old, Asian like the man who they buy sweets from in the shop around the corner, black hair and eyes. It was not much to go on, but it was something.

George asked, "How do you both know Dania?"

The pair shared a glance before Poppy said, "We got into nursery sometimes and read to them. Dania was adorable and loved to be read to."

"She was like a little sister," Destiny added.

"Last question, girls," George said, his tone serious but kind. "Do you feel safe at school? Have you ever seen anything that made you uncomfortable?"

Poppy shrugged. "It's OK, I guess. Nothing weird."

Destiny nodded in agreement, but her eyes flicked briefly towards Mrs Gledhill. George caught the gesture but didn't comment.

"Well, you've both been incredibly helpful," he said, standing up. "If you remember anything else, anything at all, you can always call us." He handed them each a card with his mobile number. "Make sure your parents know you're calling us, OK?"

As the girls left, escorted by a teacher, George turned to Mrs Gledhill. "We'll need to inform their parents of the contents of the interview."

The headmistress nodded stiffly. "Of course. I'll take care

of it immediately."

Outside the office, Tashan muttered, "Did you catch that look from Destiny?"

George nodded grimly. "Yeah. We might need to have another chat with her. Alone."

They walked towards the exit, minds racing with new information. The pretty woman with the mole. The man in the white van. And underneath it all, the nagging sense that there was still more to uncover.

"We need to cross-reference this description with the one Chelsie gave," George said as they reached their car. "And find out more about this van man."

Tashan nodded, his expression determined. "We're getting closer, sir. I can feel it."

As they drove away from the school, George couldn't shake the image of Dania, quiet and subdued, walking away with a stranger. What had that little girl seen in her final days? What secrets had she taken to her grave?

Chapter Five

George steered the car through the streets of Beeston towards Elland Road, the sun low in the sky. The day's events churned in his mind, a relentless tide of information and emotion. He needed a moment to breathe, to process. And his team needed sustenance.

"Pull over here," he said to Tashan, spotting a familiar chippie. "We'll grab some tea for the team."

The smell of vinegar and frying oil hit them as they entered. George ordered a mix of sausages, both battered and not, fish, scallops, and fish cakes plus a few bags of chips, exchanging pleasantries with the owner. Small talk, mundane and comforting in its normalcy.

Back at the station, the team gathered in the Incident Room. Tired faces looked up expectantly as George and Tashan entered, arms laden with grease-spotted paper bags and cans of pop, condensation dripping down the aluminium.

"Right," George said, distributing the provisions. "Let's go over what we've got."

For the next twenty minutes, he and Tashan briefed the team on their meetings with the Bhatis, the school staff, and Mr Farooq. The room buzzed with quiet intensity as detectives jotted notes and asked questions.

"This is priority one, people," George emphasised, his voice cutting through the murmur. "We've got a child killer out there, and every minute counts."

Heads nodded in agreement, determination etched on every face. But as George scanned the room, his gaze snagged on DC Priya Patel. The young officer sat rigidly in her chair, her usually sharp eyes unfocused and distant.

"Alright, I want a plan and I want it soon," George concluded. As the team dispersed, he approached Priya. "DC Patel. A word in my office?"

She startled slightly, then nodded, following him out of the room.

George's office was a sanctuary of organised chaos. Case files teetered in precarious stacks, whiteboards covered in scrawled notes and timelines. He closed the door behind them, gesturing for Priya to take a seat.

"What's going on, Priya?" he asked, leaning against his desk. "You seem off."

Priya's hands twisted in her lap, her usual confidence notably absent. "I'm fine, sir. It's... it's nothing."

George's eyebrows rose. "Bollocks. I've known you long enough now to know when something's eating at you. Spill it."

For a long moment, Priya said nothing. Then, with a shaky breath, the words tumbled out. "It's this case, sir. It's... it's bringing up some stuff. From when I was a kid."

George waited, giving her space to continue.

"I had a best friend when I was little. Amrita." Priya's voice wavered. "We were inseparable. Did everything together. And then one day... she was gone."

George's stomach clenched, sensing where this was going.

"They found her body a week later," Priya continued, her eyes fixed on a point somewhere beyond the office walls. "It was her uncle. He'd... he'd been abusing her for months. None of us knew."

"Christ, Priya," George breathed. "I'm so sorry."

She shook her head as if trying to dislodge the memories. "It was a long time ago. I thought I'd dealt with it. But this case... it's all coming back."

George moved to sit beside her, close but not touching. "Have you considered sitting this one out? No one would think less of you."

Priya's head snapped up, fire returning to her eyes. "No. Absolutely not. I need to see this through. For Dania. For Amrita."

George studied her for a long moment, weighing her determination against his concern. "Alright," he said finally. "But you talk to me, yeah? If it gets too much, you say the word. No heroics."

Priya nodded, a ghost of a smile touching her lips. "Yes, sir. Thank you."

"We're a team, DC Patel," George said, standing. "We look out for each other. Especially on cases like this. Now, let's go catch this bastard, shall we?"

* * *

There was a sense of renewed energy in the Incident Room as George strode in, Priya close behind. Faces turned expectantly, pens poised over notepads, ready for direction. George surveyed his team, a mix of seasoned veterans and eager newcomers, all united in their determination to solve this case.

"Right," George said, his voice cutting through the low hum of conversation. "We've got a lot of ground to cover, and time isn't on our side. Let's break this down."

He moved to the whiteboard, marker in hand, and began sketching out their priorities. The squeak of the pen against the glossy surface seemed to heighten the room's tension.

"First up," George continued, "we need to identify and locate Dania's uncle. The name Bilal has come up multiple times. We need to cross-reference this with the family information Hassan Bhati provided."

DS Yolanda Williams leaned forward, her distinctive red and green Mohawk catching the fluorescent light. "Sir, I might have a lead on that. I've got a mate in customs. I can reach out and see if this Bilal character has left the country recently, as Hassan suggested."

George nodded approvingly. "Good thinking, DS Williams. Make that call. If he's done a runner, we need to know."

Yolanda was already reaching for her phone as George turned to the rest of the team. "Next, we need to dig into the Bhati family's history with social services. There might be previous concerns or reports we're not aware of."

His gaze fell on Priya, noting the determined set of her jaw. She'd bounced back quickly from their earlier conversation, her professional mask firmly in place. "DC Patel, I want you on this. Reach out to social services and get everything they've got on the Bhatis. While you're at it, review files on other missing children in the area. Let's make sure we're not missing any connections."

Priya nodded briskly, already pulling her laptop towards her. "On it, sir."

George turned to Tashan, who stood ready, notebook in hand. "Blackburn, I need you to liaise with PS Greenwood's team. They're reviewing CCTV footage from around the school and the farmhouse. Get an update on their progress."

Tashan scribbled furiously. "Anything specific you want me to focus on, sir?"

"Look for that white van the girls mentioned," George replied. "And any sign of our mystery woman with the mole. Also, I want you to start putting together a detailed timeline of Dania's last known movements. Every minute counts here."

* * *

George made his way to DSU Smith's office. Each step echoed in the quiet corridor, a rhythmic accompaniment to the thoughts racing through his mind.

He rapped his knuckles against the frosted glass of Smith's door, waiting for the gruff "Come in" before entering.

DSU Jim Smith sat behind his desk, a mountain of paperwork threatening to topple onto the floor. He looked up as George entered, his bushy eyebrows raising in question.

"Beaumont," he said by way of greeting. "What can I do for you?"

George settled into the chair opposite, leaning forward with his elbows on his knees. "Sir, I need to request a temporary DC for my team. With Candy still on sick leave and... well, given the situation with Luke, we're stretched thin."

Smith's expression darkened at the mention of Luke Mason. The betrayal of one of their own still stung, a fresh wound in the department's collective psyche.

"You've got access to the other teams' detectives," Smith

reminded him. "Not to mention regular CID. Why the need for a specific temporary assignment?"

George's jaw tightened. "After everything that's happened, sir, I need someone I can trust implicitly. Someone I've worked with before."

Understanding dawned in Smith's eyes. He nodded slowly, gesturing for George to continue.

"I was thinking of DC Susie Whitaker," George said. "We worked together on the Naughty List case a couple of years back. She's sharp, dedicated. I'd stake my career on her integrity."

Smith leaned back in his chair, considering. "Whitaker... ginger hair, blue eyes? Mid-twenties?"

George nodded. "That's her. Astute as they come. She'd be a valuable asset to the team."

For a long moment, Smith said nothing. Then he sighed, reaching for a form on his desk. "Alright, Beaumont. I'll put in the request. She should be with you first thing tomorrow morning."

Relief washed over George. "Thank you, sir. In the meantime, I'll use CID detectives for the background checks we need to run today."

"Good," Smith said, scribbling his signature on the form. "Now, about this Bhati case. We need to discuss media strategy."

George straightened in his chair, his mind shifting gears. "What did you have in mind, sir?"

Smith's eyes narrowed. "We're walking a tightrope here, Beaumont. The public needs to be informed, but we can't risk compromising the investigation. I want you to prepare for a possible media briefing."

George nodded, his mind already racing through potential scenarios. "What information are we clearing for release?"

"That's what we need to decide," Smith said, leaning forward. We confirm the victim's identity, obviously. But how much do we reveal about the circumstances? The potential link to other missing children cases?"

George considered momentarily. "We need to strike a balance. Enough information to keep the public vigilant, but not so much that we tip our hand to the killer."

Smith nodded approvingly. "My thoughts exactly. We confirm Dania's identity, appeal for any information about her movements in the days leading up to her disappearance. But we keep the details of how she was found under wraps for now."

"And the uncle?" George asked. "Do we mention him?"

Smith's brow furrowed. "Not by name. But we can say we're following several leads, including family members. It might smoke him out if he's still in the country."

George made mental notes, already crafting the statement in his head. "What about the other missing children cases? Do we hint at a potential connection?"

"Not yet," Smith said firmly. "We need more concrete evidence before we risk causing a panic. For now, we focus on Dania. But be prepared for questions about other cases. The press will smell blood in the water."

George nodded grimly. He'd faced the media circus before, but this case felt different. More volatile. The stakes impossibly high.

"One more thing," Smith added. "Has DI Wood spoken with you about the Fawcett/Morris case she's working on?"

"No, sir," George said. "She knows better."

"I thought as much," Smith said. "She's working on a missing children case too." The Geordie paused and scratched his stubbly chin. "I'm wondering whether they're linked."

"Is that permission to speak with her, sir?"

"Not yet."

George nodded.

"Also," Smith said, "we need to tread carefully around the cultural aspects of this case. The last thing we need is to inflame racial tensions."

George's jaw tightened. "Agreed. We stick to the facts. This isn't about race or religion. It's about a child who was brutally murdered. That's what matters."

Smith held his gaze for a long moment, then nodded. "Good. Draft a statement and get it to me by the end of the day. I want to review it before we go public."

As George stood to leave, Smith called out, "And Beaumont? Watch yourself on this one. I've got a feeling it's going to get a lot uglier before it's over."

George paused at the door, his hand on the handle. "I know, sir. I'll be careful."

With that, he stepped back into the corridor, his mind already racing with the tasks ahead. A new team member to brief, a media statement to craft, and always, always, the ticking clock of the investigation.

Chapter Six

George closed the door to his office. He sank into his chair, eyes fixed on the phone on his desk. The call he needed to make wasn't one he relished, but it was necessary. Vital to moving the investigation forward.

With a deep breath, he picked up the receiver and dialled the number for the pathology department. Each ring seemed to stretch for an eternity before a crisp, professional voice answered.

"Pathology, Dr Yardley speaking."

"Lindsey, it's George Beaumont," he said. "Have you got a minute to discuss the Bhati case?"

There was a brief pause, the sound of papers shuffling in the background. "Of course, DCI Beaumont. I've just finished my preliminary report. I warn you, it's not pleasant reading."

George's jaw tightened. "I didn't expect it would be. What can you tell me?"

Dr Yardley's voice took on a clinical tone, a defence mechanism against the horrors she dealt with daily. "The victim, Dania Bhati, suffered extensive abuse prior to her death. Multiple contusions and lacerations in various stages of healing suggest this was ongoing, not a single incident."

George closed his eyes, fighting to maintain his professional composure. "Go on."

"There's clear evidence of sexual assault," Lindsey continued, her voice faltering slightly. "Both recent and... historical."

The pencil in George's hand snapped, startling him. He hadn't even realised he'd been gripping it. "Christ," he muttered. "Anything else?"

"Multiple fractures," Lindsey said. "Some old, some new. Her right arm had been broken and improperly set. Two ribs showed signs of previous breaks. And her left ankle... the break there was recent. Probably within 24 hours of her death."

George's free hand clenched into a fist, nails digging into his palm. "Cause of death?"

"Blunt force trauma to the head," Lindsey replied. "A single, powerful blow. Death would have been almost instantaneous."

"Small mercies," George muttered. "Time of death?"

"Based on liver temperature and the state of rigour, I'd estimate between 48 and 72 hours before she was found. But George..." Lindsey paused, her professional demeanour slipping momentarily. "The level of abuse this child endured... it's one of the worst cases I've seen."

"I understand, Lindsey. Thank you for your work on this. Can you send over the full report as soon as it's ready?"

"Of course," she said. "It should be on your desk within the hour. And George? Catch this bastard, will you?"

"Count on it," George replied, his voice hard.

As he hung up the phone, George leaned back in his chair, running a hand over his face. The details of Dania's suffering burned in his mind, fuelling a rage he struggled to contain. He'd seen a lot in his years on the force, but cases involving children always hit hardest.

He stood abruptly, needing to move, to do something. Pacing the confines of his office, he tried to process what he'd learned. Dania hadn't just been murdered; she'd been tortured and abused over an extended period. The implications were staggering.

This wasn't a crime of opportunity or a momentary loss of control. This was sustained, deliberate cruelty. And if Priya's hunch about connections to other missing children cases panned out, they could be dealing with something far more sinister than they'd initially thought.

George's thoughts spiralled, connecting dots and forming theories. The uncle, Bilal, fleeing the country. The school's lax security procedures. The people waiting outside the school. The pretty woman with the scarf on her head that didn't cover her face. It all painted a picture of systemic failure, a perfect storm of negligence and evil that had resulted in a little girl's death.

* * *

George strode into the Incident Room, his mind still reeling from the pathologist's report. The buzz of activity hit him like a wall, phones ringing and keyboards clacking as his team worked tirelessly.

Yolanda's distinctive Mohawk caught his eye. She waved him over, her expression a mix of excitement and frustration.

"Sir!" she called. "Got an update from my customs con-tact."

George was at her side in an instant, hope flaring in his chest. "What have you got?"

Yolanda's eyes gleamed with the thrill of the chase, but her brow furrowed. "It's about Bilal Bhati, sir. But it's not what we expected."

George's stomach clenched. "Go on."

"My contact's been through every outbound flight manifest for the past week. Checked all the major airports, seaports too." Yolanda shook her head. "There's no record of Bilal Bhati leaving the country."

George's mind raced. "Are you sure? Could he have used a different name?"

Yolanda nodded. "Thought of that. They cross-checked passport photos and ran facial recognition on CCTV. Nothing."

"Bloody hell," George muttered. "So he's still here."

"Looks like it," Yolanda confirmed. "Unless he's found some way to slip past border control undetected."

George's jaw tightened. "Which means he could be anywhere. Hiding out, planning his next move."

Yolanda leaned in, lowering her voice. "There's more, sir. My contact flagged something odd. There's no record of Bilal Bhati entering or leaving the country in the past five years either."

George's eyebrows shot up. "What? But Hassan said his brother travels regularly for work."

"Exactly," Yolanda said. "Either Hassan was lying, or..."

"Or Bilal Bhati isn't who we think he is," George finished.

The implications hung heavy in the air between them. George's mind whirled with possibilities, each more disturbing than the last.

"Good work, DS Williams," he said finally. "Keep digging. I want to know everything there is to know about Bilal Bhati. If that's even his real name."

As Yolanda nodded and turned back to her computer, George felt the case shift beneath his feet. What had seemed like a straightforward lead had just become infinitely more complex.

Tashan appeared at his elbow, face grim. "Sir, I've just heard back from Greenwood. They've got CCTV footage of a man matching Bilal's description in various places near the farmhouse."

"When?"

"The night before Dania was found."

"Where?"

Tashan handed George three separate printouts showing a dark-haired and dark-bearded man of South Asian origin in different areas of Middleton and Thorpe, driving a white van, the reg number obscured by dirt.

"Any others?"

Tashan nodded and handed George a printout. "Same guy filling up a white van at the petrol station on Leeds Road, just off the A654."

George nodded. "He look familiar to you?"

"Zachary Sayed?"

George raised his brow. Zachery Sayed was one of Jürgen Schmidt's lieutenants. "It could be him. Get down there, Tashan, see if the man in the CCTV paid by cash or card."

The pieces were starting to fall into place, a picture emerging from the chaos. George felt the familiar surge of adrenaline.

"Good work, both of you," he said. "Now get cracking."

As they hurried off, Priya approached, her face a mask of controlled anger. "Sir, I've got the social services reports. Concerns were raised about Dania's home life six months ago. A neighbour reported hearing screaming, but when social workers visited, the family claimed it was just a loud argument."

George's jaw tightened. "And they left it at that?"

Priya shook her head, disgust evident in her voice. "They made a note to follow up, but it seems to have fallen through the cracks."

George made a mental note to visit social services personally.

"There's more, though," Priya said. "I've found three other cases of missing children in the area over the past eighteen months. All unsolved."

The implications hung heavy in the air. George's mind whirled with possibilities, each more horrifying than the last. "Any connections to the Bhati case?"

"Not immediately obvious," Priya admitted. "But I'm digging deeper. Two of the children were from Asian families, one Chinese and one Indian. The other, a boy, was white British."

George nodded, his expression grim. "Keep on it, DC Patel. If there's a link, I want to know about it."

As Priya returned to her desk, George surveyed the room once more. His team was in full flow now, working towards a common goal. But the clock was ticking, and somewhere out there, a killer walked free.

He moved to the centre of the room, raising his voice to be heard over the bustle. "Listen up, everyone. We're making progress, but we can't afford to get complacent. This isn't just about Dania now. If DC Patel's right, we could be looking at a serial offender."

A hush fell over the room. George continued, his voice hard. "I want updates every hour. If you find anything, no matter how small it seems, you bring it to me or DS Blackburn immediately. We're going to nail this bastard, and we're going to do it before he hurts another child. Understood?"

A chorus of affirmatives rang out. George nodded, satisfied. "Right. Let's get back to it."

* * *

George Beaumont stepped out to face the assembled press, the late afternoon sun casting long shadows across the steps of Elland Road Police Station. A forest of microphones sprouted before him, camera lenses glinting like predatory eyes. The air thrummed with anticipation, reporters jostling for position.

George straightened his tie, his face a mask of professional composure. Behind him, DS Tashan Blackburn stood at attention, a silent pillar of support.

"Thank you for coming," George began, his voice carrying across the murmur of the crowd. " I'm Detective Chief Inspector George Beaumont, leading the investigation into the death of Dania Bhati."

A hush fell over the gathering.

"At approximately 10:15 pm on Tuesday evening, the body of four-year-old Dania Bhati was discovered in an abandoned farmhouse just off the A654 near Thorpe. We are treating her death as suspicious and are carrying out a murder investigation."

Cameras flashed, pens scribbled furiously. George paused, letting the information sink in.

"Dania was last seen alive leaving her nursery school three weeks ago. We are appealing to the public for any information regarding her movements or whereabouts during this time."

A hand shot up. "DCI Beaumont! Is it true the child was abducted from the school?"

George's jaw tightened imperceptibly. "We are exploring all possibilities. The circumstances of Dania's disappearance form a crucial part of our investigation."

Another reporter called out, "Are there any suspects?"

"We are following several leads," George replied carefully. "This includes speaking with family members and associates. Normally, it would be inappropriate to comment further on potential suspects at this stage of the investigation." He paused. "However, we are currently seeking two individuals who may have crucial information regarding Dania's disappearance and subsequent murder."

The crowd hushed, pens poised over notepads.

"First, we're looking for a South Asian man, approximately 40 to 45 years old, seen on CCTV near the location where Dania's body was found, driving a white van with its reg number concealed by dirt." George held up the printouts and added, "These images will be provided to all." He paused and looked at the TV cameras. "I want you, the public, to think hard and see if you can remember any white vans you have seen recently and get in touch with my dedicated line, which I will release information about at the end of the press conference." There were more blinding flashes. "Secondly, we're seeking a young Asian woman, described as attractive with dark, curly hair and a distinctive mole above her lip, possibly wearing a scarf on her head. This woman was seen collecting Dania from her school on the day of her disappearance." Again, George held up printouts of the CCTV footage.

Once more, camera flashes erupted like lightning. George

raised his hand, stemming the tide of questions before they could begin.

"I want to stress that these individuals are persons of interest at this stage. We urgently need to speak with them to further our investigation. If anyone has information about either of these people or if you are one of these individuals, please get in touch with us immediately."

He could see the reporters' eyes narrow, scenting blood in the water. A woman near the front raised her voice, "Is there any connection to other missing children cases in the area?"

George's pulse quickened, but he kept his expression neutral. "At present, we are focusing our efforts on solving Dania's murder. We have no evidence linking this case to any other investigations."

The questions came rapid-fire now, a barrage of inquiries about timelines, suspects, and gruesome details. George fielded them with practised ease, revealing enough to satisfy without compromising the investigation.

Finally, he held up a hand. "One last thing. To the person or persons responsible for Dania's death: We will find you. There is nowhere you can hide, no rock you can crawl under that we won't overturn. For Dania's sake, for her family's sake, turn yourself in. It's only a matter of time."

With that, George stepped back from the microphones. "Thank you. No further questions."

Chapter Seven

The fluorescent lights of the Incident Room buzzed overhead, casting harsh shadows across tired faces. George stood at the head of the table, surveying his team. Exhaustion etched deep lines around their eyes, but determination still burned bright.

"Alright, we're shifting gears. Bilal Bhati is now our prime suspect. Yolanda, I need you to use those contacts of yours. Get an all-ports warning issued immediately. We can't risk him slipping out of the country."

Yolanda nodded sharply. "On it, boss. I'll make the calls as soon as we're done here."

George turned to Tashan. "DS Blackburn, I want you overseeing surveillance on any properties associated with Bilal. And start prepping for a potential armed response when we move to apprehend him. This bastard's shown he's capable of extreme violence."

Tashan's eyes hardened. "Understood, sir. I'll coordinate with the Specialist Firearms Command and have a plan ready by morning."

"Good," George said, then shifted his attention. "Priya, you're on the woman with the mole. She's either a key witness or an accomplice, and we need to find her. Get her image out to every media outlet in West Yorkshire. And I want you diving deep into HOLMES—cross-reference her description with missing persons and criminal databases."

Priya was already jotting notes. "Consider it done, sir. I'll have the overnight Digital Media Investigators working round the clock on this."

George straightened, surveying his team. "CID's started the background work on Bilal—financials, phone records, known associates. DC Whitaker will pick that up in the morning when she joins us."

He paused, making eye contact with each of them. "You've all done stellar work today, but we're just getting started. Get some rest tonight. I need you sharp tomorrow."

Tashan nodded, stifling a yawn. "What time do you want us back, sir?"

"Eight sharp," George replied. "And I want fresh eyes on everything. Sometimes a good night's sleep is what we need to spot something we've missed."

As the team began to gather their things, George caught Priya's eye. "You alright, DC Patel?"

She nodded, a ghost of a smile touching her lips. "Yes, sir. Ready for round two tomorrow."

George clapped her on the shoulder. "That's what I like to hear. Now go on, all of you. Get out of here."

The room emptied slowly, detectives trickling out in ones and twos. George remained, gathering his thoughts, mentally preparing for the battles to come.

George pulled out his phone. "Greenwood? It's DCI Beaumont. I need your uniforms to keep canvassing around the school and farmhouse. Use the photo of the woman with the mole. Someone must have seen her."

He listened for a moment, then nodded. "Good. Keep me

updated on any leads, no matter how small."

Hanging up, George looked around the now-empty Incident Room. They were making progress. And tomorrow, they'd hit the ground running.

With a deep breath, he gathered his things. It was time to head home to try and snatch a few hours of sleep before the hunt began anew.

* * *

The drive home was a blur of streetlights and late-night traffic. George's thoughts spiralled, rehashing the day's developments, plotting strategies for tomorrow. By the time he pulled into his drive in Middleton, his head throbbed.

He paused at the front door, taking a deep breath. Home was supposed to be a sanctuary, a place to shed the horrors of the job. But lately, the lines had begun to blur.

The sound of the television greeted him as he stepped inside. Isabella sat on the sofa, her eyes fixed on the screen where George's own face stared back, mid-press conference.

"You're home late," Isabella said, not looking away from the TV.

George hung up his coat, fatigue settling into his bones. He saw the look on Izzy's face. "It's been a bloody long day. How was yours?"

Isabella's jaw tightened. "Bloody awful. We're getting nowhere. But that's not..." She trailed off, biting her lip.

George frowned. "What is it, Izzy?"

Isabella muted the TV, turning to face him fully. "It's Olivia. I feel like we're failing her, George."

The mention of their daughter sent a pang through George's

chest. "What do you mean?"

"She's being passed around like a parcel," Isabella said, her voice thick with emotion. "Your mum, my grandparents, even your dad. It's not fair on her."

George ran a hand through his hair, guilt gnawing at him. "I know. But what choice do we have? The job—"

"The job is important, I know," Isabella cut in. "But so is our daughter. My grandparents are getting older, George. It's not fair to keep relying on them so much."

George nodded, thinking of Anne and Eric, Isabella's grand-parents, who had become such a crucial part of their support system. "They love having her, though. You know that."

"Of course they do," Isabella agreed. "But they're in their seventies. It's a lot to ask."

George's mind turned to his own parents. His mother, Marie, who doted on Olivia but had her own life to lead. And his father, Edward...

George had, begrudgingly, allowed Edward into Olivia's life, even trusting him to look after her once a month.

Isabella's eyes softened momentarily as if reading his mind. "Once a month at your dad's isn't enough, George. We need a more stable solution."

George leaned back, the full weight of their situation settling over him. "You're right. We can't keep doing this to her. To any of them."

"I feel so guilty," Isabella whispered, tears welling in her eyes. "We're supposed to be there for her, and instead—"

"Hey," George said softly, sitting down beside her and pulling her into his arms. "We're doing our best. We're not perfect, but Olivia knows she's loved. That's the most important thing."

Isabella nodded against his chest, but he could feel the tension in her body. "We need to do better, George. For Olivia's sake."

George pressed a kiss to the top of her head, his mind racing with possible solutions. "We will," he promised. "We'll figure something out. Maybe... maybe it's time we looked into a nanny. Or a more flexible childcare arrangement."

Isabella pulled back, meeting his eyes. "You'd be OK with that? Having someone else in the house?"

George nodded slowly. "If it means giving Olivia more stability, yes. We can't keep relying on family forever. It's not fair to them, and it's not fair to Olivia."

A small smile tugged at Isabella's lips. "Look at us, being responsible parents."

George chuckled, some of the tension easing from his shoulders. "We're trying, at least. That's got to count for something."

She smiled. "It does."

"It'll also give us a bit more time together." He grinned. "You know, to—"

Isabella stood abruptly and said, "Not this again. I'm going for a bath."

"Izzy," George started, but she was already halfway up the stairs.

"Not now, George. I can't... I can't deal with this on top of everything else right now."

Upstairs the bathroom door slammed, leaving George alone in the sudden silence. He sank onto the sofa, rubbing his temples. The adrenaline of the day ebbed away, leaving him hollow and drained.

On the TV, the news cycled through footage of the press

conference again. George watched himself, noting the tension in his shoulders and the carefully measured words. He looked older, somehow, worn down.

Upstairs, water thundered into the bathtub. George closed his eyes, letting the white noise wash over him. He should eat something, he knew. Should review his notes for tomorrow. Should call his son Jack, check in on him and Mia.

Instead, he sat motionless, letting the minutes tick by.

* * *

Isabella sank deeper into the warm bath, letting the water lap at her shoulders. The steam rose in lazy tendrils, carrying with it the scent of lavender bath oil. She closed her eyes, trying to relax, but her mind refused to quiet.

The visit to the Fawcett household a month ago played on repeat in her head. Mrs Fawcett's face, etched with years of grief and desperate hope, swam before her closed eyelids. The woman's trembling hands, her voice cracking with emotion as she spoke of her lost daughter—it all felt painfully vivid.

Isabella remembered the burden of responsibility she'd felt as she'd sat in that living room, tasked with delivering news that could shatter or reignite a mother's fragile hope. The careful words she'd chosen, trying to balance truth with compassion.

Timothy Aldred, the charismatic Crime Scene Manager, known affectionately by his nickname 'Moth', had been with her that day.

His usual cheerful demeanour had crumbled, replaced by a raw vulnerability she'd never seen in him before. The image of him clutching that small teddy bear, tears streaming down his face, tugged at her heart.

She thought about the room itself—a time capsule of a life interrupted. The faded posters, the untouched hairbrush, the dusty jewellery box—each item a testament to a childhood frozen in time, to dreams left unfulfilled.

How many more Abigails and Danias were out there? How many families were living in this agonising limbo, caught between hope and despair?

Isabella's thoughts drifted to the Morris case, to the possible connection between the two disappearances.

But with that determination came fear. If these cases were indeed connected, if there was a predator who had been operating undetected for years, how many more victims might there be?

She thought of George, working his own harrowing case. The urge to call him, to share the weight of their respective investigations, was strong. But she resisted, knowing they both needed to focus.

As the bathwater began to cool, Isabella sat up, her resolve hardening. She would solve this case, would bring closure to the Fawcetts and the Morrises.

Isabella stood, water cascading off her body. It was time to apologise to George for being a right bitch.

Things had been rocky of late, but with their winter wedding coming up, she had faith they'd get through it.

* * *

The creak of the stairs roused him from his stupor. Isabella padded into the living room, wrapped in her dressing gown, hair damp and tousled.

"I'm sorry," she said softly. "I shouldn't have snapped at you. It's not your fault my day was shit."

George opened his arms, and Isabella curled into him, her familiar scent enveloping him. "I'm sorry too," he murmured into her hair. "I should have asked about your day first."

They sat in comfortable silence for a moment, the tension of earlier melting away. Finally, Isabella pulled back, meeting George's gaze.

"How are you holding up?" she asked. "This case... it looks rough."

George sighed, the horrors of the day pressing in again. "It's bad, Izzy. Really bad. This little girl, what she went through..."

Isabella squeezed his hand. "You'll find who did it. You always do."

George nodded, wishing he felt as confident as she sounded. "I hope so.

George hesitated. But the need to unburden himself, to share his suspicions with someone he trusted implicitly, won out.

"Izzy," he began. There's something I need to tell you—something I probably shouldn't, but..."

Isabella sat up straighter, her eyes narrowing with concern. "George, what is it?"

He took a deep breath, steeling himself. "It's about the Dania case. And... possibly your case too."

Isabella's breath caught. "What do you mean?"

"Smith," George said, lowering his voice further, "he's worried there might be a connection. Between Dania and the children you're looking for."

Isabella's eyes widened. "A connection? Based on what?"

George ran a hand through his hair, frustration evident in

the gesture. "The similarities are... unsettling. Young children, abandoned farmhouses. The level of... brutality involved."

Isabella's face paled slightly. "You think we might be dealing with the same perpetrator?"

"I don't know," George admitted. "But the possibility is there. Smith wanted me to keep it under wraps for now, but... I couldn't not tell you, Izzy. Not when you're working a case that might be linked."

Isabella was quiet for a long moment, processing this new information. When she spoke, her voice was filled with a mix of determination and dread. "If these cases are connected, George... the implications are horrifying. How long has this been going on? How many more victims are out there?"

George nodded grimly. "I know. It's a nightmare scenario. But if there is a link, we need to find it. We need to stop this bastard before he hurts anyone else."

Isabella squeezed his hand, her resolve evident in her grip. "We will. Together. Thank you for telling me, George. I know it wasn't easy going against Smith's orders."

George managed a small smile. "No secrets between us, remember? Not when it comes to something this important."

* * *

That night, the darkness of the bedroom pressed in around George, broken only by the faint glow of the digital alarm clock. 3:17 am. He stared at the ceiling, his mind racing, sleep a distant impossibility.

Isabella's soft snoring filled the room, a rhythmic counter-point to the chaotic thoughts swirling in his head. He tried to focus on his breathing, in and out, slow and steady, but the technique that usually calmed him seemed useless tonight.

Images of Dania's small, broken body flashed behind his eyelids every time he closed them. The brutality of her murder, the suffering she must have endured... it churned his stomach, set his heart pounding against his ribs.

But as he lay there, listening to Isabella's breathing, he realised it wasn't just the case keeping him awake. A different kind of anxiety gnawed at him, one he'd been trying to ignore for weeks. Months.

Their wedding. December. Less than six months away.

George turned his head, studying Isabella's profile in the dim light. She'd brushed off his advances earlier, claiming exhaustion. It wasn't the first time. Lately, it felt like they were ships passing in the night, both consumed by their cases, barely finding time to connect.

But at least he'd tried. Isabella hadn't tried it on with him for months.

He loved her. God, he loved her. But were they ready for this? With their jobs, the constant pressure, the horrors they faced daily... how could they build a life together when they could barely find time to talk?

George's mind drifted to the similarities between their cases, the possible connections. If they were dealing with the same perpetrator, the implications were staggering. How could they plan a wedding, start a life together, with something so dark looming over them?

He thought about the Fawcetts, about Mrs Fawcett's haunted eyes as she spoke of her lost daughter. About the Bhatis, their world shattered by Dania's murder. How fragile happiness was, how quickly it could be snatched away.

Isabella shifted in her sleep, her hand brushing against his arm. George froze, not wanting to wake her. But part of him longed for her to open her eyes, to talk to him, to reassure him that they were solid, that they could weather any storm.

He wanted her to tell him she loved him and that this was just a slump.

But as the night crept on, George's anxiety grew. Since Olivia had been conceived, their love life had dwindled entirely. He loved Isabella and wanted a future with her. But as he lay there, listening to her sleep, he couldn't shake the feeling that something was slipping away from them. That the darkness they fought every day was seeping into their relationship, threatening to pull them apart.

The wedding loomed in his mind, no longer a joyful milestone but a deadline. A test they might not be ready to face.

George closed his eyes, trying once more to sleep. But as Isabella's snoring grew louder, he couldn't help but wonder: Were they really going to make it? Or was this case, this endless fight against evil, going to be the thing that finally drove them apart?

Chapter Eight

The sun had barely crept over the horizon when George Beaumont strode into Elland Road Police Station. The early morning quiet hung heavy in the air, broken only by the hum of fluorescent lights and the distant clatter of a cleaner's trolley. He made his way to the Homicide and Major Enquiry Team floor, his footsteps echoing in the empty corridor.

Pushing open the door to the shared office, he found Priya already at her desk, poring over a stack of files. She looked up as he entered, offering a nod of greeting.

"Morning, sir," she said, her voice steady and clear. No trace of yesterday's emotional turmoil lingered in her eyes.

"DC Patel," George replied, shrugging off his coat. "You're in early."

Priya straightened a pile of papers on her desk. "Couldn't sleep. Figured I'd get a head start on cross-referencing those missing persons reports."

George studied her for a moment, noting the determined set of her jaw. "How are you holding up?"

"Better," she said, meeting his gaze squarely. "Ready to catch this bastard."

George nodded, satisfied. He moved to the whiteboard, scanning the timeline they'd put together. "Do you have any leads on our mystery woman?"

Priya shook her head. "Nothing concrete yet. But I've got feelers out to every women's shelter and support group in West Yorkshire. If she's running scared, she might turn up there."

"Good thinking," George murmured. He turned back to face her, his expression grim. "Priya, we need to discuss something. It was on my mind last night. It's not pleasant, but we can't ignore the possibility any longer."

Priya's brow furrowed. "What is it, sir?"

George took a deep breath. "The level of organisation in this case, the multiple victims... We might be dealing with more than just one sick individual here."

Priya's eyes widened as understanding dawned. "A paedophile ring?"

George nodded, his jaw clenching. "It's a grim possibility, but we can't rule it out. The sophistication of the abduction, the use of the farmhouse... It suggests a level of planning and resources beyond a lone predator."

Priya's face hardened. "Bloody hell. You're right, though. We've seen an up-tick in these cases over the past few years."

"Exactly," George said, running a hand through his hair. The internet's made it easier for these monsters to connect and share certain... techniques." The last word came out as a disgusted snarl.

Priya stood, moving to join him at the whiteboard. "So, where do we start? We can't exactly put out an APB for a paedophile ring."

George tapped the photo of Bilal Bhati. "We start here. If Bilal's involved in something bigger, he'll have connections. Financial transactions, communications, travel patterns. We need to dig into every aspect of his life."

Priya nodded, her eyes gleaming with renewed determination. "I'll coordinate with financial crimes and see if they can spot any suspicious patterns in his accounts."

"That's great," George said. "Look into the Bhati family finances, too."

"I'll get a team on it right away."

George clapped her on the shoulder. "That's the spirit. We're going to turn over every stone until we find these bastards."

A knock at the door interrupted them. DS Tashan Blackburn poked his head in, his expression a mix of tension and excitement. "Sir, DC Whitaker's here. Where do you want me to set her up?"

George straightened. "Bring her in here, Tashan. We'll get her up to speed right away."

As Tashan disappeared to fetch their new team member, George turned back to Priya. "You ready for this? It's going to get ugly before it gets better."

Priya's eyes hardened. "I'm ready, sir. Whatever it takes to bring Dania justice."

George nodded, a grim smile tugging at his lips. "That's what I like to hear."

The door opened again, admitting Tashan and a petite woman with fiery red hair. DC Susie Whitaker's blue eyes scanned the room, quickly assessing the chaos of files and whiteboards.

"DC Whitaker, reporting for duty, sir," she said, her voice crisp and professional.

George extended his hand. "Welcome aboard, Susie. I wish it were under better circumstances."

Susie shook his hand firmly. "So do I, sir. But I'm ready to dive in. What do you need from me?"

George gestured to the whiteboard. "Tashan, bring Susie up to speed on where we are. Priya, you and I need to brief DSU Smith on our paedophile ring theory."

* * *

Priya fell into step beside George as they headed for Smith's office. "Sir," she said, her voice low, "if we're right about this ring, how far do you think it goes?"

George's jaw tightened. "I don't know, Priya. But I've got a nasty feeling we're only seeing the tip of the iceberg."

They paused outside Smith's door. George took a deep breath, steeling himself for the conversation ahead. "Ready?"

Priya nodded. "Let's do this."

George rapped his knuckles against the frosted glass. Smith's gruff voice called out, "Enter!"

They stepped into the office, finding the Detective Superintendent hunched over his desk, a scowl etched on his weathered face. He looked up as they entered, his bushy eyebrows rising in question.

"Beaumont, Patel. What's got you two looking like you've swallowed lemons?"

George glanced at Priya before addressing his superior. "Sir, we've got a theory about the Bhati case. It's not pretty."

Smith leaned back in his chair, gesturing for them to continue. "Out with it, then."

George took a deep breath. "We think we might be dealing with a paedophile ring, sir."

The words hung in the air, heavy and ominous. Smith's

face darkened, his eyes narrowing. "Christ. You're sure about this?"

Priya stepped forward. "We can't be certain, sir, but the evidence points that way. The level of organisation, the possibility of multiple victims, the sophisticated abduction techniques..."

Smith's fist came down on the desk with a sharp crack. "Bloody hell. As if one sick bastard wasn't bad enough."

George nodded grimly. "We're expanding our investigation, sir. Looking into every missing child case in West Yorkshire for the past five years. If there's a pattern, we'll find it."

Smith rubbed a hand over his face, suddenly looking every one of his years. "This is going to be a nightmare, Beaumont. The press will have a field day if they get wind of this."

"I know, sir," George said. "But we can't ignore the possibility. If we're right, there could be more children at risk."

Smith's eyes hardened. "You're right, of course. What do you need from me?"

Priya spoke up. "We'll need additional resources, sir. More staffing is needed to go through old cases, and liaisons with financial crimes are needed to track suspicious transactions."

"Consider it done," Smith said without hesitation. "Anything else?"

George glanced at Priya again before answering, "We might need to consider bringing in the National Crime Agency, sir. If this ring extends beyond West Yorkshire..."

Smith's face tightened, but he nodded. "Let's not jump the gun on that just yet. Give me solid evidence of a wider conspiracy, and I'll make the call myself."

"Understood, sir," George said. "We'll keep you updated

on any developments."

Back in the corridor, Priya let out a shaky breath. "Well, that went better than I expected."

George managed a grim smile. "Smith's a hard-arse, but he knows when to back his team. Come on, let's see how Tashan and Susie are getting on."

* * *

Detective Inspector Isabella Wood strode into her Wakefield HQ Incident Room, her mind still reeling from yesterday's emotional memories of her visit to the Fawcett household.

The weight of Mrs Fawcett's grief and the haunting remnants of Abigail's bedroom clung to her like a shroud, a constant reminder of the high stakes involved in this case.

Abigail was still missing after all this time. But not for long.

She rubbed her hand over tired eyes.

As she settled into her desk, Isabella noticed an email from Naomi Sasaki, the meticulous forensic scientist who, alongside the forensic anthropologist, had been analysing the bones found at the abandoned farm. With a sense of trepidation, she clicked on the message, her heart pounding in her chest.

The email was concise and to the point, as was Naomi's style. It read:

Detective Inspector Wood,

After careful analysis of the DNA samples obtained from the bones discovered at the abandoned farm in Walton, Wakefield, I can confirm that they belong to Ethan Morris, not Abigail Fawcett. The DNA profile matches the one on file for Ethan, who went missing over a decade ago.

The pathologist, Dr Susan Robinson, will inspect the remains today alongside Dr Agrawal, the forensic anthropologist, to determine the cause of death.

Please let me know if you require any further assistance.

Best regards,

Naomi Sasaki

Isabella leaned back in her chair, a mixture of relief and frustration washing over her. On the one hand, she was grateful that the remains did not belong to Abigail Fawcett, sparing the family from the devastating confirmation of their worst fears. On the other hand, the discovery opened up a whole new set of questions and challenges.

She called out to her team, who were scattered throughout the Incident Room. "Listen up, everyone. We've just received confirmation from Naomi Sasaki that the bones belong to Ethan Morris, not Abigail Fawcett."

A murmur of surprise and concern rippled through the room. Noah Briggs, the imposing Detective Sergeant, stepped forward, his brow furrowed. "Ethan Morris? Not Abigail Fawcett?"

Isabella nodded, her expression grim. "Yes. We need to dig deeper into the Morris case and see if there are any connections to the abandoned farm or any other leads we might have missed."

Connor Riley, the eager young detective constable, raised his hand. "I'll start combing through the old case files and see if anything jumps out."

"I'll contact Ethan's family and see if they can provide any additional information or insights," Leanne Spencer, another bright and energetic detective constable, added.

Isabella nodded. "I'll come with you and officially notify

them of Ethan's death."

Emma Brooke, the dedicated Digital Media Investigator, nodded. "I'll scour social media and online forums to see if there are any mentions of Ethan or the farm that we might have overlooked."

Isabella felt a surge of pride in her team, their determination and commitment to the case shining through. "Good work, everyone. Let's not forget, though, that this is still an active investigation. We need to be thorough and methodical but also sensitive to the fact that we're dealing with a grieving family."

As the team set to work, Isabella's thoughts turned to Mrs Fawcett and the heartbreaking scene Moth described in Abigail's bedroom. She knew that the confirmation that the bones did not belong to Abigail would bring a measure of relief to the family, but it would not ease the pain of the uncertainty that still surrounded their daughter's disappearance.

* * *

George Beaumont stood at the head of the Incident Room, his eyes scanning the faces of his team. The air hung heavy with anticipation, a palpable tension coiling in the pit of his stomach. He drew in a deep breath, steeling himself for what lay ahead.

"Right, listen up," he began, his voice cutting through the low murmur of conversation. "We're expanding the scope of our investigation. This isn't about just one child now. We might be dealing with something far bigger, far more insidious."

The room fell silent, all eyes fixed on George. He could see the mix of determination and apprehension in their gazes, mirroring his own internal struggle.

"I'm setting up a dedicated task force," he continued. "We're going to review every unsolved missing children case in West Yorkshire for the past five years. No stone left unturned, no lead left unexplored."

DC Susie Whitaker raised her hand, her brow furrowed. "Sir, five years? Is the scope going to be too wide?"

George shook his head. "We can't afford to miss anything, Susie. If there's a pattern, we need to find it. No matter how far we have to dig."

He turned to DS Tashan Blackburn. "Tashan, I need you to reach out to our neighbouring forces. Greater Manchester, West Midlands, Merseyside. See if they've got any cases matching our profile."

Tashan nodded, already reaching for his phone. "On it, boss."

George's mind flashed to Isabella, to her Fawcett/Morris case. The similarities nagged at him, a persistent itch he couldn't scratch. But he pushed the thought aside. Focus on what's in front of you, he told himself.

"We're also thinking of bringing in additional resources," he announced. "The National Crime Agency. This might be bigger than West Yorkshire, and we need to be prepared."

The team exchanged glances, a ripple of excitement and nervousness running through the room. NCA involvement meant this was serious. Deadly serious.

George turned to DC Priya Patel. "Priya, what have you got for us on those similar cases?"

Priya stood, moving to the whiteboard. She pinned up three photographs: two girls and a boy, all under the age of ten.

Their smiling faces struck a chord in George's chest, a painful reminder of what was at stake.

"Right," Priya began, her voice steady despite the gravity of the situation. "We've identified three cases in Leeds with similarities to Dania's disappearance."

She pointed to the first photo, a girl with pigtails and a gap-toothed grin. "Lily Chen, aged seven. Disappeared from a park in Harehills eighteen months ago. Witnesses reported seeing a woman matching our mystery mole lady's description nearby."

George's jaw tightened. The coincidence was too stark to ignore.

Priya moved to the next photo, a boy with a mop of curly hair. "Thomas Wilkes, aged five. Vanished from outside his school in Beeston eight months ago. Again, reports of a woman with a mole, though the description is less detailed."

The room had gone deathly quiet, the implications of these connections sinking in.

"And finally," Priya said, her voice catching slightly, "Amira Khan, aged six. Last seen at a shopping centre in Headingley four months ago. CCTV footage shows her leaving with a woman who matches our suspect's description."

George's thoughts spiralled, connecting the dots. Four children, four different areas of Leeds, all potentially linked by one mysterious woman. It was too much to be coincidence.

"What about Fawcett and Morris?" The words slipped out before George could stop them.

Priya's eyebrows rose. "Sir? The cases from Wakefield?"

George waved a hand, silently cursing his lapse. "Never mind. Let's focus on these three for now. What else have we got?"

Priya hesitated for a moment before continuing. "The circumstances of each disappearance are different, sir. Lily was taken from a busy park in broad daylight. Thomas vanished during the after-school rush. Amira was in a crowded shopping centre."

"Different MOs," Tashan mused. "But the same woman keeps popping up. Or a similar one at least. That to me isn't random."

George nodded, his mind whirling. "No, it can't be. We need to treat these cases as connected. From now on, we're working under the assumption the same person or group took these children."

He turned to address the entire team. "I want every detail of these cases combed through—witness statements, CCTV footage, forensic reports—everything. If there's a link we've missed, we find it. If there's a pattern we haven't seen, we uncover it."

The room buzzed with renewed energy, detectives already reaching for files and firing up computers.

"Sir," Susie called out, "what about the Fawcett and Morris cases that were mentioned? Should we be looking into those too?"

George hesitated, torn between his instinct to pursue every lead and the need to keep the investigation focused. "Not yet," he said finally. "Let's concentrate on what we've got here in Leeds. If we need to expand further, we will."

He could see the questions in their eyes, the curiosity about the Wakefield cases. But now wasn't the time for that.

"Alright, people," he said, clapping his hands together. "We've got work to do. Priya, I want a detailed timeline of all three disappearances. Susie, dig into the backgrounds of each family. Tashan, coordinate with the original investigating officers. I want to know if they spotted anything we might have missed."

Chapter Nine

George Beaumont strode through the automatic doors of Kernel House, the headquarters of Leeds Social Services. The building loomed over him, a concrete and glass monolith that seemed to suck the warmth from the air. Priya Patel followed close behind, her face set in grim determination.

"Bloody bureaucracy," George muttered as they approached the reception desk. "Always getting in the way of actual police work."

Priya nodded, her eyes scanning the lobby. "Let's hope they can give us something useful this time."

The receptionist, a bored-looking woman in her fifties, barely glanced up as they approached. "Can I help you?"

George flashed his warrant card. "DCI Beaumont and DC Patel. We're here to speak with someone about the Bhati family from Beeston."

The woman's eyebrows rose slightly, a flicker of interest crossing her face. "Oh, right. You'll want Nadia Shah. Third floor, room 307."

As they rode the lift, George's thoughts churned with questions. Why had the Bhati family slipped through the cracks? How many other vulnerable children were out there, their cries for help going unheard?

The lift doors opened with a soft ding, revealing a long corridor lined with identical doors. They found room 307 and knocked.

"Come in," called a soft voice from inside.

Nadia Shah looked up as they entered, her dark eyes widening slightly. She was younger than George had expected, probably in her early thirties. Her long black hair was pulled back in a neat bun, and she wore a crisp white blouse under a charcoal grey blazer.

"DCI Beaumont? DC Patel?" she asked, rising to shake their hands. "Please, have a seat. How can I help you?"

George settled into one of the uncomfortable plastic chairs, Priya taking the other. "Miss Shah, we're here about the Bhati family. Specifically, we'd like to know why they seem to have fallen through the cracks of your system."

Nadia's face fell, a look of genuine concern crossing her features. "Ah, yes. The Bhatis. I was afraid you might be here about them." She tapped a few keys on her computer, pulling up a file. "I'm so sorry about what happened to little Dania. It's... it's a tragedy."

George leaned forward, his eyes never leaving Nadia's face. "Miss Shah, can you explain why the concerns raised about Dania's home life six months ago weren't followed up on?"

Nadia sighed, rubbing her temples. "I wish I could give you a better answer, DCI Beaumont. The truth is that the case was passed on to a different social worker, who was then put on long-term sick leave. I've just checked our system, and... well, it appears the Bhati family doesn't currently have an assigned social worker."

Priya's eyes narrowed. "And why weren't we told this yesterday when we requested the information?"

Nadia had the grace to look embarrassed. "I'm afraid I was on annual leave yesterday. I only just returned this morning. I'm still catching up on everything that's happened."

George sat back, his jaw clenching. It was the same old story—overworked staff, cases slipping through the cracks, vulnerable children paying the price. "Miss Shah, I understand you're in a difficult position. But surely there must be some system in place to prevent cases from being forgotten like this?"

Nadia nodded vigorously. "There is, DCI Beaumont. Or at least, there should be. I can assure you this isn't how we typically operate. I'm as concerned about this as you are."

George studied her momentarily. She seemed genuine in her distress, but something nagged at him. Years on the force had taught him to trust his instincts, and right now, they were telling him there was more to this story.

"Miss Shah," he said slowly, "I'd like to speak with your manager, if possible. Not because I doubt your competence," he added quickly as her face fell, "but because I need to understand how this happened at a systemic level."

Nadia nodded, reaching for her phone. "Of course. I'll see if Yvette is available."

As she dialled, George exchanged a glance with Priya. The younger detective's face was a mask of controlled anger, her fingers tapping an impatient rhythm on her thigh.

"Yvette? It's Nadia. I've got two detectives, DCI Beaumont and DC Patel, here about the Bhati case. They'd like to speak with you if possible." She listened for a moment, then nodded. "Right, I'll send them up. Thank you."

Hanging up, she turned back to George and Priya. "Yvette Watkins, my manager. She'll see you now. Fifth floor, room

502."

As they stood to leave, George paused. "Thank you for your time, Miss Shah. We may need to speak with you again as our investigation progresses."

Nadia nodded, her face a mixture of concern and something else—relief? "Of course, DCI Beaumont. Anything I can do to help."

The lift ride to the fifth floor was silent; both detectives were lost in thought. When they reached room 502, George knocked sharply.

"Enter," called a brisk voice from within.

Yvette Watkins was a stark contrast to Nadia Shah. Where Nadia had been softly spoken and apologetic, Yvette radiated confidence and authority. Her steel-grey hair was cut in a severe bob, and her piercing blue eyes seemed to x-ray them as they entered.

"DCI Beaumont, DC Patel," she said, gesturing to the chairs in front of her desk. "Nadia tells me you have concerns about the Bhati case."

George nodded, settling into the chair. "Mrs Watkins, we're trying to understand how a family with known concerns could have been left without an assigned social worker for months."

Yvette's lips thinned. "I understand your frustration, DCI Beaumont. Believe me, it's not a situation we're happy about, either. As Nadia probably explained, the case was transferred to a worker who then went on long-term sick leave. It should have been reassigned, but..." she spread her hands, a gesture of helplessness. "We're understaffed, overworked. Things slip through the cracks sometimes."

Priya leaned forward, her voice tight with barely contained anger. "With all due respect, Mrs Watkins, we're not talking about misplaced paperwork here. We're talking about a child who's now dead."

Yvette's face softened slightly. "You're right, of course. It's a tragedy and one we take very seriously. I assure you that I'll be speaking with Nadia about this. We need to tighten our procedures to ensure nothing like this happens again."

George nodded, but something still bothered him. "Mrs Watkins, can you tell me a bit more about Nadia? How long has she been with your department?"

Yvette's eyebrows rose slightly, but she answered readily enough. "Nadia? She's been with us for about five years now. One of our best, actually. I'm rather proud to tell you she has an unusually high success rate in closing child protection cases."

"Oh?" George said, his interest piqued. "That's impressive. How does she manage that?"

A flicker of pride crossed Yvette's face. "Nadia has a real gift for connecting with families. She's able to build trust quickly and get to the heart of issues. Her colleagues and superiors praise her efficiency."

George nodded slowly, processing this information. "And what about her caseload? Does she handle a lot of difficult cases?"

Yvette's smile widened. "Oh yes. Nadia's known for taking on the most challenging cases, especially those involving vulnerable children. She has a particular knack for working with kids who don't have close family ties or are already marginalised. She's a rising star."

Something cold settled in George's stomach at these words. "That's... quite a talent," he said carefully. "And everyone's happy with her work? No concerns from colleagues or other managers?"

Yvette hesitated for a fraction of a second, so brief George almost missed it. "Well, you know how it is in any workplace. There's always a bit of professional jealousy. A few people find it odd that she's able to resolve cases that others struggle with. But personally, I think they're just envious of her skills."

George sat back. "Mrs Watkins," he said slowly, "I'd like to request copies of all files related to the Bhati case, including any notes or reports made by Nadia Shah."

Yvette's smile faltered slightly. "I'm afraid I can't release those without a warrant, DCI Beaumont. Confidentiality and all that."

George leaned forward. "Mrs Watkins, we're investigating the murder of a child. A child who was known to your department."

Yvette held his gaze for a long moment, then sighed. "I understand, but I'll still need that warrant." She paused and smiled. It did not meet her eyes. "Provide me with a warrant, and I'll have the files sent over to your office by the end of the day."

George stood. "Have it your way, Mrs Watkins."

As they left the office, Priya turned to him, her voice low. "Sir, something's not right here. The way Watkins talked about Nadia..."

George nodded grimly. "I know. It's too perfect, too neat. No one's that good at their job without raising eyebrows."

They rode the lift down in silence; both lost in thought. As they exited the building, George paused, looking up at the looming structure.

"Priya," he said, his voice tight with suppressed emotion, "I want you to dig into Nadia Shah's background. Everything you can find—work history, education, personal life. And I want a list of every case she's closed in the last five years."

Priya's eyes widened. "You think she's involved somehow?"

George shook his head. "I don't know."

As they climbed into the car, George sat for a moment before firing up the engine.

"Everything OK, sir?"

"Yeah, fine," he said. "Get in touch with DSU Smith and get a warrant. I want to see what's hidden in those files."

* * *

Isabella stepped up to the podium, the burden of the news she was about to deliver heavy on her shoulders. The press conference room was filled with reporters, their cameras flashing and their pens poised to capture every word. She took a deep breath, steeling herself for the difficult task ahead.

"Good afternoon, everyone," she began, her voice steady and clear. "I called this press conference to provide an update on the remains discovered at Old River Farm. After thorough DNA analysis, we can confirm that the bones belong to Ethan Morris, a young boy who went missing over a decade ago."

A hush fell over the group, the gravity of the announcement sinking in. Isabella paused, her mind drifting back to the harrowing visit she had just made to the Morris household.

She had sat with Ethan's parents, their faces etched with a mixture of grief and relief. Mrs Morris had clutched a framed photograph of her son, tears streaming down her face as Isabella delivered the news.

"I knew it," Mrs Morris had whispered, her voice trembling. "I knew in my heart that he was gone, but I never wanted to believe it."

Mr Morris had wrapped his arm around his wife, his own eyes glistening with unshed tears. "We never gave up hope," he said, his voice hoarse with emotion. "We always thought that maybe, just maybe, he would come home to us."

Isabella had felt her own tears threatening to fall as she witnessed the raw pain of a family whose worst fears had been confirmed. She had reached out, taking Mrs Morris's hand in her own.

"I promise you," she had said, her voice firm with conviction, "we will not rest until we find out what happened to Ethan. We will bring those responsible to justice."

Now, standing before the press, Isabella channelled that same resolve. "The Morris family has been informed of the discovery, and our hearts go out to them during this incredibly difficult time. They have asked for privacy as they process this news and begin to grieve for their son."

As Isabella stepped away from the podium, a voice cut through the clamour of the press.

"DI Wood! Helen Senior, Leeds Local Post," a sharp-faced woman in the front row called out. "Is there any connection between this case and the recent murder of Dania Bhati in Leeds?"

Isabella froze, her heart rate spiking. She turned back to the microphone, her mind racing. George's words from the night before echoed in her ears—the potential connection, the similarities between the cases. She took a deep breath, choosing her words carefully.

"At this time, we have no evidence linking the two cases," Isabella stated, her voice steady despite the turmoil in her gut. "The investigation into Ethan Morris's death is ongoing, as is the investigation in Leeds. It would be inappropriate to speculate on any connections at this stage."

Helen Senior pressed on, her eyes glinting with the scent of a story. "But both cases involve young children found at abandoned rural properties. Surely the similarities can't be ignored?"

Isabella's jaw tightened almost imperceptibly. "Helen, I understand the desire to draw connections, but it's crucial that we focus on facts, not speculation. Each case is unique and complex. Making premature links could potentially harm both investigations."

She paused, scanning the room. "Our priority is to bring justice for Ethan and his family. We're working closely with our colleagues across the West Yorkshire Police to ensure all avenues are explored thoroughly. If any substantiated connections emerge, we will, of course, investigate them fully."

As Isabella finished speaking, she could see the reporters scribbling furiously and could practically hear the headlines being crafted. She knew her words would be scrutinised, dissected for any hint of a larger story.

"Thank you all for your time," she said, bringing the press conference to a firm close. "We'll provide updates as the investigation progresses."

But the room erupted with questions, reporters clamouring for more information. Isabella held up her hand, silencing the crowd.

"I know that you have many questions, but I ask that you respect the Morris family's wish for privacy at this time. We will provide updates as the investigation progresses, but our focus now is on bringing closure to Ethan's loved ones and ensuring that no other family has to endure such a tragedy."

As she stepped away from the podium, Isabella's mind whirled. The question had hit too close to home, bringing George's confidential revelation into sharp focus. She knew she'd have to tread carefully in the coming days, balancing the need for transparency with the integrity of both investigations.

She thought of Mrs Morris, clutching her son's photograph, and Mr Morris, his face lined with grief. She thought of Ethan, a young boy whose life had been cut tragically short, his potential snuffed out in an act of unimaginable cruelty.

And somewhere in the back of her mind, a nagging doubt grew. What if the connection was real? What if they were dealing with something far more sinister than they'd initially thought? The implications were too horrifying to contemplate, but Isabella knew she couldn't shy away from the possibility. Whatever the truth, she was determined to uncover it—for Ethan, for Dania, for Abigail, and for every child who might be at risk.

Chapter Ten

George Beaumont leaned back in his chair and glanced at the clock on his office wall, its steady tick-tock a constant reminder of the precious minutes slipping away. With a deep breath, he reached for his phone, fingers hovering over the keypad for a moment before dialling the first number.

The line rang three times before a woman's voice answered, tight with barely contained emotion. "Hello?"

"Mrs Chen? This is DCI George Beaumont from West Yorkshire Police."

A sharp intake of breath crackled through the receiver. "Have you found Lily? Please, tell me you've found my little girl."

George closed his eyes, steeling himself. "I'm sorry, Mrs Chen. We haven't found Lily yet. But I'm calling to let you know we're re-examining her case as part of a larger investigation."

"Larger investigation?" Mei Chen's voice rose, a mix of hope and frustration. "What does that mean? It's been eighteen months, Detective. Eighteen months of not knowing if my daughter is alive or—" She broke off, unable to finish the sentence.

"I understand your frustration, Mrs Chen. Truly, I do."

George leaned forward, elbows on his desk. "We believe Lily's disappearance might be connected to other missing children cases in the area. We're dedicating more resources to the investigation."

"You said the same thing six months ago," Mei snapped. "And three months before that. What's different now?"

George paused, weighing his words carefully. "We've uncovered new evidence that suggests a potential link between several cases. I can't go into details, but I assure you, we're pursuing every lead."

"Evidence?" Mei's voice caught. "What kind of evidence? Please, I need to know something."

"Mrs Chen, I—"

"No," she cut him off. "Don't give me that 'can't discuss ongoing investigations' line again. My daughter has been missing for over a year. I deserve to know what's happening."

George sighed, rubbing his forehead. "You're right. You do deserve to know." He hesitated, then continued, "We've identified a woman who may have been involved in Lily's disappearance. She's been spotted near the locations of other missing children as well."

A sharp gasp came through the line. "A woman? The one with the mole? I told the officers about her months ago!"

"Yes, Mrs Chen. We're taking that information very seriously now. We're re-interviewing witnesses and reviewing all CCTV footage."

"Why now?" Mei's voice cracked. "Why didn't you listen before?"

The question hit George like a punch to the gut. He had no good answer, no way to explain the bureaucracy and resource limitations that had led to these cases being treated as isolated incidents for so long.

"I'm sorry," he said, the words feeling wholly inadequate. "We should have connected these cases sooner. But I promise you, Mrs Chen, I'm in charge now, and we're doing everything in our power to find Lily and bring her home."

Mei was quiet for a long moment. When she spoke again, her voice was barely above a whisper. "Do you have children, Detective?"

"I do," George replied softly. "A daughter and a son."

"Then you must know," Mei said, "what it's like to live with this fear. This... emptiness. Every day, I wake up hoping it was all a bad dream. Every night, I go to sleep praying tomorrow will be the day you find her."

George swallowed hard, pushing down the lump forming in his throat. "I can't imagine what you're going through, Mrs Chen. But I swear to you, we won't rest until we find out what happened to Lily."

"I want to believe you," Mei said, her voice thick with unshed tears. "I need to believe you. Because I can't... I can't keep living like this. Not knowing."

"We're going to find her," George said, injecting as much conviction into his voice as he could muster. "I'll keep you updated on any developments, no matter how small."

"Thank you," Mei whispered. "Please, just... find my little girl."

The line went dead, leaving George staring at the receiver, the echo of Mei Chen's plea ringing in his ears. He set the phone down, hands shaking slightly. One down, he thought grimly. Two more to go.

George allowed himself a moment to collect his thoughts. He reached for his mug, grimacing as he sipped the now-cold coffee. With a deep breath, he picked up the phone again, dialling the next number on his list.

The phone rang longer this time, each unanswered tone ratcheting up the tension in George's shoulders. Finally, a clipped voice answered. "Wilkes residence."

"Mrs Wilkes? This is DCI George Beaumont from West Yorkshire Police."

A sharp intake of breath, then, "What is it? Have you found Thomas?"

George's grip tightened on the receiver. "I'm afraid not, Mrs Wilkes. But I'm calling to inform you we're re-examining Thomas's case as part of a larger investigation."

"Larger investigation?" Catherine Wilkes's voice dripped with scepticism. "What does that mean, exactly?"

"We believe there may be a connection between Thomas's disappearance and several other missing children cases in the area," George explained, bracing himself for the reaction.

"A connection?" Catherine's voice rose sharply. "You mean more children are missing? And you're only just now putting this together?"

George winced. "Mrs Wilkes, I understand your frustration—"

"No," she cut him off, "I don't think you do. My son has been missing for eight months. Eight months of hell, of not knowing if he's alive or dead. And now you're telling me there might be others? That this could have been prevented?"

George took a deep breath, forcing himself to remain calm. "Mrs Wilkes, I assure you, we're doing everything in our power to find Thomas and the other missing children. We've uncovered new evidence that—"

"Evidence?" Catherine latched onto the word. "What

evidence? Why weren't we told about this before?"

"We've identified a potential suspect," George said carefully. "A woman who's been seen near the locations where several children, including Thomas, went missing."

"A woman?" Catherine's voice faltered. "The one I told your officers about? The one with the mole?"

George closed his eyes. That was now two mothers who had told the police about the woman with the mole. What the fuck was going on? He made a note to check on which officer had been in charge before and then said, "Yes, Mrs Wilkes. We're taking that information very seriously now. We're re-interviewing all witnesses and reviewing all available CCTV footage."

"Now?" The word came out as a strangled laugh. "You're taking it seriously now? I told your officers about her the day Thomas disappeared. I begged them to look into it!"

"I'm in charge now," George said softly. "And I'm sorry we didn't pursue that lead more aggressively at the time. But I promise you, we're leaving no stone unturned now."

"Your promises don't mean much to me, Detective," Catherine said, her voice cold. "Not after eight months of silence and dead ends."

George leaned forward, elbows on his desk. "I understand your anger, Mrs Wilkes. You have every right to be furious with us. But please, if you remember anything else, anything at all about the day Thomas disappeared or the woman you saw, no matter how small or insignificant it might seem, please let us know."

There was a long pause on the other end of the line. When Catherine spoke again, her voice was quieter, laced with a desperation that made George's chest tighten. "He was wearing his favourite dinosaur t-shirt that day. The blue one with the T-Rex. He begged to wear it, even though it was getting too small. I should have... I should have made him get changed."

"Mrs Wilkes," George said gently, "this isn't your fault. None of it is."

"Isn't it?" she whispered. "I let him out of my sight. I let him go to school alone. I—"

"You trusted your community," George interrupted. "You trusted that your son would be safe walking to school. The only person at fault here is the one who took Thomas."

Catherine's breath hitched, a soft sob escaping. "I just want him back. I want my little boy back."

"We're going to find him," George said, injecting every ounce of determination he could muster into his voice. "We're not giving up, Mrs Wilkes. Not now, not ever."

"Please," Catherine whispered. "Please find him."

As the line went dead, George set the phone down, his hand shaking slightly. They'd royally fucked up.

He barely had time to collect himself before his office door burst open. DS Tashan Blackburn strode in, his face tight with barely contained frustration.

"Sir," he said, "I've managed to get Mr and Mrs Khan on the phone, but they're refusing to speak with us."

George's brow furrowed. "What? Why?"

Tashan shook his head. "They say they've been let down by the police too many times. They don't trust us now."

George stood, pacing behind his desk. "Christ. We can't afford to lose their cooperation, not now."

"I know, sir," Tashan agreed. "But they're adamant. They said they've had enough of empty promises and dead ends."

George ran a hand through his hair, mind racing. "We need to fix this, Tashan. We need the community on our side if we're going to crack this case."

Tashan nodded. "What do you want to do?"

George paused, considering their options. "We need to show them we're taking this seriously. That we're not just paying lip service to their concerns."

"How do we do that?" Tashan asked.

"We go to them," George decided. "We need to be visible, present in the community. Let's start with door-to-door inquiries in the areas where Bilal was spotted on CCTV."

Tashan's eyebrows rose. "That's a lot of ground to cover, sir."

"I know," George nodded. "But it sends a message. Shows we're willing to put in the legwork, that we're not just sitting behind desks pushing papers."

"And the Khans?" Tashan pressed.

George's jaw set. "We organise a community meeting. Address their concerns head-on, appeal for information. Let them see we're taking this seriously."

Tashan nodded, a glimmer of approval in his eyes. "It's a good plan, sir. Might help rebuild some bridges."

"It's a start," George agreed. "But we need to back it up with results. These families have been waiting far too long for answers."

"I'll start organising the door-to-door," Tashan said. "And I'll reach out to community leaders about setting up a meeting."

"Good," George said. "And Tashan? Make sure every officer involved understands the gravity of this. We can't afford any more missteps."

As Tashan left, George sank back into his chair. He thought of Mei Chen and Catherine Wilkes, of their pain and desperation. Of the Khans, their trust in the police so thoroughly shattered.

And beneath it all, the nagging fear that had been growing since this case began. What if they were already too late? What if, despite their best efforts, they couldn't bring these children home?

George shook his head, banishing the thought. They would find them. They had to. The alternative was unthinkable.

He reached for his phone again, ready to start putting their community outreach plan into action. As he dialled, he silently renewed his vow to the missing children and their families. He would find them. No matter what it took, no matter how long it took, he would bring them home.

The phone rang, and George steeled himself for another difficult conversation. This was the job, he reminded himself. The hard conversations, the sleepless nights, other people's grief and hope. It was a burden he'd chosen to bear, and he would bear it until they found the truth.

"Hello," he said as the line connected. "This is DCI George Beaumont. I need to speak with you about organising a community meeting..."

Chapter Eleven

Hours ticked by, the Incident Room a hive of activity. George moved from desk to desk, checking progress, offering insights, pushing his team to dig deeper. The wall behind him grew cluttered with photos, timelines, and scribbled notes, a visual representation of the web they were trying to untangle.

"Boss," Tashan called out, waving George over to his desk. "I've been going through the witness statements from the Chen case. Something odd keeps coming up."

George leaned in, scanning the documents spread across Tashan's desk. "What have you found?"

Tashan pointed to several highlighted sections. "Multiple witnesses mentioned a white van parked near the park where Lily disappeared. It was there for hours, according to some statements."

George's eyes narrowed. "A white van? Like the one seen near the farmhouse where we found Dania?"

Tashan nodded, his expression grim. "Exactly like it. And here's the kicker—similar reports have been turned up in the Wilkes and Khan cases, too. Always a white van, always parked just out of direct view of where the kids were taken."

George straightened, his mind racing. "It can't be coincidence. We're dealing with a team here. The woman lures the children; the van provides the getaway."

He turned, surveying the room. "Susie!" he called out. "I need you to pull traffic camera footage from around each abduction site. Look for white vans in the hours before and after each disappearance."

Susie nodded, already reaching for her phone to make the necessary requests.

George moved back to the centre of the room, clearing his throat to get everyone's attention. "Listen up, people. We've got a new lead. White van, possibly used in all four abductions. I want every scrap of information you can find on vehicle sightings near our crime scenes."

The room erupted into a flurry of activity, detectives calling contacts and scouring reports with renewed vigour.

Priya approached, a troubled look on her face. "Sir, there's something else you should see."

She led him to her desk, pointing to a series of maps on her computer screen. "I've been plotting the locations of each abduction, trying to find a pattern. Look at this."

George leaned in, his eyes scanning the digital map of Leeds. Four red pins marked the abduction sites, spread across different areas of the city.

"What am I looking at, Priya?"

She clicked a button, and suddenly lines appeared, connecting the pins. George's breath caught in his throat as the shape emerged.

"It's a cross," he murmured.

Priya nodded. "And not just any cross. The proportions match those of the White Rose of York."

George's mind reeled. "Excuse me." The White Rose of York, the symbol of Yorkshire itself. And the White Rose League.

Was it deliberate? A sick joke? Or something more sinister?

He thought of Luke Mason and Clare Brack. Didn't they mention that the League groomed its members and purposely put them into the police force?

"Good work, Priya," he said, straightening. "Keep digging. See if you can find any significance to the specific locations beyond this pattern."

* * *

George Beaumont sat at his desk. The fluorescent lights hummed overhead, casting harsh shadows across the room. He rubbed his eyes, fatigue settling into his bones after hours of poring over statements.

"Priya," he called out, his voice gruff with exhaustion. "Any word from Yvette Watkins?"

Priya appeared in the doorway, a triumphant gleam in her eye. "Just got back, sir. Handed her the warrant personally. You should have seen her face—like she'd swallowed a lemon." She began stacking a paper mountain of social services files on his desk. "Good luck, sir."

George grunted in approval. "Good work. Let's hope these files give us something to work with."

As Priya left, George turned back to the documents spread across his desk.

* * *

The fallout from Isabella's press conference was immediate and intense. The revelation that the remains belonged to Ethan Morris, a child who had been missing for over a decade, sent shock-waves through the community. Media outlets clamoured for more information, their headlines stoking the flames of public outrage and demanding answers.

Isabella found herself at the centre of a maelstrom, fielding calls from concerned citizens and fending off the relentless press. She barely had a moment to catch her breath before she was summoned to a meeting with the Chief Constable, a stern-faced man with a reputation for expecting results.

As she entered his office, Isabella could feel the tension in the air. The Chief Constable sat behind his desk, his expression grim.

"Take a seat, Detective Inspector," he said, his voice tight with frustration.

Isabella settled into the chair opposite him, her posture straight and her expression neutral.

"I'll cut right to the chase," the Chief Constable continued, leaning forward. "This case has become a media circus, and the pressure is mounting. The public is demanding answers, and they want them now."

Isabella nodded, her jaw clenched. "I understand, sir. My team and I are working around the clock to uncover the truth."

The Chief Constable sighed, rubbing his temples. "I know you're doing your best, Wood, but we need more than that. We need a win, and we need it soon. The department's reputation is on the line, and if we don't deliver, the consequences could be severe."

Isabella felt a flicker of anger at the implication. "With all due respect, sir, our priority should be justice for Ethan and his family, not the department's reputation."

The Chief Constable's eyes narrowed. "Don't be naive, Wood. The two are intertwined. If the public loses faith in us, our job will be that much harder. We need to show them that we're capable of solving this case and bringing the perpetrators to justice."

Isabella took a deep breath, choosing her words carefully. "I understand the pressure we're under, sir, but I won't compromise the integrity of the investigation for the sake of a quick win. We need to be thorough and methodical, even if it takes time."

The Chief Constable leaned back in his chair, his expression unreadable. "You have one week, Wood. One week to make significant progress on this case. If you can't deliver, I'll have no choice but to bring in outside help."

Isabella felt a chill run down her spine at the thought of being pulled off the case. She knew that she was the best person to see it through, and the idea of someone else taking over filled her with dread.

"That won't be necessary, sir," she said, her voice firm. "I give you my word that we will have a breakthrough within the week."

The Chief Constable nodded, his expression softening slightly. "I hope so, Wood. For all our sakes."

As Isabella left the office, she knew that the next week would be critical and that every moment counted.

* * *

George had been at it for hours, combing through case after case handled by Nadia Shah. Something wasn't adding up, and it was driving him mad.

He picked up another file, flipping it open with a sigh. His eyes scanned the pages, looking for anything out of the ordinary. Suddenly, he sat up straighter, his brow furrowing.

"Bloody hell," he muttered, rifling through the papers more urgently now.

The pattern was there, subtle but unmistakable once he'd spotted it. Several of Nadia's case files were missing key documents—follow-up reports, detailed notes, the kind of paperwork that formed the backbone of any thorough investigation.

George leaned back in his chair, his mind racing. Was this sloppy work? Or something more sinister? He couldn't shake the feeling that these missing documents were more than just administrative oversights.

His thoughts turned to Nadia herself. The Asian woman with the mole, the one seen leading children away. Could it be her? The idea had been niggling at the back of his mind since their meeting at Kernel House.

But as he mulled it over, doubts began to creep in. According to the files, Nadia worked at Dania's school frequently. If she were the woman they were looking for, surely someone at the school would have recognised her by now?

And then there was the matter of appearance. Nadia hadn't been wearing a headscarf when they'd met, and he couldn't recall seeing a mole on her face. It was possible she could have disguised herself, but it seemed unlikely.

George stood, pacing the small confines of his office. The pieces weren't fitting together, and it was driving him mad. He needed to question Nadia again; that much was clear. But about what, exactly?

The missing documents were suspicious, no doubt about that. But were they evidence of something more sinister, or just the result of an overworked social worker cutting corners?

He wasn't sure but knew he'd be paying Nadia Shah another visit.

And soon.

Chapter Twelve

George Beaumont rubbed his eyes, exhaustion seeping into every fibre of his being.

The community meetings played out in his mind, a carousel of faces, voices, and emotions. Three distinct gatherings, each with its own flavour of desperation and hope.

Harehills. The first stop. George could still see the cramped community centre, feel the press of bodies as anxious residents packed into the space. The air had been thick with tension, a palpable undercurrent of fear and frustration.

Mei Chen had been there, her small frame seeming to shrink under her grief. George had watched her throughout the meeting, noting how she clung to her husband's hand like a lifeline.

"We understand your concerns," George had begun, his voice carrying across the hushed room. "And we're here to assure you we're doing everything in our power to find Lily and bring her home."

A murmur had rippled through the crowd. Scepticism. Disbelief. George couldn't blame them.

"You said the same thing months ago," a voice called out. "What's changed?"

George had taken a deep breath, meeting the speaker's gaze.

"We've uncovered new evidence linking Lily's disappearance to other missing children cases in the area. We believe we're dealing with an organised group, not isolated incidents."

The room had erupted then, a cacophony of voices clamouring for answers. George raised his hands, attempting to calm the crowd.

"I know you're frustrated. I know you're scared. But we need your help. If you've seen anything suspicious, no matter how small it might seem, we need to know."

Mei Chen had stood then, her voice quavering but determined. "Please," she'd said, addressing her neighbours. "If you know anything about my Lily, anything at all, tell the police. She's out there somewhere. She needs to come home."

The room had fallen silent. George had seen tears in more than one pair of eyes, a shared grief binding the community together.

As the meeting wound down, George had approached Mei. "Thank you," he'd said quietly. "For speaking up. It means a lot."

Mei had nodded, her eyes red-rimmed but determined. "Find her, Detective. Please, find my little girl."

The memory faded, replaced by the stark contrast of the Beeston meeting. A different venue, a different crowd, but the same undercurrent of fear and desperation.

Catherine Wilkes had been there, standing rigidly at the back of the room. Her eyes had never left George, burning with a mixture of hope and accusation.

"We're pursuing several new leads," George had announced, his voice echoing in the school gymnasium. "Including a potential suspect seen near the locations of multiple child disappearances."

A ripple of excitement had run through the crowd. Catherine Wilkes had stepped forward, her voice cutting through the murmurs.

"The woman with the mole?" she'd demanded. "The one I told you about months ago?"

George had nodded, meeting her gaze steadily. "Yes, Mrs Wilkes. We're taking that information very seriously now. We're re-interviewing witnesses and reviewing all available CCTV footage."

"Now?" Catherine had spat the word like a curse. "Why not then? Why did it take more children disappearing for you to listen?"

The room had fallen silent, all eyes on George. He'd felt their judgment, their fear, their anger.

"You're right," he'd said softly. "We should have pursued this lead more aggressively from the start. We made a mistake, and I'm sorry for that. But we're committed to finding Thomas and all the other missing children. We won't stop until we bring them home."

Catherine had held his gaze for a long moment, tears glistening in her eyes. Then she'd nodded, once, before melting back into the crowd.

The rest of the meeting had been a blur of questions, of frightened parents seeking reassurance, of community leaders demanding action. George had done his best to address their concerns, to offer hope without making promises he couldn't keep.

As the crowd dispersed, Catherine had approached him. "I want to believe you," she'd said, her voice barely above a whisper. "I need to believe you. Because I can't... I can't keep living like this. Not knowing."

George had nodded, understanding her words. "We're going to find him, Mrs Wilkes. I swear to you, we won't rest until we do."

The memory faded, replaced by the stark contrast of the Headingley meeting. The atmosphere there had been different from the start, a powder keg of emotion waiting to explode.

The Khan family had been there in force, surrounded by a sea of supporters. The hostility in the room had been palpable, a living, breathing thing.

George had barely opened his mouth before the first shout rang out.

"Why should we trust you? You've done nothing for us!"

Mr Khan had stepped forward, his face a mask of anger and pain. "You promised us answers. You promised to find our Amira. And what have you given us? Nothing but silence and excuses!"

The crowd had roared its approval, a wave of anger washing over George. He'd raised his hands, trying to calm the storm.

"I understand your frustration," he'd begun, only to be cut off by Mrs Khan.

"Frustration?" she'd cried, her voice cracking with emotion. "Our daughter is missing. Our beautiful Amira is out there somewhere, alone and scared. And you talk about frustration?"

George had taken a deep breath, forcing himself to remain calm. "You're right," he'd said, his voice carrying across the room. "Frustration isn't the right word. What you're feeling is anguish, fear, anger. And you have every right to those emotions."

The room had quieted slightly, surprised by his honesty.

"We've made mistakes," George had continued. "We should

have seen the connections sooner. We should have listened more closely to your concerns. And for that, I am truly sorry."

Mr Khan had stepped closer, his eyes boring into George's. "Sorry doesn't bring our daughter back."

"No," George had agreed. "It doesn't. But this will." He'd gestured to the officers flanking him. "We're dedicating more resources to Amira's case and the other missing children. We're pursuing new leads, re-examining old evidence. And we're here, in your community, because we need your help."

A murmur had run through the crowd. Scepticism, yes, but also a flicker of something else. Hope, maybe. Or at least a willingness to listen.

"We believe Amira's disappearance is connected to other missing children cases in the area," George had explained. "We're looking for a woman, possibly of South Asian descent, with a distinctive mole above her lip. Has anyone seen someone matching this description?"

The room had erupted into discussion, people turning to their neighbours, voices rising and falling. George had watched, hope blooming in his chest. This was what they needed—the community engaged, working together.

As the meeting wound down, Mr Khan had approached George. The anger was still there in his eyes, but tempered now with something else. Desperation, perhaps. Or the faintest glimmer of hope.

"You really think you can find her?" he'd asked.

George had met his gaze steadily. "We're going to do everything in our power, Mr Khan. Everything. I promise you that."

Mr Khan had nodded, once, before turning away. It wasn't forgiveness, not yet. But it was a start.

Now, sitting in his darkened office, George replayed these scenes in his mind. Three communities, three families torn apart by tragedy. The weight of their hope, their fear, their anger pressed down on him.

He stood, moving to the window. The city sprawled before him, a tapestry of lights and shadows. Somewhere out there, Lily, Thomas, and Amira were waiting. Somewhere out there, a monster walked free.

George's jaw clenched. He'd made promises today. To grieving parents, to frightened communities. Promises he intended to keep, no matter the cost.

He turned back to his desk, reaching for the case files. Sleep could wait. There was work to be done.

As he settled in, George's mind drifted to the connections between the cases. The woman with the mole, spotted near each disappearance. The white van, seen lurking in the background. The Asian man, possibly Bilal Bhati. The carefully chosen locations, each abduction executed with chilling precision.

This wasn't the work of an opportunistic predator. This was organised, methodical. A group working together, preying on the most vulnerable members of society.

The thought sent a chill down George's spine. If they were right, if this was indeed a ring of child traffickers, the implications were staggering. How many more children were at risk? How deep did this conspiracy run?

George shook his head, forcing himself to focus on the task at hand. Speculation wouldn't find these children. Facts would. Evidence. Good, old-fashioned police work.

He opened the first file, Lily Chen's smiling face looking up at him from the photograph. Eight years old. Missing for eighteen months. Last seen in Harehills Park, wearing a pink jacket and carrying a butterfly-patterned backpack.

George's eyes skimmed the witness statements, searching for any detail they might have missed. A jogger who'd seen a woman matching their suspect's description lingering near the playground. A burger van owner who remembered a white van parked illegally near the park entrance.

He made notes, connecting threads that had seemed insignificant before but now took on new importance in light of the other cases.

Next, Thomas Wilkes. Five years old. Missing for eight months. Last seen walking to school in Beeston, wearing his favourite dinosaur t-shirt during a non-uniform-day.

Again, the woman with the mole appeared in witness statements. A lollipop lady who'd noticed her watching the children. A neighbour who'd seen her speaking to Thomas, gesturing as if giving directions.

And finally, Amira Khan. Six years old. Missing for four months. Last seen at a busy shopping centre in Headingley, holding her mother's hand one moment, gone the next.

CCTV footage had captured a glimpse of their suspect, her face partially obscured but the dark hair and telltale mole visible. She'd been seen speaking to Amira, smiling, pointing towards something off-camera.

George leaned back, rubbing his eyes. The connections were there, clear as day now that they were looking for them. How had they missed this before? How many chances had they let slip through their fingers?

He thought of the community meetings, of the pain and anger in the eyes of the parents. Of Mei Chen's quiet desperation, Catherine Wilkes's simmering rage, the Khans' shattered trust.

They deserved better. The children deserved better.

George stood, pacing the length of his office. They were close, he could feel it. The pieces were there, waiting to be put together. They just needed that one break, that one crucial piece of evidence to blow the whole case wide open.

He stopped at the window again, looking out over the sleeping city. George's reflection stared back at him, determination etched into every line of his face. He'd made promises today. To grieving parents, to frightened communities. Promises he intended to keep, no matter what.

Chapter Thirteen

George Beaumont stood, stretching muscles cramped from hours hunched over his desk. The station hummed with the quiet energy of the night shift, a stark contrast to the frantic pace of the day. He reached for his suit jacket, his mind already racing ahead to tomorrow's tasks.

A sharp knock on the door jolted him from his thoughts.

"Come in," he called, recognising the distinctive pattern of Tashan's knock.

The door swung open, revealing Tashan Blackburn, his face etched with a mixture of excitement and apprehension. In his arms, he cradled a stack of worn file folders.

"Sir," Tashan said. "I've got something you need to see."

George's eyebrows rose. "What is it?"

Tashan stepped into the office, kicking the door shut behind him. "The original case files for Lily, Thomas, and Amira. I've been going through them, and... well, you'd better see for yourself."

He laid the files on George's desk, spreading them out. George leaned in, his eyes scanning the familiar details of each case. Suddenly, a name jumped out at him, repeated across all three files.

"Clare Brack," he murmured, his blood running cold. "She

was the SIO on each case."

Tashan nodded grimly. "Every single one, sir. And given what we now know about her involvement with the White Rose League..."

George's thoughts spiralled, connecting dots he'd never seen before. The White Rose League. A shadowy organisation they'd thought they'd dismantled. But if Clare had been involved in these cases...

"Christ," he muttered, running a hand through his hair. "This changes everything."

Tashan shifted uncomfortably. "Do you think the League could be behind the disappearances?"

George's jaw clenched. "I don't know. But we can't rule it out."

He straightened, his decision made. "I need to speak with DSU Smith."

Tashan nodded. "I'll keep digging, sir. See if I can find any other connections."

George clapped him on the shoulder. "Good work, Tashan. Keep this under wraps for now, yeah? Until we know more." He smiled at his young DS. "And go home. Get some rest."

With a nod, Tashan left, leaving George alone.

DCI Beaumont strode out of his office, making his way to Smith's door with quick, purposeful steps.

The door was closed, the office dark, and Jim's receptionist was nowhere to be seen. George leaned against it, fishing his mobile from his pocket. He dialled Smith's number, his foot tapping an impatient rhythm against the floor.

One ring. Two. Three.

"Beaumont?" Smith's gruff voice came through, tinged with sleep and irritation. "Do you have any idea what time it is?"

"Sorry, sir," George said, not feeling sorry at all. "But this couldn't wait. We've uncovered something about the missing children cases."

There was a rustling sound, as if Smith was sitting up in bed. George checked his watch. 10.30 pm.

"Go on, Beaumont."

George took a deep breath. "Clare Brack was the SIO on all three cases, sir. Lily, Thomas, and Amira."

A sharp intake of breath from the other end of the line. "Bloody hell."

"I think the White Rose League is involved, sir."

"Really, George?"

"It's a possibility we can't ignore," George said. "Given what we know about Clare's involvement with the League, and now this connection to the missing children..."

Smith's voice hardened. "No. Absolutely not, Beaumont. We're not going down that road again." George heard a door slam and then Smith added, "You ended it, remember."

George blinked, taken aback by the intensity in Smith's tone. "Sir?"

"The White Rose League is finished," Smith said firmly. "You took them down. End of story. This is a paedophile ring, nothing more."

"But sir," George protested, "the evidence—"

"Is circumstantial at best," Smith cut him off. "Clare Brack's involvement doesn't prove anything. She worked a lot of cases, Beaumont. It's not surprising she'd have been involved in these."

George's free hand clenched into a fist. "With all due respect, sir, we can't dismiss this connection out of hand. If there's even a chance the League is still operating—"

"There isn't," Smith snapped. "Drop it, Beaumont. Focus on the paedophile ring angle. That's an order."

The line went dead, leaving George staring at his phone in disbelief. He pushed off from Smith's door, his mind whirling with questions and theories.

* * *

The drive home to Middleton passed in a blur of streetlights and racing thoughts. George's knuckles were white on the steering wheel, his jaw clenched tight enough to ache.

Missing children. A possible paedophile ring. Clare Brack's involvement. The spectre of the White Rose League looming over it all.

Something wasn't right. The pieces fit together too neatly in some ways, not at all in others. It nagged at him, an itch he couldn't scratch.

As he pulled into his drive, the warm glow of lights from his home did little to dispel the chill that had settled in his bones. He sat for a moment, engine idling, weighing his options.

Smith's order echoed in his mind. Focus on the paedophile ring. Drop the White Rose angle.

Why?

George's jaw set. No. He couldn't. Wouldn't. Not when children's lives were at stake.

He'd follow all theories, all leads. Even if it meant going against his superior. Even if it meant risking his career.

For Lily. For Thomas. For Amira. For all the children still out there, waiting to be found.

And for Dania.

With renewed determination, George killed the engine and headed inside. The house was quiet, no sign of Isabella downstairs. He climbed the stairs, the familiar creak of the third step a welcome reminder of home.

He paused at Olivia's door, pushing it open a crack. His daughter lay curled in her cot, curls splayed across the pillow, face peaceful in sleep. George's heart clenched. How many parents were staring at empty beds tonight, praying for their children's safe return?

He clenched his fists. Those poor parents.

The sound of running water drew his attention. The shower. Isabella.

He approached the ensuite door, raising his hand to knock. "Izzy?" he called. "Fancy some company in there?"

A pause, then Isabella's voice, muffled by the water and the door. "Not tonight, George. I'm knackered."

George's hand dropped to his side, disappointment mingling with the exhaustion and stress of the day. "Right. No worries. I'll see you in bed, yeah?"

No response came. George sighed, turning away from the door. He stripped off his suit, letting it fall in a crumpled heap on the floor. Too tired to care about wrinkles or dry cleaning, he crawled into bed, the cool sheets a balm against his skin.

His eyes drifted shut, but sleep remained elusive. Images of missing children, of grieving parents, of Clare Brack's face swam behind his eyelids. Theories and questions chased each other in endless circles.

* * *

Isabella stood under the shower's spray, letting the hot water pound against her tense muscles. Steam billowed around her, but it did little to wash away the stress of the day.

The Morris case weighed heavily on her mind. Bones in an abandoned farm. A family's worst fears confirmed. And still, no answers for the Fawcetts, no closure for Abigail.

She reached for the shampoo, working it into her hair with mechanical movements. Her thoughts spiralled, rehashing every detail of the case, searching for connections she might have missed.

George's voice, muffled by the door and the rush of water, barely registered. She answered on autopilot, rejecting his offer of company without really processing the words.

As she rinsed the shampoo from her hair, a pang of regret hit her. She should have said yes. Should have let him in, both literally and figuratively. They'd been like ships passing in the night lately, both consumed by their cases, barely finding time to connect.

Isabella turned off the water, stepping out of the shower and wrapping herself in a towel. She wiped the steam from the mirror, staring at her reflection. Dark circles shadowed her eyes, worry lines etched at the corners of her mouth.

She needed to talk to George. Needed his insight, his steady presence. The Morris case was eating at her, and she could use a fresh perspective.

Quickly drying off and slipping into her pyjamas, Isabella padded out of the bathroom. "George?" she called softly. "Are you still awake? I was hoping we could—"

Her words trailed off as she took in the sight of her fiancé, sprawled across the bed, fast asleep. His face was creased with exhaustion, one arm flung out across her side of the bed as if reaching for her even in sleep.

* * *

George lay still, his eyes closed, breathing carefully regulated to mimic sleep. He'd heard Isabella's soft footsteps approaching, her gentle call. "George? Are you still awake? I was hoping we could—"

He fought the urge to respond, to open his eyes and meet her gaze. But exhaustion weighed on him like lead, and the thought of discussing cases, of diving back into the murky waters of missing children and possible conspiracies, was more than he could bear.

So he remained motionless, his arm deliberately flung across her side of the bed in a convincing facsimile of unconscious reaching. He heard Isabella's soft sigh, felt the mattress dip as she slid in beside him.

Guilt gnawed at him, mingling with relief. He knew they needed to talk, to reconnect. But not tonight. She'd only reject him again. So tonight, he decided he needed the escape of sleep, the temporary reprieve from the horrors that haunted his waking hours.

Tomorrow, he told himself. They'd talk tomorrow. For now, he let himself drift, clinging to the illusion of sleep while acutely aware of Isabella's restless presence beside him.

* * *

Disappointment washed over Isabella. She'd wanted to talk, to unburden herself of the day's worries. To ask his advice about the Morris case, about the nagging feeling that something bigger was going on.

But looking at George's sleeping form, she couldn't bring

herself to wake him. He'd been running himself ragged with his own case, she knew. He needed the rest.

With a sigh, Isabella slipped into bed beside him, careful not to disturb his slumber. She curled onto her side, watching the steady rise and fall of his chest.

Tomorrow, she told herself. They'd talk tomorrow. She'd tell him about the Morris case, about her suspicions. They'd figure it out together, like they always did.

But as she lay there, listening to George's soft snores, Isabella couldn't shake the feeling that tomorrow might be too late. That they were both missing something crucial, something that connected their cases in ways they had yet to understand.

Sleep eluded her, her mind racing with possibilities and fears. What if the Morris case was connected to George's missing children? What if this was all part of something bigger, something more sinister than either of them had imagined?

Isabella turned onto her back, staring up at the ceiling. The questions swirled in her mind, unanswered and relentless.

Tomorrow, she promised herself again. Tomorrow, they'd talk. Tomorrow, they'd start piecing it all together.

But as the night wore on and sleep remained elusive, Isabella couldn't help but wonder: Would tomorrow be soon enough?

Chapter Fourteen

George Beaumont burst through the station doors, rain cascading off his coat in rivulets. Tashan Blackburn followed close behind, equally drenched. The sudden shift from the roaring downpour outside to the fluorescent-lit quiet of the station left them both blinking, momentarily disoriented.

"Bloody hell," George muttered, shaking water from his hair. "What happened to summer?"

Tashan grimaced, peeling off his sodden jacket. "Must've taken a holiday, sir. Along with our luck."

They squelched their way towards the Incident Room, leaving a trail of puddles in their wake. The familiar bustle of the station surrounded them, phones ringing and keyboards clacking, a constant reminder of the work that never stopped.

As they entered the Incident Room, Priya Patel's face caught George's attention. She stood by the evidence board, her usually confident posture deflated, worry etched into every line of her face.

"Priya?" George called, concern colouring his voice. "What's wrong?"

She turned, her dark eyes wide with distress. "Sir, I... I made a mistake. A big one."

George's stomach clenched. In their line of work, mistakes

could cost lives. "Tell me."

Priya took a deep breath, visibly steeling herself. "It's about Bilal Bhati. I missed something in his background check. Something crucial."

George and Tashan exchanged glances. "What did you miss?" Tashan asked.

"A sexual assault charge," Priya said, her words tumbling out in a rush. "From years ago. I don't know how I missed it, I swear I was thorough, but—"

"Stop," George said, holding up a hand. He could see the panic rising in Priya's eyes, the self-recrimination. "Take a breath. Show me what you've found."

Priya nodded, leading them to her desk. She pulled up a file on her computer, her fingers flying over the keyboard. "Here. Bilal Bhati was charged with sexual assault in 2015. The case never went to trial, but..."

George leaned in, scanning the report. His jaw tightened as he read. "Christ. This changes things."

Tashan peered over his shoulder. "Sir, if Bilal has a history of sexual violence..."

"I know," George said grimly. He straightened, turning to face his team. "Alright. We need to find Bilal Bhati; we need to bring him in for questioning ASAP."

Priya nodded, relief washing over her face at having a clear directive. "I'll start digging deeper into his background, sir. See if there's anything else we missed."

"Good," George said. "And Priya? Don't beat yourself up over this. We all miss things sometimes. What matters is how we move forward." He paused. "And your honesty. I appreciate it."

She managed a small smile. "Thank you, sir."

George turned to Tashan. "I want you to interview Hassan Bhati's closest friends. We need to know everything they can tell us about Bilal, about the family dynamics. And..." he hesitated, lowering his voice. "We need to consider the safety of Hassan's other daughter, especially considering what we learnt at the school."

Uniforms had been watching the Bhati house around the clock for any irregularities. So far, there were none.

Tashan's expression hardened. "I'm on it, sir. I'll be thorough."

As his team dispersed, George allowed himself a moment to breathe. The case was growing more complex by the hour, layers upon layers of secrets and lies. But they were making progress. Slowly, painfully, they were inching closer to the truth.

He shrugged off his wet coat, hanging it to dry. No time for creature comforts now. There was work to be done.

* * *

Tashan Blackburn sat across from Zayan Afridi, studying the man's face. Zayan was in his mid-forties, with a neatly trimmed beard and kind eyes that crinkled at the corners. He fidgeted with his wedding ring, a nervous tic Tashan had noticed as soon as the interview began.

"Mr Afridi," Tashan said, keeping his voice neutral. "How long have you known Hassan Bhati?"

Zayan's brow furrowed in thought. "Oh, must be... twenty years now? We met at university. Been close ever since."

Tashan nodded, making a note. He wondered why Hassan was working in a restaurant if he had a degree. Then again, why not? It wasn't for him to judge. "And in all that time, did you ever notice anything... unusual about Hassan's behaviour? Particularly towards his children?"

Zayan's head snapped up, his eyes widening. "What? No, never. Hassan adores his kids. He'd never... Is this about what happened to Dania?"

"We're exploring all possibilities, Mr Afridi," Tashan said carefully. "What can you tell me about Bilal Bhati?"

A shadow passed over Zayan's face. "Bilal? He's Hassan's younger brother. Bit of a wild card, if I'm honest. But he loves his family."

"Have you seen Bilal recently?"

Zayan shook his head. "Not for a few weeks. He travels a lot for work, you know."

Tashan leaned forward slightly. "Mr Afridi, I need you to think carefully. Have you ever seen or heard anything that might suggest Bilal was... inappropriate with Dania? Or any other children?"

"No," Zayan said firmly. "Never. Look, I know Hassan and Alize are innocent in all this. They're good people. And Bilal... he's a bit rough around the edges, but he'd never hurt a child. Never."

Tashan nodded, keeping his expression neutral. "Thank you for your time, Mr Afridi. If you think of anything else, anything at all, please don't hesitate to contact us."

As Zayan left, Tashan sighed, rubbing his temples. One down, three to go. And so far, nothing but dead ends.

The door opened again, admitting Harnail Iqbal. He was younger than Zayan, early thirties at most, with a lean build and sharp, intelligent eyes, more Bilal's age than Hassan's. He sat without waiting to be asked, his posture radiating impatience.

"Mr Iqbal," Tashan began. "Thank you for coming in. I just have a few questions about—"

"About Hassan and Alize," Harnail interrupted. "Yeah, I figured. Look, they didn't do this. No way. They loved Dania more than anything."

Tashan blinked, taken aback by the man's directness. "I appreciate your loyalty to your friends, Mr Iqbal. But we need to explore every angle. Can you tell me about your relationship with the Bhatis?"

Harnail shrugged. "Known Hassan for about five years. Met through work. He's a good bloke, hard-working. Alize too. They don't deserve what's happening to them."

"And Bilal Bhati?" Tashan pressed. "What can you tell me about him?"

Something flickered in Harnail's eyes. Recognition? Wariness? It was gone before Tashan could be sure. "Bilal? Yeah, I know him. Decent guy. Bit of a drinker, but who isn't these days?"

Tashan leaned forward. "Drinker? Isn't that against your religion?"

"No," was all Harnail said.

"When was the last time you saw Bilal?"

Harnail's brow furrowed. "Let's see... Oh yeah, it was last Sunday. We were at the pub in Middleton. Something with a bird in the name, I think."

"The Falconers Rest?"

Harnail nodded. "That's the one."

Tashan's pulse quickened. "You're sure about that? The exact night?"

Harnail nodded. "Yeah, positive. We were watching the

match. Leeds versus some Spanish team. A friendly. Bilal was gutted when the Spaniards scored in the last minute."

Tashan leaned forward, his eyes narrowing slightly. "Can you walk me through that evening in more detail?"

Harnail shrugged, but Tashan noticed a flicker of tension in his shoulders. "Sure. Like I said, we were at the Falconers Rest. Got there around seven, I think. Match started at eight."

"What time did you leave the pub?"

"Must've been... half eleven? Maybe midnight? We had a few, you know how it is."

Tashan made a note, his mind racing. If Harnail was telling the truth, it placed him in Middleton, half a mile away from the farm. It was also smack bang in the middle of the time of death estimate Dr Yardley had given them.

"He was with you all night?"

"Yeah, course," Harnail nodded. Then he paused, frowning slightly. "Well, except when he went to the loo. And he stepped out for a fag at half-time."

Tashan made a note. "How long was he gone each time?"

Harnail's brow furrowed. "The loo? Few minutes, I guess. Half-time break was longer. Maybe... fifteen, twenty minutes?"

"Did you see him outside during his smoke break?"

A beat of hesitation. "Nah, I stayed inside. It was pissing down, wasn't it?"

Tashan nodded, keeping his expression neutral. "And after the match? You said you left around midnight?"

"That's right," Harnail confirmed. "Had a few more pints after the game. Bilal was in a right mood 'cause Leeds lost."

"Did you leave together?"

Another pause. "Not exactly. Bilal said he was gonna walk

home, clear his head. I got a taxi."

"It's a long way to walk," Tashan said, his tone casual but his gaze sharp.

Harnail narrowed his eyes, a flicker of something—confusion? alarm?—crossing his face. "It's not, he lives around the corner."

Tashan leaned forward slightly, his voice level. "Where?" As far as he knew, Bilal lived in Beeston, a good few miles from the Falconers Rest.

Harnail blinked, his composure slipping momentarily. "I... well, I mean... he said he was staying at a mate's place. Near the pub. Can't remember the exact address."

"A mate's place," Tashan repeated, his pen poised over his notepad. "Did he mention this mate's name?"

Harnail shook his head, a bead of sweat forming on his brow despite the cool temperature of the interview room. "Nah, didn't say. Just said it was someone from work."

"I see," Tashan said, his tone neutral but his mind racing. "And you didn't think to mention this earlier when I asked about Bilal's whereabouts?"

Harnail shifted in his seat, discomfort evident in every line of his body. "Didn't think it was important. It's not like he does it all the time or anything."

"What about the day Dania was abducted?" Tashan asked.

"When was that? I forget the date," Harnail asked, and Tashan told him. "I'd have been at work. I dunno where Bilal would have been."

Tashan nodded slowly, making a note. Nobody knew where Bilal was during that moment, which only added suspicion. He asked, "Mr Iqbal, I need you to think carefully. Has Bilal ever mentioned staying at other 'mates' places' before?

Particularly in areas near where children might be?"

Harnail's eyes widened, a mix of indignation and fear flashing across his face. "What? No! It's not like that. Bilal's not... he wouldn't..."

"I'm not accusing anyone of anything, Mr Iqbal," Tashan said, his voice calm but firm. "I'm simply trying to establish the facts. Now, is there anything else about that night, or about Bilal's habits, that you might have forgotten to mention?"

The silence that followed was heavy, pregnant with unspoken truths and growing suspicions. Tashan waited, pen ready, as Harnail visibly wrestled with his thoughts. Eventually, Harnail said, "No."

Tashan sighed. And you didn't see Bilal again after that?"

"Nah," Harnail shook his head. "Texted him the next day to check he got home alright, but didn't hear back. Figured he was sleeping it off."

Tashan nodded, making a final note. "Mr Iqbal, one last question. You seem to know Bilal quite well. Has he ever mentioned any... interests or hobbies that struck you as unusual?"

Harnail's eyes narrowed. "What are you getting at?"

"It's a routine question," Tashan assured him. "We're trying to build a complete picture of Bilal's life."

Harnail was quiet for a moment, then shrugged. "Nothing weird, if that's what you're asking. He likes football, obviously. Bit of a tech geek, always fiddling with computers and stuff. Oh, and he's into photography. Has a proper fancy camera and everything."

Tashan's pen paused mid-stroke. "Photography? What kind of subjects does he like to shoot?"

"Dunno, landscapes mostly, I think," Harnail said. Then he added, almost as an afterthought, "He did mention something about wanting to do more portrait work. Said he was thinking of offering to take photos at kids' birthday parties and stuff. Make a bit of extra cash, you know?"

Tashan fought to keep his expression neutral, but alarm bells were ringing in his head. "I see. And when did he mention this?"

Harnail frowned, thinking. "Couple of months ago, maybe? Haven't heard him talk about it since, though."

"Mr Iqbal," Tashan said carefully. "Are you aware that Bilal has a history of... legal troubles?"

Harnail's eyes narrowed. "You mean that bollocks sexual assault charge? Yeah, I heard about it. Load of rubbish, if you ask me."

"Oh?" Tashan kept his tone neutral. "What makes you say that?"

Harnail leaned back in his chair, crossing his arms. "It was a false accusation. Some bird at a work do had too much to drink, started coming onto Bilal. When he turned her down, she cried assault. Charges were dropped as soon as the truth came out."

Tashan nodded, making another note. "I see. And you're certain about this?"

"Course I am," Harnail said, a hint of defensiveness creeping into his voice. "She was sixteen; shouldn't have even been allowed to drink by the company. Hence why the charges were dropped."

Tashan scribbled down some notes.

"Look, Bilal's not perfect. But he's not a nonce, and he's sure as hell not a killer. Neither are Hassan and Alize. You're barking up the wrong tree, mate."

Tashan sat back, studying Harnail's face. The man seemed genuine in his belief, but something nagged at Tashan. A gut feeling he couldn't quite pin down.

"Thank you for your time, Mr Iqbal," he said finally. "If you think of anything else, anything at all, please let us know."

As Harnail left, Tashan remained seated, his mind racing. The gaps in Bilal's alibi, the interest in photography, the potential access to children—it all added up to a picture that was becoming increasingly concerning.

Two interviews down, and he was no closer to the truth. If anything, the waters seemed murkier than ever.

He stood, stretching muscles cramped from sitting. Time to brief George on what he'd learned—or rather, what he hadn't. As he made his way back to the Incident Room, Tashan couldn't shake the feeling that they were missing something. Something big.

The pieces were there, he was sure of it. They just needed to figure out how they fit together. And they needed to do it fast, before another child fell victim to whoever was behind this nightmare.

Chapter Fifteen

Tashan leaned back in his chair, fingers drumming on the desk. The next interviewee wasn't due for another hour, leaving him with a window of opportunity. He turned to his computer, the glow of the screen illuminating his determined face.

"Right," he muttered, cracking his knuckles. "Let's see what we can find about this sixteen-year-old."

His fingers flew over the keyboard, delving into databases and cross-referencing reports. As he dug deeper, a pattern began to emerge, one that made his brow furrow with each new piece of information.

After an hour of intensive searching, Tashan sat back, rubbing his eyes. The picture he'd uncovered was troubling, to say the least. He gathered his notes and headed for George's office, knocking briskly before entering.

George looked up from a stack of files. "Tashan? What have you got?"

Tashan closed the door behind him. "Sir, I've been looking into the sexual assault allegation against Bilal Bhati. Specifically, the sixteen-year-old accuser."

George's eyebrows rose. "And?"

"It's... complicated," Tashan said, settling into a chair. "The girl has a history. Three other previous allegations of sexual assault, all retracted. Two against secondary school teachers, and one against a family friend. Each time, she admitted to fabricating the claims for attention."

George's jaw tightened. "Christ. And the case against Bilal?"

"Dropped due to lack of evidence," Tashan confirmed. "Her story had inconsistencies, and given her history..."

George nodded slowly. "It casts doubt on the allegation. But it doesn't clear Bilal entirely."

"No, sir," Tashan agreed. "And given what we know about what Dania told the teacher..."

They shared a grim look.

George stood, pacing behind his desk. "We can't discount Bilal as a suspect. Not yet. We need to keep digging, find out where he really was the night Dania disappeared."

Tashan nodded. "What about the woman with the mole, sir? Harnail's alibi for Bilal puts him in Middleton that night, but it doesn't account for the woman seen with Dania."

George's eyes narrowed. "You're right. We need to put more resources into finding her. She's our best lead at this point."

"I'll get the team on it," Tashan said, standing. "We'll comb through CCTV, re-interview witnesses, the works."

George clapped him on the shoulder. "Good work, Tashan. Keep at it."

* * *

Detective Inspector Isabella Wood stood at the edge of Old River Farm in Wakefield, her eyes scanning the overgrown field before her. The air was crisp, carrying the scent of damp earth and decaying vegetation. Behind her, a team of forensic specialists unloaded equipment from a van, their movements precise and practised.

Isabella took a deep breath, steeling herself for the task ahead. This wasn't just another crime scene. This was where Ethan Morris's remains had been found, a grim discovery that had reignited a decade-old case and opened up a Pandora's box of questions.

"DI Wood?"

She turned to find Dr Naomi Sasaki approaching, clipboard in hand. The forensic scientist's face was set in its usual mask of professional detachment, but Isabella caught a flicker of something in her eyes. Anticipation? Dread?

"Dr Sasaki," Isabella nodded. "Are we ready to begin?"

Naomi glanced back at the team. "Almost. We're just calibrating the ground-penetrating radar. Should be good to go in about ten minutes."

Isabella nodded, her gaze drawn back to the field. Somewhere out there, buried beneath years of neglect and nature's reclamation, lay the answers they sought. She hoped.

"What do you think our chances are?" she asked, keeping her voice low. "Of finding anything else, I mean."

Naomi's lips thinned. "Honestly? It's hard to say. The GPR is sensitive, but we're dealing with a lot of variables. Soil composition, time elapsed, potential disturbances..."

"But it's our best shot," Isabella finished.

"Yes," Naomi agreed. "If there's anything else out there, this is how we'll find it."

A shout from behind them signalled the team was ready. Isabella squared her shoulders, pushing aside the nagging doubts and what-ifs that had plagued her since this case landed on her desk.

"Right," she said, more to herself than to Naomi. "Let's do this."

They made their way across the field, picking through knee-high grass and navigating around chunks of broken concrete—remnants of the farm's former life. The GPR unit, a bulky contraption that looked like a lawnmower crossed with a computer, was already positioned at the far end of the search grid.

"We'll start here," Naomi explained, gesturing to the marked-off area. "Work our way across in a systematic pattern. The GPR will give us real-time data on subsurface anomalies."

Isabella nodded, her eyes fixed on the screen attached to the GPR. "And if we find something?"

"We flag it, record the coordinates, and move on," Naomi said. "Once we've covered the entire grid, we'll review the data and determine which anomalies warrant further investigation."

It was painstaking work. For the next three hours, Isabella watched as the team methodically swept the field, inch by inch. The monotonous beep of the GPR became a constant backdrop, occasionally punctuated by a different tone that had everyone holding their breath.

Each time, Naomi would study the readout, her brow furrowed in concentration. And each time, she'd shake her head. "Natural formation," or "Probably a rock," she'd mutter, and they'd move on.

By midday, Isabella's initial surge of hope had dwindled to a flickering ember. They'd covered nearly two-thirds of the search area with nothing to show for it but mud-caked boots and increasingly frayed nerves.

"Maybe we should take a break," she suggested, noticing the fatigue etched on the faces of the team.

Naomi shook her head, her jaw set with determination. "We're close to finishing the grid. Let's push through."

Isabella couldn't argue with that logic, even as her stomach grumbled in protest. She'd skipped breakfast in her haste to get to the site, a decision she was now regretting.

They pressed on, the beep of the GPR now an irritating drone in Isabella's ears. She found her mind wandering, replaying the details of the case in her head. Ethan Morris, eleven years old, vanished without a trace. A decade of dead ends and false hopes. And now, his remains found in this godforsaken field.

But why here? What connection did this abandoned farm have to Ethan's disappearance? And more importantly, was he the only victim buried in this lonely stretch of land?

A sudden change in the GPR's tone snapped Isabella back to the present. She looked up to see Naomi frozen in place, her eyes wide as she stared at the readout.

"What is it?" Isabella demanded, her heart hammering in her chest.

Naomi's voice was barely above a whisper. "We've got something. And it's big."

The next few minutes passed in a blur of activity. Naomi called over the rest of the team, pointing out the anomaly on the GPR's screen. Isabella watched, her mind racing with possibilities.

"How deep?" she asked.

"About two meters," Naomi replied, her fingers flying over the device's controls. "And it's... uniform. Too uniform to be natural."

Isabella's breath caught in her throat. "Another body?"

Naomi met her gaze, the scientist's usual composure cracking slightly. "Possibly. Or..."

"Or what?"

"It could be a container of some sort. The readings are consistent with a large metal object."

Isabella's mind whirled with the implications. A metal container, buried two meters deep in an abandoned field. It could be nothing—farm equipment, perhaps, long forgotten. Or it could be everything they'd been searching for.

"How soon can we dig?" she asked, already reaching for her phone to call in additional resources.

Naomi shook her head. "Not today. We need to finish the grid, compile all the data. And we'll need specialised equipment for an excavation this deep."

Isabella nodded, forcing down her impatience. "First thing tomorrow, then. I want a full team here at dawn."

As Naomi moved off to brief the rest of the team, Isabella stood rooted to the spot, her eyes fixed on the innocuous patch of ground that might hold the key to unlocking this entire case.

What secrets lay buried beneath her feet? Was this the breakthrough they'd been hoping for, or another dead end in a case already full of disappointment?

One thing was certain—whatever lay two meters below the surface of this forgotten field was about to change everything. For better or worse, Isabella Wood was on the cusp of uncovering a truth that had remained hidden for over a decade.

* * *

George Beaumont strode into the Incident Room. The air crackled with tension as his team looked up, sensing the urgency in his demeanour. He didn't waste time with pleas-antries.

"Right, listen up," he barked, his voice cutting through the low hum of conversation. "We've got new leads on Bilal Bhati, and we need to move fast."

The team straightened, all eyes fixed on George. He could see the mixture of exhaustion and determination in their faces, a mirror of his own state.

"Yolanda," he said. "I need you to dig into Bilal's interest in photography. We've got information he might be using it to gain access to children. Birthday parties, school events, anything like that. I want to know every click of his shutter."

Yolanda nodded, her eyes narrowing. "On it, boss. I'll check with local photography clubs, online forums, the works."

George turned to Priya and Susie, who sat side by side, notepads at the ready. "You two, I want you at the Falconers Rest. Retrieve every scrap of CCTV footage from the night of the football match. And I mean every scrap—inside, outside, nearby streets, the lot."

Priya's pen was already flying across her notepad. "What about staff and regulars, sir?"

"Interview them all," George confirmed. "Anyone who might have been there that Sunday night. I want to know Bilal's every move, every word, every bloody sip of his pint. Clear?"

Susie and Priya exchanged a glance before nodding in unison. "Crystal, sir," Susie replied.

George's gaze swept the room, taking in the determined faces of CID. "The rest of you, keep pushing on your current assignments. Every lead, no matter how small, gets followed up. We're close, I can feel it. We just need that one piece to make the puzzle click."

He paused, his voice dropping slightly. "Remember, we're not just looking for a killer. We're looking for a child predator. Every minute counts."

The room hummed with renewed energy, detectives already reaching for phones and firing up computers. George allowed himself a moment of pride in his team before turning to Tashan.

"You and me, we're heading to the Bhati household," he said. "We need to talk to the parents about these accusations against Bilal."

Tashan's jaw tightened. "You think they knew, sir?"

George shook his head. "I don't know. But if Dania tried to tell them something and they didn't listen..."

He let the sentence hang, the implications clear. Tashan nodded grimly.

"Right, people," George called out, his voice rising above the bustle. "You've got your assignments. I want updates every hour, on the hour. Let's bring this bastard in."

As the team dispersed, George grabbed his coat, his mind already racing ahead to the confrontation with the Bhatis. He could feel the case teetering on a knife-edge. One wrong move, one missed clue, and it could all come crashing down.

But they were close. He could taste it.

George and Tashan strode out of the station. The weather had turned warm.

"Some summer, eh, boss?"

"Typical British one, Tashan."

The drive to the Bhati household was tense, filled with unspoken concerns and grim speculation.

"What's our approach, sir?" Tashan asked as they turned

137

onto the Bhatis' street.

George's hands tightened on the steering wheel. "We need to tread carefully. They've lost a child, Tashan. But we can't pull our punches. If they knew something and didn't act..."

Tashan nodded, understanding the delicate balance they needed to strike.

Chapter Sixteen

DCI Beaumont stood on the doorstep of the Bhati residence. Beside him, Tashan Blackburn shifted uneasily, both men acutely aware of the delicate nature of their visit. George raised his hand and rapped sharply on the door.

Moments passed, each second stretching into eternity. Then, the door swung open, revealing Hassan Bhati. His face, already lined with grief, creased further at the sight of the detectives.

"DCI Beaumont," Hassan said, his voice tight. "DS Blackburn. What's happened? Have you found something about Dania?"

George kept his expression neutral. "Mr Bhati, we need to speak with you and your wife. Privately, if possible."

Hassan's eyes darted between them, confusion and anxiety warring on his face. "Of course, come in. Alize is in the living room with Inaya. She was just heading to work."

They followed Hassan into the house, the air heavy with the scent of spices and something else—grief, perhaps, or fear. In the living room, Alize sat on the floor, watching Inaya play with a set of brightly coloured blocks. The little girl barely glanced up as they entered, lost in her own world of imagination.

"Alize," Hassan said softly. "The detectives need to speak with us."

Alize looked up, her eyes widening as she took in George and Tashan's grim expressions. She stood, wiping her hands on her jeans. "What's wrong?"

George glanced at Inaya, then back to the parents. "Is there somewhere we can talk privately?"

Hassan nodded, leading them to the kitchen. As they settled around the small table, George could see the tension in both parents' postures, the way their hands sought each other's for comfort.

"Mr and Mrs Bhati," George began. "Some troubling allegations have come to light during our investigation. Specifically, from Dania's school."

Hassan's brow furrowed. "Allegations? What kind of allegations?"

George took a deep breath. "A teacher has come forward, claiming Dania confided in them about... inappropriate touching. By Bilal. This was weeks before her disappearance."

The words hung in the air, heavy and poisonous. Hassan's face drained of colour, his grip on Alize's hand tightening visibly.

"What?" he whispered, his voice cracking. "No. No, that's impossible. Bilal would never... Dania would never say such a thing!"

Alize remained silent, her eyes wide and unblinking.

George leaned forward slightly. "Mr Bhati, I understand this is difficult to hear. But we need to address it. Can you think of any reason why Dania might have said this?"

Hassan shook his head vehemently. "No! Absolutely not. Bilal loved Dania. He would never hurt her. Never!"

"The teacher mentioned something about Bilal touching Dania's 'special place'," Tashan interjected gently. "Does that mean anything to you?"

A flicker of recognition passed over Hassan's face. "Her heart," he said softly. "Bilal used to tickle her there, call it her special place. It was a game between them."

George and Tashan exchanged glances. "A game," George repeated carefully. "And this happened often?"

"Yes," Alize spoke for the first time, her voice barely above a whisper. "Whenever Bilal visited. The girls loved it."

George nodded slowly. "I see. Mr and Mrs Bhati, I want to assure you that no immediate action will be taken based on this single allegation. But it's important that we address it."

Hassan's face contorted with a mixture of grief and anger. "Address it? How can we address such a... such a horrible lie? Why would Dania say such a thing if it wasn't true?"

"Children sometimes misunderstand things," Tashan offered. "Or they might repeat something they've heard elsewhere, not fully grasping its meaning."

Alize's hand trembled as she brought it to her mouth. "But... but Bilal was alone with the girls so often. We trusted him completely."

George's eyes narrowed slightly at this. "How often was Bilal alone with Dania and Inaya?"

Hassan ran a hand through his hair, frustration evident in every movement. "I don't know. Once a week, maybe? He'd babysit sometimes, when Alize and I both had to work. He'd pick them up from school. Have them on weekends. He loves the girls."

The room fell silent, the implications of this information settling over them like a heavy blanket. George cleared his throat, knowing he had to press on.

"There's something else you should know," he said, his voice gentle but firm. "We've uncovered information about Bilal's past. He was charged with sexual assault several years ago."

Hassan's head snapped up, shock written across his features. "What? No, that's impossible. I would have known!"

"The charges were dropped," Tashan added quickly. "But it's something we need to consider in light of these new allegations."

Alize made a small, choked sound. "I can't believe this," she whispered. "We left our babies alone with him. How could we be so blind?"

Hassan stood abruptly, his chair scraping against the linoleum. "This is too much," he said, his voice shaking. "First Dania, now these... these insinuations about Bilal. It's too much!"

George remained seated, his voice calm. "I understand this is overwhelming, Mr Bhati. But we need to consider every possibility. For Dania's sake, and for Inaya's."

At the mention of their younger daughter, both parents stiffened. Alize's eyes darted towards the living room, where Inaya could still be heard playing.

"You don't think..." she began, unable to finish the thought.

"We're not making any assumptions," George assured her. "But we need to be thorough. Has Inaya ever mentioned anything unusual about her time with Bilal?"

Hassan shook his head, collapsing back into his chair. "No. Never. This is madness. Bilal is innocent. He has to be."

George leaned back, studying the couple before him. The pain in their eyes was palpable, the weight of suspicion and fear crushing down on them.

"Mr and Mrs Bhati," he said softly. "I know this is difficult. But we need your help. Have you been in contact with Bilal recently?"

Hassan's head snapped up. "No. Not since... not since Dania disappeared. He called once, to check on us, but that's all."

George nodded, making a mental note. "And you haven't seen him? He hasn't tried to visit?"

"No," Alize said firmly. "We've barely left the house. If Bilal had come by, we'd have known."

George stood, signalling to Tashan that it was time to leave. "Thank you for your time," he said. "We'll be in touch if we need any further information."

As they made their way to the door, Hassan followed, his face a mask of anguish and frustration. "Detective," he said. "I appreciate your honesty. But you're wrong about Bilal. He's not a predator. He's not a killer. He loved Dania."

George paused, his hand on the doorknob. He turned to face Hassan, his expression unreadable. "Then why did Dania say what she did, Mr Bhati? Why accuse her beloved uncle of touching her inappropriately?"

Hassan's face crumpled, the question hanging in the air between them. "I don't know," he whispered. "I don't know."

They walked to their car in silence, each lost in their own thoughts. As they climbed in, Tashan turned to George, his face grim.

"What now, sir?" he asked.

George started the engine, his jaw set with determination. "Now," he said, "we find Bilal Bhati. And the woman with the mole."

As they pulled away from the curb, leaving the Bhati household behind, George couldn't shake the image of Inaya, playing innocently in the living room. Another potential victim, another child at risk. The clock was ticking, and they were running out of time.

* * *

Detective Inspector Isabella Wood strode into her Incident Room at Wakefield HQ, her footsteps echoing with purpose. The team looked up, sensing the urgency in her demeanour. Isabella's eyes swept across the room, taking in the tired faces of her detectives. They'd been at this for days, weeks even, but now they had a lead. A glimmer of hope in the darkness that had shrouded the Ethan Morris case for over a decade.

"Right," Isabella said, her voice cutting through the low hum of conversation. "We've got work to do."

She moved to the whiteboard, uncapping a marker with a decisive flick of her wrist. "The GPR scan at the farm has given us something to work with, but we can't put all our eggs in one basket. We need to attack this from every angle."

DS Noah Briggs leaned forward, his brow furrowed. "What's the play, boss?"

Isabella turned to face her team, her jaw set with determination. "We're going back to the beginning. I want a fresh analysis of every scrap of digital evidence we have from the time of Ethan's disappearance. CCTV footage, phone records, everything."

DC Leanne Spencer's fingers were already flying across her keyboard. "Most of that stuff's been gone over a hundred times, boss."

"I know," Isabella nodded. "But we've got tools now we

didn't have back then. I want you to use every modern data analysis technique at our disposal. If there's a pattern hidden in those old files, we're going to find it."

DMI Emma Brooke spoke up, her voice tinged with excitement. "I can run the CCTV footage through our new facial recognition software, ma'am. It might pick up on something the original investigation missed."

"Do it," Isabella ordered. "And don't just look for Ethan or known suspects. I want to know about anyone who appears in multiple locations, anyone who stands out as behaving oddly."

Noah scratched his chin, thoughtful. "What about the phone records? We've been through them before, but..."

"But now we can cross-reference them with cell tower data," Isabella finished for him. "I want to know every call made within a five-mile radius of Ethan's last known location. And I mean every call, not just the ones to or from numbers we've already flagged."

The team nodded, energy crackling through the room as they absorbed their orders. Isabella felt a surge of pride. They were good, her people. Dedicated. Relentless.

"Connor," she said, turning to DC Riley. "I want you to dig into the internet history. Not just Ethan's family computer, but every device we can link to anyone even tangentially connected to the case. Use whatever data recovery methods you need."

Connor nodded, already reaching for his laptop. "On it, boss. I'll see if I can recover any deleted emails or social media posts, too."

Isabella moved to the evidence board, her eyes scanning the timeline they'd constructed. "We're not just looking for information directly related to Ethan's disappearance. I want to know about any unusual activity in the area in the weeks leading up to it. Burglaries, vandalism, anything out of the ordinary."

Leanne looked up from her computer. "You think there might have been a dry run? The killer scoping out the area?"

"It's possible," Isabella said. "Killers like this, they often escalate. Start small, work their way up to abduction. If we can identify a pattern of smaller crimes, it might lead us to our perpetrator."

Noah stood, stretching muscles cramped from hours of desk work. "What about the farm, boss? When do we start digging?"

Isabella's eyes hardened. "First light tomorrow. But I don't want anyone fixating on that. We follow every lead, no matter how small. The answer could be buried in that field, or it could be hiding in plain sight in these old files. We don't assume anything."

The team murmured their agreement, a renewed sense of purpose filling the room. Isabella felt it too, the familiar surge of adrenaline that came with a breakthrough. They were close. She could taste it.

"One more thing," she said, her voice dropping slightly. "This case... it's not just about Ethan now. We have to consider the possibility that there are other victims out there. Other families waiting for answers."

A sombre silence fell over the room. They'd all seen the reports, the whispers of connections to other missing children cases. The spectre of a serial predator loomed large.

"We owe it to Ethan, to his family, to every child who's ever gone missing, to solve this," Isabella continued. "Whatever it takes, however long it takes, we don't stop until we have answers. Clear?"

"Clear," the team chorused.

Isabella nodded, satisfied. "Good. Now let's get to work."

As her team dispersed, each detective diving into their assigned tasks with renewed vigour, Isabella allowed herself a moment of quiet reflection.

She thought of Ethan, of the life he should have had. Of the other children who might have suffered a similar fate.

Her phone buzzed in her pocket, George's name flashing on the screen. She hesitated, torn between the urge to share her progress and the need to focus on the task at hand. With a sigh, she silenced the call. Later. She'd fill him in later.

Isabella turned back to the Big Board, her eyes tracing the familiar details of Ethan's last known movements. Somewhere in this maze of information, the truth was hiding. And she was going to find it, no matter what it took.

As the Incident Room hummed with activity, Isabella felt a familiar fire ignite in her belly. They were on the verge of something big. She could feel it. And this time, she wasn't going to let the answers slip through her fingers.

Not again.

Not ever again.

Chapter Seventeen

Later that evening, George Beaumont stood at the head of the Incident Room, his eyes scanning the faces of his team.

He nodded to Police Sergeant Greenwood and Detective Sergeant Josh Fry as they entered, their expressions grim.

"Right," George barked, his voice cutting through the low murmur of conversation. "Let's hear it. What have we got on Bilal Bhati?"

Greenwood stepped forward, a stack of papers clutched in his hand. "Sir, we've had eyes on all of Bilal's known addresses for the past seventy-two hours. No sign of him at any of them."

George's jaw tightened. "Nothing at all?"

"Not a whisper," Greenwood confirmed. "His flat in Beeston's been dark. Same for his work address and the gym he frequents."

Fry chimed in. "We've been monitoring his financials, sir. Bank accounts, credit cards, the lot. There's been no activity since Sunday night."

A ripple of unease passed through the room. George leaned forward, his hands gripping the edge of the table. "No activity since at all? That's not normal."

"No, sir," Fry agreed. "It's like he's gone completely off the grid since leaving the pub."

Tashan Blackburn, standing to George's right, frowned. "What about his mobile?"

Greenwood shook his head. "Nothing. It's either turned off or he's ditched it. We can't get a signal."

George straightened, his mind racing. "Alright. What about his other devices? Laptop, tablet, anything?"

Fry consulted his notes. "We've tracked his laptop to his flat in Beeston, but it hasn't been accessed since Sunday morning. No activity on any known email accounts or social media profiles either."

"Christ," George muttered. He turned to the rest of the team. "Thoughts?"

Priya Patel spoke up from her position near the evidence board. "He's running, sir. Has to be. No one goes dark like this unless they're trying to avoid detection."

Susie Whitaker nodded in agreement. "It's textbook flight behaviour. He knows we're onto him."

George's eyes narrowed. "Or he's been taken out of the picture."

A hush fell over the room as the implications of his words sank in.

"You think someone might have silenced him, sir?" Tashan asked.

George shrugged. "It's a possibility we can't ignore. Especially if there's more to this than just Bilal."

He turned back to Greenwood and Fry. "What about his work? Any colleagues report him missing?"

Greenwood consulted his notes. "He texted in sick the night Dania's body was found, saying he had food poisoning and wouldn't be in the following morning. He hasn't been in touch since. His boss is getting antsy, but he hasn't filed a missing persons' report yet."

George nodded slowly. "Alright. Here's what we do next. Greenwood, I want you to expand the surveillance. Check hotels, hostels, anywhere he might be laying low. DS Fry, dig deeper into his financials. Look for any accounts we might have missed, any patterns in his spending that could give us a clue to where he's gone."

Both officers nodded, already making notes.

"DS Williams," George continued, "I want you to keep going through Bilal's online presence with a fine-tooth comb. Social media, forums, anywhere he might have left a digital footprint. Look for any connections, any hints about where he might go to ground."

Yolanda nodded, her fingers already flying over her key-board.

"I want an update, Susie and Priya," George said. "What did you find at the Falconers Rest?"

Susie stepped forward, a folder clutched in her hand. "It's not good, sir. We've got confirmation that Bilal was there the night Dania's body was found, but the timeline's murky."

George's eyes narrowed. "How murky?"

Priya chimed in, her voice tight with frustration. "The CCTV footage is patchy at best. We've got Bilal arriving at 7.15 pm, clear as day. But after that, it gets complicated."

"Complicated how?" George pressed.

Susie flipped open her folder. "He's visible at the bar until about 9.30 pm. Then he disappears from view for nearly an hour."

George straightened. "An hour? Where the hell did he go?"

"That's the thing, sir," Priya said. "The pub was packed

that night. Leeds match, remember? People were coming and going constantly. It's possible he just moved to a blind spot in the camera's view."

"Or he left," George muttered. "What about after that hour?"

Susie nodded. "He reappears on camera at 10.37 pm. Stays at the bar until closing time."

George ran a hand through his hair. "Christ. So we've got a solid hour where he could have been anywhere, doing anything."

"It gets worse," Priya added. "We interviewed the staff. Most of them remember Bilal being there all night, but one bartender swears he saw him leave around 9.30."

"And return?" George asked.

Priya shook her head. "He wasn't sure. Said it was too busy to keep track."

George's mind raced. An hour. More than enough time for Bilal to have done... what? Moved Dania from wherever he had hidden her and then killed her? His stomach churned at the thought.

A knock at the door interrupted his thoughts. Yolanda poked her head in, her expression grim.

"Sir? I've got that information you wanted on Bilal's photography interests."

George waved her in. "Let's hear it."

Yolanda entered, clutching a stack of printouts. "It's not pretty, sir. Bilal's been active on several online photography forums. Mostly landscape stuff, like we were told. But in the past few months, he's been asking a lot of questions about portrait photography. Specifically, child portraiture."

The room fell silent, the implications hanging heavy in the

151

air.

"Any evidence he actually did any child photography?" George asked.

Yolanda shook her head. "Nothing concrete. But he was asking about locations, lighting setups for shooting kids. One post mentioned wanting to do a series on 'innocence lost'. It's all circumstantial, but..."

"But it's damn suspicious," George finished.

He stood, pacing the small confines of his office. The pieces were there, tantalisingly close to fitting together. Bilal at the pub, with an unaccounted hour. His interest in photographing children. Dania's accusation of inappropriate touching.

"Alright," he said finally, turning to face his team. "Here's what we do. Susie, Priya, I want you to go back to the Falconers Rest. Check every inch of that CCTV footage. If Bilal so much as sneezed, I want to know about it. Talk to every staff member again, see if anyone remembers anything else about that night."

They nodded, already gathering their things.

"Yolanda," George continued, "dig deeper into those photography forums as well as the other job I gave you. See if you can trace any of Bilal's connections. If he was involved in something bigger, there might be a trail."

"On it, sir," Yolanda said.

George's gaze swept the room. "Listen up, everyone. Nothing is adding up, which is suspicious. As such, Bilal Bhati is our prime suspect in a child murder case. But he's also potentially a victim. A scapegoat. We don't know what we're dealing with here, so stay alert. If anyone gets even a whiff of his location, you call it in immediately. Clear?"

A chorus of "Yes, sir" echoed through the room.

"Good. Let's move."

As the team dispersed, George felt the familiar rush of adrenaline coursing through his veins.

* * *

Detective Constables Susie Whitaker and Priya Patel stood outside the Falconers Rest, the pub's weathered sign creaking gently in the breeze. The late afternoon summer sun cast long shadows across the car park, giving the place an eerily deserted feel.

"Right," Susie said, squaring her shoulders. "Let's do this."

Priya nodded, her dark eyes scanning the building. "CCTV first or staff interviews?"

"CCTV," Susie decided. "Might help us ask better questions if we spot anything odd."

They entered the pub, the smell of stale beer and cleaning products hitting them like a wall. The landlord, a burly man named Mike, looked up from behind the bar.

"Back again?" he grumbled. "Thought you lot were done yesterday."

Susie flashed her warrant card. "Just a few follow-up questions, Mr Harrison. And we'll need another look at your CCTV footage."

Mike sighed but nodded towards a door marked 'Private'. "Same as yesterday. Knock yourselves out."

For the next three hours, Susie and Priya pored over grainy footage, their eyes straining in the dim light of the pub's back office. They watched Bilal Bhati arrive, order drinks, chat with other patrons. Nothing they hadn't seen before.

"This is useless," Priya muttered, rubbing her eyes. "We're

not going to spot anything new."

Susie leaned back in her chair, frustration etched on her face. "Maybe we're looking at this wrong. Let's try the staff again, see if anyone's remembered anything overnight."

They emerged from the office, blinking in the comparatively bright light of the pub. The after-work crowd had started to trickle in, the low hum of conversation filling the air.

Susie approached the bar, where a young woman was pulling pints. "Excuse me, were you working here the night of the Leeds match? Sunday?"

The barmaid shook her head. "Sorry, love. I was at 'ome on Sunday."

They worked their way through the staff, each conversation yielding the same result: nothing new, nothing useful. As the sun dipped below the horizon, casting the pub in a warm, golden glow, Susie and Priya found themselves back at the bar, defeat written in the slump of their shoulders.

"One last try?" Priya suggested, nodding towards Mike.

Susie sighed but nodded. They approached the landlord, who was busy restocking glasses.

"Mr Harrison," Susie began, "we know we've asked this before, but is there anything else you can remember about the night Bilal Bhati was here? Anything at all, no matter how small?"

Mike paused, glass in hand. "Look, I've told you everything I know. Bilal was here, watched the match, had a few pints. It was busy, but there was nothing out of the ordinary."

Just as Susie was about to admit defeat, the pub door swung open. A wiry man in his sixties ambled in, nodding to Mike as he approached the bar.

"Evening, Mike. Usual, please."

Mike's face lit up with recognition. "Jack! Where've you been hiding yourself? Haven't seen you since the weekend."

As Mike poured a pint, Priya's eyes narrowed. She leaned in close to Susie, whispering, "A regular. Could be a local? Might be worth a shot."

Susie nodded, turning to the newcomer. "Excuse me, sir. I'm DC Whitaker; this is DC Patel. We're investigating a case and wondered if we might have a word?"

Jack eyed them warily, accepting his pint from Mike. "What's this about, then?"

"We're looking into the disappearance of a young girl," Priya explained. "We believe a man named Bilal Bhati might have information. He was here the night of the Leeds match on Sunday. Did you happen to see him?"

Jack's brow furrowed. "Bilal? Yeah, I know him. Asian fella, right?" The two young DCs nodded. "Decent lad, he is. He comes in for the footie sometimes, like you say."

Susie and Priya exchanged glances, a spark of excitement igniting between them.

"You know him well?" Susie pressed.

Jack shrugged. "Well enough, I suppose. Even walked him home once when he'd had a few too many. Why? He's not in trouble, is he?"

"We just need to speak with him," Priya said carefully. "You wouldn't happen to know where he lives, would you?"

Jack took a long swig of his beer before answering. "Yeah, actually. It's not far. Just across the road in the Heritage Village. Hillthorpe Court. Number 17, I think it was. Red door, can't miss it."

Susie's heart raced. This was it. The break they'd been waiting for. "Thank you, Mr...?"

"Thornton. Jack Thornton."

"Thank you, Mr Thornton. You've been incredibly helpful."

As they left the pub, Susie and Priya could barely contain their excitement. They'd done it. They'd found Bilal's address.

"We need to call this in," Priya said, already reaching for her phone.

Susie nodded, her eyes fixed on the Heritage Village across the street. "George is going to want to handle this himself. But we should do a quick recce, make sure Bilal's actually there."

Chapter Eighteen

Detective Constables Susie Whitaker and Priya Patel crouched behind a neatly trimmed hedge, their eyes fixed on the red door of Number 17 Hillthorpe Court. The Heritage Village was quiet, almost unnaturally so.

"Anything?" Susie whispered, her breath fogging in the cool evening air.

Priya shook her head. "Not a flicker. No lights, no movement. Place looks dead."

They'd been there for thirty minutes, watching and waiting. But the house remained stubbornly silent, offering no clues about its occupants or their whereabouts.

"We should talk to the neighbours," Priya suggested. "Someone must know something."

Susie nodded, about to reply when her radio crackled to life. "DC Whitaker, this is DCI Beaumont. What's your location?"

"Sir," Susie responded, keeping her voice low. "We're outside 17 Hillthorpe Court. No sign of activity so far."

"Stay put. We're two minutes out."

* * *

True to his word, less than 120 seconds later, George's Mercedes pulled up at the entrance to the cul-de-sac. George Beaumont stepped out, followed by DS Tashan Blackburn and DC Yolanda Williams.

George approached Susie and Priya, his face a mask of controlled anticipation. "Sitrep," he demanded without preamble.

Susie straightened, her professionalism kicking in despite the excitement thrumming through her veins. "Sir, we've been observing the property for approximately 35 minutes. There's been no sign of life inside. No lights, no movement, nothing to suggest anyone's home."

George nodded, his eyes scanning the quiet street. "Priya?"

"We managed to speak briefly with the neighbour at Number 15," Priya reported. "They don't know the occupants' names, but described them as an Asian couple, both of whom wear suits to work. They couldn't provide any more details."

George absorbed this information, his mind clearly racing. After a moment's consideration, he turned to Tashan. "I want you three to canvas the rest of the cul-de-sac. Look for CCTV, doorbell cameras, anything that might give us eyes on this place. And interview every neighbour. I want to know everything there is to know about the people living at Number 17."

Tashan nodded, already moving to organise Susie and Priya for the task. As they dispersed, George turned to Yolanda. "What do you think? Do we ask for a warrant?"

Yolanda's eyes narrowed as she studied the house. "If Bilal's been here, there could be evidence inside. Forensics could tell us a lot, even if he's cleared out."

George grunted, unconvinced. "Or we could spook him if he comes back and sees we've been through the place."

"True," Yolanda conceded. "But if he's run, that evidence could be crucial. And if he hasn't, well, a search might flush him out."

They stood in silence for a moment, weighing the options. The quiet of the cul-de-sac pressed in around them, broken only by the distant sound of Tashan knocking on a neighbour's door.

"We could set up surveillance," George mused. "Wait and see if anyone comes back."

Before Yolanda could respond, they heard footsteps approaching. Priya jogged up, her face flushed with a mixture of cold and excitement.

"Sir," she said, slightly breathless. "I think we should do both."

George raised an eyebrow. "Both?"

Priya nodded eagerly as she said, "I wasn't eavesdropping".

"It's fine, DC Patel," George said. "Go on."

"Get forensics in and out as quick as possible, then set up surveillance. If Bilal or anyone else comes back, we'll know. And if they don't, we'll still have whatever evidence we can gather from inside."

George considered this, his eyes flicking between Priya and the silent house. After a long moment, he nodded. "Alright. Let's do it. Yolanda, get on to DSU Smith. I want a warrant within the hour. Priya, call forensics. Tell them to be ready to move as soon as we have authorisation."

As his team sprang into action, George felt a familiar surge of adrenaline.

The next few hours passed in a blur of activity. The warrant came through, forensics arrived in their white suits and masks, and the quiet cul-de-sac became a hive of controlled chaos.

George stood watch as the forensics team combed through every inch of Number 17. They dusted for prints, collected trace evidence, photographed rooms. But as the night wore on, a sinking feeling settled in George's gut. The house was clean. Too clean.

"It's like no one's lived here for weeks," the lead forensic technician reported, frustration evident in her voice. "We'll run everything we've collected, but I wouldn't get your hopes up, sir."

George nodded, his jaw tight. "Thanks. Let me know if anything turns up."

George gathered his exhausted detectives.

"Alright," he said. "We've done what we can here for now. I want everyone to go home, get some rest. But be back at the station by 8 am sharp. We'll regroup, go over whatever forensics gives us, and plan our next move."

The team nodded, fatigue evident in their slumped shoulders and bleary eyes. As they dispersed, heading for Priya's car, George remained, his eyes fixed on the innocuous red door of Number 17.

As George watched the SOCOs methodically work their way through Number 17, his thoughts churned with possibilities. His eyes drifted to the neighbouring houses, their windows dark and silent. But appearances could be deceiving.

"Any of them could be Bilal's allies," he muttered to himself, the thought sending a chill down his spine.

He imagined curtains twitching, phones held in trembling hands, hushed voices warning Bilal to stay away. The cul-de-sac suddenly felt less like a quiet residential area and more like a web of potential conspirators.

George pulled out his mobile, his fingers finding DS Josh

Fry's number almost on autopilot.

"DS Fry," came the answer after two rings.

"Josh, it's George. Any update on Bilal's phone?"

A sigh crackled through the line. "Nothing, sir. It's still offline. Hasn't pinged a single tower since Sunday."

George's jaw tightened. "Damn. I was hoping..."

"That he'd slip up?" Josh finished. "Not likely, sir. If Bilal's as smart as we think he is, he's probably ditched that phone entirely."

"You think he's using a burner?"

"Almost certainly," Josh replied. "It's what I'd do if I were on the run."

George rubbed his forehead, frustration mounting. "Any way to track those?"

"Not easily," Josh admitted. "We can try to isolate new activations in the area around the time Bilal disappeared, but it's a long shot. Burners are designed to be anonymous."

George's eyes scanned the quiet street once more. "What about the neighbours? Any chance we could track unusual call patterns from this area?"

There was a pause as Josh considered. "It's possible, but it would take time. And we'd need a warrant for each address we want to check."

"Might be worth it," George mused. "If Bilal has allies here, they could be our key to finding him."

"I'll get on it," Josh said. "But sir... if Bilal is using a burner, and if he's got people helping him, we might be chasing ghosts."

George's free hand clenched into a fist. "I know. But we have to try. This bastard's been one step ahead of us from the start. It's time we caught up."

"Understood, sir. I'll keep you posted."

As George hung up, he couldn't shake the feeling that they were missing something crucial. The quiet houses around him seemed to loom larger, each one potentially hiding secrets that could break the case wide open.

He watched as a SOCO emerged from Number 17, evidence bag in hand. The hunt for Bilal Bhati had taken on a new dimension, and George was determined to see it through. No matter how many doors they had to knock on, no matter how many phones they had to trace.

He stayed for another couple of hours, watching as the forensics team finished up and departed. The cul-de-sac settled back into its eerie quiet, the only sign of their presence the subtle surveillance equipment now hidden around the property.

Finally, as his watch hit midnight, George decided to call it a night. He climbed into his car, his mind racing with possibilities and theories.

As he drove home, the quiet streets of Leeds slipping by in a blur, George couldn't get the case out of his mind. Bilal Bhati was out there somewhere; he was sure of it. And George was going to find him, no matter what it took.

He pulled into his drive, the house dark and silent. Isabella's car was there, a small comfort in the turmoil of the case. George sat for a moment, gathering his thoughts, before stepping out into the cooling evening air.

* * *

George Beaumont pushed open the front door, fatigue weighing heavily on his shoulders. The house was quiet, but a soft glow from the kitchen caught his eye. He moved towards it, his footsteps echoing in the silent hallway.

Isabella sat at the kitchen table, her face illuminated by the harsh light of her laptop screen. Case files were spread out before her, a half-empty mug of coffee at her elbow. She looked up as George entered, her eyes heavy with exhaustion.

"You're still up," George said, his voice a mixture of surprise and disapproval.

Isabella's eyebrows rose. "So are you."

George moved to the fridge, pulling out a beer. The cold glass felt good against his palm. "I was working. Bilal Bhati case."

"And I'm working," Isabella replied, gesturing to the files in front of her. "The Morris case won't solve itself."

George took a long swig of beer, studying his fiancée over the bottle. "You're working too hard, Izzy. You need to rest."

A harsh laugh escaped Isabella's lips. "That's rich, coming from you. When was the last time you got more than four hours sleep?"

"That's different," George countered, feeling his irritation rise. "I'm in the middle of a critical investigation."

"And I'm not?" Isabella's voice had an edge to it now. "In case you've forgotten, I'm trying to solve a decade-old cold case. A child who's been missing for years."

George slammed his beer down on the counter, harder than he'd intended. "I haven't forgotten. But you're exhausted all the time, Izzy. When was the last time we did anything together? Just the two of us?"

Isabella's eyes flashed. "That's not fair, George. Look at the time. It's gone midnight. What exactly did you expect to be doing together at this hour?"

The argument hung in the air between them, an almost tangible thing.

"It's not just tonight," he said. "It's been weeks, Izzy. Months, even. You're always tired, always working. We barely talk now, let alone..."

He trailed off, but the implication was clear. Isabella's face flushed, a mixture of anger and embarrassment.

"Let alone what, George?" she snapped. "Go on, say it."

George ran a hand through his hair, exasperation evident in every movement. "Fine. We never have sex, Izzy. We barely touch. It's like we're flatmates, not a couple about to get married."

The words hung in the air, heavy and accusatory. Isabella stood abruptly, her chair scraping against the tile floor.

"How dare you," she hissed. "You think I don't want to be intimate? You think I enjoy feeling like this? I'm exhausted, George. I'm trying to balance a demanding job, planning a wedding, and being a mother and stepmother to your children. And you have the cheek to complain about our sex life?"

George felt a pang of guilt, but his anger overrode it. "And you think I'm not under pressure? I've got a child killer on the loose, Izzy. A monster who's targeting little kids. But I still make time for us, or at least I try to."

Isabella laughed, a bitter, hollow sound. "Make time? When, George? Between your endless overtime and your brooding silences when you are home? Don't put this all on me."

The tension in the room was palpable, months of unspoken frustrations finally bubbling to the surface. George could feel his control slipping, words spilling out before he could stop them.

"Maybe if you weren't so obsessed with your case, you'd

see what's happening to us," he spat. "We're falling apart, Izzy, and you're too buried in work to notice."

Isabella's face contorted with hurt and anger. "That's not fair, George. You know how important this case is. How can you be so selfish?"

"Selfish?" George's voice rose. "I'm selfish for wanting to spend time with my fiancée? For wanting to feel like we're in a relationship, not just co-existing?"

Isabella slammed her laptop shut, gathering her files with shaking hands. "I can't do this right now. I'm going to bed."

She brushed past George, her shoulder bumping his as she stormed out of the kitchen. He heard her footsteps on the stairs, followed by the slam of their bedroom door.

George stood in the kitchen, his beer forgotten on the counter. The silence of the house pressed in around him, suffocating. He looked at the chair where Isabella had been sitting, the ghost of her presence still lingering.

With a heavy sigh, he turned and headed for the stairs. But instead of following Isabella to their room, he veered off, pushing open the door to Jack's room. The spare bed was made up, waiting for the next time his son visited.

George sank onto the edge of the bed, his head in his hands. How had they gotten here? When had their passion for justice begun to overshadow their passion for each other?

He lay back on the bed, not bothering to undress. The ceiling above him swam in and out of focus as fatigue and emotion warred within him. Tomorrow, he'd have to face Isabella, to try and bridge this growing chasm between them. But for now, sleep beckoned, offering a temporary respite from the turmoil of his thoughts.

As George drifted off, his last coherent thought was of Dania

Bhati, and all the other children out there who needed him. He couldn't let them down, no matter the personal cost. But as consciousness slipped away, a small voice in the back of his mind whispered a troubling question: At what point does the cost become too high?

The answer eluded him as sleep finally claimed him, leaving George Beaumont alone in the dark, his responsibilities pressing down on him even in his dreams.

Chapter Nineteen

George Beaumont gripped the steering wheel, his knuckles white against the black leather. The early morning traffic crawled along, mirroring the slow churn of his thoughts. Isabella's words from last night echoed in his mind, sharp and cutting.

"You have the cheek to complain about our sex life?"

He shook his head, trying to dislodge the memory. The argument had spiralled, each barbed comment widening the gulf between them.

The radio droned on, a background hum to his brooding. He reached to switch it off when a familiar name cut through his musings.

"...vandal attack at the Bhati residence in Beeston. Reports suggest..."

George's hand froze mid-air. His breath caught in his throat as he listened, the world outside his car fading away.

"...graffiti accusing the family of being child killers. Windows shattered..."

"Bloody hell," George muttered.

He burst into the station, startling a young PC who nearly dropped his coffee. "Sir?" the constable stammered.

"Where's my team?" George barked, not breaking stride.

"Incident room, sir. They're—"

George was already gone, taking the stairs two at a time. He threw open the door to find his team huddled around Yolanda's desk, faces grim.

"You've heard," Tashan said. It wasn't a question.

George nodded. "Grab your coat. We're going."

The drive to Beeston was tense, the silence between them heavy with unspoken concerns. As they turned onto the Bhatis' street, George's stomach clenched. The house stood out like a wound, angry black graffiti stark against the walls.

"Christ," Tashan breathed.

They climbed out of the car, the acrid smell of spray paint hitting them immediately. Uniformed officers milled about, securing the scene. George approached the nearest one, flashing his warrant card.

"DCI Beaumont. What've we got?"

The officer, young and clearly shaken, gestured to the house. "It's bad, sir. They didn't hold back."

George took in the scene, his jaw tight. 'CHILD KILLERS' sprawled across the front door in dripping crimson. 'MONSTERS' adorned one wall, the 'S' trailing off as if the writer had been interrupted. Every window on the ground floor was shattered, glass glittering on the pavement like malicious confetti.

"Hassan's car?" Tashan asked, nodding towards the driveway.

The officer shook his head. "Same treatment. Windows put through with rocks. Happened late last night, from what we can gather."

George's mind raced. "Where are the Bhatis now?"

"Hospital, sir. Mr Bhati's being treated for concussion. Rock caught him while he was asleep."

George's eyebrows shot up. "He was home?"

The officer nodded. "Early shift end, apparently. Bad luck, that."

"Or good," Tashan muttered. "Might've been worse if he'd confronted them."

George grunted in agreement. "Right. We need to get to the hospital. Any CCTV?"

"Nothing useful so far," the officer replied. "But we're still canvassing the area."

"Keep at it," George ordered. "And get forensics down here. I want every inch of this place gone over."

As they climbed back into the car, Tashan's phone buzzed. He glanced at the screen, his brow furrowing. "Sir? You might want to see this."

He held out the phone. A grainy image filled the screen, clearly from a security camera. A group of figures in black, faces obscured by balaclavas, fleeing down a darkened street.

"Where's this from?" George demanded.

"Shop three streets over," Tashan replied. "Owner just sent it in. Time stamp matches our window."

George studied the image, frustration building in his chest. "Not much to go on, is it?"

Tashan shook his head. "No, but it's something. At least we know it was a group, not a lone nutter."

"Small mercies," George muttered, starting the engine. "Let's get to the hospital. I want to hear from the Bhatis themselves."

The drive was mercifully short, the early hour sparing them the worst of the traffic. As they strode through St James' Hospital A&E corridors, the antiseptic smell and harsh fluorescent lighting set George's teeth on edge. A harried-looking nurse directed them to a small waiting area.

Alize Bhati sat hunched in a plastic chair, her daughter Inaya curled up asleep beside her. As George and Tashan approached, she looked up, her eyes red-rimmed and haunted.

"Mrs Bhati," George said softly, crouching down to her level. "I'm DCI Beaumont and this is DS Blackburn, if you remember? We've heard about what happened at your house."

Alize nodded, her gaze drifting back to Inaya. "They could have killed us," she whispered. "If that rock had hit Inaya instead of Hassan..."

George's chest tightened. "I know this is difficult, but can you tell us what happened?"

Alize took a shuddering breath. "I was in bed. Hassan had come home early, said he wasn't feeling well. I heard... it sounded like fireworks at first. Then glass breaking."

She paused, her hand absently stroking Inaya's hair. "I ran to check on Inaya. She was crying, scared. I could hear shouting outside, but I couldn't make out the words. Then there was a crash, and Hassan... Hassan cried out."

Tears welled in her eyes. George waited patiently, giving her time to compose herself.

"I looked out the window," she continued. "I saw them running away. A group, all in black. Masks on their faces. They were laughing, DCI Beaumont. Laughing as they ran."

Tashan's pen scratched across his notebook. "How many would you say there were, Mrs Bhati?"

Alize frowned, considering. "Five, maybe six? It happened so fast."

George nodded encouragingly. "You're doing great, Mrs Bhati. Can you think of anyone who might harbour such hatred towards your family?"

Alize's head snapped up, her eyes flashing with a mixture of anger and disbelief. "No! We're good people, DCI Beaumont. We've never hurt anyone. Why would someone do this to us?"

George chose his words carefully. "Sometimes, in cases like Dania's, people can react... irrationally. They look for someone to blame."

"Blame?" Alize's voice cracked. "They think we killed our own daughter? How could anyone think that?"

George reached out, his hand hovering near hers before thinking better of it. "We know you didn't, Mrs Bhati. And we're going to find who did this to your home. To your husband."

A doctor appeared in the doorway, his face weary but professional. "Mrs Bhati? Your husband is awake. You can see him now."

Alize stood, gathering a still-sleeping Inaya in her arms. She turned to George, her eyes pleading. "Find them, DCI Beaumont. Please. We can't live like this."

As she disappeared down the corridor, George and Tashan exchanged grim looks.

"This complicates things," Tashan murmured.

George nodded, running a hand through his hair. "Understatement of the bloody year, that. We need to get ahead of this, fast. If word gets out about the attack..."

"It'll be open season on the Bhatis," Tashan finished.

"Exactly. And our real killer gets to sit back and watch the chaos."

They made their way out of the hospital. As they climbed back into the car, George's phone buzzed. He glanced at the screen, his stomach dropping at the sight of Isabella's name.

He hesitated, thumb hovering over the answer button. The memory of last night's argument warred with the urgency of the case. With a sigh, he hit decline, shoving the phone back into his pocket.

"Everything alright, sir?" Tashan asked, eyeing him curiously.

George grunted, starting the engine. "Fine. Let's get back to the station. We've got work to do."

As they pulled away from the hospital, George's mind raced. The vandalism, the attack on Hassan, the laughing figures in balaclavas—it all painted a grim picture. Someone was stirring up trouble, and the Bhatis were caught in the crossfire.

He thought of Alize's haunted eyes, of Inaya sleeping fitfully in the harsh hospital lighting. An innocent family, already devastated by loss, now facing a new kind of terror.

His jaw clenched. Whoever was behind this, whether misguided vigilantes or something more sinister, they'd made a grave mistake. They'd given George Beaumont a new target.

And he was proper fucked off about it!

* * *

George Beaumont drummed his fingers on the steering wheel, his eyes scanning the quiet suburban street. The Bhati house loomed in the rear-view mirror, a stark reminder of the ugliness humans could inflict on one another. Beside him, Tashan Blackburn scrolled through his phone, brow furrowed in concentration.

"Anything?" George asked, breaking the silence.

Tashan shook his head. "Nothing useful. A few posts on social media about the attack, but no names, no leads."

George grunted, frustration building in his chest. "Right. Let's talk to the neighbours. Someone must've seen something."

They climbed out of the car, the summer sun beating down on them. A group of women huddled on a nearby lawn, their voices a low murmur of gossip and speculation. As George and Tashan approached, the conversation died, replaced by wary glances.

"Ladies," George said, flashing his warrant card. "DCI Beaumont. This is DS Blackburn. We'd like to ask you a few questions about what happened last night."

A stocky woman with bottle-blonde hair stepped forward, arms crossed. "We've already talked to the plods. Told them everything we saw."

George raised an eyebrow. "And you are?"

"Dawn Hobson," she replied, chin jutting out defiantly. "I live two doors down."

"Well, Miss Hobson, I'd appreciate it if you could tell me what you saw. Sometimes details come back to us on second telling."

Dawn's eyes narrowed. "It's Miss Dobson, and I saw a bunch of lads running off, didn't I? All in black, hoods up. Couldn't see their faces."

George nodded, encouraging her to continue. "And before that? Did you hear anything unusual?"

"Course I did," Dawn snapped. "Glass breaking, shouting. Woke the whole bloody street up. My baby girl, too. Arseholes!"

Tashan scribbled in his notebook. "Can you remember any specific words you heard?"

Dawn hesitated, her gaze flicking to her friends. "They were calling Hassan a killer. Said he'd got what was coming to him. They were chanting 'Paedo Paki'."

George's ears pricked up. "Hassan specifically?"

"Yeah, Hassan," Dawn confirmed. "Everyone knows he did it, don't they? Killed his own daughter."

The words hung in the air, sharp and accusatory. George kept his face neutral, even as anger bubbled in his gut. "That's a serious accusation, Miss Hobson. Do you have any evidence to support it?"

Dawn snorted. "Evidence? You want evidence? How about the fact he was the last one to see her alive? How about the way he acted after she went missing? Cold as ice, he was. I saw him on TV. And I watch a lot of documentaries. He's defo the killer."

George pressed on, his voice level. He'd watched the footage and saw a grieving father. "And how exactly did he act, Miss Hobson? Can you give me specific examples?"

Dawn faltered, her bravado slipping. "Well... he didn't cry, did he? Not where anyone could see. And he was always going off on his own, making phone calls. Avoiding questions. Going to work. Dodgy is that."

"I see," George said, his tone betraying nothing. "And you don't think a grieving father might want some privacy? Might handle his emotions differently than you'd expect?"

Dawn's face flushed. "You don't know them like we do. They're not... they're different, aren't they?"

The implication hung heavy in the air. George's jaw tightened, but he kept his voice steady. "Different how, Miss Hobson?"

She shifted uncomfortably. "You know... they've got their own ways, don't they? Their own... culture an' that."

George exchanged a glance with Tashan, whose expression had hardened. "Miss Hobson, I'm going to ask you a direct question, and I'd appreciate an honest answer. Do you suspect Hassan Bhati of killing his daughter because of his race?"

The other women gasped, murmuring among themselves. Dawn's face contorted with anger. "Now 'ang on a minute! I never said nothing about them being Pakis. You're putting words in my mouth! I wasn't the one calling him a Paedo Paki, remember."

George held up a hand, silencing her protests. "I'm not accusing you of anything, Miss Hobson. I'm trying to understand why you're so convinced of Hassan's guilt. Do you have any concrete reasons? Anything you might have seen or heard?"

Dawn's eyes darted around, as if searching for an escape. "I... well, no. Not exactly. But you can tell, can't you? The way he looks at you, all shifty-like. Like he's undressing you with his eyes an' that."

George sighed inwardly. Vague accusations and thinly veiled prejudice—it was a familiar dance. He reached into his pocket, pulling out a sketch. "Miss Hobson, I'd like you to take a look at this. It's a sketch of a woman we believe may have been involved in Dania's disappearance. Have you ever seen her around the neighbourhood?"

He held out the drawing, watching Dawn's face carefully. For a split second, something flashed in her eyes— recognition? Fear? But it was gone as quickly as it appeared, replaced by a mask of indifference.

"Never seen her," Dawn said, a bit too quickly. "Don't know nothing about that woman."

George's suspicion deepened. "Are you sure, Miss Hobson?

Take another look. She might have been around the street, or the shops."

Dawn shook her head vehemently. "I said I don't know her, alright?" She frowned at her friends. "Are we done 'ere? I've got things to do."

George studied her for a moment longer, weighing his options. Pushing harder might shut her down completely, but letting her go meant losing a potential lead. He decided to err on the side of caution—for now.

"Alright, Miss Hobson. Thank you for your time. If you remember anything else, anything at all, please don't hesitate to contact us."

He handed her his card, which she took with obvious reluctance. As they walked away, George could hear the women's whispers starting up again, no doubt dissecting every word of their encounter.

Back at the car, Tashan let out a low whistle. "Well, that was a waste of time."

George shook his head. "Not necessarily. Dawn Hobson knows something. Did you see her reaction to the sketch?"

Tashan nodded. "Yeah, she definitely recognised her. But why lie about it?"

"That's what we need to find out," George said, leaning against the car. "What about the doorbell footage? Anything useful there?"

Tashan pulled out his phone, scrolling through some images. "Not much. We've got a few glimpses of the suspects, but they're all wearing hoodies and balaclavas. No clear faces."

George cursed under his breath. "And the other neighbours?"

"Same story," Tashan replied. "They heard the commotion,

saw some people running away, but couldn't give us any details. It's like they're all reading from the same script."

George's eyes scanned the street, landing on PS Greenwood and his team of uniforms canvassing the area. "What do you make of it, Tashan? Why is everyone so reluctant to help?"

Tashan shrugged, his expression grim. "Fear, maybe? Or they're protecting someone. Could be a bit of both."

George nodded, mulling it over. "And then there's Dawn Hobson, with her thinly veiled racism and obvious lies. She's hiding something, but what?"

"What's our next move, sir?" Tashan asked.

George ran a hand through his blond hair, frustration evident in every line of his body. "We keep digging. Someone in this neighbourhood knows something, and we're going to find out what. But first, I need food. Can't think straight on an empty stomach."

Tashan grinned. "I know a decent place not far from here. Fancy a bite?"

George's stomach rumbled in response. "Lead the way, DS Blackburn. Maybe a good feed will shake loose some ideas."

As they climbed back into the car, George cast one last look at the Bhati house. The graffiti glared back at him, a reminder of the hatred and fear swirling just beneath the surface of this quiet community.

Chapter Twenty

Detective Isabella Wood stood at the edge of the excavation site, her eyes locked on the metallic glint peeking through the dirt. The early morning sun cast long shadows across Old River Farm, the air thick with anticipation and the earthy scent of freshly turned soil.

"Careful now," she called to the forensics team. "Let's not damage anything."

The lead technician, a wiry man named Dave, shot her a thumbs up. "No worries, DI Wood. We've got steady hands."

Isabella watched, her heart pounding, as they slowly unearthed what appeared to be a large metal box. Not a body, as they'd feared. But potentially something far more interesting.

"What do you reckon?" Dave asked, brushing dirt from the lid. "Buried treasure?"

Isabella shook her head. "In my experience, Dave, buried things are rarely good news. A harvest like this usually leads to sorrow."

They carefully extracted the box, loading it into a sealed evidence container for transport back to Wakefield HQ. Isabella rode with it, unwilling to let it out of her sight. This could be the break they'd been waiting for.

At the station, the forensics team set up in a secure room.

Isabella paced as they worked to open the box without com-promising any potential evidence.

"Got it," Dave announced, the lock finally giving way with a rusty groan.

Isabella leaned in, her breath catching as Dave lifted the lid. Inside, neatly stacked and surprisingly well-preserved, were police files. Dozens of them.

"Christ," she muttered, pulling on a pair of gloves. "These are from the 90s."

She gingerly lifted the top file, her eyes widening as she scanned its contents. "This is... this is about the White Rose League. A female detective, a Mary something was investigating them for child abductions."

Dave whistled low. "Blimey. That's heavy stuff, boss."

Isabella nodded, her mind racing. "This could be huge. It could explain so much about—"

The door burst open, cutting her off mid-sentence. Chief Superintendent Morgan strode in, his face a thundercloud.

"DI Wood," he barked. "A word. Now."

Isabella followed him out, her stomach churning. In his office, Morgan rounded on her.

"What the hell do you think you're doing?" he demanded. "Those files are way above your pay grade."

Isabella stood her ground. "Sir, with all due respect, this could be crucial to our investigation. If the White Rose League was operating back then—"

"Enough!" Morgan slammed his hand on the desk. "Those files are confiscated. Security concerns. You're to focus on current cases. The Fawcett girl, remember her?"

Isabella bit back a retort. "Yes, sir. But surely—"

"No buts, Wood. That's an order. Stick to your assigned

cases."

As Morgan ushered her out, Isabella's mind whirled. Why was he so adamant about burying this? What was he afraid of?

* * *

The drive to the sandwich shop was short, but it gave George time to mull over the morning's events. Dawn Hobson's face kept flashing in his mind—her defensive posture, the flicker of recognition in her eyes when she saw the sketch. What was she hiding? And more importantly, why?

They pulled up at the curb. The smell of sizzling bacon and sausages wafted out as they entered, making George's stomach growl. They slid into a booth, the laminated menu slightly sticky under George's fingers.

"What do you reckon, sir?" Tashan asked, scanning the options. "Bacon and sausage combo?"

George shook his head. "Better not. Need to keep my wits about me. I'll go for just sausage with brown sauce, I think."

They placed their orders, the waiter disappearing into the kitchen with a nod. George leaned back, his mind still churning over the case.

"So," he said, fixing Tashan with a steady gaze. "What's your read on Dawn Hobson?"

Tashan considered for a moment, absently fiddling with his napkin. "She's definitely hiding something. The way she reacted to the sketch... she knows our mystery woman."

George nodded. "My thoughts exactly. But why lie about it? What's she afraid of?"

"Could be protecting someone," Tashan suggested. "A family member, maybe? Or she might be involved herself."

George's eyebrows shot up. "You think she could be part of it? The abduction?"

Tashan shrugged. "It's possible. Her reaction was pretty extreme. And she seemed awfully keen to pin everything on Hassan."

Their sandwiches arrived, the smell of freshly fried sausage and bacon filling the air. They ate in silence for a few minutes, both lost in thought.

"We need to look into Dawn Hobson's background," George said finally, taking a bite of his sandwich. "Family, friends, financials—the works. If she's connected to this somehow, we'll find it."

Tashan nodded, swallowing a mouthful. "What about the others? The women she was with?"

"Them too," George agreed. "And we need to keep the pressure on the community. Someone saw something last night, and I want to know what."

They finished their meal, the savoury taste lingering on George's tongue. As they walked back to the car, he felt a renewed sense of determination. They might be facing a wall of silence now, but walls could be broken down. It was only a matter of finding the right pressure point.

"Back to the station, boss?" Tashan asked as they climbed in.

George nodded, starting the engine. "Yeah. Let's see what the team's dug up while we've been out. And I want to talk to DSU Smith about setting up some covert surveillance on Dawn Hobson. If she's involved, she'll slip up eventually."

As they pulled out of the car park, George's phone buzzed. He glanced at it—another missed call from Isabella. He sighed, shoving the phone back into his pocket. He'd deal with that later. Right now, he had a case to solve and a community to crack open.

* * *

Back at her desk, Isabella stared unseeing at her computer screen. She couldn't let this go. Wouldn't. But she'd have to be smart about it.

She glanced around the office, suddenly acutely aware of who might be watching. Trust no one, a voice in her head whispered. Except...

Her eyes landed on a photo on her desk. George. Her fiancé. The one person she should be able to confide in. But as she reached for her phone, she hesitated.

George was already neck-deep in his own case. Bringing him into this... it could put him in danger. And things were already strained between them. No, she decided. She couldn't involve George. Not yet.

But she needed help. Someone she could trust implicitly. Someone with access and skills.

Isabella's fingers hovered over her contacts list, finally landing on a name. Joshua Fry. At Elland Road. Not strictly her jurisdiction, but... desperate times.

She fired off a text: "Need to talk. Privately. Urgent. Please don't tell George."

As she waited for a response, Isabella began methodically going through her notes on the Fawcett case. To any observer, she was the picture of a dedicated detective, following orders. But her mind was elsewhere, piecing together fragments of a decades-old conspiracy.

Her phone buzzed. Fry's reply: "The usual. 1 hour."

Isabella grabbed her coat, calling out to her team that she was following up a lead. It wasn't entirely a lie.

* * *

George Beaumont strode into the Incident Room, his footsteps echoing off the linoleum floor. Tashan Blackburn followed close behind, his notebook clutched in one hand. The room buzzed with activity, detectives hunched over computers or huddled in small groups, voices low and urgent.

Priya Patel looked up from her desk, dark circles under her eyes betraying long hours of work. "Sir," she said, pushing back from her computer. "Any luck?"

George shook his head, frustration evident in the set of his jaw. "Not much. A lot of vague statements and one very uncooperative witness. What've you got?"

Priya sighed, running a hand through her hair. "We've circulated the artist's sketch of the woman with the mole, but so far, nothing. It's like she's a ghost."

Susie Whitaker piped up from her desk. "I've been going through CCTV footage from around the Bhati house, but it's slow going. Whoever these vandals were, they knew how to avoid cameras."

George nodded, his mind racing. "Keep at it. There's got to be something we're missing."

He was about to say more when a commotion at the door caught his attention. A uniformed officer burst in, face flushed with exertion. "Sir! We've got a report of a child abduction at Middleton Park, near Dania's school."

The room fell silent, all eyes turning to George. He felt his stomach drop, a cold dread settling in his chest. "Details," he barked, already moving towards the door.

"Four-year-old girl, sir," the officer reported, struggling to keep up. "Taken from near the pond. Mother's hysterical."

George's jaw clenched. "Tashan, Priya, with me. Susie, hold down the fort here. I want updates every fifteen minutes."

They raced to George's Merc and set off.

His knuckles were white on the steering wheel as he tore through the streets of Leeds, his mind a whirl of possibilities and fears.

"Could it be connected?" Priya asked from the backseat, voicing the question they were all thinking.

"We can't rule it out," George replied grimly. "Same area, similar MO. But Christ, I hope we're wrong."

They screeched to a halt at the entrance to Middleton Park, Tashan flashing his warrant card, allowing them to enter the car park down the hill. The park was already swarming with uniforms and distraught onlookers. George climbed out, scanning the crowd for any sign of their mystery woman.

A constable approached, face grim. "DCI Beaumont? The mother's over there, sir. She's... well, she's not taking it well."

George nodded, steeling himself. He'd done this too many times, delivered too many pieces of devastating news. It never got easier.

Gillian Kershaw sat on a park bench, her body wracked with sobs. A friend had an arm around her, murmuring words of comfort George knew wouldn't penetrate the fog of panic and grief.

"Mrs Kershaw?" he said softly, crouching down to her level. "I'm DCI George Beaumont. Can you tell me what happened?"

Gillian looked up, her eyes red and swollen. "Rosie," she choked out. "And it's Miss." She sniffed. "My baby. She was right there, playing by the pond. I only looked away for a second, I swear. And then... then she was gone."

George nodded, keeping his voice calm and steady. "You're doing great, Miss Kershaw. Can you remember anything about the person who took Rosie? Anything at all?"

Gillian shook her head, fresh tears spilling down her cheeks. "I didn't see. Oh God, I didn't see anything."

The friend spoke up, her voice shaking. "I saw someone. A woman, I think. Leading a little girl away. I thought... I thought it was her mum."

George's head snapped up. "You saw the woman? Can you describe her?"

The friend nodded. "Youngish. Dark hair. Wearing some sort of scarf, I think."

George and Tashan exchanged looks. The description matched their suspect. "Lisa, isn't it?" George asked. Lisa nodded. "I need you to come with DS Blackburn here. We need to get a full statement, OK?"

As Tashan led Lisa away, George turned back to Gillian. "Miss Kershaw, I know this is difficult, but I need you to focus. Is there anyone who might want to hurt you or Rosie? Any custody issues with her father?"

Gillian shook her head violently. "No! No, Will's a good dad. He'd never... oh God, Will. Someone needs to tell him."

"We'll take care of that," George assured her. "What's his full name?"

"William Lambert," Gillian managed. "He works at the Royal Armouries. Please, you have to find her. My baby..."

Her words dissolved into fresh sobs. George stood, his mind racing. He caught Priya's eye and jerked his head, indicating she should join him.

"Get uniforms to do a door-to-door in the areas around each exit," he ordered in a low voice. "Every house, every shop within a mile radius. Someone must have seen something."

He ran a hand through his hair. The park and the woods covered over a million square metres, and George knew from experience that it would be a nightmare to search.

Priya nodded, already pulling out her phone. "What about the sketch, sir? Should we release it to the media?"

George hesitated. Going public could spook their suspect, but it might also be their best chance of finding Rosie quickly. "Do it," he decided. "But keep it low-key for now. We don't want a panic."

As Priya hurried off, George turned back to the scene. Uniforms were fanning out, questioning witnesses and securing the area. An ambulance had arrived, paramedics making their way towards Gillian.

"Sir?" Tashan approached, notepad in hand. "I've got Lisa's full statement. She's pretty sure about the headscarf. She also mentioned a white van parked in the car park near the ice cream van. Didn't get the reg, but it's something."

George nodded, his mind piecing together the fragments of information. "Good work. Speak with the owner of the ice cream van and see if they remember anything."

He watched as the paramedics helped Gillian into the ambulance. The poor woman had finally succumbed to exhaustion and shock, fainting as they tried to question her further.

"Any word on the father?" George asked.

Tashan nodded. "Uniforms are bringing him in now. He was at work when it happened."

"Right," George said, rubbing his tired eyes. "I'll talk to him at the hospital. You stay here, coordinate the search. I want every inch of this area of the park gone over with a fine-tooth comb."

As George climbed back into his car, his phone buzzed. Isabella's name flashed on the screen. He stared at it for a moment, torn between personal obligation and professional duty. With a sigh, he hit decline. Again, there'd be time for that later. Right now, a little girl needed him.

Chapter Twenty-one

As she drove to the meeting spot, a quiet pub on the outskirts of Leeds, Isabella's mind raced with possibilities.

The White Rose League. Child abductions dating back to the 90s. A female detective who'd gotten close, only to... what? Disappear? Be silenced?

She pulled into the pub car park, spotting Fry's battered Ford already there. Inside, she found him nursing a half-pint in a corner booth.

Isabella slid into the worn leather booth, the familiar scent of stale beer and decades of spilt spirits enveloping her. The Crow's Nest was a dive bar in every sense of the word, its shabby exterior belying the warm, if slightly grimy, atmosphere within.

Dark wood panelling lined the walls, scarred with countless initials and crude drawings etched by patrons over the years. The low ceiling was stained yellow from years of cigarette smoke, despite the smoking ban being in place for over a decade. Dim lighting cast long shadows across the room, creating pockets of privacy perfect for clandestine meetings.

The bar itself was a massive slab of oak, polished to a dull sheen by countless elbows and spilled drinks. Behind it, rows of bottles gleamed in the low light, their labels promising temporary escape from the harsh realities of life.

In the corner, an ancient jukebox wheezed out Oasis hits, the sound slightly tinny and distorted. A handful of regulars hunched over their pints, lost in their own worlds and paying no mind to the newcomers.

Isabella took in Josh Fry, slouched in the booth. He looked much the same as always—a study in controlled chaos. His black Ray-Ban rectangle glasses sat askew on his nose, the thick lenses magnifying his eyes to an almost comical degree. They gave him a perpetually surprised look, at odds with the permanent five o'clock shadow darkening his jaw.

His hair was a disaster, as usual. It stuck up in all directions, defying gravity and any attempts at styling. Isabella often wondered if he even owned a comb.

Despite his dishevelled appearance, there was a sharpness to Josh's gaze that belied his brilliant mind. Those magnified eyes missed nothing, scanning the room constantly, cataloguing every detail.

He wore his usual outfit- a rumpled button-down shirt, sleeves rolled up to reveal forearms covered in a maze of circuitry tattoos. His fingers, long and nimble, tapped an impatient rhythm on the scarred tabletop.

As Isabella approached, Josh's mouth quirked into a lopsided grin. "Took you long enough, Wood," he quipped, his voice gruff from too many late nights and too much coffee.

Isabella slid into the booth across from him, noting the dark circles under his eyes. "Rough night, Fry? Or have you been living in front of your screens again?"

Josh shrugged, pushing his glasses up his nose. "You know me. Sleep is for the weak. Besides, someone's got to keep this department dragging itself into the 21st century."

Despite his rumpled appearance and sarcastic tone, Isabella knew there was no one she'd rather have on her side for this investigation. Josh Fry might look like he'd just rolled out of bed after a three-day bender, but his mind was sharper than anyone else in Leeds CID.

As they leaned in to discuss the case, Isabella felt a surge of gratitude for this brilliant, eccentric man. Together, they just might have a chance of cracking this wide open.

* * *

The drive to the hospital was a blur. George's mind kept circling back to the woman with the mole. Two abductions, same description. It couldn't be a coincidence.

He found William Lambert in the waiting room, pacing like a caged animal. The man's face was a mask of fear and confusion, his clothes rumpled as if he'd thrown them on in a rush.

"Mr Lambert?" George approached, flashing his warrant card. "I'm DCI George Beaumont. I'm investigating your daughter's disappearance."

William's head snapped up, eyes wild. "Where is she? Where's Rosie? Gillian won't tell me anything, she's too upset."

George gestured to a nearby chair. "Let's sit down, Mr Lambert. I need to ask you some questions."

As they settled, George studied the man before him. No obvious signs of guilt or deception, only the raw panic of a parent whose child was missing. Still, he couldn't rule anything out. Not yet. Even if he hadn't abducted Rosie personally, he could still be involved.

"Mr Lambert, where were you when Rosie was taken?"

William ran a shaking hand through his hair. "At work. The Royal Armouries. I was giving a tour when my boss came and got me. Said there was an emergency."

George nodded, making a mental note to verify the alibi. "And your relationship with Gillian? Any issues there?"

William's brow furrowed. "We're... we're OK. I mean, the breakup was hard, but we're civil. For Rosie's sake."

"No custody battles? No threats?"

William shook his head vehemently. "God, no. We share custody. I'd never... Christ, you don't think I had something to do with this?"

George held up a placating hand. "We have to explore every avenue, Mr Lambert. Now, can you think of anyone who might want to hurt you or Gillian? Anyone who's shown an unusual interest in Rosie?"

William's face crumpled, the reality of the situation seeming to hit him anew. "No. No one. She's just a little girl. Who would want to take her?"

George leaned forward. "We're going to find her, Mr Lambert. I promise you, we're doing everything we can."

"What school did she go to?"

"The nursey at the school just off Town Street, I can't remember it's name. It's close to where Gillian lives. I live in Hunslet."

As he left the hospital, George's phone buzzed again. This time, it was Tashan.

"Sir," Tashan's voice crackled through the speaker. "We've got something. A witness saw a white van speeding away from the park about the time Rosie was taken. Again, the plate was dirty, which matches the one we've been looking for in connection with Dania's case."

George's pulse quickened. "Good work. Get roadblocks set up. I want that van found."

He ended the call, his mind racing. The connections were piling up, too many to be coincidence. The woman with the mole, the white van, the proximity to Dania's case. It all pointed to one chilling conclusion: they were dealing with a serial child abductor.

But were they part of a ring, or the White Rose League?

* * *

"I'm risking my neck meeting you like this," Joshua Fry said.

Isabella leaned in, her voice low. "Josh, what I'm about to tell you... it's big. And dangerous. If you want to walk away, I won't hold it against you."

Fry's eyes narrowed. "Spit it out, Izzy. You've got me curious now."

She took a deep breath, then laid it all out. The box. The files. Morgan's reaction. With each word, Fry's expression grew more serious.

"Bloody hell," he muttered when she finished. "You're right. This is big."

"I need your help, Josh," Isabella said, her voice barely above a whisper. "I can't let this go. But I can't do it alone. And I can't... I can't involve George. Not yet."

Fry studied her for a long moment. "You know what you're asking? If we get caught..."

"I know," Isabella nodded. "But think about it. If this goes as deep as I suspect, how many lives could we save? How many families could finally get closure?"

Fry drained his pint, his face set in grim determination. "Alright. I'm in. But we do this smart. No unnecessary risks."

Isabella felt a weight lift from her shoulders. "Thank you, Josh. I mean it."

As they began to plan their next moves, Isabella couldn't shake a nagging sense of guilt. She was keeping secrets from George, from her team. But the potential stakes were too high. She had to see this through, no matter the personal cost.

"First thing," Fry said, pulling out a notebook. "We need to identify that female detective. If she's still alive..."

Isabella nodded. "She could be the key to unravelling this whole thing."

As they dove into the details, Isabella pushed aside thoughts of George, of their strained relationship, of the wedding looming on the horizon. This was bigger than her personal life. This was about justice. About protecting the innocent.

And if it meant sacrificing her own happiness? Well, that was a price she was willing to pay.

* * *

Back at the station, George found the team huddled around a whiteboard, faces grim. Priya looked up as he entered, her eyes haunted. "Sir, we've got the sketch out to all major news outlets. It should be hitting the airwaves any minute."

George nodded, shrugging off his jacket. "Good. Tashan filled me in on the van. Any hits yet?"

Susie shook her head. "Nothing concrete. We've had a few sightings called in, but nothing's panned out."

George sighed, rubbing his temples. The pressure was mounting, each passing minute decreasing their chances of finding Rosie alive. He glanced at the clock. Nearly time for the press conference.

"Alright," he said, straightening his tie. "I'm going to address the media. I want everything we've got compiled and ready for distribution. And keep those phones manned. If anyone calls with information about the sketch or the van, I want to know immediately."

As he made his way to the press room, George's mind whirled with the words he needed to say. He had to strike the right balance—urgent but not panicked, informative but not alarmist. And above all, he needed to reach the one person who might have the information they desperately needed.

The room was packed, cameras and microphones pointed at the podium like accusing fingers. George took a deep breath, stepping up to face the sea of expectant faces.

"Good afternoon," he began, his voice steady despite the turmoil in his gut. "At approximately 10.15 this morning, four-year-old Rosie Kershaw was abducted from Middleton Park. We believe this abduction may be connected to the disappearance of Dania Bhati three weeks ago."

A murmur ran through the crowd. George pressed on, his voice gaining strength.

"We are releasing a sketch of a woman we believe may be involved in both cases. She is described as being in her late twenties to early thirties, with dark hair and a distinctive mole above her lip. We are also looking for a white van, its registration covered with muck."

He paused, letting the information sink in. Then, looking directly into the nearest camera, he spoke from the heart.

"To the person who has taken Rosie, I want to speak to you directly. This little girl has a family who loves her, who are desperate to have her home safe. It's not too late to do the right thing. Please, give Rosie back. We can work this out together."

George's voice softened, his eyes never leaving the camera lens. "And to anyone who might have information, no matter how small or insignificant you think it might be, please come forward. Your call could be the one that brings Rosie home."

As he stepped away from the podium, ignoring the shouted questions from reporters, George felt a mixture of hope and dread. They'd cast their net wide. Now, all they could do was wait and see what it caught.

* * *

Back in the Incident Room, the atmosphere was tense. Detectives huddled over phones and computers, following up on every lead, no matter how tenuous. George paced, his mind racing with possibilities and fears.

"Anything?" he asked, for what felt like the hundredth time.

Priya shook her head, frustration etched on her face. "Nothing solid yet, sir. We've had a few calls about white vans, but nothing concrete."

"What do you mean by 'nothing concrete'?"

"Just the usual, sir, people calling up telling us their neighbour's a bit shifty and has a white van that's dirty, etc."

George nodded, trying to quell the rising panic in his chest. Every minute that passed decreased their chances of finding Rosie alive. And if this was connected to Dania's case, as he strongly suspected it was, they were dealing with someone who wouldn't hesitate to harm a child.

"Keep at it," he said, his voice tight. "Someone out there

knows something. We just need to find them."

* * *

Hours passed as Isabella and Fry pieced together what little information they had. The pub emptied around them, the bartender shooting them curious glances as he wiped down tables.

"We should call it a night," Fry said, stifling a yawn. "Can't afford to look suspicious."

Isabella nodded reluctantly. "You're right. But we need to move fast. Morgan's not going to sit on those files forever."

They agreed to meet again tomorrow, each with their own tasks to pursue. As they stood to leave, Fry caught Isabella's arm.

"Izzy," he said. "Are you sure about this? About keeping George in the dark?"

Isabella hesitated. "I have to, Josh. At least for now. If this goes sideways... I can't risk dragging him down with me."

Fry nodded, understanding in his eyes. "Alright. But be careful. Secrets have a way of coming out, especially between couples."

As Isabella drove home, her mind buzzed with the day's revelations. The White Rose League, operating for decades. Children vanishing without a trace. And now, a cover-up reaching to the highest levels of the police force.

She pulled into her driveway, noting the darkened windows of her home. It wasn't that late so George was probably still at work, buried in his own case. Or maybe he was avoiding her, their recent arguments still hanging heavy between them.

Inside, Isabella moved on autopilot, shedding her work

clothes and stepping into the shower. As the hot water pounded against her skin, she allowed herself a moment of vulnerability. Tears mixed with the spray, the enormity of what she'd undertaken finally hitting her.

She was risking everything—her career, her relationship, possibly even her life. But the faces of the missing children flashed through her mind. Abigail Fawcett. Ethan Morris. Countless others whose names she didn't yet know.

Isabella straightened, wiping the tears from her eyes.

No, she couldn't back down now.

Chapter Twenty-two

George Beaumont leaned back in his office chair, his eyes closed. He rubbed his temples, trying to ease the tension headache building behind his eyes.

The shrill ring of his mobile jolted him from his momentary respite. He fumbled for the phone, frowning at the unfamiliar number on the screen.

"Beaumont," he answered, his voice gruff with fatigue.

"DCI Beaumont? It's Abbie Illingworth. From Middleton Academy Primary School."

George sat up straighter, instantly alert. "Miss Illingworth. What can I do for you?"

Her voice wavered slightly as she spoke. "It's about Rosie. She was... she was one of my students. I'm... I'm heartbroken, DCI Beaumont. I can't stop thinking about her."

George's jaw clenched. Another innocent life touched by this case. Another person left to grapple with the aftermath of evil.

"I understand, Miss Illingworth. This must be incredibly difficult for you."

"I was wondering..." she hesitated. "I was wondering if we could talk. About Rosie. About... everything."

George glanced at the clock. He should really send a DC, but the raw emotion in Abbie's voice tugged at him.

"Of course," he found himself saying. "Where would you like to meet?"

"My place?" Abbie suggested. "I'm in East Ardsley. I can text you the address."

George agreed, jotting down the details. As he hung up, he realised he was looking forward to the meeting more than he probably should.

The drive to East Ardsley was mercifully quiet, giving George time to gather his thoughts. He pulled up outside a small semi-detached house on Bidder Drive, its front garden neat and well-tended. As he approached the door, it swung open, revealing Abbie Illingworth.

She looked different outside of school, George noted. More relaxed, her hair loose around her shoulders instead of pulled back in its usual severe bun. She wore a soft jumper and jeans, a far cry from her professional attire.

"DCI Beaumont," she greeted him with a small smile. "Thank you for coming. Please, come in."

The interior of Abbie's home was warm and inviting, a stark contrast to the sterile environment of the police station. Soft lamplight cast a golden glow over comfortable furnishings, and the air was fragrant with the scent of vanilla and cinnamon.

"Would you like some tea?" Abbie asked, gesturing towards the kitchen.

George nodded gratefully. "Tea would be lovely, thank you."

As Abbie busied herself with the kettle, George found himself relaxing. The cosy domesticity of the scene was a balm to his frayed nerves.

"Lovely weather we've been having," Abbie commented as

she handed him a steaming mug. "Makes a nice change from all the rain."

George murmured his agreement, sipping the perfectly brewed tea. It had been pissing it down in Beeston recently, but he supposed East Ardsley could have been missed.

They chatted amiably about inconsequential things—the change in weather from cold to warm and back to cold again, the latest rugby league results, the perennial roadworks plaguing Leeds city centre.

Gradually, almost imperceptibly, the conversation shifted. Abbie's smile faded, her eyes growing serious.

"I keep thinking about Rosie," she said softly. "She was such a bright little thing. Always laughing, always eager to learn."

George leaned forward, his voice gentle. "Tell me about her. What was she like in class?"

Abbie's eyes lit up as she spoke about her former student. "Oh, she was a joy, DCI Beaumont. Curious about everything. She loved story time, especially anything with princesses."

George found himself leaning in, drawn by the warmth in Abbie's eyes. "George," he said. "Please, call me George."

Abbie smiled, a faint blush colouring her cheeks. "George," she repeated, as if testing the name on her tongue. "And she was kind, always sharing her crayons with the other children."

As Abbie spoke more about Rosie, George found himself drawn in by her passion, her obvious love for her students. He listened intently, asking questions, genuinely interested in learning more about the little girl.

The professional nature of their meeting began to blur. George found himself sharing stories from his own school days, laughing with Abbie over shared experiences of unruly students and exasperated teachers.

"I once wanted to be a teacher," George admitted, surprising himself with the confession. "Never quite made it though."

Abbie tilted her head, studying him. "What happened?"

George shrugged. "Life, I suppose. I was a bit of a naughty boy."

Abbie leaned forward, her eyes sparkling with interest. "A naughty boy, eh?" she said, her voice taking on a playful lilt. "I bet you were a handful in class."

George chuckled, feeling a warmth spread through his chest that had nothing to do with the tea. "You could say that. Spent more time in detention than out of it."

Abbie's lips curved into a mischievous smile. "You know, I've always had a soft spot for the troublemakers. They're usually the most interesting."

She shifted slightly, her knee brushing against George's. The contact, brief as it was, sent a jolt through him.

"Is that right?" George asked, his voice lower than he intended. "And here I thought teachers were supposed to prefer the well-behaved ones."

Abbie leaned in closer, her voice dropping to a near-whisper. "Well, we can't always go for what we're supposed to prefer, can we? Sometimes the heart wants what it wants."

George swallowed hard, acutely aware of how close they were sitting, of the scent of Abbie's perfume, light and floral.

He wanted to ask her, "And what does your heart want Abbie?" but he managed to stop the words from escaping.

Abbie's eyes locked with his, a mixture of desire and hesitation swirling in their depths. The air between them crackled with tension. George knew he should move away, should

201

maintain professional boundaries. But the look in Abbie's eyes—it was intoxicating.

And then reason reasserted itself. The image of Isabella flashed through his mind, followed quickly by the stark reality of the case they were supposed to be discussing.

George cleared his throat. "We should probably get back to talking about Rosie," he said, hating the disappointment that flashed across Abbie's face.

Abbie nodded, straightening up and smoothing her skirt. "Of course," she said, her professional demeanour sliding back into place. "You're right." She smiled. "But first, let me ask you. Do you ever regret it?" Abbie asked, her voice soft.

George paused, considering. "Sometimes," he said finally. "When cases like this come along. Makes you wonder if you could have made a difference..."

He trailed off, unable to finish the thought. Abbie reached out, her hand resting lightly on his arm. The touch sent a jolt through him, unexpected and not entirely unwelcome.

"You make a difference every day, George," she said earnestly. "The work you do... it matters."

Then suddenly, the atmosphere in the room shifted, charged with an unexpected intimacy. George was once again acutely aware of how close they were sitting, of the softness of Abbie's hand still resting on his arm.

"Are you married, George?" Abbie asked, her voice barely above a whisper.

The question caught him off guard. He should tell her about Isabella, about their engagement. But the words stuck in his throat. Instead, he heard himself say, "No. No, I'm not married."

It wasn't a lie, but it felt like one.

Abbie's smile widened slightly. "Neither am I," she said. "It's... it's not easy, is it? Balancing work and personal life."

George nodded, guilt gnawing at him even as he found himself drawn further into Abbie's orbit. "No, it's not easy at all."

George settled back into Abbie's comfortable sofa, his fingers wrapped around the warm mug of tea. The soft lamplight cast a gentle glow over the room, creating an atmosphere of intimacy that made it easy to forget the grim reality of why he was here.

"Abbie," he said, "can you tell me about Rosie's mother? What was your impression of her?"

Abbie hesitated, her eyes flicking away from George's. She bit her lower lip, clearly wrestling with something.

George leaned forward slightly. "You can be honest with me," he assured her. "Whatever you say stays between us. But if there's anything that might help us find Rosie, I need to know."

Abbie's shoulders sagged slightly, as if a weight had been lifted. She met George's gaze, her eyes filled with a mixture of concern and resolve.

"Gillian... she loves Rosie, I've no doubt about that," Abbie began, her voice soft but steady. "But she's... struggled. Ever since Rosie's father left."

George nodded encouragingly, staying silent to let Abbie continue.

"She'd miss parents' evenings sometimes. Forget to send Rosie in with her PE kit. Little things, you know? But they add up." Abbie sighed, running a hand through her hair. "I tried to be understanding. Single parenthood isn't easy. My mum tried her best when I was growing up, but I could see it was difficult for her."

George nodded, thinking of Mia and Jack.

"But then..." Abbie hesitated again, her brow furrowing. "About a month ago, Rosie came to school with a bruise on her arm. When I asked her about it, she said she'd fallen. But the way she said it... it didn't sound right."

George felt his stomach tighten. "Did you report it?"

Abbie nodded quickly. "Of course. Immediately. Social services came to investigate, but..." She trailed off, frustration evident in her voice.

"But what?" George prompted gently.

"But nothing came of it," Abbie said, her voice tinged with anger now. "They said there wasn't enough evidence. That accidents happen. I tried to argue, to tell them about the missed appointments, the times Rosie came to school without breakfast. But they wouldn't listen."

George's jaw clenched. Another potential failing of the system. Another child possibly slipping through the cracks.

"Who was the social worker?"

"The last time I saw Gillian," Abbie continued, her voice dropping to almost a whisper, "she smelled of alcohol. It was a morning drop-off. She was... different. Agitated. Rosie was quiet that day and wouldn't look at me."

George leaned back, processing this information. It painted a troubling picture, one that added another layer of complexity to an already complicated case.

"Thank you for telling me this, Abbie," he said softly. "I know it can't have been easy."

Abbie nodded, her eyes glistening with unshed tears. "I should have done more," she whispered. "I should have pushed harder, made someone listen."

George reached out, his hand covering hers. The touch was meant to be comforting, professional. But he couldn't ignore the spark of electricity that shot through him at the contact.

"You did everything you could," he assured her. "You reported your concerns. You looked out for Rosie. That's all anyone could ask."

"Find her, George," she pleaded, her voice cracking. "Please, find her."

George met her gaze, seeing the pain and worry etched in her beautiful features. In that moment, he wanted nothing more than to promise her everything would be alright.

But he couldn't. Because he didn't know if it would be.

Instead, he said, "I'll do everything in my power, Abbie."

The air between them was charged, heavy with unspoken emotions. George knew he should leave, should maintain professional boundaries. But the warmth of Abbie's presence... it was intoxicating.

For a moment, just a moment, he let himself imagine a different life. One where he wasn't engaged to Isabella, where the burden of missing children and broken families didn't rest on his shoulders. A life where he could stay here, in this cosy room, with this kind and passionate woman.

But reality intruded, as it always did. The case files waited for him back at the station. Rosie was still out there, scared and alone. And Isabella... Isabella was either working her arse off or waiting for him at home.

They lapsed into a comfortable silence, the air between them thick with unspoken possibilities. George knew he should leave, should maintain professional boundaries. But he couldn't bring himself to move.

Abbie broke the silence, her voice taking on a more serious

tone. "There was something else I wanted to talk to you about, George. Something that happened at school recently."

George straightened, his detective instincts kicking in. "Oh?"

Abbie nodded, leaning in closer. Her voice dropped to a near whisper, as if she was sharing a secret. "We had a school event last month. A fundraiser for the library. It was well-attended, lots of parents and community members there."

George nodded, encouraging her to continue.

"Well, Nadia Shah was there. You know, the social worker? The one who was involved with Rosie and Dania?" Abbie paused, biting her lip. "She was talking to one of our students. A boy who's been in and out of social services lately."

George's interest piqued. "Go on," he urged gently.

Abbie's brow furrowed as she recalled the scene. "It was... odd. Nadia was paying a lot of attention to this particular child. More than to any of the others. I saw her leading him away from the main event, speaking to him very quietly."

"Could she have been discussing a sensitive issue?" George suggested, playing devil's advocate.

Abbie shook her head. "Maybe, but... she kept looking around. Like she was making sure no one was watching them. And the boy... he's usually such a cheerful lad, but he looked... scared. Uncomfortable."

George leaned back, processing this information. On the surface, it didn't seem overtly suspicious. But combined with the irregularities he'd noticed in Nadia's files...

"Did you mention this to anyone?" he asked.

Abbie nodded. "I told Mrs Gledhill, our headteacher. She's the safeguarding officer. But she didn't seem concerned. Said Nadia was probably just doing her job because she knew Nadia loved kids."

George made a mental note to follow up with Mrs Gledhill. "Why did you decide to share this information with me?"

Abbie looked down into her lap. "The woman with the mole," Abbie explained. "I'm not a racist person, George, and I don't believe, like some others, that all Asian people look the same, but there's a resemblance between the woman you're searching for and Nadia Shah."

"Thank you for telling me this, Abbie. It might be nothing, but in cases like these, every detail matters."

Abbie smiled, relief evident in her expression. "I'm glad I told you. It's been bothering me ever since it happened."

As the conversation wound down, George found himself reluctant to leave. The warmth of Abbie's home, the comfort of her company—it was a stark contrast to the cold, hard reality of the case waiting for him back at the station.

But duty called. With a sigh, he stood, gathering his coat. "Thank you for the tea, Abbie. And for sharing your concerns. I'll look into it."

Abbie walked him to the door, her hand lingering on his arm. "Thank you for coming, George. It... it meant a lot to me."

Their eyes met, and for a moment, George was tempted to stay longer. Make an excuse to ask her more questions. To let himself get lost in the warmth and comfort Abbie offered. But the image of Isabella flashed through his mind, followed quickly by Rosie's smiling face they had on their Big Board.

With a final smile and a nod, George stepped out into the cool evening air. As he drove back to the station, his mind whirled with conflicting thoughts and emotions. The case, Abbie, Isabella, and Nadia Shah's strange behaviour—it all swirled together in a confusing maelstrom.

One thing was clear, though. He needed to take a closer look at Nadia Shah. Something wasn't adding up, and George was determined to find out what it was.

Chapter Twenty-three

George stepped into the house, the familiar scent of home doing little to ease the tension in his shoulders. It was early, for him at least. The sun hadn't quite set, casting long shadows across the living room floor.

"Izzy?" he called out, shrugging off his coat. "I'm home."

A muffled response came from upstairs, followed by the sound of hurried footsteps. Isabella appeared at the top of the stairs, her hair damp from the shower, a forced smile on her face.

"George," she said, surprise evident in her voice. "You're early."

He nodded, studying her. Something was off. Her eyes darted away from his, focusing on a point just over his shoulder. "Thought I'd surprise you," he said. "Maybe we could have dinner together for once."

Isabella's smile faltered for a moment before she hitched it back into place. "Of course. That sounds lovely. I'll just... I need to finish something upstairs. Won't be a minute."

She disappeared back up the stairs, leaving George standing in the hallway, a frown creasing his brow. He moved into the kitchen, opening the fridge more out of habit than hunger. As he reached for a beer, he heard Isabella's voice, low and urgent, drifting down from above.

"No, not now," she was saying. "I can't talk. He's home."

George froze, his hand on the bottle. He? Who the hell was 'he'?

The conversation continued, too muffled for him to make out the words. But the tone... secretive, rushed. Like she was hiding something.

George's thoughts spiralled, piecing together fragments of the past few weeks. Isabella's late nights at work. The way she'd jump when her phone buzzed. The distant look in her eyes when she thought he wasn't watching.

He'd been so wrapped up in his own case, in his own... distractions. Had he missed something crucial? Something happening right under his nose?

The image of Abbie Illingworth flashed unbidden through his mind. The warmth of her smile, the softness in her eyes. Guilt twisted in his gut, sharp and accusatory.

Was this karma? His own wandering thoughts coming back to bite him?

Footsteps on the stairs jolted him from his spiralling thoughts. He quickly grabbed the beer, shutting the fridge as Isabella entered the kitchen.

"Sorry about that," she said, smoothing her hair. "Work call. You know how it is."

George nodded, not trusting himself to speak. He watched as she moved around the kitchen, pulling out pots and pans with an energy that seemed forced.

"I was thinking pasta," she said, her back to him as she rummaged in a cupboard. "Something quick and easy. Unless you had other ideas?"

"Pasta's fine," George managed, his voice rougher than he

intended.

Isabella turned, concern flashing across her face. "Are you alright? You look... tense."

George forced a smile. "Long day," he lied. "Nothing a good meal won't fix."

She nodded, seemingly satisfied with his answer. As she turned back to the stove, George's eyes landed on her phone, sitting on the counter. It buzzed, the screen lighting up with a message.

Before he could stop himself, he glanced at it. A name caught his eye: Josh.

Who the hell was Josh? Somebody from work? The pieces clicked into place with sickening clarity. Her late nights. The secretive calls. The distance growing between them.

George's hand tightened on his beer bottle, knuckles turning white. He should confront her. Demand answers. But the words stuck in his throat, choking him with their hypocrisy.

After all, wasn't he guilty of the same thing? Especially today with his stolen moments with Abbie Illingworth, thoughts straying where they shouldn't?

He took a long pull from his beer, the bitter liquid doing nothing to wash away the taste of suspicion and guilt.

"George?" Isabella's voice broke through his dark thoughts. "Can you set the table?"

He nodded mechanically, going through the motions of domestic normalcy while his mind churned with doubts and accusations.

As they sat down to eat, the silence between them stretched, taut and uncomfortable. George pushed pasta around his plate, appetite gone.

"So," he said finally, his voice carefully neutral. "How's

work? Any progress on the Fawcett case?"

Isabella's fork paused halfway to her mouth. "It's... complicated," she said after a moment. "You know how these cold cases can be."

George nodded, watching her closely. "And your team? Everyone pulling their weight?"

A flicker of... something crossed Isabella's face. Guilt? Apprehension? "They're good," she said. "Dedicated. We're all working hard to crack this."

The lie hung between them, as palpable as the steam rising from their untouched meals.

"What were their names again?" George's phone buzzed in his pocket. For a moment, he thought it might be Abbie. The guilt intensified, churning in his gut.

But when he glanced at the screen, it was Tashan's name that flashed up. A welcome distraction from the tension at the table.

"Sorry, Izzy, it's Tashan," he muttered, standing. "I need to take this."

As he stepped into the hallway, George caught a glimpse of Isabella reaching for her own phone. Her fingers flew across the screen, a message sent before he was even out of sight.

The seeds of doubt, already planted, began to take root.

* * *

Isabella's heart raced as she fired off a quick text to Josh. "Can't talk now. George home early. Update tomorrow?"

She set her phone down, guilt gnawing at her. She hated lying to George, hated the distance growing between them. But what choice did she have?

The White Rose League. The cover-up. It was bigger than them, bigger than their relationship. She had to see this through, no matter the cost.

Her phone buzzed with Josh's reply: "No problem. Stay safe. Big breakthrough on female detective. Fill you in tomorrow."

Isabella's pulse quickened. A breakthrough. They were getting close, she could feel it.

"Everything alright?" George's voice made her jump. He stood in the doorway, watching her with an intensity that sent a shiver down her spine.

"Fine," she said, too quickly. "Just work stuff."

George nodded, his face unreadable. "Right. Well, I've got to head back to the station."

Isabella's stomach dropped. She should tell him. About the White Rose League, about the cover-up. About all of it.

But the words wouldn't come. Instead, she heard herself say, "Of course. I understand."

As George gathered his things, Isabella fought the urge to call him back, to confess everything. But the moment passed, and then he was gone, the door closing behind him with a finality that echoed in the sudden silence of the house.

Isabella slumped in her chair. She reached for her phone, needing to talk to someone who understood.

Josh picked up on the second ring. "Izzy? What's wrong?"

"I can't do this," she blurted out. "Lying to George, sneaking around. It's tearing me apart."

Josh's voice was gentle, understanding. "I know it's hard. But think about what's at stake here. If we're right about the White Rose League…"

"I know, I know," Isabella sighed. "It's just… you should have seen his face, Josh. He knows something's up."

"We're close," Josh assured her. "Once we have concrete evidence, we can bring him in. Make him understand why we had to keep it quiet."

Isabella nodded, even though Josh couldn't see her. "You're right. Of course, you're right. So, tell me about this break-through."

As Josh launched into an explanation of the female detective they'd identified—a Mary Sutcliffe, who'd gone missing in 1995 while investigating a series of child abductions—Isabella felt some of the tension ease from her shoulders.

They were making progress. Soon, they'd have enough to blow this whole thing wide open. And then, finally, she could come clean to George.

She only hoped their relationship would survive the fallout.

* * *

George sat in his car, parked at the circus across the road from his house. His knuckles were white on the steering wheel, his mind a whirlwind of suspicion and self-recrimination.

He should go back. Confront Isabella. Demand answers about her secretive behaviour, about the messages from this 'Josh'.

But every time he reached for the ignition, Abbie Illing-worth's face swam into view. The softness in her eyes, the warmth of her touch. His own guilty secret.

Who was he to demand honesty when he was harbouring secrets of his own?

With a growl of frustration, George started the car. He'd go to the station, bury himself in work. It was easier than facing the mess his personal life had become.

As he pulled away from the curb, George's phone buzzed. A text from Abbie: "Any news on Rosie? I can't stop thinking about her."

George's thumb hovered over the reply button. It would be so easy to call her, to lose himself in her warmth and understanding.

But he couldn't. Not now. Not with everything else going on.

He tossed the phone onto the passenger seat, focusing on the road ahead. The case.

That's what mattered now.

Finding Rosie, bringing her home safe.

* * *

George strode into the shared office on the HMET floor, his face a mask of barely contained emotion. Tashan looked up from his desk, eyebrows raising at the sight of his boss's slumped shoulders and clenched jaw.

"Sir?" Tashan asked, concern evident in his voice. "Everything alright?"

George shook his head, running a hand through his hair. "Fancy a drink, Tashan?"

Tashan studied him for a moment, then nodded. "I'll drive," he said, reaching for his keys.

The short drive to The Drysalters was silent, George staring out the window at the darkening Leeds streets. The pub was a familiar haunt, its worn wooden interior a comforting constant in their chaotic lives.

They found a quiet corner booth, away from the after-work crowd clustered around the bar. George ordered a double whisky, Tashan opting for a pint.

"So," Tashan said as their drinks arrived. "What's eating you, boss?"

George took a long pull of his whisky, the burn in his throat a welcome distraction. "It's Isabella," he said finally. "We're... struggling."

Tashan nodded, his face neutral. "Work getting in the way again?"

"Something like that," George muttered. He wanted to tell Tashan everything—about the secretive calls, the suspicions of an affair. But the words stuck in his throat.

Instead, he changed tack. "How are you, Tashan?"

Tashan's eyebrows rose slightly at the sudden shift in conversation. He studied George for a moment, sensing there was more to his boss's troubles than he was letting on. But he recognised the offered opening for what it was.

"Well, since you're asking," Tashan said, leaning back in his chair. "It's been... challenging, to say the least."

George nodded encouragingly. "Go on."

Tashan sighed, his usual composed demeanour slipping slightly. "It's not easy, you know? Being a person of colour in this job. Especially as I move up the ranks."

George's brow furrowed. "Are you facing discrimination within the force?"

"Not overtly," Tashan replied, shaking his head. "It's more... subtle than that. The looks, the whispers. The assumption that I'm only here to tick a diversity box."

George leaned forward, his own troubles momentarily for-gotten. "That's ridiculous. You're one of the best detectives I've ever worked with."

A small smile tugged at Tashan's lips. "Thanks, boss. But

not everyone sees it that way. There's always this... pressure. To be twice as good, work twice as hard, just to be seen as equal."

"I had no idea," George said softly. "Why haven't you said anything before?"

Tashan shrugged. "What's there to say? It's not like it's anything new. And complaining... well, that just reinforces the stereotypes, doesn't it? The chip on the shoulder, playing the race card."

George shook his head vehemently. "That's not right, Tashan. You shouldn't have to deal with this alone."

"I'm not alone," Tashan said, his voice firm. "I've got a good support system. Family, friends. And this team... it's different. Better. But out there," he gestured vaguely, "in the wider force, it's still a battle sometimes."

George sat back, processing this information. He'd always prided himself on running an inclusive team, on judging people solely on their merits. But had he been blind to the struggles his officers faced outside of his immediate supervision?

"What can I do?" he asked finally. "How can I help make things better?"

Tashan looked surprised, then thoughtful. "Honestly? Just listening helps. Acknowledging that it's real, that it's not all in our heads. And maybe... maybe using your position to push for more diversity in leadership roles. To challenge the old boys' network."

George nodded slowly. "I can do that. I will do that. And Tashan... thank you. For trusting me enough to share this."

Tashan smiled, a genuine one this time. "Thanks for asking, boss. And for listening."

As they lapsed into a companionable silence, George felt a renewed appreciation for his team, for the trust and openness they shared. "What do you make of Nadia Shah?" George eventually asked.

Tashan's eyebrows shot up at the sudden shift. "The social worker? You got something on her?"

George shrugged. "Call it a hunch. Something's not adding up with her."

Tashan leaned back, taking a sip of his beer. "Funny you should mention it," he said slowly. "I've been digging into some paperwork. Turns out Shah was involved, peripherally at least, with Lily Chen, Thomas Wilkes, and Amira Khan."

George sat up straighter, his personal troubles momentarily forgotten. "All three cases? That can't be a coincidence."

"My thoughts exactly," Tashan agreed. "Nothing concrete, mind you. But she'd had contact with each family at some point before the kids went missing."

George's thoughts spiralled, piecing together fragments of information. "We need to look deeper into Shah's background. Her cases, her contacts, everything."

Tashan nodded. "I'll get on it first thing tomorrow. But sir... are you sure you're alright? This thing with Isabella..."

George waved him off. "It's fine. We'll sort it out. The case has to come first."

Tashan didn't look convinced, but he let it drop. They finished their drinks in companionable silence, each lost in their own thoughts.

As they stood to leave, Tashan placed a hand on George's shoulder. "You know you can talk to me, right? About anything. Not just work."

George managed a small smile. "I know, Tashan. Thanks."

They stepped out into the cool night air, the pub's warmth fading quickly. As Tashan moved towards the car, George hesitated.

"I think I'll walk back," he said. "Clear my head a bit."

Tashan frowned. "You sure?"

George nodded. "I'm sure. I need the time to think."

As he watched Tashan drive away, George felt the burden of his secrets pressing down on him. Isabella's strange behaviour, his own conflicted feelings for Abbie, the growing suspicions about Nadia Shah—it was all tangling together in his mind, a Gordian knot of complications.

He set off down the street, his footsteps echoing in the quiet night. Somewhere out there, Rosie was waiting to be found.

Somewhere, the answers to all of this were hiding, just out of reach.

Chapter Twenty-four

DCI Beaumont drummed his fingers on the steering wheel, his eyes fixed on the imposing facade of HMP New Hall. The early Sunday morning sun did little to soften the prison's harsh lines. Beside him, DC Priya Patel shifted in her seat, her face a mask of professional detachment.

"You ready for this, sir?" she asked, her voice cutting through the tense silence.

George nodded, his jaw set. "As I'll ever be."

They climbed out of the car, the gravel crunching under their feet.

A guard led them through a series of security checkpoints, each buzz and clang of metal doors setting George's teeth on edge. His mind wandered, unbidden, to Isabella. The secretive calls, the furtive glances at her phone. The growing chasm between them.

He shook his head, forcing himself to focus. Clare Brack. The White Rose League. That's what mattered now.

The interview room was stark and cold, all harsh fluorescent lights and unyielding metal furniture. Clare Brack sat on the other side of the table, her prison jumpsuit a stark contrast to the sharp suits she'd favoured as a detective.

"DCI Beaumont," she said, her voice flat and emotionless.

"To what do I owe the pleasure?"

George settled into the chair across from her, Priya taking up position by the door. "We need to talk about your past cases, Clare. Specifically, Lily Chen, Thomas Wilkes, and Amira Khan."

Clare's face remained impassive, but something flickered in her eyes. Recognition? Fear? It was gone before George could be sure.

"I've got nothing to say about those cases," she said, her tone clipped.

George leaned forward. "Come on, Clare. We both know there's more to it. The White Rose League's involvement, for one."

Clare's lips twitched, the barest hint of a smirk. "The White Rose League? You're chasing ghosts, George."

"Am I?" George pressed. "Or are you protecting them, even now?"

Clare said nothing, her silence a wall between them. George's frustration mounted, mingling with the nagging thoughts of Isabella that he couldn't quite shake.

"What about Nadia Shah?" he asked, watching Clare's face closely. "She's a social worker. Ring any bells?"

For a split second, Clare's mask slipped. A flicker of... something crossed her face. But it was gone as quickly as it appeared, replaced by the same cold indifference.

"Never heard of her," Clare said, but her voice lacked conviction.

George's instincts screamed that she was lying, but he couldn't prove it. Not yet.

"Look, Clare," he said, leaning back in his chair. "We're not here to rehash old ground. But kids are missing. Kids are dying. If you know anything that could help..."

Clare's eyes met his, cold and unyielding. "I've told you everything I'm going to tell you, DCI Beaumont. Are we done here?"

George sighed, frustration etched into every line of his face. "For now," he said, standing. "But this isn't over, Clare. Not by a long shot."

As they left the interview room, George's mind was a whirlwind of conflicting thoughts. The case, Clare's stubborn silence, and always, always, the gnawing doubt about Isabella.

"Well, that was a waste of time," Priya muttered as they made their way back through the prison.

George shook his head. "Not necessarily. Did you see her reaction when I mentioned Nadia Shah?"

Priya nodded. "It was subtle, but it was there. You think there's a connection?"

"I think," George said, his voice low, "that we've just scratched the surface of something much bigger than we realised."

As they reached the car, George's phone buzzed in his pocket. His heart leapt, thinking it might be Isabella. Or worse, Abbie. But it was Tashan's name that flashed on the screen.

"DCI Beaumont," he answered, trying to quash the disappointment in his voice.

"Sir," Tashan's voice crackled through the speaker. "We've got a lead on the white van. ANPR picked it up heading north on the M1."

George's pulse quickened. "How long ago?"

"Twenty minutes. I've already alerted traffic units in the area."

"Good work," George said. "I'm on my way back now. Keep

me updated."

As he hung up, George caught Priya watching him, concern etched on her face. "Everything alright, sir?"

George nodded, not trusting himself to speak. How could he explain the turmoil in his mind? The case, Isabella, Abbie Illingworth—it was all tangled together, a knot of complications he couldn't seem to unravel.

They climbed into the car, the drive back to Leeds stretching out before them. George's thoughts spiralled, jumping from the case to his personal life and back again. The white van, a potential breakthrough. But always, always, the image of Isabella, secretive and distant, hovered at the edges of his thoughts.

He gripped the steering wheel tighter, knuckles turning white. Focus, he told himself. The case. That's what matters now.

But as they merged onto the motorway, George couldn't shake the feeling that everything was about to come crashing down around him. The case, his relationship, his entire world—it was all balanced on a knife's edge.

And he was powerless to stop it.

* * *

Clare Brack watched the door close behind DCI Beaumont, her face a mask of indifference. But inside, her thoughts churned.

George was getting close. Too close. And Nadia Shah... that was a complication she hadn't anticipated.

She waited until the sound of footsteps faded, then turned to the guard. "I need to make a phone call," she said, her voice low and urgent.

The guard hesitated. "It's not your designated time…"

Clare leaned in, her voice dropping to a whisper. She murmured something in the guard's ear, watching as his eyes widened in recognition.

"I… I suppose we can make an exception," he stammered, fumbling for his keys.

As Clare was led to the phone, a grim smile played at the corners of her mouth. George thought he was unravelling a conspiracy. He had no idea how deep the rabbit hole went.

She picked up the receiver, her fingers hovering over the keypad. One call. That's all it would take to set things in motion. To protect what needed to be protected, no matter the cost.

Clare took a deep breath, steeling herself. Then she dialled, the numbers as familiar to her as her own name.

It was time to raise the alarm. The White Rose was under threat.

And Clare Brack would be damned if she'd let George Beaumont tear it all down.

* * *

George hunched over his desk, the glow of his computer screen casting harsh shadows across his face. Files scattered around him. Nadia Shah's name glared up at him from every page, a taunting reminder of the mystery he couldn't quite crack.

He rubbed his eyes, fatigue warring with determination. The clock on the wall ticked relentlessly, a constant reminder of the time slipping away.

"Sir?" Tashan's voice cut through his concentration. "You might want to see this."

George looked up, blinking away the after-images of endless spreadsheets. Tashan stood in the doorway, a folder clutched in his hand, his face grim.

"What've you got?" George asked, gesturing for him to come in.

Tashan laid the folder on the desk, flipping it open. "Nadia Shah's success rates. They're... well, they're off the charts."

George leaned in, scanning the figures. His eyebrows shot up—Nadia's boss had been right. "Looks dodgy to me. Nobody's this good."

"That's not all," Tashan continued. "I've been going through her case files. There are discrepancies. Missing documents, incomplete reports. It's like..."

"Like someone's been covering their tracks," George finished, his mind racing. "I've noticed the same and was about to call a meeting."

Instead, George stood abruptly, grabbing his coat. "We need to bring her in. Now."

Tashan blinked, caught off guard by the sudden decision. "Sir? Shouldn't we get a warrant first?"

George shook his head, already halfway out the door. "No time. We've got enough for reasonable suspicion. Let's go."

The drive to Kernel House was tense, the silence broken only by the occasional crackle of the police radio. George's knuckles were white on the steering wheel, his jaw clenched tight enough to ache.

They burst into the social services building, warrant cards out, startling the receptionist. "Nadia Shah," George barked. "Where is she?"

The woman behind the desk stammered, "I... she's not here. She called in sick this morning."

George cursed under his breath. "I need to speak to her boss. Now."

Minutes later, they were in Yvette Watkins' office, the woman's face a mask of confusion and growing alarm.

"DCI Beaumont," she said, her voice tight. "What's this about?"

"Nadia Shah," George said, leaning over her desk. "We need her home address."

Yvette hesitated. "I can't just give out personal information without—"

"This is a criminal investigation," George cut her off. "Nadia Shah is a suspect in multiple child abductions. Now, her address. Please."

The colour drained from Yvette's face. She fumbled with her computer, her fingers shaking slightly. "Here," she said finally, scribbling on a notepad. "It's a semi-detached house on Monkwood Road in Outwood, Wakefield. Blue door. Easy to find."

George snatched the paper, already turning towards the door. "Thank you for your cooperation, Mrs Watkins. I really appreciate this."

Back in the car, George radioed for backup. "I want a full team at that address. Tactical support, the works. But no sirens, no lights. We don't want to spook her."

The drive to Outwood was a blur of adrenaline and anticipation. George's thoughts spiralled, piecing together the fragments of evidence. The missing documents, the impossibly high success rates, the connection to the missing children. It all pointed to Nadia Shah.

They pulled up a block away from the address, killing the engine. Other unmarked cars slid into position around them, a net closing in on their target.

George stepped out, adjusting his stab vest. "Remember," he said to the assembled officers. "We don't know what we're walking into. Stay alert, stay safe."

They approached the house, a nondescript semi-detached that could have belonged to anyone. No signs of life from within, no curtains twitching at their approach.

George nodded to the tactical team. They moved in, swift and silent, securing the perimeter. The Big Red Key made short work of the front door.

"Police!" George bellowed as they swarmed inside. "Nadia Shah, show yourself!"

But the house was empty. Eerily so. No dirty dishes in the sink, no clothes strewn about. It was as if no one had ever lived there at all.

"Clear!" came the shouts from upstairs, then the basement.

George stood in the middle of the living room, frustration etched into every line of his face. "Where the hell is she?"

Tashan shrugged.

"Get forensics in here," he snapped. "I want every inch of this place gone over. Fingerprints, DNA, the works. If Nadia Shah so much as sneezed in this house, I want to know about it."

As the forensics team swarmed in, their white suits a stark contrast to the empty beige walls, George paced the living room.

Nadia Shah wasn't just a social worker with questionable practices. She was something more. Something darker. And she'd known they were coming.

"Sir?" Tashan's voice cut through his thoughts. "What's our next move?"

George took a deep breath, forcing his racing mind to focus. "We put out an APB. Every copper in West Yorkshire needs to be on the lookout for Nadia Shah. Check airports, train stations, and bus depots. She can't have gone far."

He paused, his eyes scanning the room one last time. "And get tech forensics in here. I want her computer, her phone records, everything."

As the team bustled around him, George couldn't shake the feeling that they'd just scratched the surface of something much bigger. The White Rose League, Nadia Shah, the missing children—it was all connected. He could feel it in his bones.

But how? And more importantly, why?

George's phone buzzed in his pocket. He fished it out, his heart skipping a beat when he saw Isabella's name on the screen. For a moment, he considered ignoring it. The case, Nadia's disappearance, it all seemed more pressing.

But the memory of her secretive behaviour, the growing distance between them, made him pause. With a sigh, he answered.

"Isabella? What is it?"

Her voice came through, tinny and distant. "George? Where are you? I've been trying to reach you all day."

He glanced around the empty house, at the forensics team combing through Nadia Shah's life. "I'm working," he said, his voice gruffer than he intended. "Big break in the case."

"Oh," Isabella said, and was it his imagination, or did she sound... relieved? "Well, don't work too late. We need to talk."

Those words sent a chill down George's spine. We need to talk. Nothing good ever followed that phrase.

"Right," he said, his mind already drifting back to the case. "I'll be home when I can."

He hung up, shoving the phone back into his pocket. Personal drama would have to wait. Right now, he had a suspect to find and children to save.

"Tashan," he called out. "I want background checks on everyone Nadia Shah has ever worked with. Colleagues, clients, everyone. Someone must know where she's gone."

As Tashan hurried off to make the necessary calls, George found himself drawn back to the study. He stood in the doorway, surveying the sparse room. It was too empty, too clean. Like a stage set, waiting for the actors to arrive.

What are you hiding, Nadia? he thought. And why do I get the feeling we're playing right into your hands?

The forensics team worked methodically, dusting for prints, swabbing for DNA. But George couldn't shake the nagging feeling that they were already too late. That Nadia Shah was long gone, taking her secrets with her.

He clenched his fists, frustration and determination warring within him. He'd find her. And fast.

Chapter Twenty-five

George Beaumont stepped up to the podium, his shoulders squared. Camera flashes exploded like silent lightning, illuminating the grim determination etched on his face. He cleared his throat, the sound amplified by the microphone, cutting through the hushed murmurs of the assembled press corps.

"Good afternoon," he began, his voice steady and authoritative. "I'm here to provide an update on the ongoing investigation into the disappearance of Rosie Kershaw and the murder of Dania Bhati."

He paused, letting the gravity of the situation settle over the room. The journalists leaned forward, pens poised over notepads, hungry for every scrap of information.

"We have identified a person of interest in connection with these cases," George continued. He nodded to an officer off-stage, who stepped forward with a large photograph. "This is Nadia Shah, a social worker employed by Leeds City Council. We believe Miss Shah may have crucial information regarding the whereabouts of Rosie and Dania."

The photograph was held up for the cameras. Nadia's face, unremarkable yet somehow unsettling, stared out at the assembled crowd. George's eyes swept the room, gauging reactions.

"We are asking for the public's help in locating Miss Shah. If you have any information about her whereabouts, please contact the police immediately. Do not approach her directly."

A forest of hands shot up. George pointed to a familiar face in the front row.

"Helen Senior, Leeds Local Post," the sharp-faced woman announced. "DCI Beaumont, can you confirm reports of a white van seen near both abduction sites?"

George's jaw tightened imperceptibly. "We are pursuing all leads in this investigation, including reported sightings of vehicles in the vicinity of the incidents."

"But is it the same van?" Helen pressed. "And what about the man reportedly seen driving it?"

"At this time, we cannot confirm whether the vehicles are connected," George replied, his tone measured. "As for the individual you mentioned, we are following up on all witness statements and CCTV footage. However, our primary focus remains on locating Miss Shah and, most importantly, finding Rosie."

Another hand shot up. "Jake Thornton, Yorkshire Evening Post. DCI Beaumont, how long has Nadia Shah been a person of interest in this case? Why are we only hearing about her now?"

George's thoughts spiralled, weighing the need for transparency against the risk of compromising the investigation. "Miss Shah became a person of interest as our investigation progressed. We are releasing this information now because we believe public assistance is crucial in locating her."

He scanned the room, bracing himself for the inevitable follow-up. It came from a young reporter near the back.

"Sir, are you saying the police lost track of a suspect in a child abduction case?"

The room fell silent, all eyes on George. He took a deep breath, choosing his words carefully.

"What I'm saying is that we are pursuing every lead with the utmost diligence. Miss Shah's disappearance is a recent development, and we are allocating all available resources to find her."

More hands shot up, a barrage of questions threatening to overwhelm him. George held up a hand, silencing the crowd.

"I want to speak directly to Nadia Shah," he said. He stared straight into the nearest camera. "Nadia, if you're watching this, come forward. Whatever you know, whatever you've done, we can work through it. But Rosie and Dania need your help. Their families need closure. Do the right thing."

He paused, letting the words hang in the air. Then, straightening his shoulders, he addressed the room one final time.

"That's all for now. We'll release further updates as the investigation progresses. Thank you."

George stepped away from the podium, ignoring the shouted questions that followed him. As he exited the press room, Tashan fell into step beside him.

"How'd it go, sir?" Tashan asked.

George grunted. "About as well as could be expected. Any updates?"

Tashan shook his head. "Nothing concrete yet. But the team's waiting to brief you."

They strode through the station, a palpable energy humming in the air.

They entered the Incident Room, a hive of activity despite the hour. Detectives hunched over computers, phones pressed to ears, voices a low murmur of frustration and dogged persistence.

"Right," George said, his voice cutting through the background noise. "What have we got?"

Priya stepped forward, dark circles under her eyes betraying long hours of work. "We've been following up on every lead, sir. Checking CCTV, interviewing neighbours, the works. But Nadia's gone to ground. It's like she vanished into thin air."

George's jaw clenched. "What about her finances? Phone records?"

"That's the thing," Susie chimed in, pushing her glasses up her nose. "Her bank accounts haven't been touched since yesterday morning. And her phone's been off since around the same time."

"She knew we were coming," George muttered, more to himself than the team. He turned to Tashan. "The white van?"

Tashan shook his head, frustration evident in every line of his body. "We lost it again, sir. Last confirmed sighting was near Scotch Corner services. After that, nothing."

George paced the length of the room, his mind racing. "So we've got a missing social worker, a vanishing van, and some missing children somewhere." He stopped, facing his team. "What are we missing?"

The room fell silent. George's eyes swept over his team, taking in their exhausted faces, the determination still burning beneath the fatigue.

"Alright," he said. "We go back to basics. Priya, I want you digging deeper into Nadia's past. School records, employment history, everything. There's got to be something we've overlooked."

Priya nodded, already reaching for her notebook.

"Susie, keep on those phone records. If Nadia's made so much as a single call in the last 48 hours, I want to know about it."

"On it, sir," Susie replied, turning back to her computer.

"Tashan," George continued, "coordinate with traffic. I want every CCTV camera between here and Scotland checking for that van. And get onto the ports and airports. If Nadia's trying to leave the country, I want to know about it."

Tashan nodded grimly, reaching for his phone.

George paused, his eyes scanning the evidence board. Photos of Rosie and Dania smiled out at him, a stark reminder of what was at stake.

"I also want to point out the elephant in the room," he said.

"Sir?" asked Tashan.

"Bilal Bhati."

"CID is still working on finding him, sir; they haven't let up."

"Good."

He turned back to his team, determination hardening his features. "No one goes home until we've got something solid. Clear?"

A chorus of affirmatives echoed through the room. George nodded, satisfied. "Good. Let's get to work."

* * *

Tashan Blackburn drummed his fingers on the steering wheel, eyes scanning the road ahead. Beside him, Priya Patel pored over a stack of witness statements, her brow furrowed in concentration.

"Anything?" Tashan asked, breaking the tense silence.

Priya shook her head, frustration evident in her voice. "Nothing concrete. Half our witnesses say the van was white, the other half swear it was off-white or cream. Nobody got a clear look at the number plate."

Tashan grunted, turning onto a side street. "Typical."

"Wait a minute," Priya said, sitting up straighter. "Look there."

Tashan followed her gaze to a CCTV camera perched on the corner of a building. "Good spot. Let's see if we can get that footage."

An hour later, they sat in their dimly lit video room at the station, eyes glued to a grainy video playing on a monitor. The white van appeared on screen, moving at a steady pace down the street.

"There," Priya pointed. "Can you zoom in on that?"

Tashan leaned forward, squinting at the pixelated image. "It's blurry, but... is that a logo on the side?"

Priya nodded, excitement creeping into her voice. "Looks like it. Can we enhance this?"

"I can't, but Josh can."

Priya and Tashan spent the next few hours poring over enhanced images, cross-referencing with local business directories and vehicle registrations. Progress was slow, each lead seeming to fizzle out as quickly as it appeared.

"This is useless," Tashan groaned, leaning back in his chair. "We're getting nowhere."

Priya rubbed her eyes, fatigue etched across her face. "Maybe we're approaching this wrong. Instead of focusing on the van itself, what if we look at where it's been?"

Tashan sat up, intrigued. "Go on."

"We've been tracking its movements, right? Let's plot every

sighting on a map, see if we can establish a pattern."

They set to work, marking each confirmed sighting of the van on a large map of Leeds and the surrounding areas. Slowly, a picture began to emerge.

"Look at this," Priya said, pointing to a cluster of marks. "It keeps circling back to this area here."

Tashan leaned in, studying the map. "That's... Bramham, isn't it? What's out there?"

Priya was already typing furiously on her laptop. "Not much. It's mostly farmland. Wait a second..." She paused, eyes widening. "There's an old farm there. Crossroads Farm. It used to belong to Leeds University, but it was sold off a few years ago."

Tashan's pulse quickened. "To who?"

"That's the thing," Priya said, frowning at her screen. "The records are... vague. It's listed as belonging to a private company, but the details are buried under layers of bureaucracy."

Tashan stood, energy thrumming through him. "We need to check this out. It could be nothing, but..."

"But it could be everything," Priya finished. She grabbed her coat, already heading for the door. "I'll tell Yolanda to dig into the ownership records. We might need to get a warrant."

* * *

Detective Inspector Isabella Wood hunched over her desk at home. The clock on the wall ticked relentlessly, a constant reminder of the precious hours slipping away. She rubbed her eyes, fatigue warring with determination as she pored over the stack of dusty files before her.

"Anything?" Josh Fry's voice cut through the silence,

startling her from her concentrated state. He'd just arrived at the Beaumont household after helping Tashan and Priya.

Isabella looked up, blinking away the after-images of endless reports and grainy photographs. Josh stood in the doorway, two steaming cups of coffee in his hands, his dishevelled appearance a mirror of her own exhaustion.

"Maybe," she said, reaching for the proffered cup. "Come take a look at this."

Josh crossed the room, settling into the chair beside her with a weary groan. His glasses sat askew on his nose, magnifying his bloodshot eyes to an almost comical degree.

"What've you got?" he asked, peering at the file she'd pushed towards him.

Isabella tapped a grainy photograph, her finger tracing the outline of a woman's face. "Mary Sutcliffe," she said, her voice low and intense. "The detective who went missing in '95. I think I've found something."

Josh leaned in, squinting at the image. "Christ," he muttered. "She looks familiar, doesn't she?"

Isabella nodded. "I can't tell why, though." She flipped to another page, this one a heavily redacted report. "It's the last case Mary was working on before she disappeared. A series of child abductions, all bearing the hallmarks of the White Rose League."

Josh's eyebrows shot up, disappearing beneath his unruly fringe. "Bloody hell," he breathed. "You think she got too close?"

Isabella nodded, her mind racing. "It fits, doesn't it? She uncovers something big, something that goes all the way to the top. And then, poof. She vanishes without a trace."

"So what do you want to do?"

"We need to dig deeper. Mary's personal life, her contacts, everything. There's got to be something we've missed."

Josh nodded. "Good thinking," he said, his eyes scanning the cluttered desk. "I'll focus on her case files. There's got to be a pattern we're not seeing."

They worked in companionable silence, the only sounds the clacking of keyboards and the rustle of papers.

Chapter Twenty-six

Detective Sergeant Tashan Blackburn hunched over his desk, eyes burning from hours of staring at CCTV footage. The incident room hummed with quiet intensity, the air thick with caffeine and determination.

"Anything, sarge?" Detective Constable Priya Patel's voice cut through his concentration.

Tashan blinked, refocusing on his colleague. Priya stood before him, two steaming mugs in hand, her own exhaustion evident in the shadows beneath her eyes.

"Cheers," he said, accepting the coffee. "And no, not yet. This bloody van's like a ghost."

Priya settled into the chair beside him, her gaze flicking to the screens. "We've got to be missing something. A vehicle can't disappear into thin air."

Tashan grunted in agreement, taking a long swig of coffee. The bitter liquid jolted him awake, sharpening his focus. "Right," he said, straightening. "Let's go over it again. What do we know?"

Priya pulled out her notebook, flipping to a well-worn page. "White van, Mercedes Sprinter, early 2000s model. Reg plate obscured by mud in all sightings. Last confirmed location was the Scotch Corner services, heading north on the A1."

"And after?" Tashan prompted.

Priya shook her head. "Nothing concrete. A few potential sightings along the A1, but nothing we can verify."

Tashan leaned back, his mind racing. "So we're assuming they stayed on the A1. But what if they didn't?"

Priya's eyebrows shot up. "You think they doubled back?"

"Or took a different route entirely," Tashan mused. He turned to his computer, pulling up a map of the area. "Look, there are dozens of minor roads branching off. If they wanted to disappear..."

"They could have taken any one of them," Priya finished, excitement colouring her voice. "Tashan, you're a genius."

He allowed himself a small smile. "Don't get ahead of yourself. We still need to prove it."

They spent the next hours poring over traffic camera footage from every road within a fifty-mile radius of Scotch Corner. It was mind-numbing work, but the possibility of a breakthrough kept them going.

"Wait," Priya said suddenly, her hand shooting out to grab Tashan's arm. "There. Rewind it."

Tashan obliged, his eyes narrowing as he focused on the grainy image. A white van flashed across the screen, its reg plate obscured by a conveniently placed splash of mud.

"That's got to be it," Priya breathed. "Where is this?"

Tashan checked the camera details. "A659, heading towards Bramham. About an hour after the Scotch Corner sighting."

Priya was already reaching for her phone. "I'll get uniform to canvas the area. Someone must have seen something."

As Priya made the call, Tashan delved deeper into the traffic system, tracking the van's progress. It appeared on three more cameras before disappearing again, each sighting leading them further into the countryside.

"Priya," he called, excitement building in his chest. "I think I've got something."

She hurried over, leaning in to peer at his screen. "What am I looking at?"

"The last sighting of the van," Tashan explained, pointing to a frozen image. "It's turning onto a dirt road. And guess where that road leads?"

Priya squinted at the map he'd pulled up. "Crossroads Farm? Never heard of it."

"Me neither," Tashan admitted. "But it's the only property for miles around. If they were looking for a place to lie low..."

"It's perfect," Priya finished. She straightened, determination hardening her features.

* * *

An hour later, Tashan Blackburn leaned back in his chair, rubbing his eyes. The glow of the computer screen cast harsh shadows across his face, highlighting the fatigue etched into every line. Beside him, Priya Patel hunched over a stack of papers, her brow furrowed in concentration.

"Anything?" Tashan asked, his voice rough from too many hours of silence.

Priya looked up, shaking her head. "Nothing concrete. But I've got a hunch."

Tashan straightened, interest piqued. "Let's hear it."

Priya spread out a series of documents on the desk between them. "Crossroads Farm. It's been abandoned for years, right? But someone's been paying the taxes, keeping it off the radar."

Tashan leaned in, scanning the papers. "Leeds University?"

"Used to be," Priya nodded. "But they sold it five years ago. To a private company called Meadowland Holdings."

Tashan's eyebrows shot up. "Never heard of them."

"Exactly," Priya said, a hint of triumph in her voice. "Because they don't exist. Not really. It's a shell company, sarge. No employees, no office, nothing but a PO box and this one property."

Tashan sat back, his mind racing. "So someone went to a lot of trouble to hide their ownership of an abandoned farm. Why?"

Priya's eyes gleamed. "That's what we need to find out."

They shared a look, the same thought passing between them. This could be it. The break they'd been waiting for.

Tashan stood, grabbing his jacket. "We need to tell the boss."

George Beaumont's office was a hive of activity when they entered. The DCI looked up from a pile of reports, his eyes sharp despite the hour.

"What have you got?" he demanded, not bothering with pleasantries.

Tashan and Priya laid out their findings, watching as George's expression hardened with each new detail.

"Good work," he said when they finished.

The trio headed into the Incident Room.

"Yolanda, I want you digging deeper into this Meadowland Holdings. Find out who's really pulling the strings."

Detective Sergeant Yolanda Williams nodded, already reaching for her computer.

George turned back to Tashan and Priya. "You two, head out to Crossroads Farm. Do a recce, but keep it low-key. We don't want to spook anyone if there's something going on out there."

* * *

Detective Chief Inspector George Beaumont stood before the imposing gates of HMP Leeds. The prison loomed before him, a stark reminder of the consequences of crossing the line between law and disorder.

He'd come here seeking answers, but as he was processed through security, a maelstrom of emotions churned within him. Anger, betrayal, a bone-deep weariness he couldn't seem to shake.

His footsteps echoed off the concrete walls, and the familiar smell of unwashed man, disinfectant and despair assaulted his nostrils, a grim reminder of the lives wasted behind these walls.

He'd been here before, of course. Too many times to count. But this visit was different. This time, he was here to see Luke Mason.

Luke Mason had been his friend, his mentor. Now, he was a convicted criminal with ties to a shadowy organisation they were still struggling to understand. The thought of his former colleague, his friend, sitting in a cell turned George's stomach. But he pushed the feeling aside. He needed answers, and Luke might be the only one who could provide them.

The guard led him to a small interview room, stark and oppressive under the harsh fluorescent lights. Luke was already there, hands cuffed to the table, a ghost of his former self.

George settled into the uncomfortable chair, his mind racing through the questions he needed to ask.

"George," Luke said, a ghost of his old smile playing across his features. "To what do I owe the pleasure?"

Luke had aged years in the short time he'd been incarcerated, his once-sharp eyes now dull and sunken.

George leaned forward. "I need information, Luke. About Nadia Shah, Bilal Bhati, and the White Rose League."

Luke's eyebrows rose, and a flicker of something passed across his face. "Straight to business, eh? No warm welcome for an old friend?"

"We're not friends, Luke," George said flatly. "You saw to that when you betrayed everything we stood for."

Luke's smile faded, replaced by a weariness George had never seen in him before. "Fair enough," he sighed. "What do you want to know?"

George pulled out a photograph, sliding it across the table. "Nadia Shah. Social worker. We think she's involved in recent child abductions. What can you tell me about her?"

Luke studied the image, his brow furrowing.

Luke sat back, the chains on his cuffs clinking softly. "What makes you think I know anything?"

"Because you were one of them," George said, his voice hard. "You were the Ghost. You were deep in the League's operations."

Luke's eyes narrowed, a calculating look George knew all too well. "And what do I get out of this little chat?"

George's jaw clenched. "The satisfaction of doing the right thing for once in your miserable life."

A bark of laughter escaped Luke's lips. "Oh, George. Still the idealist, I see. Even after everything you've been through."

They sat in silence for a long moment.

Finally, Luke spoke. "I never met her personally," he said slowly. "But the name... it came up in League business. Someone to be protected, I think."

"Protected?" George pressed. "Why?"

Luke shrugged, leaning back in his chair. "I don't know the details. The League operates on a need-to-know basis. Keeps everyone in the dark about the bigger picture."

George's frustration mounted, a tide of anger rising within him. "Damn it, Luke," he snapped. "I'm not here for your cryptic bullshit. I need answers."

Luke's eyes widened slightly at the outburst. "George—"

"No," George cut him off. "You don't get to 'George' me. Not after what you did. Do you have any idea what your betrayal cost us? Cost me?"

The words hung in the air between them, charged with years of unspoken pain and resentment.

Luke's shoulders slumped. "I never meant to hurt you, George. You have to believe that."

"Believe you?" George's laugh was harsh, devoid of humour. "Why should I believe a word you say? You lied to me for years, Luke. Years. I trusted you. I looked up to you. And all the while, you were working for the very people we swore to bring down."

Luke flinched as if the words were physical blows. "It wasn't like that," he said softly. "Not at first. I thought... I thought I was doing the right thing."

"The right thing?" George's voice rose, echoing off the bare walls. "How was any of this the right thing? Children are missing, Luke. Families torn apart. And you were part of it. You helped make it happen."

Luke's face crumpled, the mask of indifference finally

cracking. "I didn't know," he whispered. "I swear to you, George, I didn't know about the children. Not until it was too late."

George wanted to believe him. Part of him, the part they still clung to the memory of their friendship, desperately wanted to accept Luke's words as truth. But the detective in him, hardened by years of lies and betrayal, couldn't let it go.

"Even if that's true," he said, "it doesn't change what you did. The lives you ruined. The trust you shattered."

Luke nodded, his eyes fixed on the table between them. "I know," he said. "And I'll have to live with that for the rest of my life. But George, you have to understand—the White Rose League, it's not what you think it is. It's not what I thought it was."

George's eyes narrowed. "What do you mean?"

Luke leaned forward, his voice dropping to a near-whisper. "The League... it goes deeper than you can imagine. There are people involved who you'd never suspect. Pillars of the community. People beyond reproach."

George's thoughts spiralled, connecting dots he'd never seen before. "Give me names, Luke."

But Luke was already shaking his head. "I can't. I don't know them. Nobody does, except the inner circle."

Frustration welled up in George, threatening to overwhelm him. "Then what good are you?" he spat. "Why am I even here?"

Luke met his gaze, and for a moment, George saw a glimmer of the man he'd once called friend. "Because I want to make it right, George. As much as I can. I can't undo what I've done, but I can help you stop them."

George sat back, studying Luke's face. He wanted to believe

him. God, how he wanted to believe that some shred of the man he'd known and trusted still existed.

"Why should I trust you?" he asked finally. "After everything you've done, why should I believe a word you say?"

Luke's answer was immediate, his voice steady. "Because you know me, George. Better than anyone. You know when I'm lying. Look me in the eye and tell me if I'm lying now."

George held his gaze, searching for any sign of deception. But all he saw was regret, determination, and a flicker of something he hadn't expected—hope.

"Alright," he said finally. "Talk. Tell me everything you know about Bilal Bhati and Nadia Shah, and their connection to the League. And Luke?"

"Yeah?"

"If I find out you're lying to me again, I'll make sure you never see the outside of this prison. Clear?"

Luke nodded, a grim smile playing at the corners of his mouth. "Crystal."

"Start with Bilal Bhati. Where does he fit into all this?"

"Bilal?" Luke frowned. "I don't know him. But if he's mixed up in this, I'd bet my life he's another pawn. Someone to take the fall when things go wrong."

George sat back, processing this information. It aligned with what they'd uncovered so far, but it still didn't give them the breakthrough they needed.

"What about the children, Luke?" he asked, his voice hardening. "What happens to them?"

Luke's face clouded, a mix of guilt and something darker passing across his features. "I don't know," he said finally. "And trust me, George, you don't want to know either."

The implications hung heavy in the air between them. George's stomach churned at the possibilities.

"One last thing," he said, pushing down his revulsion. "Crossroads Farm. Mean anything to you?"

Luke's reaction was subtle, but George caught it. A slight widening of the eyes, a tightening of the jaw.

"Never heard of it," Luke said, but his voice lacked conviction.

George leaned in, his eyes boring into Luke's. "Don't lie to me. Not now. Not about this."

Luke held his gaze for a long moment before sighing heavily. "I'm not lying to you."

"Why are you telling me this, Luke?" he asked finally. "Why now?"

Luke's eyes met his, and for a moment, George saw a glimmer of the man he'd once called friend. "Because it has to stop, George. What they're doing... it's evil. And I may be a lot of things, but I never signed up for this."

George nodded slowly, standing to leave. George felt a shift within himself. The anger was still there, the betrayal a wound too deep to heal easily. But alongside it, a spark of the old connection flared to life. But Luke's voice stopped him at the door.

"Be careful, George," he said, his voice laden with warning. "These people... they'll stop at nothing to protect their secrets. And they've got eyes and ears everywhere."

"Thanks for the warning."

"Oh, and George."

Beaumont turned on his heel. "What?"

"I'm sorry."

They weren't friends. Not now. But in this moment, united

against a common enemy, they were allies. And for now, George thought, that would have to be enough.

George said, "So you should be."

Chapter Twenty-seven

The drive to Crossroads Farm was tense, anticipation thrumming through the car. Tashan's knuckles were white on the steering wheel as they turned onto the narrow country lane leading to their destination.

"There," Priya said suddenly, pointing through the windscreen. "Up ahead."

Tashan slowed the car, taking in the scene before them. Crossroads Farm sprawled across the landscape, a collection of dilapidated buildings surrounded by overgrown fields. At first glance, it appeared abandoned, forgotten by time.

But as they drew closer, details emerged that belied first impressions. Fresh tire tracks cut through the muddy driveway. A glint of metal behind one of the barns suggested recently moved equipment.

"Charming," Priya muttered, stepping out of the car. "Looks like nobody's been here in years."

Tashan nodded, eyes scanning the property. "Perfect hideout, though. Isolated, lots of space..."

Priya nodded.

They approached the main building cautiously, years of training kicking in. Tashan tried the door, finding it locked.

"No signs of forced entry," he noted. "But look at this."

He pointed to a patch of ground near the door. Tire tracks, fresh ones, cut through the overgrown grass.

Priya crouched down, examining the marks. "Someone's been here recently. And often, by the looks of it."

"We need to get inside," Tashan said, frustration edging his voice. "But we can't risk compromising potential evidence."

Priya nodded, her hand instinctively checking her radio. "What's the play?"

Tashan considered their options. They were here to observe, not engage. But the site was large, and time was of the essence.

"We split up," he decided. "You take the outbuildings, I'll check the main house. Keep in radio contact, and at the first sign of trouble, we fall back. Clear?"

"Crystal, sarge," Priya agreed, "You alright?" Priya asked, noticing his unease.

Tashan shook his head, trying to clear it. "Yeah, just... something about this place gives me the creeps."

Priya nodded, understanding in her eyes. "I know what you mean. It's too quiet. Too... empty." The silence was oppressive, broken only by the distant call of birds and the whisper of wind through abandoned fields.

Tashan approached the farmhouse, every sense on high alert. The porch steps creaked ominously under his weight, the sound unnaturally loud in the stillness.

He peered through a grimy window, cupping his hands around his eyes to block the glare. The interior was dark, filled with shadows and half-seen shapes. But something caught his eye—a flicker of movement, there and gone in an instant.

Tashan's pulse quickened. He reached for his radio, about to call Priya, when a new sound cut through the air. The rumble of an engine, growing louder by the second.

He spun around, watching in disbelief as a white van burst from behind one of the barns, tires spinning in the loose gravel.

"Stop! Police!" Tashan bellowed, already sprinting towards their car.

The van careened past them, missing Priya by inches. It fishtailed onto the dirt road, engine roaring as it accelerated away.

"Fuck," Tashan spat. Tashan threw himself into the driver's seat, Priya scrambling in beside him. He gunned the engine, tires squealing as they gave chase.

"Call it in," he barked, eyes fixed on the van ahead. "All units in pursuit."

As they peeled out after the van, Tashan's mind raced. Who had been driving? How had they known to run? And most importantly, what or who were they running from?

The chase led them back towards the main road, the van weaving dangerously across the narrow country lanes. Tashan pushed the accelerator, closing the gap inch by agonising inch.

"They're heading for the A1," Priya said, clinging to the dashboard as they took a corner at breakneck speed.

Tashan nodded grimly. If the van made it to the motorway, their chances of catching it would plummet.

They burst onto the A1 slip road, the van now barely a car length ahead. Tashan could see the driver now, a figure hunched low over the wheel.

"Come on," he muttered, urging the car faster.

For a heart-stopping moment, it seemed they might catch up. But then the van swerved, cutting across three lanes of traffic. Horns blared, tyres screeched, and Tashan was forced to brake hard to avoid a collision.

By the time they recovered, the van had disappeared into the sea of traffic ahead.

"Shit," Tashan slammed his hand against the steering wheel. "We lost them."

Priya was already on the radio, coordinating with other units. But they both knew the chances of picking up the trail again were slim.

As they pulled over onto the hard shoulder, the adrenaline of the chase fading, Tashan's mind whirled with questions. What had they stumbled upon at Crossroads Farm? And how deep did this rabbit hole go?

* * *

Isabella's fingers danced across her laptop keyboard, the soft tapping a counterpoint to Josh's rustling papers. The clock ticked relentlessly, marking the passage of time as they delved deeper into Mary Sutcliffe's past.

"This is like searching for a needle in a bloody haystack," Josh grumbled, pushing his glasses up his nose. "Half these files are handwritten. Who even does that nowadays?"

Isabella glanced up, a wry smile tugging at her lips. "Welcome to policing in the 90s, Josh. No fancy databases or digital archives. Just good old-fashioned legwork and a lot of paper cuts."

Josh snorted, flipping through another stack of yellowed reports. "Makes you appreciate modern technology, doesn't it? How did they get anything done back then?"

"They managed," Isabella murmured, her eyes fixed on her screen. "And sometimes, old school methods turn up things our shiny new systems miss."

As if to prove her point, she let out a low whistle. "Josh, come look at this."

He pushed back from the desk, wheels squeaking as he rolled his chair over. "What've you got?"

Isabella pointed to her screen, where a scanned newspaper article from 1995 filled the display. "It's a small piece, buried in the back pages of the Yorkshire Evening Post. 'Local Detective Commended for Bravery in Child Rescue Operation.'"

Josh leaned in, squinting at the grainy image accompanying the article. "That's her, isn't it? Mary Sutcliffe?"

Isabella nodded, excitement colouring her voice. "Yeah, but look at the date. This was published just two weeks before she disappeared."

"Christ," Josh breathed. "Talk about timing. What does the article say?"

Isabella skimmed the text, her brow furrowed in concentration. "It's vague on details. Mentions Mary leading a raid on a suspected paedophile ring, rescuing several children. But there's no follow-up, no names of those arrested."

Josh's fingers drummed a restless rhythm on the desk. "That's odd, isn't it? You'd think a big bust like that would generate more press coverage."

"Unless someone wanted to keep it quiet," Isabella mused. She clicked through a few more scanned articles, her frown deepening. "There's nothing else. No court reports, no sentencing news. It's like the whole case just... vanished."

"Along with Mary," Josh added, his voice grim.

Isabella nodded, her mind racing. "We need to find out more about this raid. Who was involved, where it happened, what became of the children."

Josh was already reaching for the phone. "I'll ring the Yorkshire Evening Post, see if they've got any archived material that didn't make it to print."

As Josh dialled, Isabella turned back to her stack of files. There had to be something here, some clue they'd overlooked. Her eyes fell on a thin folder, tucked beneath a pile of more official-looking documents. Curiosity piqued, she pulled it out.

Inside, she found a collection of personal effects. A half-empty packet of mints, a tattered paperback novel, a few crumpled receipts. The detritus of a life interrupted.

But it was a small, leather-bound notebook that caught her attention. She flipped it open, her breath catching as she recognised Mary's handwriting, cramped and hurried as if she'd been writing in secret.

"Josh," she called, her voice urgent. "I think I've found something."

He hung up the phone, wheeling back over. "What is it?"

Isabella held up the notebook. "Mary's personal notes. And look at this entry, dated the day before she disappeared."

Josh leaned in, reading aloud. "'Meeting C at the usual place. This goes deeper than we thought. Trust no one.'" He looked up, meeting Isabella's gaze. "Who's C?"

Isabella shook her head, frustration evident in the set of her jaw. "I don't know. But whoever they are, they might have been the last person to see Mary alive."

Josh's eyes widened as the implications sank in. "Or the person responsible for her disappearance."

"Exactly," Isabella nodded. She flipped through more pages, her excitement growing. "There are other mentions of C throughout the notebook. Coded messages, locations... This could be the break we've been looking for."

Josh was already pulling his laptop closer. "I'll start cross-referencing the locations with any known White Rose League activity from that time. Maybe we can establish a pattern."

As they dove back into their research, the room hummed with renewed energy. The pieces were starting to fall into place, a picture emerging from the fog of decades-old secrets.

Hours slipped by, marked only by the steadily emptying coffee pot and the growing pile of notes. The sun had long since set, casting the room in the eerie glow of computer screens and desk lamps.

"Izzy," Josh's voice broke through the concentrated silence. "I think I've got something."

Isabella looked up, hope flaring in her chest. "What is it?"

Josh turned his laptop towards her, pointing at a map on the screen. "I've plotted all the locations mentioned in Mary's notebook. Most of them are scattered around Leeds and the surrounding areas. But there's one outlier."

Isabella leaned in, her eyes narrowing as she studied the map. "That's... that's miles from anywhere. What's out there?"

Josh clicked a few keys, zooming in on the location. "According to old land records, it used to be a farm. Owned by a family called the Thorpes. But it was abandoned in the late 80s and taken over by Leeds University."

Isabella's pulse quickened. "An abandoned farm in the middle of Bramham? That's perfect for—"

"A hideout," Josh finished. "Or a base of operations."

They shared a look, the same thought passing between them. This could be it. The key to unravelling the whole mystery.

Isabella stood, her decision made. "We need to check it out. First thing tomorrow."

Josh nodded, already reaching for his coat. "I'll pull to-gether a team. We'll need backup if we're walking into a potential White Rose League stronghold."

"No," Isabella said sharply, then softened her tone at Josh's startled look. "We can't risk alerting anyone. If this place is as important as we think it is, the League might have eyes and ears everywhere. We go alone."

Josh hesitated, concern etching lines across his forehead. "Izzy, that's not protocol. It could be dangerous."

Isabella met his gaze, her voice steady and determined. "I know. But we can't risk this lead slipping away. Not when we're so close."

After a long moment, Josh nodded. "Alright. But we take precautions. Full tactical gear, and we let someone know where we're going. Just in case."

"Agreed," Isabella said, relief washing over her. She glanced at the clock, surprised to see it was well past midnight. "Get some rest. I'll pick you up at dawn."

As Josh gathered his things and headed out, Isabella turned back to Mary's notebook. She ran her fingers over the worn leather cover, a strange mix of excitement and trepidation churning in her gut.

Tomorrow, they might finally uncover the truth about Mary Sutcliffe's disappearance. And with it, the key to finding Abigail Fawcett and the mystery of the White Rose League.

Chapter Twenty-eight

The shrill ring of George Beaumont's mobile pierced the pre-dawn darkness. He fumbled for it, sleep still clouding his mind.

"Beaumont," he grunted, squinting at the clock. 5.47 am.

"Sir, it's Greenwood. A body has been found at Crossroads Farm."

George sat bolt upright, sleep forgotten. "A body? Adult or child?"

"Child, sir. Female, we think, though we're not entirely sure. Buried in the grounds."

George's stomach clenched. "I'm on my way. Have you notified my team?"

"Not yet, sir."

"I'll do it. Get Dr Yardley out there. I want her team all over this."

George ended the call, already reaching for his clothes. His thoughts churned as he dressed. Another child. Another innocent life snuffed out. The bastards responsible would pay.

He dialled Tashan's number as he headed for his car. The younger detective answered on the third ring, voice thick with sleep.

"Boss?"

"Tashan, they've found a body at the farm. I'm heading there now. Meet me."

"On my way."

George navigated the early morning traffic, his hands tight on the steering wheel. His phone rang again. Tashan.

"Stuck in traffic on the M1," Tashan reported. "Accident near Junction 45. It's a bloody nightmare."

George grunted in acknowledgement. "Same here. M621's a car park."

"Any more details on the body?"

"Female child. No age yet. Buried in the grounds."

Tashan's sharp intake of breath crackled through the line. "Christ. You don't think it's one of ours, do you? Lily? Amira?" He paused. "Rosie?"

George's jaw clenched. "God, I hope not. But we can't rule anything out at this stage."

They lapsed into silence, each lost in their own grim thoughts. George's mind whirled with possibilities. Who was this child? How long had she been there? And most importantly, how did she fit into the larger puzzle they were trying to solve?

After what seemed like an eternity, George finally pulled up to Crossroads Farm. The place was a hive of activity, police tape cordoning off a large section of the grounds. SOCOs in white suits moved carefully across the area, cataloguing every detail.

George spotted Dr Lindsey Yardley near a freshly dug pit. Her face was grim as she looked up at his approach.

"George," she greeted him. "It's not good."

He nodded, steeling himself. "Show me."

Lindsey led him to the edge of the pit. George's breath caught in his throat. The body was small, too small. A child who should have been playing, laughing, living. Instead, she lay here, discarded like rubbish.

"What can you tell me?" George asked, his voice rough.

Lindsey crouched by the pit. "Female, probably between 8 and 10 years old. Caucasian. Brown hair."

George's mind raced. Not Lily, Rosie or Amira, then.

"Cause of death?"

Lindsey shook her head. "Too early to say definitively. But there are signs of blunt force trauma to the skull."

George's fists clenched at his sides. "Time of death?"

"That's the interesting part," Lindsey said. "Based on decomposition, I'd say she's only been here a few months. Maybe six at most."

George frowned. "But the farm's been abandoned for years."

"Exactly. Someone's been using this place recently."

A commotion at the farm's entrance drew George's attention. Tashan had arrived, his face set in grim determination as he ducked under the police tape.

"What have we got, sir?" he asked, joining George and Lindsey.

George filled him in quickly. Tashan's eyes darkened as he took in the scene.

"So not Lily or Amira," he said. "Who is it?"

George shrugged. "Lindsey says it's a girl. Brown hair. Older than Rosie, Lily, or Amira."

Tashan ran a hand through his hair, frustration evident in every line of his body. "So who the hell is she?"

Before George could respond, Stuart Kent approached, evidence bags in hand.

"We've got hair and tissue samples," he reported. "I'm rushing them back to the lab for DNA analysis. With any luck, we'll have an ID within 24 hours."

George nodded. "Good work, Stuart. What else have you found?"

Stuart's face tightened. "Not much yet. The grave was shallow, probably dug in a hurry. No murder weapon, no clothes, nothing to immediately identify her."

"Keep looking," George ordered. "Every blade of grass, every grain of dirt. I want to know everything about this place."

As Stuart moved off to continue his work, George turned to Tashan. "We need to widen our search. This girl might not be one of our known victims, but she's definitely connected."

Tashan nodded. "I'll head back to the station, start going through HOLMES. Check for any missing children reports in the last two years, not just in West Yorkshire but Yorkshire as a whole."

"Why two years?" George asked.

"Because she may have only been in the ground for a few months, but she could have been held captive."

George nodded. "Good work."

Tashan was already moving, phone in hand. "On it, boss. I'll call you as soon as I have anything."

As Tashan's car pulled away, George turned back to the grave. The first rays of sunrise were peeking over the horizon, casting a deceptively peaceful glow over the grim scene.

* * *

The crunch of gravel announced new arrivals. George turned, his brow furrowing as he spotted a familiar face. Isabella Wood strode towards the scene, Josh Fry close behind. Their expressions shifted from determination to shock as they took in the police presence.

Isabella's steps faltered as her eyes met George's. A mix of emotions flashed across her face—surprise, guilt, resolve.

George's jaw clenched as he approached them. "Isabella? What are you doing here?"

She straightened, squaring her shoulders. "George, I... we need to talk. Not now, but tonight. There's something I need to tell you."

George's eyes narrowed, darting between Isabella and Josh. His voice dropped, low and dangerous. "What's going on? Why are you here with Fry?"

Isabella opened her mouth to respond, but George cut her off, his voice rising. "No, I want answers now. What the hell is this?"

Josh stepped forward, hands raised placatingly. "DCI Beaumont, if I could explain—"

"Shut it, Fry," George snapped. His face contorted with fury as he glared at them both. "I want to know what you're playing at, turning up at my crime scene unannounced."

Dr Lindsey Yardley appeared at George's side, placing a gentle hand on his shoulder. "George," she said softly, "this isn't the right place or time. We have work to do here."

George's shoulders sagged slightly. He nodded, taking a deep breath. "You're right, Lindsey. Thanks."

He turned back to Josh, his voice cold and professional. "DS Fry, you're suspended from field duty until further notice. Return to Elland Road immediately and wait for me there."

CHAPTER TWENTY-EIGHT

Josh's face fell, but he nodded, knowing better than to argue.

George's gaze shifted to Isabella. The anger in his eyes was tempered now by hurt and confusion. "We'll talk tonight," he said, his tone leaving no room for argument. "For now, I need you to leave. This is my investigation, and I can't have you compromising it."

Isabella nodded, her eyes shining with unshed tears. "I understand. I'm sorry, George. I'll explain everything later, I promise."

As Isabella and Josh retreated, George watched them go, his mind whirling with questions and suspicions. But he pushed them aside, focusing on the grim task at hand. There was a dead child here, and she deserved his full attention.

* * *

DCI George Beaumont strode the corridors of Elland Road Police Station. He pushed open the door to the Missing Persons Department, scanning the room until his eyes landed on a familiar face.

"Kalani," he called out, voice tight with urgency. "I need your help."

Kalani Akana looked up from her computer, dark eyes widening at George's expression. She nodded, already clearing space on her desk. "What've we got, DCI Beaumont?"

George settled into the chair opposite her, leaning forward. "A body. Female child, found at Crossroads Farm. Brown hair, Caucasian, between 8 and 10 years old. We need to ID her, fast."

Kalani's fingers were already flying over her keyboard. "Time frame?"

"Lindsey estimates she's been dead between three and six months, though the forensic anthropologist will confirm it."

Kalani nodded, her brow furrowed in concentration. "Right. I'll start with West Yorkshire, then widen the search if we don't get any hits."

George watched as she navigated through databases, her efficiency a small comfort in the face of their grim task. Minutes ticked by, stretching into hours as they pored over missing persons reports, cross-referencing details and eliminating possibilities.

"What about this one?" Kalani asked, turning her screen towards George. "Eva Sharp, aged 9. Reported missing from Middleton thirteen months ago."

George leaned in, studying the photograph. A young girl with long brown hair and a gap-toothed smile stared back at him. His stomach clenched. Middleton again. What was happening to the place. "It could be her. What else do we know?"

Kalani pulled up the full report. "Last seen walking home from Middleton Academy Primary School. Parents divorced, lives with her mum on Newhall Garth. No history of running away, and according to teachers, a good student. The usual story—vanished without a trace."

George nodded, his mind racing. "We need to confirm it." He pulled out his phone and called Yolanda. "Can you get me everything on a missing girl named Eva Sharp? School records, medical history, the lot."

"On it," Yolanda said.

As Yolanda worked her magic, George found himself staring at Eva's photograph. Another life cut short, another family torn apart. The anger he'd been holding at bay since the morning threatened to boil over.

"Got it!" Yolanda's voice, coming through the speaker phone, cut through his dark thoughts. "I've got everything on Eva Sharp, including dental records."

George said, "Good work, Yolanda. Get it to Lindsey immediately, see if we can make a positive ID."

He went to ring off but Yolanda's voice stopped him. "Sir? There's one more thing." She hesitated, her usual confidence faltering. "The detective handling Eva's case—DI Midgley. He's... well, he's got a reputation."

George's eyebrows rose. "What kind of reputation?"

"Let's just say he's not known for his delicate touch with victims' families. Or his cooperation with other teams."

George nodded, filing the information away. "Thanks for the heads up. I'll handle Midgley."

Chapter Twenty-nine

"Tell me you've got something," George said to Dr Yardley by way of greeting.

Lindsey looked up from her microscope, her face grim. "I've got plenty, George. None of it good."

She led him to a light-box, where X-rays of the victim's skull were displayed. "Blunt force trauma to the back of the head. Massive cranial fracture. It would have been quick, at least."

George nodded, his jaw clenched. "Cause of death?"

"Almost certainly," Lindsey confirmed. "But George, there's more. The bruising patterns, the bone density... this wasn't the first time she'd been hurt."

George's fists clenched at his sides. "Abuse?"

Lindsey nodded, her eyes shadowed. "Long-term, by the looks of it. Whoever had her, they'd been hurting her for a while."

George took a deep breath, suppressing the rage that threatened to overwhelm him. "Did Yolanda send over the data?"

Lindsey picked up a freshly printed stack of documents, flipping to the dental records. Comparing them to the X-rays, her face set in concentration, she looked up after what seemed like an eternity.

"It's a match," she said softly. "Your victim is Eva Sharp."

George closed his eyes, allowing himself a moment of grief for the little girl. "Thanks, Lindsey," he said, his voice rough. "I need your full report as soon as possible."

She nodded, understanding the urgency. "You'll have it within the hour."

George left the lab, his mind racing to the next steps. He needed to inform DI Midgley and arrange for the family to be notified.

He dialled the number Tashan had given him for DI Midgley, drumming his fingers impatiently as he waited to be connected.

"DI Midgley," a gruff voice answered.

"DI Midgley, this is DCI George Beaumont. I'm calling about Eva Sharp."

There was a pause on the other end of the line. When Midgley spoke again, his voice had an edge to it. "What about her? Far as I know, that's still my case."

George took a deep breath, reminding himself to tread carefully. "We've found a body, John. At a farm just outside Leeds. We've made a positive ID. It's Eva."

The silence stretched for so long that George wondered if the call had been disconnected. Finally, Midgley spoke, his voice tight with suppressed emotion. "You're sure?"

"Dental records confirm it," George said. "I'm sorry, John. I know you've been working this case hard."

Midgley grunted, a non-committal sound. "Right. Well, I appreciate the call. I'll inform the family—"

"Actually," George cut in, "I was hoping to do that myself. Given the circumstances where we found her, there might be a connection to an ongoing investigation, and I'm SIO."

He could practically hear Midgley bristling on the other end of the line. "Now wait a minute, Beaumont. This is my case. You can't just—"

"I can and I will," George said, keeping his voice level. "It appears Eva's death is connected to other cases we're working on, and we need to handle this carefully. I'm happy to keep you in the loop every step of the way."

There was another long pause. George could almost see Midgley weighing his options, pride warring with practicality.

"Fine," Midgley said finally. "But I want to be there when you talk to the family. And I want full access to your investigation."

"Deal," George agreed, relief washing over him. "I'll send you the address. We'll meet there in an hour."

"Thanks, George."

"It's, sir, to you, DI Midgley, not George." He let the silence build for a moment before adding, "I will not be disrespected. Do I make myself clear?"

"Crystal, sir."

As he hung up, George allowed himself a moment to collect his thoughts. Notifying families was always hard, but this... this was going to be brutal.

He gathered his team, briefing them on the situation. Tashan and Priya would continue following leads at Crossroads Farm. Yolanda would dig deeper into Eva's background, looking for any connections to their other cases.

An hour later, George found himself standing on the doorstep of a block of flats on Newhall Garth in Middleton. DI Midgley stood beside him.

"You ready for this?" George asked quietly.

Midgley nodded, his jaw set. "Let's get it over with, sir."

George rang the doorbell, steeling himself for what was to come. The door opened, revealing a woman in her late thirties. Her eyes widened as she took in the two detectives on her doorstep.

"Mrs Sharp?" George asked gently. "I'm DCI George Beaumont, and this is DI John Midgley. May we come in? We need to talk to you about Eva."

Mrs Sharp's face crumpled, tears already welling in her eyes. She stepped back, wordlessly inviting them in.

As they settled in the living room, surrounded by photos of a smiling Eva, George took a deep breath. There was no easy way to do this, no words that could soften the blow they were about to deliver.

"Mrs Sharp," he began. "I'm so sorry to have to tell you this, but we've found Eva. She... she's no longer with us."

The wail that tore from Mrs Sharp's throat would haunt George for years to come. He watched, helpless, as she collapsed into sobs, her entire world shattering around her.

Midgley moved to comfort her, his earlier brusqueness replaced by a surprising gentleness. George hung back, giving them space. His eyes roamed the room, taking in the details of Eva's life. School awards on the mantelpiece. A half-finished art project on the coffee table, despite her missing for just over a year. The trappings of a childhood cut tragically short.

When Mrs Sharp's sobs had subsided to quiet weeping, George spoke again. "I know this is incredibly difficult, Mrs Sharp. But if you feel up to it, we need to ask you some questions. It might help us find who did this to Eva."

She looked up at him, her eyes red-rimmed and haunted. "You mean... it wasn't an accident?"

George shook his head, hating himself for having to cause

her more pain. "No, Mrs Sharp. We believe Eva was murdered."

Fresh tears spilt down her cheeks, but there was a new determination in her gaze. "What do you need to know?"

George settled into the armchair, his notepad balanced on his knee. "Mrs Sharp, I know this is difficult, but can you tell us about Eva's routine? What was a typical day like for her?"

Mrs Sharp took a shaky breath, her hands twisting in her lap. "She... she'd get up around seven. I'd make her breakfast—Weetabix, always Weetabix. Then she'd walk to school with her friend Gemma from next door."

"And after school?" Midgley prompted gently.

"Usually straight home. She had piano lessons on Tuesdays, swimming on Thursdays." Mrs Sharp's voice cracked. "She loved the water."

George nodded, scribbling notes.

Looking around, John asked, "How did you afford all of that?"

"Why do you think we live this way, detective?"

John nodded, embarrassed, and George asked, "Did Eva ever mention anyone new in her life? Someone who made her uncomfortable, perhaps?"

Mrs Sharp frowned, thinking. "There was... oh, what was his name? A new teaching assistant at her school. Eva said he was creepy."

"Do you remember anything else about him?" George pressed.

"Not much. Eva said he stared too much. Made her skin crawl, she said."

Midgley leaned forward. "Mrs Sharp, what about Eva's father? What's your relationship like with him?"

A flash of anger crossed Mrs Sharp's face. "James? He's useless. Barely sees Eva. Always too busy with his new family."

George made a note to follow up on the father. "Anyone else in Eva's life we should know about? Family friends, neighbours?"

Mrs Sharp shook her head. "No one... wait. There was a woman. I saw her talking to Eva outside the school gates a few times."

George's pen paused. "Can you describe her?"

"Youngish. Dark hair. Pretty, I suppose. I thought she might be a new mum at the school, a dinner lady, maybe, but Eva said she didn't know her."

George and Midgley exchanged a glance. The description was eerily familiar.

"Mrs Sharp, can you tell us about the day Eva went missing? What was different about that day?"

Mrs Sharp's eyes grew distant, reliving the memory. "It was a Tuesday. I remember because she should have had piano lessons, but her teacher was ill."

"So her routine was different that day?" George prompted.

Mrs Sharp nodded. "Yes. Usually, I'd pick her up after piano, but since it was cancelled, she was meant to come straight home."

George made a note. "Was it usual for Eva to walk home alone?"

"No," Mrs Sharp said, shaking her head emphatically. "Never. She always walked with Gemma or I'd pick her up. But that day..."

"What was different that day?" Midgley interjected.

Mrs Sharp's voice wavered. "I had a doctor's appointment.

271

I couldn't reschedule. I told Eva to wait at school, that I'd be there as soon as I could."

George's brow furrowed. "And the school was OK with her waiting?"

"They said they would be," Mrs Sharp replied, a note of bitterness creeping into her voice. "But when I got there, they told me she'd already left."

"Left?" George repeated. "On her own?"

Mrs Sharp nodded, tears welling in her eyes. "They said she insisted she was old enough to walk home alone. That lots of kids her age did it."

George exchanged a glance with Midgley. "Mrs Sharp, in your opinion, was Eva the type to insist on walking home alone?"

She shook her head vehemently. "No. Never. She was always so careful, so... aware of dangers. It wasn't like her at all."

George made another note. "And what time was this? When did the school say she left?"

"Around 3.30," Mrs Sharp said. "I got there at 4.15. They said she'd been gone for about 45 minutes." She burst into tears. "Bloody stupid doctors were behind as usual."

"And when did you report her missing?" Midgley asked.

"As soon as I got home and she wasn't there," Mrs Sharp replied, her voice breaking. "I called all her friends, checked the park. When she still hadn't turned up by 6, I called the police."

George nodded, his mind piecing together the timeline. "One last question, Mrs Sharp. Did Eva have a mobile phone?"

Mrs Sharp shook her head. "No. We'd been talking about getting her one for her next birthday, but..." She trailed off, unable to finish the thought.

George closed his notebook, offering Mrs Sharp a sympa-thetic smile. "Thank you, Mrs Sharp." The information meant he couldn't shake the feeling that Eva's disappearance had been meticulously planned. Someone had known her routine, known it would be disrupted that day. And they had taken advantage of it in the worst possible way.

"One last thing, Mrs Sharp," George said gently. "Did Eva ever mention anything about a farm? Or show any interest in farming?"

Mrs Sharp looked confused. "A farm? No, never. Why?"

George shook his head. "Just covering all bases. Thank you, Mrs Sharp. You've been incredibly helpful."

As they wrapped up the interview, George's mind was racing. The teaching assistant, the mysterious woman, the seemingly absent father—each a potential lead to follow.

"We'll be in touch if we need anything else," he told Mrs Sharp. "And please, if you remember anything else, no matter how small it seems, call us immediately."

As they prepared to leave, Mrs Sharp caught George's arm. "You'll find them, won't you?" she asked, her voice barely above a whisper. "The person who took my baby?"

George met her gaze, his own resolve hardening. "We'll do everything in our power, Mrs Sharp. I promise you, we won't rest until we bring Eva's killer to justice."

Outside, the sun was setting, casting long shadows across the quiet suburban street. George and Midgley stood in silence for a moment, each lost in their own thoughts.

"What now?" Midgley asked finally. "Sir."

George's jaw set, his eyes fixed on the horizon. "Now we do our jobs, John. We follow every lead, turn over every stone.

273

And we don't stop until we find the bastard who did this."

Chapter Thirty

George Beaumont pushed through the doors of the primary school, his mind a whirlwind of questions and suspicions. The familiar smell of school food and disinfectant hit him, a stark contrast to the grim scenes he'd witnessed earlier.

As he approached the office, a flash of movement caught his eye. Abbie Illingworth was just leaving, her face lighting up with surprise when she saw him.

"George," she said, her voice soft with concern. "Are you alright?"

He shook his head, unable to find the words. The urge to confide in her, to share the burden of the investigation, was almost overwhelming. But professionalism won out.

"I'm here to see the head," he managed, his voice gruffer than he intended.

Abbie nodded, understanding in her eyes. She reached out, squeezing his hand briefly. The touch sent a jolt through him, a moment of warmth in the cold reality of the day.

"If you need anything..." she started, but was cut off by the receptionist's voice.

"DCI Beaumont? Mrs Gledhill will see you now."

The moment shattered, Abbie gave him a small smile before slipping out the door. George watched her go, a mix of emotions churning in his gut.

Mrs Gledhill's office was as he remembered it, neat and impersonal. She greeted him with a tight smile, gesturing for him to sit.

"What can I do for you, DCI Beaumont?"

George leaned forward, cutting straight to the chase. "I need information about Eva Sharp. She was a student here."

Mrs Gledhill's face fell. "Ah, yes. Poor Eva. A tragedy." She paused. "Wait, does this mean you've found her? After all this time?"

George nodded. "Who was her teacher?" George asked, watching her reactions closely.

"That would have been Miss Illingworth," Mrs Gledhill replied. "Before she moved to nursery this current academic year."

George's heart skipped a beat. Abbie. Of course it was Abbie. He pushed down the surge of conflicting emotions, focusing on the task at hand.

"And there was a male teaching assistant? Eva had mentioned him to her mother."

Mrs Gledhill's brow furrowed. "You must mean Mr Siddiqui. He's no longer with us, I'm afraid."

"Why not?"

She shifted uncomfortably. "There were... concerns. Nothing concrete, but we felt it best to part ways."

George's eyes narrowed. "I'll need his address. And Miss Illingworth's, for the record."

Mrs Gledhill hesitated. "I'm not sure I can—"

"This is a murder investigation," George cut in, his voice hard. "I can come back with a warrant if I have to."

She capitulated, scribbling the addresses on a piece of paper.

George took it, and headed to his Merc.

Back in his car, he dialled the Incident Room. Tashan answered on the second ring.

"Boss?"

"Tashan, meet me at Bidder Drive, East Ardsley." He provided the number. "It's Abbie Illingworth's address."

There was a pause on the other end of the line. "Abbie? The teacher? What's she got to do with this?"

George sighed, rubbing his temples. "She was Eva's teacher. And Dania's. And Rosie's."

"Christ," Tashan muttered. "You don't think..."

"I don't know what to think," George admitted. "But we need to talk to her. And Tashan? Get Yolanda to run background checks on Abbie and a Mr Siddiqui, former teaching assistant at the school."

As he hung up, George couldn't shake the growing unease in his gut. Three children, all connected to Abbie. It couldn't be coincidence. Could it?

But another part of him, the part that had been drawn to Abbie's warmth and understanding, rebelled against the suspicion. He thought of her gentle touch, her concerned eyes. How could someone like that be involved in something so horrific?

And beneath it all, the anger at Isabella simmered. The secrets, the lies by omission. It all tangled together in his mind, a knot of personal and professional complications he couldn't seem to unravel.

George started the car.

As he pulled away from the school, George couldn't shake the feeling that he was driving towards a reckoning. One that would change everything, for better or for worse.

* * *

George Beaumont's knuckles whitened on the steering wheel as he pulled up to Abbie Illingworth's house. Tashan sat beside him, his face a mask of professional detachment.

"Remember," George said, his voice tight, "we're here as investigators. Nothing more."

Tashan nodded, his eyes sharp. "Understood, sir."

They approached the front door. George rang the bell, steeling himself for what was to come.

Abbie answered, her smile faltering as she took in their grim expressions. "George? What's going on?"

"Miss Illingworth," George said, forcing his voice into professional neutrality. "We need to ask you some questions. May we come in?"

Confusion and hurt flashed across Abbie's face at his formal tone. She stepped back, wordlessly inviting them inside.

The living room was as George remembered it, warm and inviting. But now it felt different, tainted by suspicion and duty. He deliberately chose a chair opposite Abbie, rather than beside her as he had before.

"What's this about?" Abbie asked, her eyes darting between them.

George leaned forward, his elbows on his knees. "We're investigating the disappearance of Eva Sharp. We understand you were her teacher."

Abbie's face paled. "Eva? Do you have news?"

"We've found her body," Tashan said bluntly. "We believe she was murdered."

Abbie's hand flew to her mouth, a choked sob escaping. "Oh God. No. Not Eva."

George watched her reaction closely, searching for any sign of deception. But all he saw was genuine grief and shock.

"Miss Illingworth," he pressed, "can you tell us about Eva? What was she like as a student?"

Abbie took a shaky breath, visibly pulling herself together. "She was... she was brilliant. Bright, curious. Always asking questions, always wanting to learn more."

"Did you notice any changes in her behaviour before she disappeared?" Tashan asked.

Abbie frowned, thinking. "Not really. She was her usual self. Happy, engaged."

George made a note, his pen scratching against paper. "What about outside of school? Did you ever see Eva with anyone unusual? Someone who didn't seem to belong?"

Abbie shook her head. "No, never. Eva's mum always picked her up, or she'd walk home with her friend Gemma."

"Always?" Tashan pressed. "There were never any exceptions?"

"Always."

Tashan leaned forward, his eyes intent. "Miss Illingworth, tell us about Mr Siddiqui?"

Abbie's expression shifted, a flicker of... something passing across her face. "I don't know what to tell you; I only worked with him briefly. Why?"

"Even little details help," George prompted.

Abbie shrugged. "There's not much to tell. He was... odd. The kids didn't like him much. He left quite suddenly, if I remember correctly."

George made another note. "Did you ever see Mr Siddiqui interacting with Eva? Or any of the other children who've gone missing?"

Abbie's eyes widened. "What do you mean? Dania and Rosie weren't at the school last year."

Tashan leaned in, his voice gentler than George had ever heard it. "Miss Illingworth, I'm going to tell you something, and I need you to listen carefully."

Abbie nodded, her face a mask of confusion and growing dread.

Tashan took a deep breath. "When I was a kid, my best friend went missing. For weeks, we searched. Put up posters, knocked on doors. But nothing. Then one day, they found him. He'd been... he'd been murdered."

Abbie gasped, her hand flying to her mouth. "I'm so sorry. That must have been awful."

Tashan nodded, his eyes never leaving Abbie's face. "It was. But you know what the worst part was? Finding out later that someone had seen something. A neighbour who'd spotted a strange car, but didn't think it was important enough to mention."

He leaned forward. "So I'm asking you now, Miss Illingworth. Is there anything, anything at all, you might have seen or heard that could help us? Even if it seems small or unimportant?"

Abbie's face crumpled, tears welling in her eyes. "I... I did see something. But I didn't think... I didn't want to believe..."

George's pulse quickened. "What did you see, Abbie?"

She took a shaky breath. "Mr Siddiqui. I saw him talking to Eva once, after school. He was... he was touching her hair. It made me uncomfortable, but when I approached, he acted like nothing was wrong."

George's jaw clenched. "Why didn't you report this?"

Abbie shook her head, tears spilling down her cheeks. "I

told Mrs Gledhill. She said she'd handle it. The next day, Mr Siddiqui was gone. I thought... I thought it was over."

George and Tashan exchanged a look. This was the break they'd been waiting for.

"Thank you, Miss Illingworth," George said, his voice softer now. "You've been very helpful."

Abbie nodded, wiping her eyes. "I'm so sorry. If I'd known... if I'd said something sooner..."

Tashan shook his head. "You can't blame yourself. The only person responsible is the one who took these children."

George stood, signalling the end of the interview. "We may need to speak with you again. Please don't leave town without informing us."

Abbie nodded, her eyes red-rimmed but determined. "Of course. Anything I can do to help."

As they headed for the door, Abbie called out. "George?"

He turned, one hand on the doorknob. "Yes?"

"When this is all over..." she hesitated, biting her lip. "Maybe we could grab a coffee? Talk about something other than missing children?"

George felt a pang in his chest, guilt and temptation warring within him. "I... we'll see," he managed, before hurrying out into the fading daylight.

On the way to their cars, Tashan raised an eyebrow. "Coffee, sir?"

George grunted, opening the door. "Focus on the case, Tashan. We need to interview the teaching assistant next. Let's not lose sight of what matters here."

Tashan said, "Sir, about what happened back there..."

George glanced at him. "I said to focus on the case, DS Blackburn."

"No, I meant the story I shared."

George nodded, a wave of relief washing over him. "You mean your story about your friend?"

Tashan nodded. "Yeah. I... I hope you don't mind that I shared that. I know it's not standard procedure."

George shook his head. "It was good work, Tashan. Sometimes a personal touch can get results where official questioning fails."

A small smile tugged at Tashan's lips. "Thanks, boss. I've been trying to... well, to be more than just the muscle, you know?"

George nodded, a surge of pride warming his chest. Tashan had come a long way since joining his team. "You're doing well, Tashan. Keep it up."

As he pulled away from the kerb, George wound his window down. "I'll meet you there, Tashan."

"OK, boss."

George's phone buzzed in his pocket. Isabella's name flashed on the dash-screen. He hesitated for a moment, then hit decline. Whatever was going on in his personal life, it would have to wait. Right now, there were missing children out there.

Tashan watched him, his expression unreadable. "You alright, boss?"

George nodded curtly. "Fine. Let's focus on Siddiqui. You got his address?"

As Tashan confirmed the details, George's mind raced. The connection between Siddiqui and Eva was troubling, but it didn't explain the other missing children. Or the woman with the mole. There were still too many pieces missing from this puzzle.

As he neared Siddiqui's address, George's focus sharpened. Whatever personal complications were swirling around him—Isabella's secrets, his conflicted feelings for Abbie—they had to take a backseat. Right now, there was a potential child predator to question and missing children to find.

* * *

"Remember," George said as they met outside Siddiqui's house, "this guy's smart. He managed to get a job working with kids despite whatever red flags there might have been. Stay sharp."

Tashan nodded. "Got it, boss."

They approached the front door. George rang the bell, his other hand resting near his warrant card.

The door swung open, revealing a man in his late thirties. George's breath caught in his throat. The face staring back at them was far from unremarkable—it was the same face they'd been studying on grainy CCTV footage for days. The face they'd assumed belonged to Bilal Bhati.

"Mr Siddiqui?" George asked, his voice hard, fighting to keep his surprise in check. "DCI Beaumont. This is DS Blackburn. We need to ask you some questions about your time at Middleton Academy Primary School."

Siddiqui's face remained impassive, but George caught the slight tightening around his eyes. Fear? Guilt? Or simply surprise at unexpected visitors?

"Of course," Siddiqui said, his voice carefully neutral. "Please, come in."

Chapter Thirty-one

George exchanged a quick glance with Tashan as they stepped inside. The living room was sparsely furnished, almost impersonal. No photos, no personal touches. It set George's teeth on edge.

"Take a seat," Siddiqui offered, gesturing to a worn sofa.

George remained standing. "We'll keep this brief, Mr Siddiqui. First, can you confirm your full name and occupation?"

"Samuel Siddiqui. I'm currently between jobs."

George nodded, his mind racing. "And before that? You worked at Middleton Academy, correct?"

Siddiqui shifted slightly. "Yes, as a teaching assistant."

"Why did you leave?" Tashan asked, his tone deceptively casual.

Siddiqui shrugged. "It wasn't a good fit. I decided to pursue other opportunities last June."

George's eyes narrowed. "Mr Siddiqui, we're investigating the disappearance and murder of several children. Some of whom attended Middleton Academy while you were working there."

Siddiqui's face paled slightly, but his voice remained steady. "That's... that's terrible. But I don't see how I can help."

"Let's start with Eva Sharp," George pressed. "You knew

her, correct?"

Siddiqui nodded slowly. "Yes, she was in Miss Illingworth's class. Bright girl."

"And what about Dania Bhati? Rosie Kershaw?"

Siddiqui shook his head. "I don't recall those names. There were many children at the school."

George leaned in. "What about Bilal Bhati? Does that name ring any bells?"

"No, I'm sorry. I don't know any child by that name."

George's frustration mounted. "Bilal Bhati is not a child but a person of interest in our investigation."

Samuel narrowed his eyes. "OK."

He pulled out a photo of Nadia Shah, sliding it across the coffee table. "How about her? Nadia Shah. Ever met her?"

Siddiqui's reaction was subtle, but unmistakable. A flicker of recognition, quickly suppressed. "I... I'm not sure. She looks vaguely familiar, but I can't place her."

Tashan stepped in, his voice deceptively calm. "Mr Siddiqui, we have CCTV footage of a man matching your description driving a white van near the locations where several children disappeared. Can you explain that?"

Siddiqui's composure cracked slightly. "I... I don't own a van. You must be mistaken."

George pressed harder. "What about Lily Chen? Thomas Wilkes? Amira Khan? Any of those names mean anything to you?"

Siddiqui shook his head vehemently. "No, I've never heard of them. Look, I don't know what you think I've done, but you're wrong."

George stood, looming over Siddiqui. "We think you're lying, Mr Siddiqui. We think you know a lot more than you're letting on. About the children, about Nadia Shah, about all of it."

Siddiqui's eyes darted between George and Tashan, panic creeping into his voice. "I'm not lying. I swear, I don't know anything about missing children or murders."

Tashan leaned in. "Then explain the van. Explain why you look exactly like the man we've been hunting."

"No doubt the CCTV is blurry, and I have dark hair and a dark beard." Sammy paused. "No doubt you're after a Pakistani man." He narrowed his eyes again. "We all look the same to you."

Tashan's jaw clenched, his eyes flashing with barely contained anger. "Don't try to make this about race, Mr Siddiqui. We're not here because of your ethnicity. We're here because evidence puts a man matching your description at multiple crime scenes."

George stepped in, his voice calm but firm. "We deal in facts, Mr Siddiqui. What we know is this: a man who looks remarkably like you was seen in a white van near locations where children disappeared. Three children have gone missing from a school you worked at. And you knew one of the girls personally. That's not racial profiling. That's following leads."

Siddiqui's shoulders slumped, the fight draining out of him. He looked between the two detectives, seeing the unwavering determination in their eyes.

"We're not here to persecute you," Tashan added, his tone softening slightly. "We're trying to find missing children. If you're innocent, help us understand why you match our suspect's description so closely."

The silence stretched for a long moment, tension thick in

the air. Finally, Siddiqui said, "Coincidence."

"My team is in the process of looking into you, Mr Siddiqui," George said, "so it's better for you to tell me the truth about everything now before one of my team members finds something I'll have to come back for."

Siddiqui's resolve finally crumbled. "OK, OK. I... I did know Nadia. We were in a relationship, briefly. But I swear, I didn't know anything about missing children. She never mentioned anything like that."

George's pulse quickened. "When was this relationship? And why did it end?"

"About a year ago," Siddiqui said, his voice shaky. "It lasted a few months. She ended it suddenly, saying she had to leave for Dubai for work. I never heard from her again."

George and Tashan exchanged glances. This was the first solid connection they'd found between Nadia Shah and someone in Leeds.

"Mr Siddiqui," George said, his voice hard, "I'm going to need you to come down to the station with us. We have a lot more questions, and I think it's in your best interest to answer them fully and honestly."

Siddiqui nodded, defeated. "I'll cooperate. But I swear, I don't know anything about these missing children."

As they led Siddiqui out to Tashan's car, George's thoughts churned. They'd assumed the man in the CCTV was Bilal Bhati, but now... Now the whole case had shifted. Siddiqui's connection to Nadia Shah, his presence at the school, his resemblance to their suspect—it all pointed to something bigger, more complex than they'd imagined.

George's phone buzzed in his pocket. Isabella's name flashed on the screen again. He hesitated, then hit decline.

Whatever was going on in his personal life, it would have to wait. They finally had a solid lead, and he wasn't about to let it slip away.

As they drove back to the station, George couldn't shake the feeling that they were on the verge of cracking this case wide open. But with each new piece of information, the picture became more twisted, more disturbing. What kind of monster were they really dealing with?

One thing was certain—they were closer than ever to finding out.

* * *

George Beaumont tightened his hands on the steering wheel as he and Tashan pulled up to the address in Halton. The sun hung low in the sky, casting long shadows across the quiet suburban street.

"You ready for this?" George asked, glancing at his partner.

Tashan nodded grimly. "Never gets easier, does it? Telling a parent their child is dead."

They approached the front door. George rang the bell, steeling himself for what was to come.

The door swung open, revealing a man in his early forties. James Sharp's eyes widened as he took in their serious expressions.

"Mr Sharp?" George asked, his voice gentle but firm. "I'm DCI George Beaumont, and this is DS Tashan Blackburn. May we come in? We need to speak with you about Eva."

James's face paled, but he stepped back, wordlessly inviting them inside. In the living room, a blonde woman in her late twenties—presumably Sophie, James's new wife—looked up from a magazine, her expression shifting from curiosity to concern.

"What's this about?" James asked, his voice tight with barely contained panic.

George took a deep breath. There was no easy way to do this. "Mr Sharp, I'm very sorry to have to tell you this, but we've found Eva. She... she's no longer with us."

The silence that followed was deafening. Then, as if a dam had burst, James let out a strangled cry, collapsing onto the sofa. Sophie rushed to his side, her own face a mask of shock and grief.

"No," James moaned, his voice muffled by his hands. "No, not my little girl. Not Eva."

George and Tashan stood silently, allowing the couple a moment to absorb the devastating news. When James finally looked up, his eyes were red-rimmed and haunted.

"How?" he asked, his voice barely above a whisper.

"We're still investigating the exact circumstances," George said carefully. "But we believe Eva was murdered."

Sophie gasped, her hand flying to her mouth. James's face hardened, grief giving way to anger.

"Who?" he demanded. "Who did this to my daughter?"

Tashan stepped forward, his voice gentle but firm. "That's what we're trying to find out, Mr Sharp. And we need your help. Can you think of anyone who might have wanted to hurt Eva?"

James shook his head vehemently. "No, never. Everyone loved Eva. She was... she was perfect."

George nodded sympathetically. "We understand this is difficult, but we need to ask you some questions. Is there anyone new in Eva's life? Someone who might have shown an unusual interest in her?"

James and Sophie exchanged glances, both shaking their heads. "No one," Sophie said. "Eva was always with us or her mother."

George pressed on, his instincts telling him they were missing something. "What about a man named Bilal Bhati? Or Samuel Siddiqui? Do either of those names mean anything to you?"

James frowned, shaking his head. "No, I've never heard of them. Who are they?"

"They're persons of interest in our investigation," Tashan explained. "What about a woman named Nadia Shah? Does that name ring any bells?"

James's reaction was subtle, but George caught it—a slight stiffening of his shoulders, a flicker in his eyes.

"Nadia?" James repeated, his voice carefully neutral. "I'm not sure. It sounds vaguely familiar, but I can't place it." He turned to his wife. "Sophie, love, would you mind making some tea for the detectives?"

Sophie nodded, rising to her feet. As she left the room, George's eyes narrowed. He pulled out his phone, bringing up a photo of Nadia.

"Mr Sharp," he said. "I'm going to show you a picture. I need you to be completely honest with me. Have you seen this woman before?"

He held out the phone, watching James's face carefully. The man's expression crumbled, a mix of guilt and fear washing over him.

"I... yes," James admitted, his voice barely above a whisper. "I know her. We... we were seeing each other last year. Around the time Eva went missing."

Tashan leaned forward, his voice sharp. "And you didn't think to mention this earlier?"

James's eyes darted towards the kitchen, where they could hear Sophie moving about. "It was a mistake. A stupid, brief affair. I was... I was seeing Sophie at the same time. I ended it with Nadia when things got serious with Sophie."

George's thoughts spiralled, connecting dots he hadn't seen before. "Mr Sharp, we need Nadia's contact information. A phone number, an address, anything you can give us."

James nodded, reaching for a notepad on the coffee table. His hand shook slightly as he scribbled down a number and address from memory. "This is the mobile number she used. And this was her address, though I never actually went there."

George took the paper, his eyes widening slightly as he recognised the Middleton address—the same one they'd found abandoned earlier. But the mobile number was new.

"Thank you, Mr Sharp," he said, his voice tight with barely contained excitement. "This could be crucial to our investigation."

As Sophie returned with the tea tray, George and Tashan stood. "We appreciate your time," George said, pulling out a business card. "If you remember anything else, anything at all, please don't hesitate to call."

Outside, the cool evening air did little to calm George's racing thoughts. They had a new lead—a direct connection between Nadia Shah and Eva's family.

"We need to track that number," Tashan said, voicing George's thoughts. "It could lead us straight to her."

George nodded grimly. "You're right. And I know exactly who to call."

He pulled out his phone, his jaw clenching as he dialled a

familiar number. On the third ring, a voice answered.

"DS Fry."

"Josh," George said, pushing down his personal feelings. "I need you to track a mobile number. It's urgent."

There was a pause on the other end of the line. "Of course, sir. What's the number?"

George rattled off the digits, his foot tapping impatiently against the pavement. "This is top priority, Fry. I want updates every hour, even if you've got nothing. Understand?"

"Yes, sir," Josh replied, his voice professional despite the tension between them. "I'll get right on it."

As George hung up, he couldn't shake the feeling that they were on the verge of a breakthrough. Nadia Shah was the key to this whole twisted puzzle, and now they had a direct line to her.

"What now, boss?" Tashan asked, watching him closely.

George's eyes hardened with determination. "Now we wait. And we prepare. Because when we find Nadia Shah, we're going to need every resource at our disposal to bring her in."

Chapter Thirty-two

George Beaumont sat at his desk, paperwork strewn across the surface, when his phone buzzed. Abbie's name flashed on the screen, sending a jolt through his stomach.

"Abbie?" he answered, his voice carefully neutral.

"George," she said, her tone warm. "I was wondering if you'd like to come over for a drink. A chat. No work talk, I promise."

He hesitated, guilt and temptation warring within him. He shouldn't. He knew he shouldn't. But the pull was undeniable.

"I... alright," he found himself saying. "I'll be there in twenty."

The drive to East Ardsley was a blur of streetlights and inner turmoil. Was this lust? Suspicion? Or something deeper, more dangerous?

Abbie answered the door with a smile that made his heart skip. "Come in," she said, ushering him inside. "I've opened a bottle of red."

The evening unfolded with an ease that surprised him. They talked about books, films, life beyond the confines of their jobs. George found himself relaxing.

As the teacher drank more wine and George drank tea, Abbie's expression grew serious. "George," she said softly, "there's something I want to tell you—something I haven't shared with many people."

He leaned in, intrigued. "What is it?"

Abbie took a deep breath. "When I was a child, I... I was abused. Neglected. My parents, they weren't fit to raise a child."

George's heart clenched. "Abbie, I'm so sorry."

She shook her head. "Don't be. It's why I became a teacher. I had a social worker, you see. A great foster mother. And an incredible teacher. They saved me. Gave me a chance at a real life."

Understanding dawned on George. "And now you want to do the same for other children."

Abbie nodded, her eyes shining. "Exactly. It's why these cases hit so hard. I see myself in every child we fail to protect."

In that moment, George's suspicions evaporated. He saw Abbie for who she truly was—a survivor, a protector, a beacon of hope in a world too often shrouded in darkness.

"You're incredible," he murmured, reaching for her hand.

Abbie's fingers intertwined with his. "So are you, George. The way you fight for these children... it's inspiring."

The air between them charged with electricity. George found himself leaning in, drawn by an irresistible force. Abbie's eyes fluttered closed, her lips parting slightly.

Just as their lips were about to meet, George's phone shattered the moment. He jerked back, fumbling for the device.

"Beaumont," he answered, his voice rough.

"Sir, it's Fry," came the response. "We've traced the number. It's registered to a house in Morley, under the name Nadezhda Shah. It's the traditional form of Nadia."

George's heart raced. "Text me the address. I'm on my

way."

He turned to Abbie, apology written across his face. "I'm sorry, I have to go. It's—"

"The case," she finished for him. "I understand. Go. Do what you do best."

He hesitated for a moment, torn between duty and desire. Then, with a quick squeeze of her hand, he was gone.

In the car, George's mind whirled. The near-kiss with Abbie, the breakthrough in the case—it all blurred together in a dizzying cocktail of emotion and adrenaline.

He dialled Tashan's number as he sped towards Morley. "Tashan, we've got a location on Nadia Shah. I need you to organise a raid. Full tactical support. Meet me at the address I'm sending you."

"On it, boss," Tashan replied, his voice taut with anticipation.

As George navigated the darkened streets, his resolve hardened. They were close. So close to cracking this case wide open. Whatever his personal complications—Isabella, Abbie, the turmoil of his own heart—they had to take a backseat.

Right now, there were children to save and a monster to catch.

* * *

The night air crackled with tension as George Beaumont surveyed the quiet Morley street. His team was in position, a well-oiled machine poised to strike. PS Greenwood's squad had the perimeter locked down. Tashan and Yolanda flanked him, eyes sharp and focused.

George's radio crackled. "AFO team in position, sir."

He nodded, adrenaline surging through his veins. "Right. Let's go over the health and safety one last time."

Tashan stepped forward. "Team's fully briefed, sir. Non-lethal weapons only. We've got ambulance support on standby. All officers are wearing stab vests."

George nodded, his mind racing through countless scenarios. "Good. Remember, we don't know what we're walking into. Stay alert, stay safe."

He took a deep breath, steeling himself for what was to come. "Alright. On my mark."

The seconds ticked by, each one an eternity. Then, with a sharp nod from George, the world exploded into action.

The AFO team surged forward, the Big Red Key making short work of the front door. It splintered inward with a thunderous crack.

"Police! Nobody move!" The shout echoed through the house as officers poured in, fanning out with practised precision.

George followed, heart pounding. The acrid smell of fear and surprise hung in the air. Room after room, cleared with military efficiency.

Then, from upstairs, a shout. "Target acquired! Bedroom, second floor!"

George took the stairs two at a time, Tashan hot on his heels. He burst into the bedroom, eyes locking onto the figure huddled in the corner.

Nadia Shah. The woman they'd been hunting. She looked smaller somehow, more vulnerable than her photos suggested. But her eyes... they burned with a cold intelligence that sent a chill down George's spine.

"Nadia Shah," he said, his voice hard. "You're under arrest

for—"

A commotion from outside cut him off. George's radio crackled to life. "Sir! We've got a situation out here!"

He hesitated, torn between securing Nadia and investigating the new development. "Tashan, stay with her. Don't let her out of your sight."

George raced downstairs and out onto the street. The scene that greeted him was chaos. A white van was tearing down the road, PS Greenwood's team in hot pursuit.

"What the hell is going on?" George demanded.

A breathless constable skidded to a stop beside him. "Van showed up, sir. Driver spotted us and bolted."

George's mind raced. The white van. The one they'd been looking for all this time. "After them!" he barked. "Do not let that van get away!"

He sprinted to his car, engine roaring to life. The chase was on, streetlights blurring as he pushed the vehicle to its limits.

Ahead, he could see Greenwood's team closing in. The van weaved erratically, desperation evident in every move. Then, with a screech of tires, it skidded around a corner.

George's heart leapt into his throat as he rounded the bend. The van had hit a lamppost, crumpled bonnet smoking. Greenwood's officers swarmed the vehicle, dragging the driver out.

He slammed on the brakes, leaping out before the car had fully stopped. As he approached, recognition dawned on him. "Samuel Siddiqui," he breathed, a mixture of triumph and disbelief in his voice.

Siddiqui's face was a mask of defiance and fear as George approached. The former teaching assistant's eyes darted between George and the officers surrounding him, panic evident in every twitching muscle.

"It's over, Siddiqui," George said. "We've got Nadia. We've got you. Your only chance now is to cooperate."

Siddiqui's jaw clenched, a bead of sweat trickling down his temple. His silence spoke volumes.

George leaned in closer, his voice barely above a whisper. "Where are the children, Samuel? Where have you taken them?"

For a moment, something flickered in Siddiqui's eyes—regret? fear?—but it was quickly replaced by steely resolve.

"Fine," George spat, frustration boiling over. "Have it your way." He straightened, addressing the nearest officer. "Arrest him. Multiple counts of child abduction, for starters. I've got a feeling the charges are going to stack up pretty quickly."

As Siddiqui was cuffed and led to a waiting squad car, George felt a mix of triumph and unease. They'd captured a key player, but the game was far from over.

He turned to PS Greenwood, who was overseeing the securing of the van. "This vehicle is our best lead. Once Kent arrives, I want it gone over with a fine-tooth comb. Every inch, inside and out. If there's so much as a stray hair in there, I want to know about it."

Greenwood nodded, already barking orders to his team.

George's phone buzzed. Tashan. "Boss, we've got Nadia secured. She's not talking either."

"Bring her in," George ordered. "I'll meet you at the station. And Tashan? Good work tonight."

As he climbed back into his car, following the squad car carrying Siddiqui, George's mind whirled. They'd captured Nadia Shah and her accomplice. It should have felt like a complete victory. But something nagged at him, a persistent doubt he couldn't shake.

How deep did this conspiracy go? Was Siddiqui really the mastermind, or just another pawn in a larger game? And most importantly, where were the missing children?

George gripped the steering wheel tighter, determination setting his jaw. They had Siddiqui and Nadia. One way or another, he'd make them talk. The children's lives depended on it.

* * *

George Beaumont stood outside the interview room, his hand on the door handle. He took a deep breath, steeling himself for what lay ahead. Nadia Shah sat on the other side of that door—the key to unlocking this entire twisted case.

He pushed the door open, striding in with a purposeful gait. Nadia looked up, her eyes cold and calculating. George settled into the chair opposite her, letting the silence stretch between them.

"Nadia Shah," he said finally, his voice level. "You've been a hard woman to find."

She said nothing, her face a mask of indifference.

George leaned forward. "We know about the children, Nadia. We know you were involved in their disappearances. The question now is, how deeply?"

A flicker of something—fear? regret?—passed across Nadia's face. But when she spoke, her voice was steady. "You don't understand. I never wanted to hurt them."

"Then explain it to me," George pressed. "Make me understand."

Nadia's eyes darted to the two-way mirror, then back to

George. "It wasn't me. It was him. The man with the van. He... he made me do it."

George's eyebrows rose. "Made you? How?"

"He threatened me," Nadia said, her voice dropping to a whisper. "Said he'd hurt my family if I didn't help him."

George sat back, studying her face. "And you expect me to believe that? That you had no choice but to help abduct innocent children?"

Nadia's composure cracked slightly. "You don't know what he's capable of. The things he's done..."

"Then tell me everything about him," George urged.

Nadia shook her head vehemently. "I can't. He'll kill me."

George leaned in, his voice softening. "Nadia, listen to me. We can protect you. But you have to help us. Those children— they're out there somewhere, scared and alone. You can help us bring them home."

Doubt flickered in Nadia's eyes. "How do I know I can trust you?"

"Because right now, I'm your only hope," George said bluntly. "You're looking at multiple life sentences, Nadia. But if you cooperate, if you help us find those children and bring down the man responsible... I can talk to the CPS. Make sure they take your assistance into account."

Nadia's eyes widened slightly. "You'd do that?"

George nodded slowly. "If you tell us everything. Starting with the location of the children."

Nadia bit her lip, indecision written across her face. "I... I don't know if I can."

"You can," George pressed. "Think about those children, Nadia. Think about their families. You have a chance to make this right."

Nadia's resolve wavered, a battle playing out behind her eyes. "If I tell you... you swear you'll protect me?"

George held her gaze steadily. "You have my word. But I need the truth, Nadia. All of it."

She took a deep, shuddering breath. "Alright. I'll tell you."

Chapter Thirty-three

Isabella Wood sat at her dining room table, papers spread out before her like a map of secrets. The Mary Sutcliffe documents had consumed her for hours, each page revealing another piece of a decades-old puzzle.

Her eyes burned from strain, but she couldn't stop. Not when she was so close to... something. She wasn't sure what yet, but her instincts screamed that the answer was hidden in these yellowed pages.

A name caught her eye. Mill Beck Farm. Located between Middleton and Morley. Isabella's heart raced. Could this be the missing link?

She glanced at the clock. 11.47 pm. Late, but not too late. Before she could talk herself out of it, Isabella grabbed her keys and jacket. She had to see this farm for herself.

The night air was crisp as she drove, streetlights giving way to darkness as she left the city behind. Her mind whirled with possibilities. Could this farm hold the key to Abigail Fawcett's disappearance? To the entire White Rose League mystery?

As she neared the area, a flicker of movement in the sky caught her attention. A helicopter, its searchlight sweeping across the fields. Police? What were they doing out here?

Isabella's grip tightened on the steering wheel. Something

was happening. She could feel it in her bones.

* * *

In the air, Sergeant Mike Donovan squinted through the helicopter's window. The searchlight illuminated patches of darkness below, revealing nothing but empty fields and the occasional startled sheep.

Until suddenly, there it was. An old farmhouse, roof partially caved in, nature reclaiming its walls. But something about it seemed... off.

"Control, this is Echo-1," Donovan radioed. "We've got a possible location. Abandoned farmhouse, grid reference..."

On the ground, PS Greenwood received the coordinates, his pulse quickening. "Copy that, Echo-1. Stand by."

He turned to his team, already mobilising. "Let's move! And someone get DCI Beaumont on the line. He'll want to be here for this."

* * *

George Beaumont's phone buzzed as he was leaving the station, Nadia Shah's revelations still ringing in his ears.

"Beaumont," he answered, striding towards his car.

"Sir, it's Greenwood. We've got a location. Abandoned farmhouse between Middleton and Morley. Helicopter spotted it during the search."

George's heart raced. This could be it. The breakthrough they'd been waiting for. "I'm on my way. Get a team ready for entry. Full tactical support."

He hung up, already planning the raid in his head. Whatever

they found in that farmhouse, he'd be ready for it.

* * *

Isabella's headlights cut through the darkness as she approached Mill Beck Farm. The old building loomed before her, a silent sentinel guarding its secrets.

She pulled over, killing the engine. The silence was oppressive, broken only by the distant hum of the police helicopter.

As she stepped out of her car, the sound of approaching vehicles made her freeze. Headlights appeared on the horizon, growing brighter by the second.

Isabella's heart hammered in her chest. She should leave. This was foolish, coming out here alone. But curiosity rooted her to the spot.

The vehicles screeched to a halt, doors flying open. Armed officers poured out, their movements precise and practised. And there, in the midst of it all, a familiar figure.

George.

Their eyes met across the yard, mutual shock written across their faces.

"Isabella?" George's voice was a mix of confusion and anger. "What the hell are you doing here?"

She opened her mouth to respond, but George cut her off. "Never mind. Get back in your car. Now. And stay there."

Isabella bristled at his tone but complied. She watched from her vehicle as George barked orders, his team moving into position around the farmhouse.

PS Greenwood approached, the Big Red Key in hand. At George's nod, he swung it at the door. It splintered inward with a thunderous crack.

"Police! Nobody move!" The shout echoed through the night as officers poured into the building.

Isabella held her breath, straining to hear any sound from inside. Seconds stretched into minutes, the tension unbearable.

Then, a shout from within. "Sir! You need to see this!"

George disappeared into the farmhouse. Isabella's hand was on her door handle before she could think better of it. She had to know what they'd found.

She crept closer, heart pounding. From inside, she could hear muffled voices, urgent and tense.

Then George reappeared in the doorway, his face ashen. His eyes met Isabella's, and in that moment, she knew.

They'd found a body.

Chapter Thirty-four

George Beaumont stood at the head of the Incident Room. The faces of his team reflected his own exhaustion and frustration. He took a deep breath, steeling himself to deliver the news.

"Right," he began, his voice rough with fatigue. "The body we found at the farmhouse... it's been identified as Bilal Bhati."

A collective gasp rippled through the room. Tashan's brow furrowed. "Bilal? But I thought..."

George shook his head. "We all did. There was an ID on the body. And Lindsey's already compared dental records. It's him."

Priya leaned forward, her eyes sharp despite the late hour. "And the children?"

"No sign," George said, the words tasting bitter in his mouth. "The place was clean. Too clean."

The silence that followed was heavy, laden with unspoken fears and bitter disappointment. They'd been so close. And now this.

Susie cleared her throat, breaking the oppressive quiet. "Sir? I've got an update on Samuel Siddiqui."

George's head snapped up, a flicker of hope igniting in his chest. "Go on."

Susie shuffled her papers, a hint of disbelief in her voice. "It turns out Siddiqui worked as a supply teaching assistant at Lily, Thomas, and Amira's schools. All around the times they went missing."

The room erupted in a flurry of muttered curses and exclamations. George's thoughts churned. "How the hell did we miss this?"

Susie shook her head, bewildered. "That's the thing, sir. The information was right there. It should have been picked up ages ago."

George's jaw clenched, a familiar anger rising in his gut. "Clare Brack," he spat. "She was SIO on those cases. She must have buried it."

Tashan leaned in. "You think it's League business? Siddiqui working for them?"

George nodded grimly. "It fits. Too well to be coincidence."

He straightened, a new determination hardening his features. "Right. I want everything we've got on Siddiqui. School records, employment history, the lot. And I want to talk to him. Now."

The team sprang into action. George strode towards the interview rooms, Tashan falling into step beside him.

"Be careful, boss," Tashan warned. "If Siddiqui is League, he'll be trained to resist questioning."

George's eyes narrowed. "Let him try."

The interview room was stark and cold, designed to unsettle. But as George entered, he found himself taken aback. The nervous, defensive man they'd questioned earlier was gone. In his place sat a figure of cool confidence, a smirk playing at the corners of his mouth.

"Mr Siddiqui," George began, settling into the chair opposite. "We need to talk about your employment history."

Siddiqui leaned back, an air of casual disinterest about him. "Do we? Sounds frightfully boring."

George's eyes narrowed. "Cut the crap, Siddiqui. We know you worked at Lily Chen's school. And Thomas Wilkes'. And Amira Khan's. All around the time they went missing."

A flicker of... something passed across Siddiqui's face. Amusement? Pride? It was gone before George could be sure.

"Did I?" Siddiqui drawled. "My, what a coincidence."

Tashan leaned forward, his voice hard. "It's not a coincidence and you bloody well know it. Where are those kids, Siddiqui?"

Siddiqui's smirk widened. "Kids? What kids? I'm a teaching assistant, remember? I see lots of kids."

George's fist clenched under the table. "You're not a teaching assistant now, Siddiqui. You're a suspect in multiple child abductions. Start talking, or—"

"Or what?" Siddiqui cut in, his voice dripping with disdain. "You'll what, exactly? Glare at me some more? Please. You've got nothing."

George leaned in. "We've got Nadia Shah. We know about the League. It's over, Siddiqui. Your only chance now is to cooperate."

For a moment, something flickered in Siddiqui's eyes—a hint of the nervous man they'd first encountered. But it was quickly replaced by that infuriating smirk.

"The League? What's that? Some sort of clandestine group?" He chuckled. "Oh, you are reaching, aren't you? Next you'll be telling me the Illuminati are involved."

George's patience snapped. He slammed his hand on the table, the sound echoing in the small room. "Enough! Those children are out there somewhere, scared and alone. You know where they are. Tell us!"

Siddiqui didn't flinch. He leaned forward, matching George's intensity. "I don't know anything about any missing children, Detective. And even if I did, why would I tell you? What's in it for me?"

The silence that followed was electric, charged with unspoken threats and barely contained fury. George stared into Siddiqui's eyes, searching for any crack in his armour, any hint of the man they'd questioned earlier.

But there was nothing. Just cold, calculated defiance.

George stood abruptly, his chair scraping against the floor. "This interview is over. For now."

As they left the room, Tashan shook his head in disbelief. "What the hell was that? It's like he's a completely different person."

George's jaw clenched. "He's playing us. But why? What changed?"

They walked back to the Incident Room in silence, both lost in thought. The cocky, uncooperative Siddiqui was a far cry from the nervous wreck they'd questioned earlier. It didn't make sense.

Unless...

George stopped short, a terrible realisation dawning. "Tashan," he said. "What if Siddiqui isn't working for the League?"

Tashan frowned. "What do you mean?"

"What if he is the League?" George's mind raced with the implications. "Or at least, a high-ranking member. It would explain the change in behaviour, the confidence."

Tashan's eyes widened. "Bloody hell. You think we've

stumbled onto something bigger than we realised?"

George nodded grimly. "I think we've barely scratched the surface. And I think Siddiqui knows it."

They shared a grim look. Whatever game Siddiqui was playing, whatever secrets he was hiding, they would uncover them. The missing children were counting on it.

* * *

George Beaumont stood at the head of the Incident Room, his eyes scanning the tired faces of his team.

"Right," he began, his voice cutting through the tense silence. "We've got Nadia and Samuel in custody, but we're far from done. Those kids are still out there, and time is not on our side."

Priya leaned forward, her eyes sharp despite the late hour. "Sir, what about their belongings? Nadia and Samuel's, I mean. There might be something there we've missed."

George nodded, a flicker of approval crossing his face. "Good thinking, Priya. I want you to take charge of that. Go through everything with a fine-tooth comb. Receipts, notes, anything that might give us a clue to where those children are being held."

Priya was already on her feet, determination etched into every line of her body. "On it, boss."

George turned to Susie and Tashan. "You two, I need you to liaise with Stuart Kent. His team is searching Nadia and Samuel's properties as we speak. I want updates every hour, no matter how small the find."

Tashan nodded grimly. "We'll stay on top of it, sir."

The door to the Incident Room swung open, and Josh

Fry strode in. The atmosphere shifted, a palpable tension crackling through the air. Josh's eyes met George's.

"I'm here for Siddiqui and Nadia's electronic devices, sir," Josh said, his voice carefully neutral. "IT forensics is ready to start their analysis."

George nodded, fighting down the guilt gnawing at his gut. He'd been so quick to assume the worst, to believe Isabella capable of betraying him. And with Josh, of all people. A loyal friend, a dedicated officer.

"Of course," George said, gesturing to the evidence lockers. "Take what you need. And Josh... good work on tracing that number earlier."

A flicker of surprise crossed Josh's face, quickly replaced by a professional nod. "Just doing my job, sir."

As Josh gathered the devices, George's phone buzzed in his pocket. Abbie's name flashed on the screen. He hesitated for a moment, then hit decline. There wasn't time for personal complications now. Not when children's lives hung in the balance.

"Yolanda," George called. "I need you to come up with an interview strategy. We're going to play Nadia and Samuel against each other."

Yolanda's eyes lit up with understanding. "A prisoner's dilemma situation, sir?"

George nodded, a grim smile tugging at his lips. "Exactly. Make each of them believe the other has confessed and is negotiating a deal. Let's see if we can crack their solidarity."

Yolanda was already scribbling notes. "I'll have a plan for you within the hour, boss."

George surveyed the room, taking in the determined faces of his team. "Listen up, everyone. We are running out of time.

Those kids have been without food or water for God knows how long. Every minute counts."

He paused, letting his words sink in. "I know you're all exhausted. I know it feels like we've hit dead end after dead end. But we are closer than we've ever been. Nadia and Samuel are the key to cracking this case wide open. We just need to find the right pressure point."

The team nodded, a renewed energy pulsing through the room. George felt a surge of pride. They were good, his people. Dedicated. Relentless.

"Alright," he said, his voice ringing with authority. "You've got your assignments. Let's bring these kids home."

As the team dispersed, each rushing to their tasks, George allowed himself a moment of quiet reflection. The case had consumed him, pushing everything else to the periphery. His relationship with Isabella, the growing complications with Abbie, even his own moral compass—all had been overshadowed by the urgency of finding those missing children.

But now, with Nadia and Samuel in custody, with the end potentially in sight, those personal entanglements pressed down on him. He'd have to face it all soon enough. The confrontation with Isabella, the unresolved tension with Josh, the dangerous pull he felt towards Abbie.

George shook his head, pushing the thoughts aside. There would be time for all of that later. Right now, there were lives at stake. Children counting on him and his team to bring them home.

Chapter Thirty-five

George Beaumont leaned forward, his eyes locked on Nadia Shah. Yolanda Williams sat beside him, coiled like a spring, ready to pounce on any inconsistency in her story.

Nadia fidgeted in her chair, her once-pristine appearance now dishevelled after hours of questioning. Dark circles shadowed her eyes, a stark contrast to the crisp white walls surrounding them.

"Let's go over this again," George said. "Your involvement with the White Rose League. Start talking."

Nadia's eyes darted between the two detectives. "I've told you already. I don't know anything about any White Rose League."

Yolanda snorted, disbelief etched across her face. "Come off it, Nadia. We've got you dead to rights on the abductions. Eva Sharp. Dania Bhati. Lily Chen. Thomas Wilkes. Rosie Kershaw. Amira Khan. And let's not forget Bilal Bhati, the poor sod you tried to frame for your sick games."

A flicker of something—fear? guilt?—crossed Nadia's face. She opened her mouth, closed it again, indecision warring in her eyes.

George pressed his advantage. "We know you're involved, Nadia. The evidence is overwhelming. The only question now is how deep it goes. How many others are out there, doing what you did?"

Nadia's eyes darted between the two detectives. "I've told you everything I know."

Yolanda snorted, disbelief etched across her face. "Come off it, Nadia. We know everything already. Siddiqui's been singing like a canary. He's already cut a deal."

A flicker of fear crossed Nadia's face. "What? No, you're lying. Sammy wouldn't..."

George pressed his advantage. "He's given us names, dates, locations. The only question now is where you fit in. How deep does your involvement go?"

Nadia's composure cracked. Her shoulders slumped, the fight draining out of her. "Fine," she whispered. "Fine. You want to know what I did? I'll tell you."

George leaned back in his chair, studying Nadia's face. Her confession had been a breakthrough, but something still nagged at him. He decided to push further.

"Nadia," he said, his voice calm but firm, "I need to ask you about something else, first. Something that doesn't quite add up."

Nadia looked up, wariness creeping back into her expression. "What?"

George exchanged a glance with Yolanda before continuing. "We spoke to Luke Mason. He mentioned your name in connection with the White Rose League. Said you were someone to be protected."

Nadia's brow furrowed, genuine confusion crossing her face. "Luke Mason? I don't know who that is. And I've told you, I don't know anything about any White Rose League."

Yolanda leaned forward, her voice sharp. "Come on, Nadia.

You've already admitted to your involvement in the abductions. Why lie about this?"

Nadia shook her head vehemently. "I'm not lying. I swear, I don't know what you're talking about. Who is Luke Mason?"

George studied her carefully, looking for any sign of deception. But all he saw was bewilderment and fear.

"Luke was a high-ranking member of the White Rose League," George explained. "He seemed certain that your name had come up in League business. That you were someone important, someone to be protected."

Nadia's eyes widened. "I... I don't understand. Why would they want to protect me? I've never heard of this League. The only person I was involved with was Sammy."

George leaned back. He believed her. The confusion in her eyes, the genuine distress in her voice – it all rang true. But if Nadia wasn't lying, then what did it mean?

George leaned in. "Nadia, I need you to think carefully. Is there any reason, any reason at all, why a powerful organisation might want to keep you safe? Anything in your past, maybe?"

Nadia shook her head, tears welling in her eyes. "No, nothing. I'm nobody. Just a social worker who... who made terrible mistakes. I don't understand any of this."

George nodded slowly, his mind working overtime. If Nadia was telling the truth – and he believed she was – then either Luke had been lying, or...

Or the White Rose League had been protecting Nadia without her knowledge. But why? What made her so important to them? Was it something to do with Samuel Siddiqui?

"Alright, Nadia," he said finally. "I believe you. But this... this complicates things. We're going to need to dig deeper into your background, try to figure out why the League might have taken an interest in you."

Nadia nodded, looking lost and overwhelmed. "I'll help however I can. I just want this nightmare to be over."

"You can start then by telling us everything you do know."

The room seemed to hold its breath as Nadia gathered herself. When she spoke again, her voice was hollow, devoid of emotion. "I took them. The children. And Bilal. I... I set him up to take the fall."

Yolanda leaned forward, her voice sharp. "How? Why Bilal?"

Nadia laughed, a brittle sound. "Why not? He was perfect. Vulnerable. Lonely. Easy to manipulate. I played the doting girlfriend, made him think we had something special."

George's stomach churned at the cold calculation in her voice. "And the children? What was your role there?"

"I chose them," Nadia admitted. "Through my work as a social worker. I identified the vulnerable ones, the ones no one would miss. Or at least, the ones whose disappearances could be explained away."

Yolanda's fist clenched on the table. "You heartless bitch. Do you have any idea what you've done to those families?"

Nadia flinched at her words, but pressed on. "I didn't kill them. Eva and Dania. It wasn't me."

"No?" George's voice dripped with scepticism. "Then who did?"

"Samuel did," Nadia said, her voice barely above a whisper. "My... my boyfriend. My real boyfriend. He's the one who killed them. I was at work when it happened. I swear it."

Yolanda pushed harder, her voice rising. "But you knew. You knew he was going to do it, didn't you? You handed those girls over to him, knowing full well what would happen."

"No!" Nadia protested, the tears now flowing freely. "I didn't... I didn't know he would kill them. I thought... I thought they were going somewhere else."

George's eyes narrowed. "Where, Nadia? Where did you think they were going?"

Nadia hesitated, her gaze dropping to her hands. "To... to other people. People who would pay for them."

The admission hung in the air, heavy with implications. George fought to keep his voice steady. "You're talking about human trafficking. About selling children to paedophiles."

Nadia nodded, unable to meet their eyes. "Samuel's boss... he runs the whole operation. I never met him, never knew his name. But Sammy... Sammy was scared of him. Said he had connections everywhere."

"And you expect us to believe you were what? An unwilling participant?" Yolanda's voice dripped with disgust. "You could have stopped this at any time."

"You don't understand," Nadia pleaded, her composure crumbling entirely. "Samuel... he would have killed me. He told me what would happen if I ever tried to leave, if I ever breathed a word to anyone." Her voice began trembling. "Said he had people everywhere, that I'd never be safe."

George exchanged a glance with Yolanda. The fear in Nadia's voice rang true, but something didn't add up.

"If you were so afraid," Yolanda pressed, "why didn't you come to us? Why keep helping him find more victims?"

Nadia's eyes filled with tears. "You don't understand. Sammy... he has a way of getting inside your head. Making you believe you have no choice."

George sat back, studying her. The tears, the trembling

hands, the look of abject terror in her eyes. It could all be an act. A ploy for sympathy. But there was something in her voice, a rawness that spoke of genuine fear. "So you kept quiet," he said, his voice softer now. "Kept feeding them children. Kept destroying lives."

Nadia nodded, her shoulders shaking with silent sobs. "I'm sorry," she whispered. "I'm so, so sorry."

Yolanda stood abruptly, her chair scraping against the floor. "Sorry doesn't cut it," she spat. "Those kids... Christ, do you have any idea what you've done?"

George placed a calming hand on Yolanda's arm. "Easy," he murmured. George leaned forward, his eyes narrowing as he studied Nadia's body language. "Tell me about Samuel," he said. "How did you two meet?"

Nadia's gaze dropped to her hands, which twisted nervously in her lap. "We... we met at a support group," she said, her voice barely above a whisper. "For survivors of childhood abuse."

Yolanda exchanged a glance with George, surprise flickering across her face. "Go on," George prompted, his tone softer than before.

Nadia took a shaky breath. "Sammy and I... we connected immediately. We understood each other in a way no one else ever had. The pain, the shame, the constant fear..." She trailed off, lost in the memory.

George pressed gently, "And how did that lead to... this?"

A bitter laugh escaped Nadia's lips. "How does it ever start? Small things at first. Sharing our darkest thoughts, our most twisted fantasies. It was cathartic, you know? To finally have someone who didn't judge, who understood the darkness inside us."

CHAPTER THIRTY-FIVE

Yolanda's jaw clenched, but she remained silent, letting her continue.

"Then one day, Sammy came to me with an idea. A way to take control, to stop being victims and become... something else." Nadia's voice hardened, a glint of something dangerous flashing in her eyes. "He said we could save other children from going through what we did. Give them a better life."

"By abducting them?" George's voice was incredulous. "By handing them over to paedophiles?"

Nadia flinched at the harsh truth of his words. "It sounds insane now, I know. But back then... God, we were so messed up. So desperate to feel powerful, to believe we were doing something good."

"And your relationship with Samuel?" Yolanda prodded. "How would you describe it?"

Nadia's eyes closed, pain etching deep lines around her mouth. "Toxic. Codependent. We... we needed each other. Fed off each other's darkness. Every time I wanted to stop, every time the guilt became too much, Sammy would remind me of our past. Of how the world had failed us."

George leaned back, his mind racing to process this new information. "So you became each other's enablers. Justifying your actions through your shared trauma."

Nadia nodded, tears welling in her eyes. "We thought we were saving each other. But really, we were just dragging each other deeper into hell."

Yolanda's voice was rough with barely contained emotion. "And the children? Did you ever stop to think about what you were doing to them?"

A sob tore from Nadia's throat. "Every day. Every single day. But Sammy... he had a way of twisting things. Making me believe we were giving them a chance at a better life than we'd had."

George's stomach churned at the implication. "By selling them to paedophiles? How could you possibly believe that was better?"

Nadia's eyes snapped up, a mixture of desperation and defiance burning in their depths. "You don't understand. The system failed us. Left us at the mercy of monsters. We thought... we thought we could control it. Choose who got the children. Make sure they went to people who would care for them, not..."

She trailed off, unable to finish the thought. The room fell silent, the weight of her confession hanging heavy in the air.

George broke the silence, his voice firm but not unkind. "Nadia, I need you to understand something. What you and Samuel went through as children... it was horrific. Unforgivable. But it doesn't justify what you've done."

Nadia nodded, her shoulders slumping in defeat. "I know," she whispered. "I know."

Yolanda leaned forward, her voice softer now. "It's not too late to make things right, Nadia. Tell us everything. Help us stop this from happening to any more children."

George added, "We're going to need names. Dates. Locations. Everything you can remember about Samuel's operation, about this boss of his."

Nadia looked up, hope flickering in her tear-stained eyes. "If I help you... if I tell you everything... what happens to me?"

George's expression hardened. "You're going away for a long time, Nadia. Nothing's going to change that. But cooperate fully, and maybe—maybe—we can talk to the CPS about reducing your charges."

Nadia looked up, meeting their eyes for the first time since her confession began. Then she nodded, a mixture of relief and resignation washing over her face. "OK," she said, her voice barely above a whisper. "OK. I'll tell you everything I know. About Sammy, about the operation, about all of it."

For the next two hours, Nadia Shah laid bare the inner workings of a nightmare. Names, dates, locations poured out of her in a torrent of guilt and fear. George and Yolanda took copious notes, their faces growing grimmer with each new revelation. It wasn't much—he had kept her largely in the dark—but every scrap of information was potentially crucial.

By the time Nadia fell silent, exhausted and spent, the scope of the operation she'd been involved in had become horrifyingly clear. It wasn't just a local paedophile ring. It was a sprawling network that reached across the country, its tendrils burrowing deep into positions of power and influence.

George stood, his mind reeling from the implications of what they'd uncovered. "We'll need you to make a formal statement," he said. "Everything you've told us today, on the record."

Nadia nodded, her eyes vacant and haunted. "Whatever you need. I... I want this to be over."

By the time they led Nadia back to her cell, George's mind was reeling. They had cracked her, yes, but the picture that emerged was far from complete. Samuel Siddiqui remained the key to unravelling this nightmare.

"We need to push harder on Siddiqui," George said to Yolanda as they walked back to the Incident Room. "He's the one holding all the cards."

Yolanda nodded, her face grim. "And the kids? You think they're still alive?"

George's jaw clenched. "They have to be. We have to believe that, or what's the point of any of this?"

Chapter Thirty-six

George Beaumont strode into the interview room, Tashan close behind. Samuel Siddiqui sat at the table, his posture relaxed, a smirk playing at the corners of his mouth.

"Mr Siddiqui," George began, settling into the chair opposite. "We've just had a very interesting conversation with your girlfriend, Nadia."

Samuel's eyebrow arched slightly. "Oh? And what tall tales has dear Nadia been spinning?"

Tashan leaned forward, his voice hard. "Cut the crap, Siddiqui. She's told us everything. The abductions, the trafficking network, your boss. It's over."

A flicker of something—uncertainty? fear?—passed across Samuel's smug face, quickly replaced by his usual cocky demeanour. "I highly doubt that. Nadia doesn't know anything worth knowing."

George pressed on. "She told us about the support group where you met. About how you manipulated her, used her childhood trauma to turn her into your accomplice."

Samuel's jaw clenched momentarily. "Interesting theory. Got any proof to back that up?"

"We will," Tashan growled. "Nadia's cooperating fully. In exchange for a reduced sentence."

For a split second, genuine surprise flashed in Samuel's eyes. But he recovered quickly, his voice dripping with disdain. "Good for her. I'm sure her imagination will provide you with hours of entertainment."

George leaned in. "This isn't a game, Samuel. We know about the children. About what happened to Eva and Dania. Nadia's given us names, dates, locations. It's only a matter of time before we find the others."

Samuel's smirk widened. "If you say so, Detective. But I think you'll find that Nadia's word against mine doesn't count for much in court."

Before George could respond, a sharp knock at the door interrupted them. He exchanged a glance with Tashan before calling out, "Come in."

Josh Fry stepped into the room, his face flushed with excitement. "Sir, we've got something."

"Interview terminated." George stood, moving to the door. "Watch him," he muttered to Tashan before stepping out into the corridor with Josh.

"What have you got?" he asked, keeping his voice low.

Josh's words tumbled out in a rush. "We've cracked their communication network. It's all on the dark web, heavily encrypted. But we've managed to trace it to several physical locations—dead drops."

George's eyebrows shot up. "Dead drops? Like in espionage?"

Josh nodded eagerly. "Exactly. It's a common tactic for OCGs. Avoiding direct meetings, maintaining operational security. We've got GPS coordinates for at least five locations across Leeds."

George's mind reeled with the implications. "Good work,

Josh. Really good work. Get onto PS Greenwood, have him put surveillance on those spots immediately."

As Josh hurried off, George took a deep breath, steeling himself. Then he re-entered the interview room, a new confidence in his step.

"Well, Mr Siddiqui," he said, settling back into his chair. "It seems we've stumbled onto something rather interesting. Care to tell us about your dead drops?"

Samuel's composure slipped for a fraction of a second, his eyes widening almost imperceptibly. But he recovered quickly, his voice steady. "I have no idea what you're talking about."

George leaned forward. "No? Then let me enlighten you. We've traced your dark web communications. We know about the locations where you exchange information. It's only a matter of time before we catch one of your associates making a drop."

Samuel's jaw clenched, a muscle twitching in his cheek. "You're bluffing."

"Am I?" George countered. "We've got teams en route to those locations as we speak. So I'll ask you one more time, Samuel. Where are the children?"

For a long moment, silence hung heavy in the room. Samuel's eyes darted between George and Tashan, calculation evident in every line of his face.

Finally, he spoke, his voice cold and precise. "I want a deal."

George sat back, studying him. "That depends on what you're offering."

Samuel leaned forward, his eyes glinting. "Full immunity. In exchange, I'll give you everything. Names, dates, locations. The entire network."

Tashan snorted in disbelief. "You can't be serious. After

what you've done?"

But George held up a hand, silencing him. "And the children? Where are they?"

Samuel's smile was razor-sharp. "That's part of the deal, Detective. Take it or leave it."

George stood, his face a mask of barely contained fury. "We'll take your offer under advisement, Mr Siddiqui. But know this—one way or another, we will find those kids. And when we do, deal or no deal, you're going down for this."

As they turned to leave, Samuel called out, his voice laced with a mixture of amusement and warning. "Be careful, Detective. You're playing a very dangerous game. There are people in this city who would do anything to keep their secrets buried. Anything at all."

George paused at the door, looking back over his shoulder. "Let them try," he said. "We're coming for all of them."

With that, he stepped out of the room, Tashan close behind.

The door swung shut, cutting off Samuel's mocking laughter.

* * *

George strode through the empty corridors of Elland Road Police Station, his footsteps echoing in the late-night silence. He reached DSU Smith's office, finding it dark and locked. Cursing under his breath, he pulled out his mobile and dialled Smith's number.

The phone rang three times before Smith's gruff voice answered. "Beaumont? This is now twice you've called me at a ridiculous hour."

"Sorry, sir," George said, not sounding sorry at all. "But this couldn't wait. We've got a situation with Samuel Siddiqui."

He could hear Smith shifting, probably sitting up in bed. "Go on."

George took a deep breath. "Siddiqui's offered us a deal. Full immunity in exchange for everything. Names, dates, locations. The whole network."

There was a pause on the other end of the line. Then, "And the children? Does he know where they are?"

"He claims he does," George replied, his frustration evident. "But he won't give us anything without the deal."

Smith's voice sharpened. "Then we give him the deal, Beaumont. What's the problem?"

George's free hand clenched into a fist. "The problem, sir, is that this man is responsible for the abduction and potential deaths of multiple children. He doesn't deserve to walk free."

"I understand your feelings, George," Smith said, his tone softening slightly. "But we have to look at the bigger picture here. If Siddiqui can give us the entire OCG network, think of how many children we could save in the long run."

"And what about justice for the ones we've already lost?" George countered, struggling to keep his voice level. "What do we tell their families? Sorry, we let the monster who took your child go free, but it was for the greater good?"

Smith sighed heavily. "Sometimes, George, this job requires us to make difficult choices. Choices we don't like, but that serve a greater purpose."

"With all due respect, sir," George said, his voice tight with restrained anger, "I didn't become a detective to let child abusers walk free."

"And I didn't become a DSU to let personal feelings interfere with an investigation," Smith snapped back. "Think, Beaumont. If we can bring down this entire network of Schmidt's, we could prevent countless future abductions. Isn't that worth the cost?"

George paced the corridor, his mind racing. "There has to be another way. We can't just—"

"Enough," Smith cut him off. "This isn't a debate, Beaumont. It's an order. You will offer Siddiqui the deal. You will get the information we need to save those children and bring down this network. And if you can't do that, you can hand in your warrant card right now, and I'll find someone else who can."

The silence stretched between them, heavy with unspoken tension.

Finally, George spoke. "Understood, sir."

"Good," Smith said, his tone softening slightly. "I know this isn't easy, George. But sometimes we have to do distasteful things to achieve a greater good. Get it done."

The line went dead, leaving George standing alone in the darkened corridor.

He took a deep breath, squaring his shoulders. He didn't like it. Every fibre of his being rebelled against the idea of letting Siddiqui walk free. But if it meant saving those children, bringing down an OCG network...

With a grim determination, George turned and headed back towards the interview rooms. It was time to make a deal with the devil.

* * *

George pushed open the door to the Incident Room, his mind still reeling from Smith's orders. The team looked up expectantly, sensing the tension radiating from their boss.

Before George could speak, Priya jumped up from her desk, waving a battered notebook. "Sir! You need to see this."

George frowned, momentarily distracted from his dilemma. "What've you got, Priya?"

She thrust the notebook into his hands. "I found this in Siddiqui's belongings. At first glance, it's just gibberish— random numbers and letters. But look closer."

George flipped through the pages, his frown deepening. "A code?"

Priya nodded eagerly. "That's what I thought. I've already contacted Josh Fry. He's brought in a cryptography expert. They're working on cracking it now."

George's pulse quickened. This could be the break they'd been waiting for. If the notebook contained the locations of the missing children...

"How long until we know anything?" he asked, his voice tight with anticipation.

Priya shrugged. "Hard to say. Could be hours, could be minutes. Depends on how complex the cipher is."

George ran a hand through his hair, his mind racing. On one hand, Smith's orders were clear—make the deal with Siddiqui, get the information directly from him. It was a guaranteed path to the children's locations and the wider network.

But this notebook... if it contained the same information, they could potentially crack the case without having to let Siddiqui walk free.

The team watched him, sensing his internal struggle. Tashan stepped forward. "What's the play, boss?"

George took a deep breath, weighing his options. Smith's words echoed in his head—"This isn't a debate, Beaumont.

It's an order." But the potential in that notebook...

"Alright," he said finally, his decision made. "We wait. Give the cryptography team one hour. If they haven't cracked it by then, we go with Smith's plan and make the deal with Siddiqui."

He turned to Priya. "Stay on top of this. The second they have anything, I want to know."

Priya nodded, already reaching for her phone.

Chapter Thirty-seven

George Beaumont's phone buzzed, jolting him from his restless pacing. He snatched it up, heart pounding.

"Beaumont," he barked.

"Sir, it's Josh. We've cracked the code."

George's breath caught. "Go on."

"It's a series of GPS coordinates. Four locations, all farmhouses. We think—"

"The kids," George finished. "They've got to be there."

He was already moving, striding out of his office. "Send the coordinates to the team. Now."

The Incident Room erupted into controlled chaos as George burst in. "Listen up," he called, his voice cutting through the noise. "We've got locations. Four farmhouses, likely holding our missing children."

His eyes swept the room, landing on each of his team members. "Tashan, Yolanda, Susie—you're each taking point on one of the first three locations. They're near the dead drops in Meanwood we identified earlier."

The three detectives nodded, already grabbing gear.

"Priya," George continued, "you're on the fourth. It's further out, less likely, but we can't take any chances."

Priya's eyes widened slightly, but she nodded, determination setting her jaw.

"I'll be mobile, ready to support wherever needed. These locations are all within a mile of each other, so we can respond quickly if anything goes sideways."

George paused. "We don't know what we're walking into. Siddiqui might have fail-safes in place. Be careful, be thorough, and for God's sake, be fast. Those kids are counting on us."

As the team moved out, George felt the familiar surge of adrenaline. This was it. The culmination of months of work, sleepless nights, and relentless pursuit.

They were going to bring those children home.

* * *

The night air crackled with tension as George Beaumont sat in his car, positioned strategically between the four target locations. His fingers drummed an impatient rhythm on the steering wheel, eyes constantly flicking between the road ahead and the radio on his dashboard.

"Tashan, what's your status?" he barked into the handset.

A burst of static, then Tashan's voice came through, tight with frustration. "Approaching the first location now, sir. It's... hang on."

George's grip tightened on the radio. The silence stretched, each second an eternity.

Finally, Tashan's voice crackled back to life. "Sir, this place is a bust. Looks like it's been abandoned for years. No sign of recent activity."

George's jaw clenched. "Are you sure? Check every room, every outbuilding."

"Already on it, boss," Tashan replied. "But I'm telling you, there's nothing here but dust and cobwebs."

Before George could respond, Yolanda's voice cut in. "Sir, I'm at the second location. It's the same story here. Place is completely deserted."

George slammed his hand against the dashboard, frustration boiling over. "Damn it! Susie, what about you?"

"Just pulling up now, sir," Susie's voice came through, slightly breathless. "I'll let you know what I find."

The minutes ticked by, each one feeling like an hour. George's thoughts churned. Had they misinterpreted the code? Were they too late? The image of those missing children flashed before his eyes, their faces etched with fear and desperation.

"Sir?" Susie's voice broke through his spiralling thoughts. "I've done a thorough sweep of the third location. It's... it's empty, sir. Looks like it hasn't been used in years."

George closed his eyes, fighting back a wave of despair. Three locations, all dead ends. The hope that had surged through him when they cracked the code was rapidly fading, replaced by a cold, sinking feeling in the pit of his stomach.

"Alright," he said, his voice rough with suppressed emotion. "Tashan, Yolanda, Susie—I want you to go over those locations again. Every inch, every corner. There has to be something we're missing." He paused. "Meet me here after."

A chorus of "Yes, sir" came through the radio, but George could hear the doubt in their voices. They were all thinking the same thing—they'd been led on a wild goose chase.

George leaned back in his seat, running a hand over his face. Those kids were counting on him, on his team. And they'd let them down.

He reached for his phone, thumb hovering over DSU Smith's number. Maybe it was time to take the deal with Siddiqui after all. The thought made his stomach churn, but if it meant saving those children...

Just as he was about to make the call, the radio crackled to life once more. "Sir!" Priya's voice, high with excitement. "I've got movement. Fourth location. Someone's inside."

George's heart leapt. "On my way. All units, converge on Priya's location. Now!"

He gunned the engine, tyres squealing as he tore down the country lane. Within minutes, he screeched to a halt outside a dilapidated farmhouse, its windows dark and forbidding.

Priya was crouched behind her car, eyes fixed on the building. "First floor, sir," she whispered as George joined her. "Saw a shadow move past the window."

George nodded, already assessing the situation. The AFO team was pulling up, their movements swift and practised.

"Alright," he said, voice low and intense. "We go in hard and fast. Priority is the children's safety. Watch for booby traps or hidden assailants."

The team moved into position, the familiar tension of a raid thrumming through the air. At George's signal, the AFOs breached the door, the splintering wood echoing in the pre-dawn stillness.

"Police! Nobody move!"

George and Priya followed close behind, weapons drawn. They cleared the ground floor quickly, finding nothing but dust and abandoned furniture.

As they approached the stairs, a floorboard creaked overhead. George froze, signalling the team to hold the position. Then, a child's muffled whimper reached their ears.

George's blood ran cold. They were here. So close.

He took the stairs two at a time, Priya right behind him. As they reached the landing, a figure burst from a side room, wild-eyed and desperate.

George recognised him instantly.

Dark hair. Dark beard.

Zachary Sayed, a known lieutenant of the Jürgen Schmidt OCG.

"Stop right there!" George bellowed. But Zach was already moving, lunging towards a closed door.

Time seemed to slow. George saw Zach's hand reaching for the doorknob, knew with sickening certainty what he intended.

"Priya!" he shouted. "Cut him off!"

His young detective reacted instantly, diving forward. She collided with Zach just as he wrenched the door open, sending them both sprawling.

George was on them in an instant, wrestling Zach into submission. The man fought like a cornered animal, all teeth and nails and desperation.

"It's over, Zach," George growled, finally pinning him down. "Where are the kids?"

Zach's eyes darted to the open door, and George's heart clenched. There, huddled in the shadows, were four small figures.

"Priya, get them out of here," he ordered, keeping Zach firmly restrained.

As Priya coaxed the children from their prison, George hauled Zach to his feet. The man's composure had returned, a cold smirk playing at his lips.

"You think this changes anything?" Zach sneered. "You

have no idea how deep this goes. I'll be out before you can file the paperwork."

George tightened his grip. "Keep telling yourself that, dickhead. You're going down for this. All of you are."

As the AFOs took Zach into custody, George turned his attention to the children. His breath caught as he recognised their faces from the missing persons reports. Lily. Thomas. Rosie. Amira.

They blinked in the harsh light of the police torches, faces pale and drawn. George knelt before them, his voice gentle.

"It's alright now," he said softly. "You're safe. We're going to take you home."

Lily, the oldest, stepped forward hesitantly. "Really?" she whispered, hope and disbelief warring in her eyes. "We can go home?"

George nodded, fighting back the lump in his throat. "Really. Your parents are waiting for you. They never gave up hope."

The floodgates opened. The children surged forward, clinging to George and Priya, sobs of relief and joy echoing through the old farmhouse.

As George held them, murmuring reassurances, Amira's small voice caught his attention.

"I thought I'd never see the stars again," she said, her eyes fixed on the lightening sky outside. "Or feel the sun on my face."

George exchanged a glance with Priya, seeing his own emotions mirrored in her eyes. The magnitude of what these children had endured, the resilience they'd shown, was staggering.

The scene outside was organised chaos. Social services had arrived, along with paramedics and additional police units.

The children clung to George and Priya, reluctant to let go of their rescuers.

"Sir," Priya said softly, "shouldn't we go with them? To the hospital?"

George understood her reluctance to leave the girls. He felt it too, the fierce protectiveness that came with being the one to bring them out of that dark place.

But he shook his head. "They're in good hands now, Priya. And we've still got work to do."

He knelt down, meeting each child's eyes in turn. "You've been so brave," he said. "Braver than anyone should ever have to be. Now it's time to let the doctors check you over, make sure you're alright. And then you'll see your families."

Lily nodded, squaring her small shoulders. "Will you come see us? After?"

George smiled, a genuine warmth breaking through his professional facade. "Nothing could keep me away."

As the paramedics loaded the children into ambulances, George turned to Priya. The young detective's eyes were bright with unshed tears.

"You did good work today," he said quietly. "Those kids are alive because of you."

Priya nodded, swiping at her eyes. "What now, sir?"

George's expression hardened, his mind already racing ahead to the next steps. "Now we make sure this never happens again. We've got names, locations, evidence. It's time to bring the whole network down."

As the sun crested the horizon, painting the sky in shades of pink and gold, George allowed himself a moment of quiet triumph. They'd done it. Against all odds, they'd brought those children home.

But the battle was far from over. The White Rose League, Jür-gen Schmidt's OCG, the shadowy figures pulling the strings— they were still out there.

And George Beaumont was coming for them all.

Chapter Thirty-eight

Knackered, George Beaumont stood in the lab, the harsh fluorescent lights casting an eerie glow over the stainless steel surfaces. The chill in the air seemed to seep into his bones, a physical manifestation of the dread coiling in his gut.

Stuart Kent approached, his face a mask of professional detachment. But George had known the man long enough to see the tension in his shoulders, the tightness around his eyes.

"What've you got for me, Stuart, that meant I had to come down here so quickly?" George asked, bracing himself for whatever bombshell was about to drop.

Kent took a deep breath, his fingers drumming a nervous rhythm on the file clutched in his hands. "It's about Clare Brack, George."

"What about her?"

"Her DNA matched that of a record on the DNA Database."

George's eyebrows narrowed. "What do you mean?"

"System's been backed up with all these missing kids cases," Kent explained, a hint of frustration creeping into his voice. "But when it did come through... Christ, George. You're not going to believe this."

He handed over the file. George flipped it open, scanning the contents. His eyes widened, disbelief warring with a sick

A HARVEST OF SORROW

sort of understanding.

"This can't be right," he muttered, more to himself than to Kent.

"I ran it three times myself," Kent said, his voice grim. "There's no mistake. Clare Brack is Abigail Fawcett."

The words hung in the air, heavy with implications. George's thoughts spiralled, piecing together fragments of a puzzle he hadn't even known existed.

"Bloody hell," he breathed. "All this time…"

Kent nodded, his face etched with a mixture of professional fascination and human horror. "Abducted as a child and raised by God knows who to be somebody else."

George's jaw clenched. "The White Rose League. It has to be."

"Makes sense," Kent agreed. "They've had their hooks in deeper than we ever imagined."

George paced the length of the morgue, energy thrumming through him despite the late hour. "We need to talk to her. Now."

Kent glanced at his watch. "It's gone midnight, sir. HMP New Hall won't—"

"I don't give a damn what time it is," George snapped. "This changes everything. I'll make it happen."

Kent nodded. "What about DI Wood? She's been working the Fawcett case for months. She should be there."

George paused, considering. Isabella. With everything going on between them, the secrets and suspicions… But Kent was right. She deserved to be there for this.

"Yeah," he said finally. "I'll call her. But Stuart? This stays between us for now. No one else needs to know until we've got Clare's side of the story."

340

Kent nodded, understanding the gravity of the situation. "Of course, George."

As George left the forensics lab, his mind whirled with possibilities, with the staggering implications of what they'd uncovered.

Clare Brack. Abigail Fawcett. A missing child turned corrupt cop. How many lives had been destroyed because of her actions? How deep did this conspiracy really go?

One thing was certain: by the time the sun rose, nothing would ever be the same.

* * *

The drive to HMP New Hall was tense, the silence in the car broken only by the occasional pothole that George couldn't avoid. George's knuckles were white on the steering wheel, his mind racing with questions he wasn't sure he wanted answered.

Beside him, Isabella sat rigid. George could see the storm brewing behind her eyes, the maelstrom of emotions she was fighting to keep in check.

"You OK?" he asked, breaking the silence.

Isabella's laugh was bitter, bordering on hysterical. "Am I OK? Christ, George. I've spent months searching for Abigail Fawcett. And now you're telling me she's been right under our noses the whole time? That she's responsible for..." She trailed off, unable to finish the thought.

George reached out, his hand hovering over hers before thinking better of it. The distance between them, once a mere crack, now felt like a yawning chasm.

"I know," he said softly. "It's a lot to process. But we need to keep our heads on straight for this interview. Clare... Abigail... whoever she is, she's going to try to manipulate us. We can't let her."

Isabella nodded, squaring her shoulders. "You're right. We do this by the book. No matter what."

They lapsed back into silence as the imposing walls of HMP New Hall loomed before them. George parked the car, killing the engine. For a moment, neither of them moved.

"Ready?" he asked.

Isabella took a deep breath, steeling herself. "As I'll ever be."

They made their way through the prison's security checkpoints, the buzz and clang of metal doors setting George's teeth on edge. Finally, they were led to an interview room, stark and clinical under the harsh fluorescent lights.

And there she sat. Clare Brack. Abigail Fawcett. The woman who had been both victim and villain, her very existence a paradox that threatened to upend everything they thought they knew.

"Hello, Clare," George said, his voice carefully neutral as he took a seat across from her. "Or should I say Abigail?"

Clare's head snapped up, her eyes widening with a mixture of shock and... was that relief? "So you know?" she whispered.

Isabella leaned forward, her voice tight with barely suppressed emotion. "Yes, but what we don't know is why. Start talking, Clare. From the beginning."

Clare's shoulders slumped, as if a great weight had been lifted. And then, in a voice raw with pain and long-buried truths, she began to speak.

"I was four years old when they took me," she said, her eyes focused on some distant point. "The White Rose League.

They... they raised me. Trained me. Brainwashed me into believing their twisted ideology."

George's fists clenched under the table. "And then they planted you in the force."

Clare nodded, a bitter smile twisting her lips. "Their perfect mole. A missing child, presumed dead, now grown and working to protect the very organisation that destroyed her life."

"But why?" Isabella pressed. "Why go along with it? You were a victim, Clare. You could have come forward, could have stopped all of this."

Clare's laugh was hollow, devoid of any real humour. "Could I? They were my family, Isabella. The only one I'd ever known. By the time I realised how wrong it all was... I was in too deep. There was no way out."

George leaned back, studying her face. The face of a woman who had been both predator and prey. "So you kept going. Kept feeding them information. Kept covering up their crimes."

"I had no choice," Clare whispered, tears welling in her eyes. "They would have killed me. Killed anyone I cared about."

"And the children?" George's voice was hard, unyielding. "Lily? Thomas? Amira? What about them? What about Eva and Dania? They're both dead because of you."

Clare flinched as if she'd been struck. "I never... I never meant for anyone to die. I thought... I thought we were saving them. Giving them a better life."

"A better life?" Isabella's voice cracked with disbelief. "You tore them from their families, Clare. You destroyed lives." She paused and shook her head. "You did to them what the League did to you!"

Clare's composure crumbled. She buried her face in her hands, her shoulders shaking with silent sobs. "I know," she choked out. "God help me, I know. I can't... I can't take it back. I can't undo what I've done."

George watched her, his heart a battlefield of conflicting emotions. Part of him wanted to comfort her, to acknowledge the trauma she'd endured. But the faces of the missing children, of their grieving families, loomed large in his mind.

"No," he said finally. "You can't undo it. But you can help us now. Tell us everything, Clare. Every name, every location, every scrap of information about the White Rose League. It's the only way to make this right."

Clare looked up, her face a mask of anguish and desperate hope. "And if I do? What then?"

"Then maybe," Isabella said, her voice softening slightly, "maybe you can start to make amends. For Lily. For Thomas. For Amira. For Eva and Dania. For all the lives you've touched."

Clare nodded, wiping her eyes. "OK," she whispered. "OK. I'll tell you everything."

And so, as the night deepened outside the prison walls, Clare Brack—Abigail Fawcett—began to unravel the tangled web of lies and betrayal that had defined her life. With each revelation, each name spoken aloud, the true scope of the White Rose League's influence became clear.

It was bigger than they'd imagined. More insidious. More deeply rooted in the very institutions meant to protect the innocent.

Yet Clare still didn't know who the Rose was.

As Clare's story wound down, George stood, his mind reeling. He paused at the door, turning back to face the broken woman before him.

"One last thing, Clare," he said, his voice heavy with the ghosts of countless shattered lives. "Spare a thought for Abigail Fawcett's family. For the people who've spent decades wondering, hoping, grieving. They deserved better than this. We all did."

With that, he stepped out into the corridor, Isabella close behind. The door swung shut with a finality that echoed through the empty hallways.

The truth was out. The White Rose League's darkest secret had been dragged into the light.

But as George and Isabella made their way back to the car, both lost in their own thoughts, one question loomed large:

Where do we go from here?

The war wasn't over. In many ways, it was just beginning. But armed with the truth, with Clare's confession and the names she'd provided, they had a fighting chance.

For the first time in months, years even, George felt a glimmer of hope. It was a small flame, fragile and flickering. But it was there.

And he'd be damned if he'd let it go out.

Chapter Thirty-nine

George Beaumont stood outside the paediatric ward of St James's University Hospital, his team gathered around him. There was a lightness in their eyes, a sense of triumph that couldn't be dampened.

"Right," George said. "Remember, these kids have been through hell. They're going to be fragile, scared. We need to be gentle, supportive. No pressing for details about their ordeal unless they volunteer the information. Understood?"

Tashan, Yolanda, Priya, and Susie nodded.

"Good," George continued. "Let's go make some kids smile, shall we?"

They pushed through the double doors, the antiseptic smell of the hospital washing over them. A nurse led them down a brightly painted corridor, cartoon characters grinning from the walls in stark contrast to the gravity of their visit.

"They're in here," the nurse said, gesturing to a private room. "They've been asking for you."

George took a deep breath, then pushed the door open.

Four small figures sat huddled on two beds, their faces lighting up as the team entered. Lily, Thomas, Rosie, and Amira - the children they'd searched for so desperately, now safe and sound.

"DCI Beaumont!" Lily called out, a smile breaking across her face. "You came!"

George moved to her bedside, his own smile genuine and warm. "Of course I did. I promised, didn't I?"

Thomas piped up from the other bed, his voice small but eager. "Are you all police officers?"

Tashan stepped forward, crouching down to the boy's eye level. "We sure are, mate. I'm DS Blackburn, but you can call me Tashan if you like."

The other officers introduced themselves, spreading out among the children. Priya gravitated towards Amira, the youngest of the group, while Yolanda sat with Rosie, and Susie joined Lily and George.

"How are you all feeling?" George asked gently, his eyes scanning each child in turn.

"Better," Lily said, her voice stronger than he'd expected. "The doctors said we're all OK. Just need to eat more, drink more, and rest."

Amira nodded shyly from her perch beside Priya. "The food here is nice. And there's sunlight."

George's heart clenched at the simple joy in her voice. He exchanged a glance with Priya, seeing his own emotions mirrored in her eyes.

"That's great," he said, forcing cheer into his voice. "I bet your parents are thrilled to have you back."

At the mention of parents, Thomas's face fell. "When can we go home?" he asked, his lower lip trembling slightly.

Yolanda answered, her voice gentle. "Soon, love. The doctors just want to make sure you're all healthy first. Your mum and dad have been here, haven't they?"

Thomas nodded. "Yeah. But they had to go home to sleep.

They said they'd be back soon."

"And they will be," George assured him. "They've missed you so much."

Rosie, who had been quiet until now, suddenly spoke up. "Did you catch the bad men? The ones who took us?"

A hush fell over the room. George chose his words carefully. "We've caught some of them, yes. And we're going to find the rest. You don't need to worry about them now."

Lily's eyes narrowed, a spark of the sharp girl she must have been before her ordeal shining through. "But there are more? Out there?"

George nodded, seeing no point in lying. "There are. But we're going to find them all. I promise you that."

"Good," Lily said firmly. "They need to be stopped. So they can't hurt any more kids."

The room fell silent momentarily. Then, as if by unspoken agreement, the team steered the conversation to lighter topics.

Tashan regaled Thomas with stories of high-speed chases (sanitised for young ears, of course). Yolanda and Rosie bonded over a shared love of football, debating the merits of various Leeds United players. Susie produced a deck of cards from her pocket, teaching Lily a simple magic trick that soon had the girl giggling.

George found himself drawn to Amira, the quietest of the group. He sat beside her bed, Priya on the other side.

"How are you doing, Amira?" he asked softly.

The little girl looked up at him, her dark eyes wide and solemn. "I'm OK," she said. "But I keep thinking... what if it wasn't real? What if I wake up and I'm back there?"

George's heart broke. He reached out, gently taking her

small hand in his. "It's real, Amira. I promise you. You're safe now, and we're not going to let anyone hurt you ever again."

Amira's lower lip trembled, tears welling in her eyes. "I was so scared," she whispered. "I thought I'd never see my mummy and daddy again."

Priya leaned in, her voice soft and soothing. "But you did, didn't you? And now you're going to go home with them soon. You're so brave, Amira. So, so brave."

The little girl nodded, wiping at her eyes. "Can... can I have a hug?"

George and Priya exchanged glances, then both enveloped Amira in a gentle embrace. The child clung to them, her small body shaking with silent sobs.

Across the room, George caught Tashan's eye. The younger detective nodded, understanding passing between them. This was why they did the job. For moments like these, when they could offer comfort and safety to those who needed it most.

As the visit wore on, the children began to tire. Yawns punctuated the conversation, eyelids growing heavy.

"I think it's time we let you get some rest," George said, standing up. "But we'll come back to see you again soon, if that's OK?"

A chorus of eager agreement met his words. As the team said their goodbyes, each child reaching out for final hugs or high-fives, George felt a tugging on his sleeve.

He looked down to see Lily, her face serious. "DCI Beaumont?"

"Yes, Lily?"

"Thank you," she said solemnly. "For finding us. For not giving up."

George crouched down, meeting her eyes. "You don't need

to thank me, Lily. It's my job. But more than that, it's a privilege. You kids... you're the bravest people I've ever met."

Lily's face broke into a smile, a real one that reached her eyes. She threw her arms around George's neck, hugging him tightly.

As they left the room, George paused in the doorway, looking back at the four children. They were already settling down, exhaustion finally claiming them. But there was peace on their faces now, a safety they hadn't known for far too long.

In the corridor, the team gathered around George, their faces a mix of emotions.

"That was..." Susie began, her voice thick.

"Yeah," Tashan agreed, running a hand over his face.

George nodded, understanding the sentiment they couldn't quite express. "You all did brilliantly in there," he said. "Those kids... they're going to need a lot of support. But thanks to you, they've got a fighting chance."

Priya spoke up, her eyes shining with unshed tears. "Sir, I was thinking... maybe we could set up some kind of ongoing support? For the kids and their families? They're going to need help adjusting, dealing with the trauma."

George smiled, pride swelling in his chest. "That's an excellent idea, Priya. Why don't you take point on that? Liaise with social services, see what we can put together."

As they walked out of the hospital, George felt a renewed sense of purpose. The case wasn't over - there were still loose ends to tie up, more arrests to be made. But they'd done the most important part. They'd brought those children home.

"Right," he said as they reached their cars. "Take the rest of the day off. You've all earned it. But I want you bright-eyed and bushy-tailed tomorrow. We've still got work to do."

The team nodded, the determination in their eyes matching his own. They'd won a significant battle, but the war was far from over.

As George climbed into his car, his phone buzzed. A text from Isabella: "How did it go? Are the kids OK?"

He smiled, warmth spreading through his chest. Despite everything – the long hours, the strain on their relationship – she still cared. Still supported him.

He typed out a quick reply: "It went well. Kids are tough, resilient. We're making a difference."

As he hit send, George realised something. For the first time in months, he felt truly, unequivocally good about his job. About the impact they were having.

They'd saved those kids. Given them a second chance at life, at happiness. And no matter what came next, no matter how dark the road ahead might be, George would hold onto this feeling. This reminder of why he became a cop in the first place.

To protect the innocent. To bring light to the darkest places. To make a difference.

With a renewed sense of purpose, George started the engine. There was still work to be done, still battles to be fought. But for now, for this moment, he allowed himself to bask in the glow of a job well done.

Those kids were safe. They were going home. And George Beaumont had played a part in making that happen.

It wasn't a bad day's work, all things considered.

As he pulled out of the hospital car park, George's mind was already racing ahead to the next steps. The White Rose League was still out there, their tendrils reaching far and wide. As was the Jürgen Schmidt OCG. But they'd dealt them a significant blow today, and they wouldn't stop until the whole rotten structure came tumbling down.

For Lily, Thomas, Rosie, and Amira. For all the children still out there, waiting to be found. For the families torn apart by unimaginable evil.

George Beaumont and his team would keep fighting. Keep pushing. Keep shining a light into the darkest corners of human depravity.

Because that's what they did. That's who they were.

And God help anyone who stood in their way.

Chapter Forty

George Beaumont stood on Abbie Illingworth's doorstep, his heart racing with a mixture of elation and dread. The news of Rosie's rescue burned in his chest, a bright spot of hope in the darkness they'd been wading through for months. But his deception, the lies by omission, hung heavy on his shoulders.

He raised his hand to knock, hesitated for a moment, then rapped sharply on the door.

Footsteps approached from inside. The door swung open, revealing Abbie's face, etched with worry and exhaustion.

"George?" she said, surprise and hope warring in her voice. "What is it? Is it about Rosie?"

He nodded, a smile breaking through his professional facade. "We found her, Abbie. Rosie's safe. She's at the hospital now, being checked over."

For a moment, Abbie stood frozen, her eyes wide with disbelief. Then, with a cry of pure joy, she launched herself at George, wrapping her arms around him in a fierce embrace.

"Oh my God," she sobbed into his shoulder. "Oh, thank God. She's really OK?"

George patted her back awkwardly, acutely aware of the line he'd been toeing for weeks now. "She's OK. A bit shaken up, but physically unharmed. She's going to be fine."

Abbie pulled back slightly, her face radiant with relief and gratitude. Their eyes met, and for a heartbeat, the world seemed to hold its breath.

Abbie leaned in, her intention clear. But George, his conscience screaming at him, turned his head at the last moment. Her lips grazed his cheek instead of their intended target.

The moment shattered. Abbie stepped back, confusion and hurt clouding her features. "George? What's wrong?"

He took a deep breath, steeling himself for what he knew he had to do. "Abbie, I... I owe you an apology. I haven't been entirely honest with you."

Her brow furrowed. "What do you mean?"

"I'm engaged," he said, the words tasting like ashes in his mouth. "I should have told you from the start. I'm so sorry for leading you on."

The colour drained from Abbie's face. She took another step back, as if his words had physically struck her. "Engaged? But... I thought... All this time, you've been..."

"I know," George said, his voice heavy with regret. "I got caught up in... I don't know what. The case, the connection we seemed to have. But it doesn't excuse my behaviour. I should have been upfront from the beginning." He paused, looking down at his shoes. "I'm sorry."

Anger flashed in Abbie's eyes, replacing the hurt. "Get out," she said, her voice low and dangerous. "Get out of my house. Now."

George nodded, accepting her fury as his due. "I'm sorry, Abbie. Truly. I never meant to—"

"I said get out!" she shouted, tears springing to her eyes. "I don't want to hear your excuses. Just go."

He turned and walked away, each step feeling like lead. As

he reached his car, he heard the slam of Abbie's front door echoing in the quiet street. It sounded like the final nail in the coffin of what might have been.

* * *

The drive home was a blur of self-recrimination and dread. George knew he had one more difficult conversation ahead, one that could potentially cost him everything.

Isabella was waiting for him when he walked through the door. One look at his face, and she knew something was wrong.

"George? What is it?"

He sank onto the sofa, gesturing for her to join him. "We need to talk, Izzy. There's something I need to tell you."

Isabella sat beside him, her body tense with apprehension. "OK. I'm listening."

George took a deep breath, forcing himself to meet her eyes. "First, I owe you an apology. I... I had suspicions. That you might be having an affair."

Isabella's eyes widened in shock. "What? George, how could you think—"

He held up a hand, stopping her. "I know. I know it was wrong. I let my insecurities, the stress of the case, cloud my judgment. I'm so sorry for doubting you."

She shook her head, disbelief written across her features. "I can't believe you'd think I'd do that. After everything we've been through together."

"I know," George said, shame colouring his voice. "I was an idiot. But there's more."

Isabella's eyes narrowed. "More?"

George nodded, steeling himself. "There's... there's someone else. A teacher at one of the schools involved in the case. Abbie Illingworth."

The colour drained from Isabella's face. "What are you saying, George?"

He rushed to clarify, the words tumbling out in a desperate stream. "Nothing happened. Not really. But... we got close. Too close. We almost kissed."

Isabella stood abruptly, putting distance between them. "Almost kissed? What does that mean, exactly?"

George ran a hand through his hair, frustration and guilt warring within him. "We went to kiss, but I got a call from the station. But... the intent was there. On both sides, if I'm being honest."

"And are you?" Isabella's voice was sharp, cutting. "Being honest? Is that all that happened?"

He nodded, forcing himself to hold her gaze. "That's all. Physically, at least. But... I think I was starting to develop feelings for her. I didn't... I swear... It just... happened."

Isabella turned away, her shoulders shaking with silent sobs. George ached to comfort her, but he knew he had no right. Not now.

"How could you?" she whispered, her voice thick with pain. "After everything... how could you do this?"

George's head dropped. "I don't know," he said softly. "I got caught up in the case, in the connection we seemed to have. But it's no excuse. I betrayed your trust, and I'm so, so sorry."

Isabella whirled to face him, anger flashing in her tear-filled eyes. "Sorry? You think sorry makes this OK? You were going to marry me, George. We were supposed to spend our lives together. And all this time, you've been... what? Fantasising about someone else?"

"No," George protested weakly. "It wasn't like that. I love you, Izzy. I never stopped loving you."

"But it wasn't enough, was it?" she spat. "Our love, our life together, it wasn't enough to keep you faithful."

George stood, taking a tentative step towards her. "Izzy, please. I know I've messed up. And really fucking badly. But can we... please is there any way we can work through this?"

Isabella held up a hand, stopping him in his tracks. "I don't know, George. I honestly don't know if I can forgive this. I need... I need time. Space."

He nodded, accepting her words as the sentence they were. "I understand. I'll... I'll pack a bag. Stay at my mum's for a while."

"I..."

"Yes?" George asked.

Isabella took a deep breath, visibly steeling herself. "I need to understand, George. How did this happen? When did we start drifting so far apart that you could... that you could develop feelings for someone else?"

George ran a hand over his face, searching for the right words. "I don't know, Izzy. It wasn't... it wasn't a conscious thing. The case, it consumed me. And Abbie, she was there, she understood the pressure, the darkness of it all."

"And I didn't?" Isabella's voice cracked. "I'm a detective too, George. I know what the job is like."

"I know," George said, frustration colouring his voice. "But you were working your own case, and I... I didn't want to burden you with mine. I thought I was protecting you."

Isabella laughed bitterly. "Protecting me? By shutting me out? By turning to another woman for comfort?"

George flinched at her words. "I never meant for it to

happen. I swear, Izzy. It just... it snuck up on me. And I hate myself for it."

They sat in silence for a moment, the weight of their shared pain hanging heavy between them.

"Do you love her?" Isabella asked suddenly, her voice small and vulnerable.

George's head snapped up. "No," he said firmly. "No, I don't love her. I love you, Izzy. Only you. What I felt for Abbie, it was... it was a connection, yes. But it wasn't love."

Isabella nodded slowly, processing his words. "But it could have been. If things had gone differently."

George shook his head. "No. I was an idiot to risk it."

"Yes, you were," Isabella agreed, but there was less venom in her voice now. "I'm glad you told me. That you didn't continue behind my back. That you didn't keep the truth from me."

"Does that not make this better?" he asked.

Isabella narrowed her eyes, so George continued. "That I told you. Even though nothing happened."

Isabella opened her mouth to say something, and then she stopped. Then she grimaced and shook her head. "So I'm meant to be grateful that you told me the truth, am I?"

"No, Izzy, I didn't mean it like that." He tried to close the distance.

"Stop!" She held out a hand.

"I'm so sorry, Izzy," George said, his own eyes stinging. "I know it's not enough, but I am. I'll do anything to make this right. To earn back your trust."

Isabella was quiet for a long moment, her gaze fixed on her hands. When she finally spoke, her voice was barely audible. "I don't know if I can trust you again, George. But... but I don't want to throw away everything we have without trying."

Hope flared in George's chest, fragile and tentative. "What are you saying?"

"I'm saying," Isabella took a deep breath, "that maybe we should consider counselling. Couples therapy. If we're going to have any chance of moving past this, we need help."

George nodded eagerly. "Yes. Absolutely. Anything you want, Izzy. I'll do whatever it takes."

Isabella held up a hand. "This isn't a quick fix, George. It's going to take time. And work. A lot of work. And I can't promise... I can't promise it will be enough."

"I understand," George said solemnly. "But I'm willing to put in that work. To fight for us. If you'll let me."

Isabella met his gaze, her eyes filled with a mixture of pain, anger, and a tiny glimmer of hope. "OK," she said softly. "We'll try."

George reached out tentatively, taking her hand in his. When she didn't pull away, he squeezed gently. "Thank you," he whispered. "For giving me a chance I don't deserve."

As they sat there, hands clasped, both acutely aware of the long road ahead, George made a silent vow. He would do whatever it took to rebuild what he'd nearly destroyed. To be worthy of the love and trust Isabella was willing to fight for.

It wouldn't be easy. The shadow of his mistake would linger for a long time. But as he looked at Isabella and saw the strength and resilience in her eyes, George knew one thing for certain.

They were worth fighting for. And he would never, ever take that for granted again.

Epilogue

The holding cell at HMP New Hall reeked of disinfectant and despair. Nadia Shah sat on her narrow bed, a dog-eared paperback clutched in her hands. The fluorescent light flickered overhead, casting harsh shadows across her face.

The cell door creaked open. Nadia's head snapped up, eyes narrowing. "Who the fuck are you?"

A figure stepped inside, face obscured by the glare. Without a word, they raised their hand, a signet ring glinting on their finger.

Nadia's breath caught. The book slipped from her grasp, forgotten.

The Rose.

"You've got some nerve showing up here," Nadia spat, rising to her feet. Her fists clenched at her sides, knuckles white with rage.

The Rose remained impassive, studying her with cold, calculating eyes. "Now, now, Nadia. Is that any way to greet an old friend?"

"Friend?" Nadia's laugh was bitter, bordering on hysterical. "You fed me lies. Promised me safety if I delivered the children."

The Rose's lips curled into a mirthless smile. "And you believed me. How... quaint."

Nadia lunged forward, stopping inches from the Rose's face.

"You manipulated me. Used me. And for what? Your sick little games?"

"Games?" The Rose's voice dropped to a dangerous whisper. "This is no game, Nadia. This is power. This is control. This is the future."

Nadia stepped back, disgust etched across her features. "You're insane."

"Perhaps," the Rose conceded. "But I'm also the one standing on this side of the bars."

Silence stretched between them, thick with unspoken accusations and shattered trust.

"Why are you here?" Nadia finally asked, exhaustion seeping into her voice.

The Rose's eyes glittered with something akin to amusement. "To thank you, of course. Your loyalty has been… invaluable."

Nadia scoffed. "My loyalty? I'm rotting in a cell because of you." She shook her head. "I didn't even kill Eva and Dania, that was Samuel."

"You rot in there for now," the Rose said, voice smooth as silk. "But loyalty, true loyalty, deserves its rewards. In time, Nadia, you will get what you truly deserve."

"And what about the children?" Nadia's voice cracked. "What about their families?"

The Rose's expression hardened. "Collateral damage. Necessary sacrifices for a greater good." They shook their head. "You didn't care about their families when you took their children."

Nadia shook her head, revulsion twisting her gut. "You're a monster."

"Perhaps," the Rose repeated. "But I'm a monster who

keeps their promises. Remember that, Nadia. Your time will come."

With a final, cryptic smile, the Rose turned and rapped on the cell door. It swung open, and they stepped through without a backward glance.

Nadia sank onto her bed, head in her hands. The weight of her choices, her complicity, threatened to crush her. She'd believed in the cause, in the twisted logic of it all. Now, faced with the cold reality of the Rose's machinations, she felt hollowed out. Used up.

* * *

The penthouse suite overlooked Leeds, its twinkling lights a poor imitation of the stars hidden behind the smog. Inside, two people faced each other across a polished oak desk.

Jürgen Schmidt paced like a caged animal, his bulk at odds with the sleek, modern furnishings. "This is unacceptable," he growled, accent thickening with rage. "Samuel Siddiqui and Zachary Sayed were two of my best. And now they're rotting in cells because of your incompetence!"

The Rose lounged in a high-backed leather chair, seemingly unperturbed by Schmidt's outburst. "Sacrifices must be made, Jürgen. You understand this, surely?"

Schmidt whirled, face mottled with fury. "Sacrifices? What have you sacrificed, eh? You sit here in your ivory tower while my men do the dirty work. While my organisation bleeds!"

"Calm yourself," the Rose said, voice like ice. "Your short-sightedness is... disappointing."

"Short-sighted?" Schmidt slammed his fists on the desk. "Beaumont is dismantling everything we've built. He's too close. Too persistent. He needs to be dealt with."

A ghost of a smile played across the Rose's lips. "Oh, he will be. Plans are already in motion."

Schmidt's eyes narrowed. "What plans?"

"Our mole is in place," the Rose said, fingers steepled beneath their chin. "The seeds of doubt have been planted. Beaumont's world is about to come crashing down around him. The end of Beaumont is nigh."

"Pretty words," Schmidt sneered. "But I've heard them before. I want results."

The Rose's eyes flashed with something dangerous. "You forget yourself, Jürgen. I made you. I can unmake you just as easily."

Schmidt opened his mouth to retort, but the words died on his lips. The threat, unspoken but palpable, hung in the air between them.

"Now," the Rose continued, voice deceptively pleasant, "shall we discuss more... productive matters? Or would you prefer to continue this little tantrum?"

Schmidt's jaw clenched, but he sank into the chair opposite the Rose. "Tell me about this plan of yours."

The Rose's smile widened, predatory and cold. "It's quite simple, really. We're going to destroy George Beaumont from the inside out. His team, his family, his very sense of self... all of it will crumble."

"And how, exactly, do you plan to accomplish this?" Schmidt asked, scepticism dripping from every word.

"Patience, my friend," the Rose chided. "The pieces are already in play. Our mole has been feeding us information, sowing discord within Beaumont's inner circle. His fiancée, that ambitious DI Wood, is already hurting. His team is fraying at the edges, doubt and suspicion spreading like a cancer."

Schmidt leaned forward, interest piqued despite himself. "Go on."

"We've planted evidence, manipulated witness statements. Every lead Beaumont follows will only serve to tangle him further in our web. And when the moment is right..." The Rose trailed off, savouring the anticipation.

"What?" Schmidt pressed. "What happens then?"

The Rose's eyes glittered with malevolent glee. "We spring the trap. Beaumont will find himself implicated in the very crimes he's been investigating. His career, his reputation, his entire life... all of it will be reduced to ashes."

Schmidt sat back, a grudging respect dawning on his face. "And the White Rose League?"

"Will emerge stronger than ever," the Rose finished. "With Beaumont disgraced, the investigation will crumble. We'll have carte blanche to continue our... operations."

A slow smile spread across Schmidt's face. "I underestimated you, it seems."

"A common mistake," the Rose said, voice dripping with condescension. "One I trust you won't make again."

Schmidt nodded, properly chastised. "And Samuel? What about him?"

The Rose waved a dismissive hand. "A regrettable loss, but a necessary one. His sacrifice will not be in vain."

Schmidt's eyes hardened. "See that it isn't. I've lost too many good men to your schemes."

"Your men knew the risks when they signed on," the Rose countered. "As did you, Jürgen. Or have you forgotten our arrangement?"

The tension in the room ratcheted up a notch. Schmidt's

hand twitched, as if longing for the comfort of a weapon. "I haven't forgotten anything."

"Good," the Rose said, voice dangerously soft. "Then let's not have this conversation again, shall we? Your role is to provide muscle, to grease the wheels of our operation. Leave the strategy to those better equipped to handle it."

Schmidt bristled at the insult, but held his tongue. He'd pushed his luck far enough for one night.

"Now," the Rose continued, all business once more, "we have work to do. Beaumont's recent success has stirred up unwanted attention. We need to ensure our assets remain protected."

"What do you need from me?" Schmidt asked, resigned to his role as enforcer.

The Rose's smile was cold and sharp as a knife. "What you do best, Jürgen. Make people disappear."

Schmidt nodded, a grim satisfaction settling over him. This, at least, was familiar territory. "Consider it done."

"Excellent," the Rose purred. "Oh, and Jürgen? Do try to be discreet. We can't afford any more... complications."

The threat, thinly veiled, hung in the air between them. Schmidt stood, eager to be gone from this place, from the Rose's calculating gaze.

"One last thing," the Rose called as Schmidt reached the door. "Remember your place, Jürgen. You may be a big fish in your little pond, but in my ocean? You're barely a minnow."

Schmidt's hand tightened on the doorknob, knuckles white with suppressed rage. But he said nothing, merely nodding stiffly before stepping out into the night.

The Rose watched him go, a satisfied smirk playing across their lips. Pawns, all of them. Useful, for now, but ultimately expendable.

George Beaumont's days were numbered. The White Rose League would flourish, its roots spreading deeper, its influence growing stronger with each passing day.

And at the centre of it all, pulling the strings, manipulating the players like pieces on a chessboard... the Rose would reign supreme.

The game was far from over.

In fact, it was only just beginning.

Also by Lee Brook